ALSO BY MYRA HARGRAVE MCILVAIN:

Six Central Texas Auto Tours
Texas Auto Trails: The Southeast
Texas Auto Trails: The Northeast
Shadows on the Land: An Anthology of Texas Historical Marker Stories
Texas Auto Trails: The South and Rio Grande Valley
Legacy

STEIN HOUSE

Myra Hargrave McIlvain

iUniverse LLC
Bloomington

STEIN HOUSE

iUniverse books may be ordered through booksellers or by contacting:

iUniverse
1663 Liberty Drive
Bloomington, IN 47403
www.iuniverse.com
1-800-Authors (1-800-288-4677)

Special thanks go to the Calhoun County Museum in Port Lavaca, Texas, for allowing use of the diorama of Indianola in 1875. Jeff Underwood researched and built the diorama that depicts the thriving coastal city. Philip Thomae of Port Lavaca provided the photograph.

ISBN: 978-1-4917-0954-2 (sc)
ISBN: 978-1-4917-0953-5 (hc)
ISBN: 978-1-4917-0952-8 (e)

Library of Congress Control Number: 2013917547

Printed in the United States of America.

iUniverse rev. date: 10/17/2013

This book is dedicated to Stroud, my best friend,
who held my hand and encouraged me
every step of the way.

Acknowledgments

My life has been a rich texture of love, encouragement, and support from more folks than I can ever name, but there are a special few who have blessed me throughout this project.

The top of the list belongs to my husband, Stroud, for the many times he patiently read the manuscript, asking questions that helped me hone my craft and advising this city girl about mules and woodstoves and gardens.

My sister, Doris Hargrave, pored over the manuscript with her red pen, offering critique that pushed me to tighten my writing, keep to the storyline, and not veer into a history lesson.

A dear friend, Barbara Wagner, set aside time to carefully read the manuscript twice, using her keen eye for detail to mark my spelling errors and note the places that needed clarity.

Earl Russell, a friend and memoir writer, served as my mentor, pushing me to write my Texas history blog and generously sharing his publishing tips and accolades along the way.

Thanks must go to a woman who was in her midnineties when I interviewed her in 1974. She shared many fascinating tales about her ancestors who had settled around Indianola. But the story that stayed with me and haunted me and finally came alive for me in *Stein House* was an incident she mentioned only casually: a widow and her children arrived in Indianola after watching their drunken papa and husband leap between the ship and the dock before falling to his death in the waters of Germany's Weser River. After all these years, that widow became Helga Heinrich of Stein House.

Stein House, which is set during a period of great tumult in Texas and the US, required months of research and many sources. I owe a tremendous debt to Brownson Malsch for his *Indianola: The Mother of*

Western Texas, an award-winning detailed history of the thriving seaport and its residents.

Finally, there are the supporters that kept telling me how eager they were to read *Stein House.* To all of you I say, "Here it is. I hope you enjoy the journey as much as I enjoyed writing it."

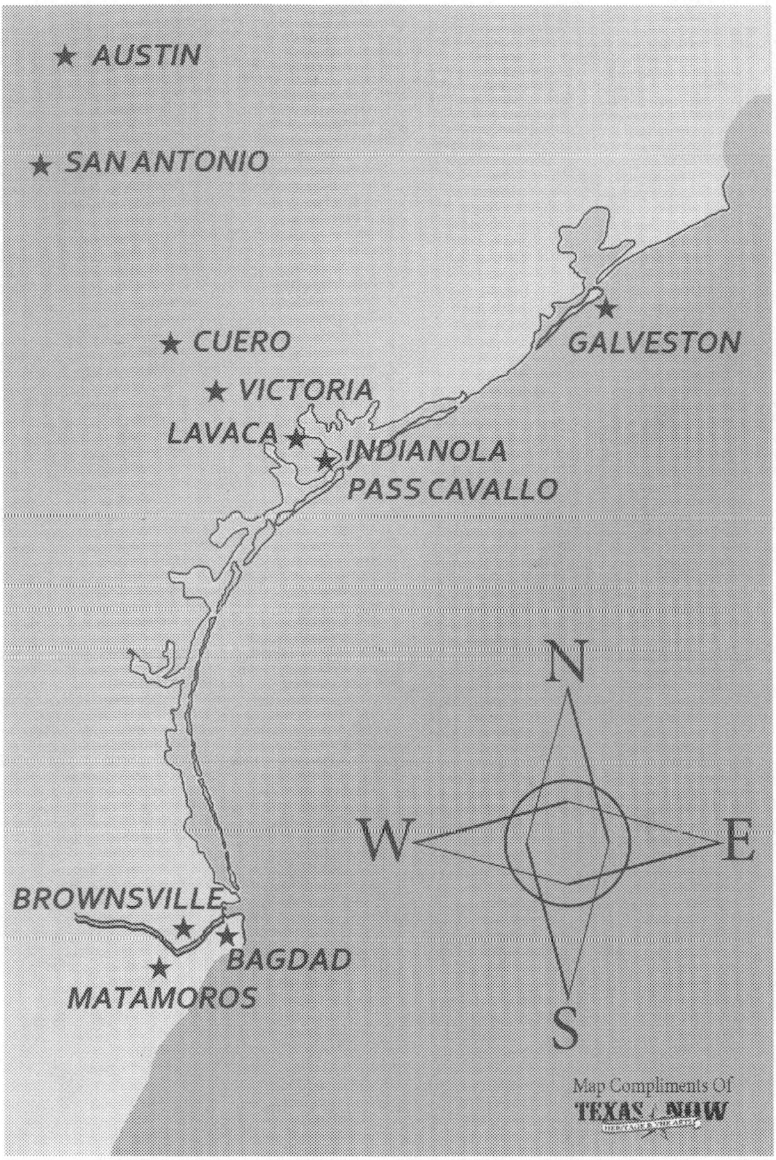
AUSTIN
SAN ANTONIO
GALVESTON
CUERO
VICTORIA
LAVACA
INDIANOLA
PASS CAVALLO
N
W
E
S
BROWNSVILLE
BAGDAD
MATAMOROS
Map Compliments Of
TEXAS NOW

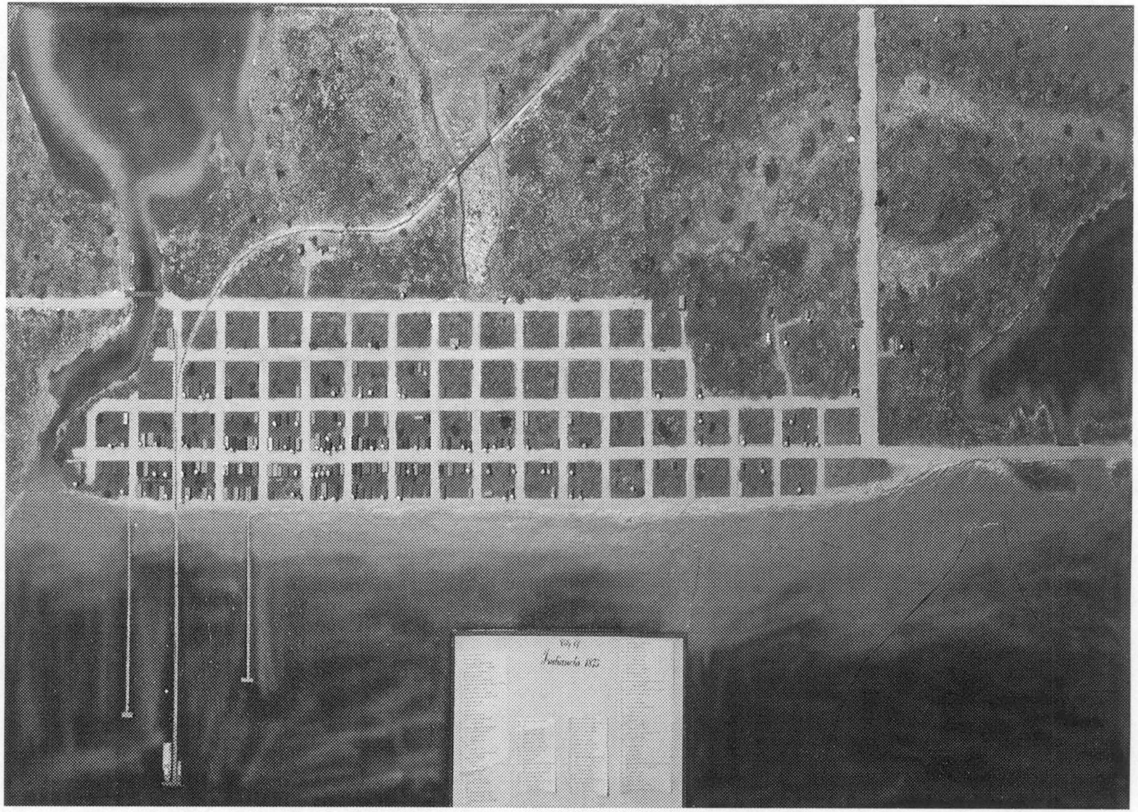

This diorama, created by Jeff Underwood, depicts Indianola in 1875. Philip Thomae is the photographer. It is from the Collection of the Calhoun County Museum, Port Lavaca, Texas.

This sign, copied from the diorama on the previous page, is located at the Indianola ghost town. Note just below the sign one of the surviving shellcrete cisterns built during a drought in Indianola.

Chapter 1

1853

HELGA GRIPPED THE SHIP RAILING, straining to see the slowly materializing shore, lulled by the sweet sounds of Paul's harmonica as he roamed among the passengers. His music had become part of the voyage, always in the background, adding energy when the hours dragged, lifting spirits during the after-supper sing-alongs. Now, the passengers leaned over the ship rail, chattering excitedly, as unaware of Paul's music as they were of the gentle breeze blowing against their faces. Heaving its way through the waves, the ship seemed as eager as everyone on board to reach Indianola, the tiny speck of buildings stretching across the flat Texas landscape.

Then, like a storm wave rising black and angry out of the sea, the memory washed over Helga, forcing her back to the horror that had begun their trip: Max leaped wildly over the ship rail to the dock. The crowd on board roared its delight, enjoying another of his hilarious antics. He whirled to face his audience on deck, tilted the rounded brim of his hat over one eye, spread his feet apart like the maestro of a grand orchestra, and played a few bars of "Die Huehle" on his harmonica while the passengers clapped or rapped the rhythm on the ship rail. Then his long, graceful legs sprang gleefully into the air, and he clicked his heels together in a final salute and raced into the inn. The children's hysterical laughter stopped the instant Max disappeared. A cold wind of fear blew over them. Helga caught her breath and pulled the children tight against her, apprehension forcing bile into her mouth.

Gretchen whispered, "No, Papa ..." as she clutched little Anna and buried her face in the two-year-old's shoulder. Paul trembled like a leaf, and Hermie stood as rigid as a poker, his face still flushed from howling at his papa's performance. The sailors ignored it all, kept to their steady pace, never looking up from their work of hauling in the gangplank. The ropes slid like gigantic reptiles onto the deck, the sails billowed, and the vessel heaved as it inched ever so slowly from the dock.

Max reappeared in the doorway of the inn, and the crowd on deck shouted in delight as he stopped, bowed to his audience, and took a huge gulp from the open bottle.

Gretchen shuddered against Helga's shoulder, and Hermie's fist pounded the rail as he muttered between clenched teeth, "Come on, Papa."

"It's all right. The captain will wait." Paul breathed into his cupped hands.

The ship began its laboring surge as the black, swirling water of the Weser River churned up waves that grew from undulating ripples to frothy caps. Still Max whirled and danced and tipped his bottle as he headed almost casually toward the departing ship. The laughter died, and in a body the crowd began coaxing him to jump, to make one mad leap, to entertain them one more time.

Helga pulled the children tighter against her, holding them, willing them not to watch.

And then Max jumped, tossing the empty bottle into the water as his body floated, suspended, arms extended, fingers spread, wildly grasping for the slowly arching rail. His face suddenly twisted to disbelieving shock as his fingers missed their grip, and he dropped like a slender arrow straight down into the roiling, icy water without causing the slightest splash.

* * *

"Mama, are you sick?" Helga felt Gretchen's arm slip around her waist, forcing her back to the present.

Catching her breath, Helga shook her head and cuffed the sweat off her upper lip. "Just excited. Tante Amelia is probably jumping up and down watching our ship head toward port."

"Paul makes me think of Papa when he plays that harmonica with such joy." Gretchen's lip trembled. "Sometimes I wish he wouldn't."

"When he plays, I can see your papa—even at ten, he's so tall and thin." Helga did not add that she worried, as she watched Paul on shipboard, that he might be as much of an entertainer and as eager to please the crowd as Max.

As they had waited for their small transfer ship to be loaded with the sea trunks and equipment and foodstuffs they had been advised to pack for Texas, Helga had watched in amazement as Max became acquainted with all the passengers. He quickly discovered if they were merchants, or farmers, or professionally trained. The men delighted in his wild tales, such as the one about stacking his manure pile on top of old farm implements to form such a mountain of manure that his neighbors thought he owned a huge herd of milk cows.

Max managed the introductions by strolling about the dock playing his violin or his harmonica. The first night after supper, crowds gathered as his rich bass led them in familiar folksongs. By the second night, people of all ages accompanied him in four-part harmony. It passed the time, and it seemed to cheer those in grief over leaving the fatherland.

At night, when Helga tried getting the children to sleep, Max kept all four of them in gales of laughter with his whispered tales of the other passengers: Frau Brugh's gas explosions every time she bent over, Herr Schmidt's big toe peeking from his shoe, and Frau Mueller bringing enough bedding for every person on the ship.

Growing up, Helga had listened to her papa's favorite sermons about Job and character and the test of a believer when faced with adversity. It all seemed so simple: like Job, girded with trust and faith, a person could weather any test, any storm God sent his way.

Then their lives changed abruptly. Helga stood paralyzed at the railing, staring at the place that had swallowed Max, her mind telling her to comfort the children, to ease the terror gripping them, but she could not move.

Hermie raised his head, staring at her in disbelief. "He's drowned. Papa's drowned in the Weser."

"Won't they get him out? Won't they help him?" Gretchen pleaded.

The passengers moved close, some of the women enfolding them in the circle of their arms, whispering gentle consolations:

"He was so happy."

"He was such a good man.

"Everyone loved him."

"He kept our spirits up as we waited all these long days."

If there had been some place to go on the tiny transfer ship, somewhere off the crowded deck, she would have pulled the children away. There was nothing to do but stand in ice-cold silence, nodding as well-intended strangers offered what comfort they could muster.

Gretchen cried softly, stroking Anna's blonde curls and straining to see through the crowd as though watching for her papa. Hermie stood as white and cold as a piece of marble, and Paul wailed, his face pressed against Helga's breasts.

Herr Weilbacher pushed through the crowd and gently laid his hand on Helga's shoulder. "Frau Heinrich, the captain says if they find his body in time, they'll cart it the few miles downriver to Brake where we're transferring to the *Margarethe.* We'll carry him out to sea for a proper burial."

"Bury Papa in the ocean?" Gretchen's face twisted in pain.

Helga sucked in the cold spring air. She could not break down. She could not let the children see the desperation settling over her like an icy quilt. "Remember how Papa loved the water? How he jumped from way up on the bank of the river? I think he'd love being buried at sea like a sailor." She reached for Gretchen and Anna, circling them in her arms, pulling them to the ship railing where Hermie held onto Paul, who gazed into the water softly calling, "Papa." The cluster of women moved with them, silent at last.

The wind picked up, propelling the ship swiftly toward the village of Brake, where they planned to wait while the crew loaded all they owned onto the giant sailing ship bound for Texas without Max.

Someone handed Helga a cup of hot tea. "Captain said for you to decide if you want to continue or have your belongings unloaded at Brake."

Helga held the hot cup between her fingers, surprised at how cold they had become. "My sister at Indianola expects us. We must continue." She did not add that Amelia and Dr. Stein were expecting Max to run their mercantile store. She could only hope that they would still want her to operate their new boarding house.

Arriving in Brake as darkness settled, they found an additional hundred people at the inn that were scheduled to join them on the ship. At last, and despite the overcrowding, the innkeeper allowed Helga and the children the privacy of a tiny attic room. They spread their blankets in silence and stretched out across the sagging bed in complete exhaustion.

Soon Helga heard their steady breathing, all except fourteen-year-old Hermie, who lay on the far side of the line of bodies in the position that should have been Max's, way too young to move into his papa's place.

What was she going to do without Max to lift her spirits when they faced the new and strange land of Texas, without Max to warm her on the cold nights? Tears, held back since Max disappeared in the dark waters of the Weser, poured unchecked in the darkness.

Morning dawned cold and clear. Helga went downstairs before the children woke. Outside the door of the inn, a peasant farmer standing solemnly beside his cart nodded toward the body wrapped in a heavy shawl. "I walked the whole way with him, Frau."

"My thanks to you, sir. What pay do you require for so much effort?"

"I'd thank you for his boots. I'm in need, and they look to be about my fit." The skinny little man, who had no teeth, opened a coat Helga recognized as Max's. It was still damp and so large it hung off both his shoulders like pointed wings. She recognized Max's fine leather boots by the brass hooks shining through the clods of mud.

"Of course." She wanted to tell him Hermie needed those boots and the coat far more than Max had needed them, but it seemed the least she could pay for his effort in such cold weather.

"When I slipped off the boots, out tumbled this old silver Thaler. It's the biggest I've ever seen. Your man saved it in the top lining of his boot."

The sight of the one-pound coin emblazoned with the worn image of the Wild Man of the Harz Mountains, so large it covered both the man's palms, caused such a jolt of surprise Helga felt faint.

"Are you all right?"

Helga nodded and took a deep breath as she accepted the heavy silver piece. "Thank you for your honesty. It's such a blessing to have it returned. It was passed to my old *grossvater,* who gave it to my papa when he was a boy." She did not say that Max had insisted they pack it in their sea chest, that he had always claimed it held more value than her papa knew and that it would be their assurance against catastrophe. If Max found that running her brother-in-law's mercantile store didn't work out, they had the old silver Thaler to get them started with their own land.

She hadn't planned to look at Max, to see how he suffered before he gave up and let the water freeze his lungs, but the realization he had secretly taken the Thaler and risked losing it, that he had gambled with their future, and that his drunken antics had left them alone, forced a trembling surge of fury through her body. In one quick motion she yanked the shawl back and gazed at his swollen, discolored face. His cavalier grin, his flippant air of confidence, was gone. His mouth gaped open in one last desperate scream before he sucked his last breath.

She tucked the huge Thaler in the pocket of her woolen shawl, asked the gentleman with the fine new coat and boots to pull the cart to the dock for loading, and walked back into the inn to wake the children for breakfast.

With nothing to do but wait for the ship to be loaded, the passengers roamed the dock and watched the sailors. Two sailors quickly built Max's coffin and left it to be loaded with the luggage.

"Papa's in there, isn't he?" Gretchen's voice trembled.

Helga folded her arm around the frail shoulders already stooped from Gretchen's insistence on carrying Anna.

"I don't like snow on it," Anna said.

Hermie brushed the powdery flakes off the coffin. "Let's go up to our room," he said, surprising Helga by reaching for Anna and carrying her to the inn.

Passengers continued to express their sympathy. One after another came to their room with little packages—cookies for the children, smoked sausage, and jars of sauerkraut—supplies prepared for the trip. And then Herr Schmidt, whose toe peeked from his shoe, came to their door with a harmonica.

"It belonged to my grossvater, but I don't play like your papa. Herr Heinrich gave us so much joy with his music. I thought his sons would be sad to lose his harmonica."

Paul reached for the instrument, rubbing his hand across its shiny surface. "Thank you, Herr Schmidt. I'll play it for my papa." He blew softly, surprising Helga at how much command he had of the sound. "Think I'll go out on the dock." He sounded like Max when he said he thought he'd go down to the tavern—half question, half statement.

To the surprise of everyone, as the trip progressed, Paul mastered many of Max's lively songs. He rekindled the passengers' interest in nightly sing-alongs, with Hermie adding his sweet tenor to round out the harmony. Several passengers brought out their violins and guitars, and the sailors led the young ones in lively dances.

* * *

Now, after three months of endless ocean, the long piers of Indianola jutted into the bay like outstretched fingers welcoming them.

"The buildings are so small and painted so many colors." Hermie sounded disappointed.

Helga had tried to read between the lines of Amelia's letters and had cautioned Max and the children about Tante Amelia's knack for finding beauty in a hog wallow. Yet as she gazed at the flat, treeless Texas prairie stretching away from the bay, Helga found herself agreeing with Amelia's glowing description of the port. The bright colors of the buildings shining in the morning light gave the tiny village sprawling along the shore an energy that sent a surge of hope through her body. She remembered Amelia writing that with hard work they could make a good life.

"They say the land begins rising about fifty miles inland." A woman's voice carried over the crowd. "They say trees shade the road to New Braunfels."

"We can trust the letters from Friedrich Ernst," a man said. "There will be green meadows."

"We can plant green meadows," Hermie declared. His determined jaw made him look like Helga, but he sounded like his papa. Helga felt the sting of tears as this man-child, standing so tall, laid his hand on her shoulder.

"We'll plant our own garden," she said.

The women on board often reminded her to direct her mind toward positive images to lift her spirits. By day she controlled her anguish, but at night, lying in their family berth and hearing couples talking softly, privately behind the makeshift walls of quilts hung between the wood frames, she missed Max, missed him terribly. It always began as a pain in her chest, then it moved to a gnawing ache in her belly, and finally the yearning took shape in her groin. At first she fought the growing need, and then she let it carry her, finally soothing her until exhausted sleep made her body forget the constant sway of the ship and the night cries of children.

"Isn't that Tante Amelia?" Gretchen pointed toward the end of the pier.

The children began waving at their only relative in America.

Amelia threw up both arms to wave and then—too quickly, Helga thought—lowered them demurely to her sides. Not at all like the rambunctious Amelia who had left for her Texas adventure.

The final good-byes started as the crew began lashing the ship to the pier. Only Helga and the children planned to remain in Indianola. The others sought inland communities in rich farming country, places Friedrich Ernst described so glowingly in his letters that were published in the Oldenburg newspaper and in a book about travel in Texas.

Most of the passengers had offered advice throughout the trip, and now their tight embraces showed genuine love and concern for the new widow and her children. A warm bond of friendship had developed over the months as the mass of strangers facing the unknown quickly took comfort in one another's lives.

When parents had realized Helga intended to ignore seasickness and spend each day continuing with the schooling and English lessons she had started with her children long before Amelia made her trip to Texas, they began asking if she had room for their children in the class, which she held under the shade of the billowing sails. Many of the parents soothed their German pride at asking for free education by saying Helga made a wise choice to stay busy.

The children quickly learned to speak and read English, as did many of the adults who sat quietly on the fringes of the classroom silently mouthing the lessons as their children went through the drills. Most people on shipboard, including the crew, followed an unwritten rule to speak English as much as possible.

Max would have disapproved; he would have said she was foolish to teach thirty children without pay, that she and Amelia had spent too many years learning English to prepare Amelia for life in Texas to give away all that knowledge. But the passengers paid in cherished copies of newspapers and books, clothing, and respect. Max would have laughed about the respect. He had always claimed their neighbors respected her because she was Parson Anton's daughter. The past three months had proved him wrong as more and more parents expressed admiration for her teaching skills. She followed the guidance Papa preached in his powerful sermons—she used the gifts God (and Papa) had given her.

Anna tugged at Helga's skirt, demanding to be held so she could be seen and receive the special attention she had grown to expect from the doting passengers. From the time they pulled up anchor, Anna had scampered among the families making friends and jabbering a mixture of English and German.

Old Herr Helfin had become one of Helga's most faithful adult students. He sat on the edge of the classroom mouthing all the drills while cradling Anna on his lap. The first time he settled quietly on the deck beside the children, Anna had headed straight for him, backed into his lap, and begun stroking his full white beard.

Now, as the ship slowed, the breeze subsided and the warmth and humidity became oppressive. Amelia had warned them to change to cotton clothing as soon as they reached the Gulf, but they didn't own cotton garments. Cotton was impractical even for Oldenburg's balmy summer days.

Anna pulled at a prickly rash on her neck, and the other three sweated in profusion. The women who insisted on wearing their wool scarves either abandoned their coverings or looked faint as they mopped the sweat creasing their faces.

Helga was startled to see Negroes moving like a steady stream of ants along the pier. Amelia had written about slaves, yet Helga hadn't expected to see black-skinned men everywhere. Their powerful, bare arms glistened with sweat as they tied down the mooring lines; a group of about ten sang a deep, melodious song as they heaved huge crates into the hold of a neighboring ship. Several others loaded an enormous wagon waiting on the pier, grunting in low, gentle tones to quiet a team of skittish mules.

Did white men not work? Negroes made up the entire labor force on the pier.

Gretchen helped Anna find Tante Amelia among the throng waiting on the pier, and the child waved eagerly, happy to finally see the relative who held such importance in their family conversations. Amelia responded like the same young girl who had left home years before; she jumped and waved, ignoring the sideways glances of the frock-coated gentleman standing next to her.

After their mama died, Amelia, the adventurous one, had come to Texas with a prominent family to tutor their son. The boy had died on shipboard, and his mother had died of yellow fever soon after they landed in Galveston. Amelia had taken work as a maid at Galveston's Tremont Hotel, and that's where she had met Dr. Joseph Stein.

After Helga buried their papa, Amelia's glowing reports of opportunities at Indianola, combined with the landlord's three-month deadline for Helga and Max to vacate the manse's property, had convinced Max to accept Dr. Stein's offer to operate his mercantile store. Now, if Dr. Stein no longer wanted her to run his boarding house ... She automatically touched the ancient silver Thaler riding securely in the leather money belt around her waist.

Hermie led the way down the gangplank followed closely by Paul. Amelia pulled them both into a fierce hug. Hermie had been seven when Amelia left for Texas, but he often talked of those days when Amelia romped with him in the meadow behind his *grossmutter*'s cottage. Paul gazed at her as though he were trying to capture an early memory.

Amelia's once-spindly body sagged with weight. Even her lovely blonde hair, which she always had brushed with such vigor and pulled back in tight, smooth braids, hung in an unkempt bun on her neck. She came to Helga in a rush, throwing her arms around her. "Seven years, and you've not changed."

Helga cupped Amelia's face between her palms. "Are you well?"

Amelia looked fondly at all four children and clasped Gretchen and Anna by the hand. "Now that my people are here, I'm fine. Hermie, you're a man. Paul, I thought you were your papa when I first saw you. Sweet Gretchen, you were a precious five-year-old. Now you're a lovely young lady."

Gretchen self-consciously smoothed her dress and turned a bright pink that highlighted the prickly rash on her neck. "Thank you, Frau Stein."

"Aw, I'm your tante Amelia." Amelia looked around. "Where's Max?"

Hermie stepped quickly to Helga's side. "An accident. He was lost as our ship sailed."

"Oh, not Max," Amelia cried.

Helga saw the suspicion in her sister's face, knew Amelia understood and would not ask how it happened.

"Do you think Dr. Stein will still need me to operate his boarding house?"

"Of course. He's desperate. And don't let him scare you. He's full of hot steam. Dr. Stein has patients this afternoon. He wants you to come by our house before you go home. He has a man who'll haul your trunk to the boarding house. We'll walk."

As they stepped off the long pier onto the dock, Hermie said, "All the buildings are made of wood. They're so small."

"We don't have stone here. Ships bring in our lumber. Those warehouses by the docks are made of cypress. It weathers to that handsome silver color." Amelia's voice held pride, and when she saw Hermie looking skeptically at the buildings, she playfully tousled his already lawless brown hair.

"What's that white dust?" Paul asked as he skipped to catch up with Amelia bustling along ahead of them.

"We have oyster shell all along the coast. Our streets are all shell, and many buildings have shell foundations. When it's dry, wagons crush the shell to dust."

Huge mule-drawn wagons clogged the street. Large carts that looked like open-sided baskets balanced between giant wheels painted in bold reds, yellows, and greens crept behind sluggish yokes of oxen. The snorts and grunts of animals added to the bedlam of shouts and curses.

Paul stepped up beside a cart painted like a flower garden of bright colors. The wheels rose taller than the top of his head. Hitched to the cart, eight yoke of oxen stood silently, their heads hanging low. Helga didn't notice the fierce-looking cock, its leg secured with a rusty chain, until its screech made Paul jump back and stare transfixed into the intense, beady eyes and sharp beak of the bright orange rooster. Its comb was gone, making its head look like a ball of blood.

Amelia laughed. "That's a *carreta,* a Mexican cart. They always carry a fighting cock for games at the end of the day. Those carts come in here loaded with gold and silver from the mines in Mexico."

"Gold and silver?" Hermie breathed in shocked awe.

"Sometimes there are 150 Mexican carts or freight wagons in a long train. They ship the gold and silver to the mint in New Orleans."

"Do they get robbed?"

"Sometimes. That's why you see men with rifles everywhere. They ride with the wagons and carts on the Chihuahua Trail to Mexico. The stages headed for California all have a man with a Winchester sitting up on the seat beside the driver."

Paul and Hermie could hardly walk for staring at the milling, whinnying, shouting activities jamming the streets. Men wearing grotesquely colored shirts fringed with silver tips that swayed along the edges of their sleeves hid deeply tanned faces under wide-brimmed hats stained with greasy circles of sweat. They sat atop jittery, prancing horses like grandees, impatiently kicking their mounts with jangling spurs to press them forward between the maze of wagons and carts.

Amelia leaned close to Helga and shouted above the din, "They are cowboys. They're riding Spanish ponies, way livelier than our German plow horses. The mules pulling freight wagons haul supplies from the ships to the towns and farms and even the military bases out west." Amelia obviously delighted in pointing out things that made Indianola different from Oldenburg.

Paul rose on tiptoe to peek into the back of an open freight wagon. "I'd like to ride in that." His pure blue eyes held the same dreamy excitement Helga had seen so often in Max.

All the activity stirred the dust, and it settled on everything, turning the colorful buildings lining Water Street to a faded gray and making Helga's lips and tongue feel gritty.

Amelia led them over to Main Street, where they stepped onto a wooden walkway built high against two-story buildings. The second floors extended over the walk, offering welcome shade from the springtime heat. Wagons and animals milling so close together stirred the fishy odor from the dock, blending it with a manure smell so strong Helga wanted to cover her face.

It felt safer to be on the walkway, well above the nervous, pawing animals. Amelia and Hermie in the lead carried in each hand a valise filled with everything they had needed on the ship. Gretchen tucked Anna's blanket under one arm and clutched Anna's hand with the other, while Paul helped Helga carry their tightly rolled feather mattresses.

They moved quickly along the plank walk, the echo of their feet joining the busy throng hurrying into businesses or tossing supplies into wagons backed up to the walk. Men shouted, horses snorted, and the grinding roar of wagons moving along the street made the activity feel like chaos.

Anna whimpered, "Scratchy, scratchy," and pulled at the front of her dress, ignoring Gretchen's attempt to distract her by pointing out eight mules harnessed two abreast to a huge freight wagon.

"Helga, she's still wearing wool?" Amelia peered first at Anna and then the other children. "I've been saving some cotton cloth. It'll make fine dresses for Anna and Gretchen. We'll get shirt material for the boys at Regan's Dry Goods." Amelia took Helga's arm and covered her mouth to inquire, "How about you, Sister? Is there a place where you aren't scalded?"

Helga covered her mouth and whispered, "Between my legs."

Amelia's hands flew to her mouth, and she snorted the way Helga remembered. On those warm summer afternoons when they had finished work in the garden and had a few minutes before Papa required their help in the barn, they used to lie in the haystack, making up stories about the clouds. To keep Papa from hearing the gales of laughter, they had clamped both hands over their mouths, and Amelia always had snorted like a pig. Helga wondered if they could still find the princess with her breasts bare and her head slung back waiting for her prince to carry her away or the pregnant elf.

Amelia clutched Helga's arm and leaned close. "Take down your stockings."

"No." Helga giggled.

Amelia's eyes sparkled with the old mischief. "I'm serious. You must set the example for the girls. It's too hot here for stockings. And, dear Sister, this is spring. Summer will be torture unless you adjust your clothing."

Amelia hurried on ahead toward a white frame, two-story house built straight up and plain like so many along Main Street with its second floor extended over the plank sidewalk.

"Dr. Stein's office is downstairs. We go around." Amelia led them through a high gate and along a narrow shell walk that ran between her house and a mercantile store next door. At the rear, a kitchen and carriage house opening to an alley formed an L around a lush, raised vegetable garden.

"We live above, like most businesses here." Amelia led them into the kitchen. Despite windows, open shutters, and the door flung wide, heat radiating from the iron stove made the kitchen almost unbearable.

Amelia passed a gourd of cool cistern water and then dipped a rag in the wash pan and dabbed tenderly first at Anna's neck and then inside Paul's collar.

"Helga, take the girls into the washroom to freshen up." Amelia raised both eyebrows, signaling the time had come for Helga to roll down her stockings.

Out of the sun and away from the stove, the washroom felt cooler. As Gretchen closed the door, Helga lifted her skirt and began solemnly rolling her black cotton stockings down to her ankles. "Let me help you, Anna. This will make you cooler."

"Mama!" Gretchen scolded.

Helga sat down hard on the overturned washtub. "This is survival. Roll down your stockings." In silence, Gretchen carefully rolled down her stockings without looking at Helga. Anna laughed, lifted her skirt, and looked at her bare white legs. Gretchen grabbed the baby into her arms, looking accusingly at Helga.

* * *

The upstairs offered shade, and a breeze blew pleasantly through the windows. They all rose formally from benches lining both sides of the dining table as Dr. Joseph Stein's massive figure loomed in the doorway.

He peered with hard black eyes at each of them as Amelia made the introductions and then took his seat at the end of the table in the only single chair in the room. He did not remove his black coat despite sweat beading on his face and coursing in rivulets into his thin gray beard.

Moving directly to business, he began, "My man just returned from delivering your trunk and informed me Max drowned as the ship left the dock." Both eyebrows shot up in curly gray arches.

"Yes." Helga sat straight, her angular chin set and tilting slightly upward. She would not let Dr. Joseph Stein see her flinch.

"Drunk?"

"Yes." She didn't look at the children, but she felt Paul's body grow rigid beside her. She'd shielded them for as long as she could. Now they had to survive. Dr. Stein looked like their best hope.

Dr. Stein nodded, studying the space in the middle of the table. "I had plans for Max, of course. I heard when sober he made a fine merchant, excellent with customers." His sharp eyes circled the table, stopping at Hermie. "The circumstances leave you responsible. Are you prepared to care for your mama and three young ones?"

"I am, sir." Hermie's eyes were as brown as Helga's, and they never left Dr. Stein's gaze. He kept his shoulders pulled tightly back, his boy chest thrust forward. "After, the … accident, the ship's helmsman obliged me with chores. I'll get work on the docks."

"Your brother calls it an accident. And what do you say it was, lad?" Dr. Stein looked directly at Paul, the frail, handsome image of Max.

Helga's hand flew out protectively to Paul's trembling shoulder. "Dr. Stein, if you still plan to offer me the position operating your boarding house, I'll accept."

Dr. Stein scraped back his chair, unfolding his massive body to its full six-and-a-half feet. "Frau Stein will direct you to the house. To compensate my expenses, and they've been considerable, as you'll see, I'll require 40 percent of the monies you take in. Frau Stein will show you the book and the pricing." He withdrew a folded handkerchief from his breast pocket and rubbed it vigorously across his face. "I'll come round the first of each month."

Helga rose, and the children stood with her. "Thank you, Dr. Stein."

"Thank Frau Stein. She's gotten the house in order. I expected that would be your job, but she insisted. You're fortunate to have such a devoted sister." He looked for the first time at Amelia, and Helga saw the softening of his gaze. Amelia had won this rigid man's heart.

"Since Max will not be here, I think the one room across from the kitchen will be large enough for Frau Heinrich and the children."

Amelia nodded and smiled sweetly into her husband's face.

Anna slipped off the bench, the first move she'd made since Dr.

Stein entered the room. Holding her blanket against her chest, she said, "Hello," in clear English, her brown eyes never wavering from his face.

Turning to gaze at her, the great, lumbering man melted to one knee, his pasty white face turning crimson. "Hello. And you are Anna?"

"I am." Anna leaned forward and stared solemnly, her face inches from his.

"I must get back to my patients." Dr. Stein looked at no one as he rose awkwardly and hurried from the kitchen.

Amelia removed from the pie safe a pot of potato soup and ladled generous servings for each of them. The cornbread tasted odd, so gritty it hung in Helga's teeth. "We serve a lot of cornbread. Meal's more plentiful than flour."

"I like it," Paul volunteered.

Helga took a deep, cleansing breath upon hearing those positive words from Paul.

After they cleared away the dishes, Amelia opened the lower doors of a cabinet and withdrew a carefully folded piece of sky-blue cloth. "This is from a dress I wore when I was thin," she said. "It'll be enough for Anna and Gretchen."

Gretchen took the cloth and rubbed its softness against her cheek. Then Anna insisted on her turn.

"Thank you, Tante Amelia. I'll help Mama sew as soon as we're settled." Gretchen smiled at Helga for the first time Helga could remember since Max died.

"We must take you to your new home."

As they walked along Main Street, men and women spoke formally in German to Frau Stein, nodding courteously to Helga. Amelia led them through the tall double doors of D. H. Regan's Dry Goods. The orderly interior brimmed with bolts of cloth of every imaginable color, neat piles of blue work pants, and wide-brimmed sunbonnets swaying prettily from overhead lines.

"Afternoon, Frau Stein. This must be your sister from Bremen." Mr. Regan smiled broadly, his short, stubby fingers resting on his ample chest.

Helga nodded. As she had suspected, the word had spread. The woman whose husband jumped drunkenly from the ship to the dock and then fell stupidly into the ship's churning wake was indeed an interesting immigrant. Helga did not lower her eyes. She meant to begin this instant to show her children and the world she was not ashamed.

"Frau Heinrich needs cloth for the boys' shirts and some work pants. Place the charge on my bill."

When they stepped back onto the street, Helga reached for Amelia's hand. "Thank you, dear Sister."

"We can't make you sick before you're settled. Besides, I feel alive again with you here."

A crowd had gathered in front of an impressive white two-story building. A sign over the door read Casimir House.

Amelia whispered, "Let's cross to the other side. It's a slave auction."

Helga's breath caught, and she stood transfixed, staring at a black boy, not more than ten, chained by his ankle and wrist to a giant black man. Both slaves had been oiled until their flesh shined like polished ebony, outlining every detail of their muscles.

"They look so strong." Hermie spoke barely above a whisper. "Have you ever seen such muscles on a boy?"

Helga had not. The child's massive shoulders bulged under the faded, sleeveless shirt, his powerful arms hanging loosely at his sides, seemingly waiting for the next command. She looked down at the round softness of Hermie and Paul. How could she think their life was hard? Yet in this new land she intended to see their lives improve.

Suddenly the crowd parted, and Helga recognized the top of Anna's blonde head as the child stepped onto the porch and very lightly stroked the black, manacled hand of the boy. The contact made the boy jump—the only indication of his fright. The crowd burst into merry laughter as Anna examined her fingertip for color.

Helga pushed her way into the throng and took Anna firmly by the hand. "Please forgive her," she whispered, her eyes riveted to the black child's steady gaze.

The amused spectators patted Anna's head and made comments about the lovely little German lass until the auctioneer began chanting excitedly. Almost immediately, the bidding reached a fever pitch.

Gretchen said, "Is that man selling those people?"

"It's legal. A few locals use slaves as domestics. Mostly, they're sold to planters who take them upriver." Amelia kept her voice low.

Helga couldn't speak. She clutched Anna's hand and stared at the boy, who continued to look into her stricken face, his eyes bold and defiant, so little remaining of the child within that fully developed body.

"We must go. You don't want to see them taken away." Amelia tugged at Helga's arm.

"I've got to see where he goes," Helga whispered.

A planter stepped forward wearing a big, broad-brimmed hat and a green satin vest that made his stomach bulge like he was about to strut at the head of a parade. He paid an amazing $900 for the boy and $1,200 for the man. The auctioneer nodded dismissively at the slaves, who trotted behind the planter in a rhythm that kept them from entangling their jangling chains. With one smooth motion, both black bodies heaved themselves into the back of a wagon. It creaked slowly away, the older slave glaring sullenly into upturned faces, the boy continuing to stare over the crowd at Helga.

Amelia pulled at Helga's arm. "Come. You can make yourself sick over something you can't change."

Anna tucked her finger protectively into the fold of her skirt.

Chapter 2

HERMIE FELT AWKWARD FOLLOWING TANTE Amelia into D. H. Regan's Dry Goods. Mama seemed so pleased that Tante Amelia had cloth for Gretchen and Anna's dresses, and now she seemed perfectly content to have Tante Amelia buy shirts and work pants for him and Paul. He couldn't understand what was happening to him. He was almost a grown man. Even Dr. Stein said he should be taking care of the family, and yet he felt like crying. His insides shook, and he feared any minute he might burst, like Paul, into loud sobs. He was embarrassed that someone from home had told Dr. Stein about Papa's drinking, that they had said Papa would be a good merchant when he was sober. He had felt the same humiliation as all the passengers on the ship gathered around saying such nice things about Papa to make them feel better. It was just like Papa to wait until they had a chance to have a better life to pull another stunt and get himself killed.

He kept holding his breath to keep back tears. It felt shameful to stand in front of Mr. Regan while Tante Amelia selected his clothing and then said to put it on her account so loudly her voice filled the whole store.

When he was a little boy, she had made him laugh harder than anyone. Somehow she knew when Papa had been drunk for days. When she came for a visit, everything changed. Papa rose up on one elbow and talked as if he'd just stretched out for a short nap. She always took Hermie on a secret trip through the woods. She'd boost him into a tree, toss her skirt over her shoulder until her bloomers showed, and clamber right up beside him, which somehow seemed perfectly okay for Tante Amelia to expose herself.

From their castle in the treetops they made up stories about a silly giant who got lost in the woods and had to help an elf climb up into the trees so they could look each other in the eye when they talked, and the elf always showed the giant the way home.

Sometimes, they sang songs and pretended a wealthy landlord came by and asked them to come live with him and teach his sad daughter to laugh.

By the time they returned home, Papa was always washed and shaved and wore fresh clothing. Then he'd get out his violin and play happy tunes before bedtime.

Now everything was changed. Tante Amelia came to Texas and became Frau Stein, and she had position. People on the street bowed their heads to her and called her Frau Stein. And Mr. Regan hurried around the store helping her like she was his only customer.

Hermie felt relieved when they finally left Regan's store and continued walking to their new home. The downtown buildings that backed up to the dock gave way to open beach, and houses facing the water sat behind fences far back from the road. Away from the protection of the buildings lining the waterfront, the wind blew in steady gusts off the bay. The road spread out wide, offering plenty of room to walk even as a steady stream of freight wagons, Mexican carts, and horseback riders heading in both directions rumbled past, stirring the shell dust into gritty clouds.

Farther up the beach, Hermie noticed children playing in the edge of the water, jumping the waves as they broke into rolling whitecaps before hitting shore. Crossing the Atlantic, he had seen enough waves and had felt the icy dousing as much as he cared to for a while. Even the daydreams he and Paul had shared of swimming in the salty water seemed like silly talk of little children.

Tante Amelia made Mama laugh as she kept Paul and Gretchen guessing how much farther it was to their house. Hermie didn't want to spoil their fun, but he could see their big, barrel-top sea chest by the front door of a plain two-story wood house. He wanted to shout to them to look at that huge white house. Steep steps rose almost as high as his head to the wide front porch wrapped around both sides of the house; more stairs climbed to the porch circling the second floor. A sign with neat black lettering that said Stein House Room and Board swung from a pole extending above the steps.

Tante Amelia stopped at the gate separating the house from the shell road and spread her arms triumphantly. "This is it. You're home."

The gasp was audible. They stood like statues, staring in amazement.

Finally Tante Amelia said, "The houses along this part of the beach are raised on piers to protect them if a storm kicks up big waves. Ship carpenters built this house for Dr. Stein. The corner posts are set six feet into the ground and fastened together with metal crosspieces to make it one of the sturdiest houses in town. He thinks this is a good location, because this road goes to Old Town and on to the far reaches of Texas settlements. Everyone going west and coming back to town passes this way."

They trailed Tante Amelia as if she were the Pied Piper up the stairs onto the porch built so high they could look across the bay and see land on the other side.

"Dr. Stein had it furnished; the smokehouse is stocked." Amelia opened plain double front doors leading into a wide hall. The air felt instantly cooler. Her steps echoed as she rushed along the wood floor to the rear of the hall and threw open two doors onto the back porch, allowing a soothing breeze to sweep through the house.

Hermie had never been inside such a large house. Their cottage at home, which connected to his grossvater's barn, sat at the rear of the landlord's property, where he had built Grossvater's manse as his church tithe. Their cottage, originally built as a storage shed for farm tools, consisted of only one room and a tiny alcove for Mama and Papa.

From the hall, Hermie peered into the parlor opening on the right. All the furniture was wood; even a bench long enough for three grown men had wood arms and a wood back. The plank walls were painted white, and the floors smelled of clean, new wood. Slatted shutters on the west windows were tilted to keep out the afternoon sun and allow a cool breeze to slip through. The dining room beyond the parlor held two long tables with benches on both sides and a cabinet with a mirror across the top.

"Dr. Stein says the two front rooms opposite the parlor should each rent for sixteen dollars a month for one person. The rooms also have doors opening onto the porches." Tante Amelia led them to the room at the back of the house across from the kitchen that Dr. Stein said for them to share since Papa wasn't there to run the mercantile store. Three beds and a washstand holding a bowl and pitcher filled the room; windows looked out on the back and side porches. "Hermie and Paul will probably want to sleep on the back porch until next winter," she said.

"Me too," Anna shrieked as she ran up and down the hall fanning her skirt, exposing her white legs, and ignoring Gretchen's stern looks.

"The porch is just for the boys, isn't it, Mama?" Paul said.

Mama didn't respond. Since Papa died, she seemed silent, Hermie thought, sort of faraway even when she sat right next to him.

The biggest iron stove Hermie had ever seen sat in the kitchen on great round legs. Three teakettles waited to be heated.

"Where do we get wood?" Hermie asked as he opened the firebox stuffed with neatly stacked split wood.

"The Howerton family's schooners make daily runs up the Navidad River to Texana to keep their wood yard supplied. Their drays deliver cords to the back porch."

Hermie watched Mama stroke the stove like it might be magic. Then she opened the cupboard and gazed at the sacks of sugar, coffee, and cornmeal. "I don't know how we'll ever repay you and Dr. Stein for all of this." She kept shaking her head like she expected to wake from the dream at any minute.

Tante Amelia placed her knuckles on both hips and grinned like a big, mischievous elf. "Believe me, Sister, Dr. Stein knows what he's doing. This place will make money. He doesn't believe in charity."

The back porch extended behind the kitchen to a washroom with big tubs for washing clothes and another one for people. The back stairs went up onto a porch, and the hall ran between three big rooms on each side of the house. Each room held two or three beds, a washstand, a bowl, and a pitcher.

"Dr. Stein thinks with all the teamsters, salesmen, and sea captains coming to town, you'll be full most of the year."

After she finished showing off everything, even the raised garden she'd put in that was already producing despite it only being April, she hurried home to cook Dr. Stein's supper.

As Tante Amelia stepped off the front porch, Anna rushed in the back door, proudly carrying an egg in each hand. When she handed her gift to Mama, they all laughed, but Mama laughed the hardest, dabbed at her eyes with the hem of her skirt, and said, "How like Amelia to have everything ready for us, even laying hens." Mama kept dabbing at her eyes, and Gretchen began wiping Anna's muddy dress. Hermie hurried to the tall wood cistern next to the back porch and drew a bucket of water to fill the basin for Gretchen.

Later, in the backyard, Hermie watched as Paul shoved both hands into his pockets. "It's big and ugly. No flowers. No trees for miles," he muttered as he kicked at the gravel walk leading beyond the henhouse and smokehouse and back to the privy. Then he stopped and stared across the alley where a jumble of prickly pear cactus formed a fence around a cow lot.

"We'll plant lots of flowers, enough for a fairyland," Gretchen said as Mama came down the walk.

"We'll make our privy path as pretty as the one at home." Mama laid her hand on Paul's shoulder. It didn't seem to bother her when he pulled away, kicking gravel all the way to the back porch. "We'll plant trees right away," Mama called after him. "As they grow, they'll be our measure of how long we've lived here."

"Let's plant big trees," Anna shouted in delight.

As darkness came, the wind died down, and mosquitoes began their barrage. The tiny stinging creatures had attacked them when they docked at Galveston. For two nights, no one had slept. The ship's crew gave them a mixture of salt and lard to ease some of the itching; they said mosquitos plagued all the towns along the coast, but Hermie had expected Indianola to be different. Tante Amelia sounded so sure in her letters that Indianola was a wonderful town, that life would be much better for them in Texas.

* * *

Hermie heard Mama calling from the back porch. She had lit a candle in the kitchen, intending for their lessons to continue without interruption. If success was possible in this new land, his mama meant for them to have it. While they took turns reading from the Bible, Mama used Anna's wool dress for a pattern to cut out Tante Amelia's soft cotton material.

She demanded expression when they read, and she corrected them without lifting her head when they mispronounced one of the names in the Old Testament. Even onboard ship, she had insisted every student read with expression.

Hermie didn't plan for Mama ever to know her classes on the ship had filled up because of his lie. When one of the boys asked Hermie in front of everyone why his mama made them read and do numbers every day, the lie that Helga was a teacher came out so easily. It was partially true; for as long as he could remember she had taught them what Grossmutter and Grossvater Anton taught her—to read Holy Scripture, to spell, and to do numbers so they knew how much was due on a bill. When Tante Amelia began planning to come to Texas, she and Mama had added English to their lessons.

At first Hermie lived in dread of the passengers finding out Mama wasn't a real teacher; she had never been to a real school. As the children began reading and drawing numbers and letters and speaking in English, Mama gained the respect of all on board. It seemed like no one remembered Papa's humiliation.

Hermie held mixed feelings about the gifts Mama received for teaching. He was pleased to get Herr Helfin's shoes. His toes rubbed the ends in his old pair. And he still pored over the copy of *Leipzizer Illustrierte Zeitung* with its articles on the London Fair, the California Gold Rush, and the German migration to America. But sometimes it felt dishonest to take the gifts when she wasn't a real teacher.

After their lessons ended, Hermie and Paul strung mosquito net over the corn shuck mattress on the porch the way Tante Amelia showed them. She insisted her corn shuck mattresses were cooler and did not get moldy and stinky like their feather mattresses did on the ship.

Lying on the porch, Hermie watched the faint glow of Mama's candle from the doorway of the kitchen. He imagined her long, slender fingers moving rapidly as she drove the needle through the cloth. He wondered if she cried, if she missed Papa.

As crickets began a wild chorus, Hermie thought of all the nights Papa stretched out with them in the garden. While crickets rubbed their wings together to call their mates, they gazed with Papa at the stars and imagined flying through the heavens using starlight as their guide.

Mosquitoes buzzed incessantly outside the net, a freight wagon rolled past, and a drunk sang a mournful song as he staggered home.

Hermie rolled over, covering his ears with both hands. He did not ever again have to listen to Papa come down the lane singing, letting all the neighbors know he'd earned enough money to go to the village tavern.

The image came again: the ship pulling steadily away from the dock, the water swirling black and angry where Papa had disappeared. When Hermie could hold his breath no longer, he had known it was over. Papa was gone, and he felt profound relief.

* * *

The loud rap on the front door woke him with a start.

"I'm here to see Frau Heinrich. I'm Captain William Whipple." In the morning light filtering through dense fog, he looked like a giant shadow. "I've come seeking a room."

Hermie rushed to the kitchen and found Mama asleep, her head on the table and Anna's new dress clutched in her lap. The candle had burned down.

Hermie followed her to the door as she smoothed her hair and shook out her skirt.

"I'll put you in this downstairs front room. It's our best, most private. I charge twenty dollars a month, with three meals a day except on Sunday night." She led the way and then stood aside while the bulk of Captain Whipple moved into the room.

Captain Whipple's pink face hid behind a mask of white whiskers. "When I saw you yesterday at the auction, I knew you wouldn't be using slaves. I've stayed my last night at the Casimir House. I can't be waited on by slaves." He took the valise from Hermie, sat it firmly beside the bed, and counted out the silver dollars.

"Welcome, Captain," Mama said as the heavy coins clattered into her apron pocket.

"I gather yesterday was your first slave auction?"

To Hermie's surprise, Mama said, "I'll never forget the eyes of that Negro child."

"There are many I can't forget." He shook his grizzly head. "I can no longer live at the Casimir House."

"Breakfast will be soon," Mama said as she motioned for Hermie to come help.

"You made a mistake," Hermie whispered. "Dr. Stein said sixteen dollars for downstairs and fifteen for upstairs."

"I'll give Dr. Stein his forty percent of sixteen dollars the first of every month."

"But this is Dr. Stein's house."

"And I'm running it. That's what I charge."

Relief swept over Hermie as he realized he didn't have all the responsibility for caring for the family. Mama knew how to care for them.

Captain Whipple returned just before lunch in a wagon with a bookshelf and lots of books Hermie and Paul helped carry into his room.

"You must read a lot." Paul spoke with reverence, holding a volume in each hand.

"That's one of the books of Homer's *Iliad.* You may borrow it sometime."

"That would be nice. We get tired of reading from the Bible every night." Paul carefully slid the book onto the shelf with all the others. "We have some newspapers the passengers gave us on the ship."

"If you enjoy the news, I'll share my paper. I get one off every ship that docks at my pier."

* * *

Later, when they unpacked their sea chest, Hermie realized how much of it belonged to Papa—two black suits and matching silk shirts for wear in Dr. Stein's mercantile store, Papa's violin, an extra pair of shoes, and his French playing cards.

Mama carefully unwrapped a hand-painted cookie dish. "A gift from Grossmutter ... to remind us we aren't peasants."

As she closed the chest, she said to Hermie, "You'll grow into Papa's clothes very soon."

"And I'll learn to play the violin," Paul said. Mama nodded and smiled, "I'm sure you will."

"Me too," Anna said. A knock on the front door echoed loudly through the house, sending her racing to throw open the door.

"I'm Eli Cox." The man stood with his hat in his hand, his white collar bound tightly around his neck, his black hair and moustache sprinkled with scaly white flakes. "They're full at Mrs. Angelina Eberley's House. She sent me here." He sniffed as though testing for an unpleasant odor. "I'm a commission and forwarding agent ... been elected to the commissioners court. Since all the members live either downtown or in Old Town, I decided I should represent this area."

Mama kept nodding her head as if she knew what a county commission was or what in the world a commission and forwarding agent did. She acted as if she understood every word of what Eli Cox said. "And my rates are lower."

Eli Cox finally smiled.

Mama led him to the middle room behind Captain Whipple's. "It's one of our best, with a private door onto the porch. It's twenty dollars a month including three meals a day, except for Sunday supper."

At supper, Eli Cox glared at the small bench sitting at the end of the table. He walked out abruptly and returned from his room carrying a heavy chair covered in shiny blue cloth. He placed it at the end of the table and then introduced himself to Captain Whipple. "I'm your newest member of the commissioners court. It's good for business now that Indianola is the county seat."

When Captain Whipple only nodded amiably, Eli Cox said, "I recognize your name, sir. Wasn't it two years ago when you escaped with your life from the *Bounty?*"

Captain Whipple nodded. "True."

"How many died? Six, I believe … tremendous loss of cargo."

"Correct."

For the first time Eli Cox acknowledged the others at the table. "I'm sure you remember coming through Pass Cavallo, Frau Heinrich. There's a treacherous bar in the channel."

"Did the *Bounty* wreck on the bar at the pass?" Mama asked.

"Exactly," Captain Whipple said.

"Where does your ship sail?" Mama asked.

"Between New Orleans and Matamoras, Mexico, but I'm no longer captaining. You came in at my wharf."

Eli Cox leaned back in his chair and announced, "After the good captain … left Harris & Morgan, he extended his wharf into deeper water in the bay. He made it possible for larger ships to access our port."

When Captain Whipple did not respond, Eli Cox said, "Appears Charles Morgan's our mutual enemy." Eli Cox turned to Mama. "He rules shipping from New York to this bay. Morgan lost a fine ship captain when he fired Whipple. If I can be as successful as the good captain's been at overcoming Morgan's power, I'll have no complaints."

"Why is Charles Morgan your enemy?" Hermie asked Eli Cox.

"Uses his shipping business to control ports. When Lavaca foolishly upped its dockage rates, Morgan moved his shipping terminus down here to Powder Horn. I had to quickly move from Lavaca or see my commission business go under."

Captain Whipple smiled genially and continued eating his baked hen.

Hermie wondered how long Captain Whipple would keep smiling at Eli Cox's constant prattle.

Chapter 3

PAUL DID NOT TELL MAMA he wanted to walk in the fog to Tante Amelia's so he could pretend he was at home, pretend the forest grew tall and dark right up to the side of the road, pretend he was going to see Grossmutter Anton, who would pour him a mug of fresh milk and tell him tales of fairies riding on the raven's back and elves hiding in the cabbage patch.

"I'll watch for freight wagons in the fog, and I'll get news about the next brig from Bremen," Paul said.

Mama stopped peeling potatoes and looked at him as if she were checking for a fever. "Bremen? Paul?"

He shuddered and quickly closed the front door to avoid responding. Fog spread so thick he could feel its wetness on his tongue. He listened for the roar of the surf, but the bay lay still, like a tamed bear licking the shore, waiting for a chance to rouse from its sleep. The gate creaked shut, and the white shell road blended with the fog, erasing the line where the road stopped and fog began. The road seemed to rise like the steep hill at Grossmutter's, curving up like the inside of a ball. He had to stop and stare at the ground to steady himself to keep from losing his balance.

He stepped in a puddle before he saw it. Water oozed over the top of his shoe, making a squishing sound as he walked. He saw the next puddle, leaned over its milky whiteness in search of his reflection, and then carefully placed his other foot in the cool, murky hole, watching the water bubble into his shoe. Both shoes squished, and his toes slipped freely inside the shoes, which had belonged to Hermie until last summer.

Puddles stood all along the street like on the roads at home after spring rains washed down from the hills. He looked into each water hole and then stomped sharply in its center, enjoying the clinging coolness of his new trousers against his legs. By the time he reached downtown, the sun had started burning through the fog, creating eerie building silhouettes. He heard the mules' snort and the creaking of the freight wagon before it materialized out of the fog. Within touching distance of him, the driver pulled the team to a halt. The mules stood perfectly still—two across and four deep. Smelling of wet leather and manure, the big lead mule stood so near that Paul closed his eyes and reached for the animal, imagining he was in Grossvater's barn.

"Hey, Oscar," he whispered.

"It's Henry." The driver tugged at the harness, moved the lines up across Henry's back.

Paul kept his eyes closed as he stroked the slight indention along Henry's nose.

"You like mules, boy?"

"My grossvater's mule was Oscar. I fed him every evening."

"You just ship in?"

"From Bremen. Three weeks ago."

"I'm Eagle Stone. You speak good English." All the time he talked, the freighter's powerful hands ran along Henry's bridle, adjusted the bit, and then moved along the lines, easing tension on the traces.

"I'm Paul Heinrich." He continued to whisper the words that had calmed Oscar as he moved his hand along Henry's thick neck.

"Check at the livery stable. Ole Man Fisher could use a hand that likes mules. Get rid of his no-count son."

"You want a place to stay, good meals? My mama runs Dr. Stein's boarding house out Main Street."

"I might do that. Me and my boy Jackson need a permanent place." Eagle Stone looked for the first time directly at Paul. He had more freckles than Paul. His carrot-colored hair curled like fuzz from under a floppy felt hat. He took off his glove to shake Paul's hand. His hard, crusty hand, like Paul's, was covered in freckles.

Paul knew Eagle Stone liked him. He didn't know how he knew, but it felt good.

Paul skipped the rest of the way to Tante Amelia's. As the sun continued burning through the fog, the air felt lighter, and everyone smiled when Paul spoke.

Tante Amelia met Paul in the garden. "How'd your new trousers get so muddy?"

"Why're puddles in the street? It didn't rain last night."

"High tide leaves puddles. We have to be careful where we step."

"High tide comes into the streets?"

Tante Amelia refused to be distracted. "Your mama works hard to keep your clothes clean. Get along to the washroom, strip off your pants, and wrap in a towel. Wash your pants, and you better wash your underdrawers. Hang them up behind the washroom."

"Mama will worry."

Tante Amelia picked up her bonnet and tied it under her chin. "I plan to stop by and leave one of my outgrown dresses for your mama. I'll tell her you're cleaning out my hen house." She held out a rake, her eyes daring him to refuse.

Paul tied the towel around his waist. He didn't care what Tante Amelia said; he wasn't taking off his drawers. He had hoped Tante Amelia would offer him some milk and cookies or tell him a story, but she was Hermie's friend, not his. Hermie always stayed clean. He didn't even sweat when he worked.

He scared an old hen off her nest. When she stopped flying and began clucking around the hen house, he shook the rake at her and chased her outside. By the time he dumped the last of the droppings in the compost heap, the sun had baked dry all but the waist of his trousers.

Paul waited for a team of sweating mules making the wide turn from Main Street into the livery stable near the end of the block. He hurried behind the wagon as it pulled to a halt and the driver jumped down.

"Ira not around today?" The driver spoke with a wad of tobacco in his jaw. He spat a streak of brown juice onto the powdery dirt floor.

"Hell no, and I got me a full house."

Paul knew the twisted little man in the blacksmith apron must be Mr. Fisher.

"I'll help you out," Paul said, pulling himself as tall as he could. "Eagle Stone sent me."

Both men turned, and as their eyes ran down the scrawny length of Paul's body, he pulled his shoulders back, set his jaw, and waited.

Mr. Fisher nodded toward a long hayfork hanging on the wall. "Pitch that hay to the team of mules in the back lot," he said, gesturing toward a stack of hay. "Soon as I get these unhitched, rub them down."

Paul moved at a fast trot. A job—the first one in the family to get a job.

All afternoon Paul felt Mr. Fisher's eyes following him. He loved working for Grossvater, because Grossvater's eyes always stayed on him, and Paul liked hearing Grossvater tell his neighbors what a worker that boy was. Paul never questioned why Grossvater didn't tell him directly; overhearing the warm tone in Grossvater's voice had been enough.

Paul had been hungry when he stopped at the livery stable. By the time the sun started slipping low over the bay, his stomach hurt. When Mr. Fisher handed him a half-dollar, he forgot everything except the feel of that shiny coin.

"Be here by sunup tomorrow, and you'll earn a dollar," Mr. Fisher said.

Paul kept his hand deep in his pocket, his fingers curled tightly around the coin, as he hurried along Main Street. Big-wheeled Mexican carts rumbled past, their fighting cocks bowing their necks from their perch at the top of the load. Freight wagons ground dents in the shell street, the drivers intently watching their animals. People on the wooden walk seemed in a hurry, but Paul didn't mind. He had a job, and he was busy too.

At the end of the block, where Crockett Street extended down to the dock, his heart lurched. How could he have forgotten Papa? He had planned to check the ship arrivals after he left Tante Amelia, but he had forgotten all about it when Eagle Stone told him about Ole Man Fisher needing a hand. He began running toward the pier extending into the bay. He could see a ship being loaded. Had Papa come in and found no one to meet him?

Gasping for breath, Paul ran to first one and then another of the Negroes who flexed rounded, sweating muscles as they heaved enormous crates onto their backs and moved like twisted grapevines up the gangplank and onto the ship.

Bremen? They didn't know about a ship from Bremen. This ship came in near noon loaded with a bunch of Germans, but they were all gone now.

Paul turned and ran back down the pier. He completely forgot his half-dollar. He could see Papa waiting for him. He'd tell Papa he was sorry for not jumping into the water to help him. He'd practiced over and over in his head since the ship left Papa struggling underwater how he would make Papa understand he hadn't meant to let him drown.

Dusk had turned the bay to roaring blackness with just a speck of light painted across the horizon by the time Paul reached the big, white house. His breath came in gasping sobs, and tears mixed on his face with snot and hay dust.

"Your mama will be glad to see you." The voice came from the end of the porch. Paul recognized Captain Whipple's white whiskers showing in the darkness.

"Where's my papa?" Paul gasped.

"Your papa?" Captain Whipple's giant hand closed tightly around Paul's shoulder. "What're you saying, young man?"

"I've got to find him. Keep him from feeling bad we let him drown."

The front door opened, and Hermie shouted, "He's here."

Mama and Tante Amelia, both wearing aprons, rushed up the hall. Mama clasped Paul in her arms, crushed him against her, and then shoved him away and demanded, "Where have you been? Go wash yourself. Why did you frighten us this way?"

She tried to push him down the hall, but Paul balked, searching the faces staring at him. "Where's Papa?"

The hall fell silent except for Paul's whimpering. "I missed his ship."

Anna threw her arms around Paul's legs and shrieked, "You stink."

Tante Amelia said, "It looks like you've got to wash your new clothes again."

Paul nodded—not in agreement about his clothes but in awareness from the stunned looks on their faces that Papa was not there, and was not expected.

Mama placed her hand on his shoulder, gently guiding him down the hall. "I forget too. Sometimes I look up and expect to see Papa."

"He'll come," Paul whispered to himself, because he was the only one who still believed.

"Wash yourself. We've already had supper. I'll give you a plate in the kitchen."

As Paul scrubbed lye soap on his new trousers, the half-dollar slipped from his pocket to the bottom of the pan. He placed it on the washstand. It didn't seem so important anymore. He pulled on his nightshirt and crawled under the mosquito net on the back porch.

Something made his eyes pop open. He sat up quickly, realizing Hermie lay asleep beside him. Fog dampened everything. Someone moved on the porch. "Papa?" he whispered.

"It's me, Paul," Mama said. "I'm starting breakfast."

His pants had not dried in the dampness. They felt like layers of ice against his body.

Mama held out the half-dollar when he stepped into the kitchen. "I found this in the washroom."

"I got a job at the livery stable. Today I'll make a whole dollar." His body grew warm at the surprised expression on Mama's face.

She sat down on the bench next to the table, almost reverently touching his shoulders. "You were so tired you fell asleep without supper or your lessons."

"I'll be home tonight." He didn't say he wouldn't go to the pier again. He knew he shouldn't go, but he didn't know if he could stay away. Believing could make anything happen.

Mama handed Paul the half-dollar. "Use your money to get some work clothes at Regan's Dry Goods."

Paul ran all the way to the livery stable, his half-dollar thumping with importance against his leg.

Mr. Fisher pointed over his shoulder. "Ira, my boy, is asleep in the hayloft. Don't pay him no mind."

Paul tried to be quiet as he pitched hay to the mules in the back lot. He smelled Ira before he spotted him sprawled out in the hay. Paul recognized the rancid odor.

By the time the sun burned off the fog, he had fed two teams and started brushing down a third. The powerful hand came down so hard on his shoulder his knees buckled.

"So you're the little bastard who took my job." Ira Fisher's face was square and red. His sand-colored hair lay fine and cropped on his wide forehead.

"Ira!" Mr. Fisher spit out the name like an oath. He stood with both feet spread apart, holding a hayfork on its end.

"You watch out, bastard," Ira whispered. "I'm not going to be pushed aside."

Paul kept an eye over his shoulder all afternoon, but Ira had disappeared.

After Mr. Fisher paid him, Paul hurried toward Regan's Dry Goods, enjoying the sound of the coins jingling in his pocket.

As he crossed the alley next to the stable, Ira stepped from behind a wagon. His hands ground into Paul's shoulders, lifting him like a sack of potatoes to the far end of the wagon. "I believe you got something for me, bastard." Ira's hand popped Paul hard on the leg and then, feeling the coins, he ripped fiercely at Paul's pocket. "You tell my ole man, and you'll be sorry, bastard."

Ira vanished as quickly as he had appeared. Paul wanted to scream, to run into the street and tell people he'd been robbed, but he didn't know where Ira was hiding. Maybe he was watching. Paul's shoulders throbbed and his leg burned, but the sight of his torn pants brought tears.

They missed lessons again that night because Paul argued with Mama, begging her not to visit Mr. Fisher. He didn't want to tell Mama he knew it'd be a while before Ira came back; Paul's money would keep Ira asleep for a few days.

In just a few days Paul felt better about their house, because Mama kept her word and planted flowers that made the path to the privy look pretty like their privy path at home. Several days later he saw bushes planted along the fence. "They're oleanders," Mama said. "After supper I'll show you the new trees." As they walked around the house, Mama pointed out all the trees she'd planted. "The pink-flowering tamarisk is small, but Tante Amelia says it'll be a good windbreak. The Texas umbrella is a good shade tree, and the oleanders from Galveston will have pretty flowers all summer. They're small, but we'll keep them watered and manured. Won't be long until you'll be surprised at what good shade they provide."

Chapter 4

OF ALL THE BOARDERS, GRETCHEN liked Captain Whipple best. Unlike Eli Cox, who insisted on sitting at the head of the table and kept asking questions about Mama's boarding-house experience, Captain Whipple seemed content to slide his bulk onto a bench at the back side of the table. He also loved Gretchen's potato soup and did not mention that Mama still had much to learn about making good cornbread.

How to cook with cornmeal was one of Tante Amelia's first lessons for Mama. Gretchen stayed busy in the kitchen so she could watch Tante Amelia, who threw off her bonnet and let it dangle down her back while she paced the kitchen, instructing Mama on all the uses for cornmeal. She showed her how to make pancakes and how to mix cornmeal with hot water and salt and fry it in pork fat to make delicious corn pones.

Gretchen tried copying Tante Amelia's gestures—elbows close to her waist while her hands flew about in excited, bird-like gestures. Anna encouraged Gretchen's efforts by laughing, marching behind her, and saying, "Tanty, Tanty."

Unlike the boys, who worked and ran errands all over town, Gretchen and Mama spent their days being trailed by Anna as they cooked, washed, and cleaned.

Gretchen's contact with the outside world came at mealtimes while listening to the boarders and in continuing excursions into the old newspaper articles and books given to them by grateful parents aboard the ship. As she worked, she recited to herself the last words of Ferdinand von Roemer in his book *Texas:* "I had grown to love the beautiful land of meadows; to which belongs a great future ... May its broad, green prairies become the habitation of great and happy people!"

She had not seen the meadows or broad green prairies, but she wanted to believe they lay out there waiting to welcome her.

Stirring sheets boiling in the black pot in the backyard, her skirt tied up behind her to keep the hem out of the fire, her mind roamed to the meadows she remembered outside their village—deep valleys waving in thick grass with big, fat cows grazing contentedly, their collar bells ringing a deep, rich melody.

After supper one night, Captain Whipple showed them how to soak cornbread in clabbered milk. "It's as good as bread pudding."

Eli Cox looked down his hooknose like a witch in a black suit and said Captain Whipple obviously had never charmed his palate with really fine French pastries.

"I like plain food," Captain Whipple said.

Eli Cox had a habit of shaking his thick black hair, which made white flakes sprinkle his shoulders. Amid the shower, he said, "Alhambra and Casimir houses have wonderful pastries."

"And slaves who serve it." Captain Whipple scooped the last bite of cornbread from the bottom of his mug of clabber.

Gretchen felt Mama's hand on her shoulder, the signal to finish clearing the table and come out to the kitchen. She found her mama marching up and down the hot little room, ignoring the sweat bubbling on her upper lip and breaking through the back of her dress. "I'll show Mr. Eli Cox who can cook," she snorted. "And I'll get some flour."

"It costs nine dollars a barrel."

"We'll manage. As soon as one more boarder comes, we'll have flour."

Without further comment, Gretchen poured hot water in the pan and began washing dishes. She had grown up understanding that Mama's angry outbursts remained private, a determined side of herself she only allowed Gretchen and Anna to witness.

* * *

Standing at the front door, Herr Richard Pressler looked like Gretchen imagined a headmaster should look—black suit, black bow tie, black hair parted in the middle, and a thin black moustache. He patted Anna's head and smiled kindly at Gretchen, but he obviously was most concerned with inspecting their upstairs back room. Mama acted so eager to have him and Frau Pressler that Gretchen wondered if Mama missed the company of a grown woman.

Herr Pressler explained that he had been hired to teach at Indianola's new private girls' academy. He fretted about Frau Pressler climbing the stairs at the Stein House, as Mama insisted it be called. Gretchen wished Mama would listen to the boarders who kept calling it the Heinrich House.

"Frau Pressler wants a family environment ... away from the impersonal Alhambra or Casimir houses," Herr Pressler explained as he examined the entire house, even the kitchen and washroom.

"Let her look for herself," Mama said.

"She trusts me."

"Really?" That was Mama's response when she didn't believe a word of what she heard.

"She's not strong enough to run a house, but she wants a family environment."

"Really?" Mama said again.

As soon as he paid the first month's rent and left, Mama announced, "Now we can buy some flour."

When Herr Pressler arrived with a wagon loaded with trunks and boxes and Frau Pressler's harp, Mama muttered under her breath, "She's not too delicate to play the harp."

The massive, gold instrument was the most beautiful thing Gretchen had ever seen. She couldn't believe it was sitting in the front corner of their parlor.

Mama knew about fine musical instruments. As a young girl, she sometimes had gone with Grossvater to worship services, baptisms, and weddings at the landlord's fine manor house. When Papa was not there to laugh at her, Mama had told them stories of the grand occasions, the lovely dresses, and the beautiful music of Bach and Handel. She had always ended her stories by saying, "You see, we aren't peasants."

Sometimes it felt like Mama put on airs about her past. Before Grossvater died, he hadn't been called to the landlord's house for many years. Mama insisted the landlord believed the strain of conducting a wedding or a baptism was too much for Grossvater.

Sometimes Papa would fall backward on their bed and say he wanted his peasant woman. Mama hated being called a peasant woman, and when Papa called her that she always pulled the curtain across the doorway of their little room and refused to answer. Gretchen wanted to tell Papa if he called her his little peasant, she would come to him.

When Frau Pressler arrived, Gretchen could not believe such a beautiful woman wanted to live in their house. She smiled kindly and repeated each name as Herr Pressler introduced her. Then, following her husband, she lifted her black skirt and sailed up the back stairs, as graceful as a long-necked black swan.

Enchanted with the way Frau Pressler glided across the upstairs porch, Gretchen tried walking slowly, moving only her feet to make her skirt slip smoothly along the floor.

In a short time Herr Pressler rushed out to the kitchen, little beads of sweat making his white face shine. "She's resting," he whispered. "I'll return to the academy until dinner."

"Really?"

Gretchen felt embarrassed that Mama kept her head down, packing the crock with newly pickled cucumbers.

Immediately after Herr Pressler left, Anna began squealing, shouting to Hermie as he came down the alley that a harp lady lived upstairs. "Now we can buy flour."

Hermie was just returning from a long day preparing the soil for a commercial fall garden at a ten-acre plot Mama rented down by Powder Horn Lake.

Gretchen left the butter half churned on the porch and began shushing Anna.

"Let her be," Mama said.

"She'll disturb Frau Pressler."

"This is not a toy shop. We don't have china dolls here. Herr Pressler wanted her to have company. She'll have it here."

Anna climbed onto Hermie's back, stretching her arms around his neck and nuzzling her face against his sweat-soaked shirt. "Ask her to play music, Hermie. You play Papa's violin."

"I'd love to play with you." Frau Pressler stood at the railing on the upstairs porch, her black hair a mass of soft curls around her face that waved softly into a huge bun on the back of her head. A fluffy white blouse that looked as soft as goose down peeked from the front of her black jacket. Her hands, which looked far too tiny to play a harp, rested like graceful doves on the banister, which Gretchen feared might be dusty.

"After supper?" Hermie smoothed awkwardly at his grimy clothes.

"We have lessons after supper," Mama said to no one in particular.

"How wonderful," Frau Pressler called. "I'll be ready when you finish." She disappeared into her room, but Hermie didn't stop staring up at the porch until Mama asked him if he'd finished turning the garden.

"Not until we have more manure. I'm going to offer to clean some of the cow lots and chicken coops along the alley. I'll charge twenty-five cents for each one."

"Good. The new wheelbarrow will pay for itself in no time." Mama lifted Anna off Hermie's sweat-soaked back.

Gretchen went back to the churning, her face burning with embarrassment. Mama acted like a peasant sometimes.

As they headed into the house to set the table for supper, Anna ran ahead and turned back, shouting, "The harp lady's playing."

Gretchen heard the rich tones of the harp as soon as she entered the house.

"Don't be long," Mama said as Gretchen hurried up the hall following Anna, who stood in the doorway of the parlor transfixed, staring at the beautiful lady whose fingers made such lovely music.

Frau Pressler nodded slightly and went on playing.

Herr Pressler, standing statue still, his hands clasped behind his back, his skinny chest bulging proudly, whispered, "Bach."

Mama stood in the dining room doorway, the hem of her apron pressed to her lips, tears making her gentle brown eyes look like pools of rich molasses.

If Gretchen could have named a moment when she embraced her new life, it happened as Frau Pressler's music transformed the bleak parlor. The room glowed in the warmth of the late-afternoon sun, throwing slatted rays across the scrubbed wood floor.

Mama called Gretchen to help her move the two dining tables to form one grand banquet table. "This will make it more like family," Mama said.

As always, Eli Cox arrived first for supper. He called Mama immediately. "Why have you moved my chair? I've always been at the head of the first table."

"We didn't move your chair. We arranged the tables to seat everyone together. You're at the center of the head table."

"Head table, my foot. All sides are equal."

"You're in the middle, sir, a prominent enough spot." Captain Whipple stood as tall as Gretchen had ever seen him, his head back and his eyes looking narrowly at Eli Cox.

Eli Cox's black eyebrows wriggled, and he sniffed his big hooknose. "I guess it will have to do." He pulled out his fancy blue chair and sat down.

After introductions, Mama and Gretchen began serving.

Eli Cox looked at the Presslers. "Since you've been recently enjoying the luxury of hotels here and in New Orleans, do you find it unusual that Frau Heinrich and her family always join us at meals? In my experience the household staff serve and then take their meals in the kitchen."

"We've selected Frau Heinrich's home especially because it's a family place." Frau Pressler smiled like an angel.

"I've said before, I'm here because slaves aren't serving our food." Captain Whipple's voice sounded extra loud.

As they cleared away the supper dishes, Frau Pressler followed them to the kitchen carrying several serving dishes. "While the men smoke, may I help you out here?"

Gretchen opened her mouth to protest such a fine lady coming into their hot kitchen but fell silent as Mama stammered her appreciation.

"You might hear Hermie read," Mama said, not letting on that Hermie usually read aloud without supervision while they washed dishes. Mama quickly sat a bench near the doorway to offer the best light and ventilation.

Anna leaned against Hermie's knee as he began reading in a shaky, embarrassed voice from the chapter on raising sheep in Leipzig's *Good Advice for Emigrants.*

Gretchen noticed Anna shifting her position, leaning instead on Frau Pressler's beautiful black linen knee.

Gretchen shook her head at Anna, who pretended not to notice. Frau Pressler laid her tiny white hand on Anna's shoulder, and Gretchen watched Anna cut her brown eyes smartly around to see if Gretchen noticed.

After Paul, whose stable odor filled the kitchen, labored through his portion of the book, Frau Pressler said, "Are you learning French?"

"Spanish," Mama said so quickly Gretchen flinched. "There're so many Mexicans in and out of here hauling goods on the Chihuahua Trail, I believe the children must be able to communicate."

"Exactly what I tell Herr Pressler. He insists on French for the girls at the academy." Frau Pressler smiled faintly, and Gretchen's heart almost burst with love for such a delicate, misunderstood lady.

While Mama washed a loudly protesting Anna, Hermie and Paul carefully removed Papa's violin from the sea chest. Hermie labored to tune it, but when he entered the parlor, Herr Pressler's sensitive ear immediately heard the discord and added the final touch.

Gretchen joined very softly with the others in singing to Frau Pressler and Hermie's accompaniment. That night she dreamed Frau Pressler and Captain Whipple asked her to sing for them. She opened her mouth, expecting to hear her lilting soprano, only to awaken to gurgling in the stifling May heat.

Chapter 5

HELGA WAITED EACH DAY UNTIL the boarders left and especially for Hermie to be off to work in the garden plot, before she cleaned out the privy. Hermie had acquired such odd notions since they arrived. Helga did not see the harm in using dried human dung along with dried chicken and cow dung in the garden. Every family at home successfully used all the waste to fertilize their gardens and fields. The American newcomers working the plots next to Hermie filled his head with ideas and shamed him unmercifully when they discovered the kind of fertilizer he used. "They say my garden smells," Hermie complained. "And they laugh at me for eating raw cucumbers. They say pickled is the only way to prepare cucumbers. They don't know about kohlrabi or mustard or parsley or even leeks. They think I'm a dunce."

Helga began mixing the dung with weeds and vegetable scraps each day and watched Hermie silently eye the ever-growing pile before loading it on his cart without asking how one cow and a few chickens produced so much.

As she crossed the alley dividing the house lot from the cow lot, she noticed Gretchen carefully sweeping the upstairs porch, her hair freshly washed and twisted into a high bun on her neck—the same style as Frau Pressler's. In just a few months in this new country, her children were changing into such different people.

All except Anna, who spilled over with so much love and energy she pulled the entire household into her charm. Anna had led Frau Pressler out to the kitchen. "Frau Pressler wants to cook," Anna announced.

"To … help?" Frau Pressler said. "And please call me Battina." Her plain blue cotton dress hung in a cool, loose fashion from her shoulders. It was much the way Helga and Gretchen dressed as the days grew hotter.

Helga stammered that she didn't need to help, but Battina brushed her protests aside. "I love to cook, and I want something to occupy my time." She hovered over the huge black pot of stew, ignoring sweat streaking down her back. Over the next few days she taught Helga to use leftover bread to make delicious bread pudding flavored with Herr Pressler's rum. She stood for hours patiently stirring the roux and then showed Gretchen and Helga how to blend the roux into thick shrimp gumbo for Herr Pressler's birthday. She knew several ways to prepare the red fish and trout Helga and Gretchen caught several days a week by simply crossing the road and casting into the bay.

"I grew up in New Orleans," Battina explained. "My parents lived a busy life. My nanny and our cook cared for me. I stayed in the kitchen when I wasn't having my school lessons. Cooking became my passion."

Helga admitted to herself, but to no one else, that she had been wrong. Battina was not a china doll. She wanted to be busy, to feel needed.

Helga felt pleased that she and Gretchen had settled into a comfortable rhythm for managing the constant pressure of running such a huge household. It was Paul that caused Helga the most worry. He wanted only men in his life. She'd not noticed so much when Max was alive. The boy always had trailed his grossvater or his papa when he was at home; now Paul seemed willing to put up with Ira robbing him at least twice a week to reap Mr. Fisher's praise, and he demanded that Helga stay out of it.

Paul didn't complain about the beatings the way Hermie complained about the taunts he received from the other gardeners. Paul seemed to keep everything to himself. Helga knew when Ira robbed the child only when the silver dollar failed to appear on the washstand.

One evening when Hermie wasn't home to play Max's violin and accompany Battina at the harp, Paul stood stiffly in the doorway, hay dust only partially washed from his face. He clutched Max's violin under his arm like a maestro, just the way Max carried it.

"We have a new violinist tonight." Captain Whipple rose graciously from his regular evening seat on the wooden bench and guided Paul to stand beside Battina.

"Launch a song for us," Gretchen said. She sat on a stool near Battina and glowed every time Battina looked in her direction.

As the sweet strains of "Der Tannenbaum" came from Paul's bow, Battina allowed Paul her full attention, chording softly in the background.

"Bravo, bravo." Herr Pressler led the applause. "You've got a sensitive touch, and such fine fingers ... but you must practice. How often do you practice?"

"I don't ..."

"But you must. You have a gift." Herr Pressler guided Paul into the hall, eagerly listing scales and practice pieces the boy should play each day.

Helga found Paul slumped on the back porch, the violin nowhere in sight. "Herr Pressler doesn't insist that Hermie practice."

"Hermie doesn't have your natural talent. Herr Pressler sees musical promise if you practice."

"I just want to play."

Helga sat down beside her son, who seemed to permanently carry the odor of hay and mule dung. She did not take his hand as she would have a few months before. She sat silently, staring with him at the sparkling blanket of stars spreading as far as she could see. *Oh Max,* she thought, *why did you desert me? This child needs you and I need you.*

* * *

Their finances improved more quickly than she expected. When the rented garden plot produced enough for Hermie to sell in town, she planned to save most of his income just as she saved most of Paul's in a pickle jar with her profits from the boarders.

Her papa would have been very upset if he knew Helga did not insist the children give money to the church. She no longer felt confident God noticed what they did from day to day—at least not confident enough to claim it as truth to the children.

The boarders paid promptly, mostly in silver dollars. Anna charmed Dr. Stein so thoroughly that his monthly visits to collect his 40 percent became family occasions, with Dr. Stein devoting most of his time to following Anna to the garden to see a bug or the progress of the turnips he had helped her plant.

When Anna wasn't trailing some member of the household, she manned the front door, watching the traffic along the road and telling anyone who slowed long enough to listen that they still had rooms to rent. One day Helga heard her shouting as she burst inside. "We have another boarder."

A young man stood at the door, obviously unsure if he should follow the child into the hallway. His curly blonde beard and moustache, stained orange from tobacco smoke, barely showed over the burden of the sketches clutched to his chest. "I'm Otto von Reider. I'm here to decorate your parlor, dining room, and hallway with my art. And I shall provide instruction for your children … for a reduced room rate, of course."

Helga looked over the seascapes, bold drawings of women in saloons, and sketches of stilted men. "I don't need any of this art."

"Oh, but I do lovely stenciling around the borders of the ceiling and around the fireplace. It's the style in fine homes today." He quickly slipped a pencil from his breast pocket and sketched a bunch of grapes along the front door frame. "It must be painted, of course. I mix blood with my paints to ensure my work endures for generations."

Helga envisioned the lively colors of fruits and flowers circling the plain walls. "You do lovely work. I can reduce your rate to seventeen dollars a month if you share one of the upstairs rooms."

Von Reider appeared pleased at the deal. "I'll move in this afternoon and begin transforming your home in the morning."

Helga had quickly realized Dr. Stein held no interest in what she actually charged so long as he received his 40 percent of his original price. Since Helga had grown up being warned about the demands of a landlord—care for the property and avoid asking for special favors—she found their arrangement quite satisfactory.

As for von Reider, he enjoyed full run of the public rooms, where prospective students viewed his work. A week after he moved in, he completed stenciling around the front door and partway down the hall.

The rich border of bright-colored birds and flowers taking shape along the top edge of the walls, and the evenings filled with music, lifted Helga's spirits, easing the burden of the long hours of work.

Soon after von Reider started his work, Battina came to the kitchen, smiling broadly as she held out a crystal vase. "This belonged to my mother. I thought with all the art we are enjoying we might cut some oleanders for the dining table."

Anna jumped from a bench where she was trying to snap beans with Gretchen. "I'll help," she said, and in a short time the table boasted an array of rose-colored blossoms.

Then Anna stood guard at the door, collaring each boarder, explaining how she and Frau Battina had gathered and arranged the centerpiece.

"Here comes another boarder," Anna announced.

Helga rushed from the kitchen, wiping her hands on her apron. She stopped short as she stared at the redheaded, freckled man covered in a thick coat of dust.

"My name's Eldred Erchel Stone. People call me Eagle. Your boy told me you cook good meals. In New Braunfels I heard you are a fine teacher—two standards I hold important for my boy."

"I don't run a school."

"You teach your own?"

"After supper."

"That'll do. Herr Helfin—you remember him from the *Margarethe?*"

"Goodness, yes. He was wonderful to my children. Have you seen him?"

"He said to send his regards … and this." Eagle Stone fished a lace handkerchief from his breast pocket. Dust flew as he slapped it against his knee. "I'm a teamster, been on the road three weeks."

Helga stared at the delicate handkerchief outstretched in Eagle Stone's rough, freckled hand.

"Herr Helfin said you were the finest teacher I could find for Jackson."

"I operate a boarding house."

"I need that too … for me and Jackson. He's nine—a smart nine. But he needs schooling while I'm freighting. I've dragged him with me for four years since his ma died. I've taught him all I know of numbers and reading from the Bible." Eagle Stone started kneading his old felt hat in both hands like it was a loaf of bread dough. "I tell him reading makes a person sharp. But those stories with all the *thees* and *thous* are hard to decipher. Herr Helfin says you teach from more than the Bible." Eagle Stone bent over until his face became level with hers, his blue eyes pleading.

"You want to leave him with me?"

"He'll be a big help." Eagle Stone glanced about. "Keep your garden clean as a whistle. And he knows how to wash and cook. Me and him been washing and cooking for ourselves for a long time. And I'll pay for my board just like I was here."

"I ask twenty-five dollars a month for two, but with the schooling …"

"I'll pay thirty." Eagle motioned with his finger, and immediately a boy with curly, sand-colored hair hopped onto the porch and bowed. "This here's Jackson. Jackson Stone."

Helga could not resist returning Jackson Stone's smile.

"He's a hard worker. Eats and sleeps without prodding." Eagle placed his hand on Jackson's shoulder, kept working his lips as though forming his next thought. "He's a fine young man."

"I can see that. Would you like to see the room?" Helga could smell the sweat and mule odor on Eagle Stone.

"Nope. I hear it's clean and sparse. I know you're German, so that says it's clean. I see your manner, and that says it's sparse."

Helga looked closely at his unblinking blue eyes, trying to guess what he meant. She smoothed her hair and immediately felt disgusted with herself for being so vain.

"Well, then supper's at half past six, Mr. Stone. And Jackson."

Helga looked in the mirror over the dining room serving board. She pulled her plain brown hair straight back over her ears. Severe described the look. Her plain dress looked neat, loose fitting for comfort in the kitchen, not for attracting men's eyes.

She quickly dusted the room over the kitchen, placing fresh sheets on the bed and leaving Eagle Stone a note saying she had failed to mentioned the price included three meals a day except Sunday supper and clean sheets on the bed once a week. A bath in the washroom with soap and hot water cost an extra half-dollar.

By supper Eagle and Jackson had moved their few belongings into the upstairs back room and occupied themselves in uproarious laughter in the washroom. Both looked slicked down and clean as they solemnly took their seats.

"Captain Whipple usually sits on that bench beside you. He left for New Orleans on business the first of July. He returns this week." Eli Cox spoke from his cushioned chair in the middle of his side of the table where, to Hermie and Paul's obvious irritation, he served as self-appointed introducer of all new arrivals.

Helga hid her own irritation.

"Pa's been to New Orleans. Lots of times," Jackson said.

"Your freighting business takes you that far, Mr. Stone?" Eli Cox looked down his great hooked nose.

"Not anymore. Now I plan to haul to San Antonio, New Braunfels, and Austin. Keep the steamers' schedule. That way I see my boy regularly."

"Pa and I used to freight the Chihuahua Trail clear to Santa Fe."

"If you've got good springs on your wagon, it may not be so bad. Try riding forty-eight hours in a stagecoach to San Antonio. Feels like riding your coffin down the side of a cliff," Eli Cox said.

"I don't notice a bit of discomfort from spring to the first cold front in the fall. Too busy looking at the wildflowers. As far as you can see looks like the world is one dancing color after the next."

"You must take a different route. I never saw one bloom." Eli Cox looked like a sour toad with his lips puckered and his nostrils flaring.

"What are your favorite wildflowers, Mr. Stone?" Helga asked.

"Bluebonnets. Especially when a storm's coming. The sky gets purple and blue, and the prairie all tucked under a quilt of bluebonnets just rises up and welcomes the rain."

"And that's another peculiar thing, calling them bonnets. They don't resemble any bonnets I've ever seen," Eli Cox said.

Eagle Stone did not look at Eli Cox; he looked down the table at Helga. "I'll bring you some. All along the stem the petals are shaped like bonnet hoods, and then there's another petal to protect the back of your neck from the sun."

The room fell silent the way rooms do when everyone wants to say something pertinent and no one can match what has just been said.

Jackson interrupted the silence. "Tell about the deer, Pa."

"White tail deer are thick. They feed a while on grass and then daintily reach over and nip off a primrose bloom."

"Pa says it's dessert."

"We hope you like it here as much as we do," Battina said. "We want to hear more about what you've seen in your travels."

"I like this ice," Jackson said as he took another sip of chilled tea.

"All the better establishments began using it last summer when refrigerated ships brought it in from New England. Real surprise when Frau Heinrich served it," Eli Cox said.

Helga was glad Battina did not announce that Amelia had enlisted her support to convince Helga daily deliveries from the icehouse would be good for business.

Battina had said, "Don't tell Herr Pressler I told you that last summer when the Casimir House began serving ice they raised our board a half-dollar."

Amelia had argued, "You operate a first-rate business, and you demand first-class prices." Amelia had marched up and down the kitchen trying to make her point.

"Don't push her, Amelia. It must be her decision." Battina didn't lift her head from the tiny stitches in the new dress she was sewing for Anna.

Helga didn't know when she had stopped resenting Battina. She still dressed for supper and sat very formally in Herr Pressler's presence. Perhaps Helga's attitude had changed as she watched the tenderness Battina displayed to each child. Or maybe it had begun when Battina asked Herr Pressler to help Hermie and Gretchen with advanced algebra. Or maybe the resentment had ended as Helga watched sweat pour from the body of such a frail and grand lady without hearing a word of complaint.

The day Captain Whipple returned from New Orleans, Battina received a letter from the same city. She tore it open eagerly and then, turning abruptly, hurried upstairs.

"Should I go check on her?" Gretchen asked.

"When she wants to talk about the news in that letter, she'll come down."

She did not come down until time for supper, her face ashen. Finally, she lifted her head and looked directly at Captain Whipple. "Is yellow fever in New Orleans as bad as I've heard?"

Captain Whipple set down his fork. "It's fearsome. Some say it's as bad as the Black Plague that devastated Europe in the Middle Ages. I heard that the editor of a local newspaper bragged in May about the city going without a case for six years. That's about when it started. Entire families are dying."

"Yes." She lifted her chin and gazed steadily around the table. "I received news it's taken my father and Hattie, the dear woman who raised me and cooked every meal I ate until I came to Indianola."

Professor Pressler placed his arm gently around her shoulder. "Don't make yourself sick talking about it."

"I need to talk about it."

Helga flinched in surprise. Battina never said a contrary word to Professor Pressler. He dropped his arm, obviously surprised at the rebuke.

"I'll be glad to arrange passage for you to return as soon as you wish," Captain Whipple said.

"I can't leave during summer classes, and my wife can't possibly make such a hazardous journey without me." Professor Pressler had regained his composure and his control.

Battina sat very still while everyone around the table looked at her. She seemed to be absent, her face without expression.

Like a burst of unexpected hot air, diners erupted in talk, asking for second servings, and then concentrating with extreme seriousness on the meal before them.

When the meal ended, Professor Pressler rose and waited for Battina to join him.

Instead of following her husband, Battina turned away and began helping to clear the table. Helga reached for the serving dishes in her hands and felt the trembling. "You don't need to help now."

"I need to. I don't want to go back upstairs until bedtime."

Chapter 6

HERMIE'S ASSOCIATION WITH THE OTHER gardeners quickly taught him about success paving the way to acceptance. As the summer days grew longer, the garden became more manageable, the dream of rows of crisp winter greens, eagerly sought by townspeople, drove him as he chopped weeds and turned the soil with the dried dung that Mama tried to disguise. And as his vegetables grew taller and looked healthier than those in the other plots, the ridicule began slowly turning to admiration.

Zachary Culpepper, the man who had started all the meanness about the dung, was the nastiest man Hermie knew except for Ira Fisher, who continued to rob Paul every few days. Hermie had not seen Ira Fisher, but he saw the terrible distress he caused Paul. Zachary Culpepper hung around where Hermie worked in the garden, constantly boasting that his corn stalks were the tallest in all the garden plots or bragging about putting Ole Man Swartz in his place. Zachary had noticed in the spring that Hermie's dung wasn't all animal. He had whooped and slapped his dirty britches leg and then trotted like a mare in season to every garden plot until every one of the gardeners cast glances at Hermie as if he were dung.

Now, as his crop thrived, his garden was the richest one of all, and he was beginning to have a lot more produce to sell than any of the others.

Every Saturday night Hermie slipped into the kitchen and looked in Mama's money jar. The collection of silver coins grew steadily. In fall, when all his greens came in, he expected the money to grow faster. Hermie didn't intend to be like Paul, who had decided Mama should keep his money separate. Hermie wanted to combine it all and watch how quickly the jar filled. He didn't notice when callouses replaced the blisters on his hands. He was too preoccupied with meeting his daily goal of weeding enough soil for two more garden rows and with planning his business.

When Jackson Stone moved in, Hermie saw hope for expanding.

After supper the first night, Hermie motioned for Jackson to follow him to the back porch. "You want to earn two bits a day?"

Jackson grinned, his wide-spaced teeth showing in the moonlight. "Sure do. I always wanted to work in a garden, but Pa and me never stayed anywhere long enough to get one going."

"My dung customers want me to haul off their slop. The freedmen do it near downtown, but they don't get out this way. With you helping, we can add slop hauling. We can sell it to the hog farmers out by the lake. Do a good job, and I'll up your pay."

"I will. You're gonna like my work."

Hermie grinned, and the two boys shook on the deal.

Many townspeople owned one cow and kept a hen house. As Hermie pulled his cart on the one-mile trip to the public garden plots, he collected their chicken and cow dung. With Jackson's help, they hauled two piles of dung every day except Sunday. On Sunday, Mama insisted they all go to church and spend the afternoon reading and playing music with Frau Pressler.

When the *Texian Advocate* from Victoria reached town, Eli Cox and Captain Whipple raced to be first to bring a copy to the supper table, and they always waited until Mama sat down at the table to share the news. In September both men eagerly told about the mail coach overturning in Peach Creek near Gonzales.

"It says the northbound coach made it through the ford just two hours earlier," Eli Cox read.

"My pa says it's a treacherous crossing. No markers along the bank to let drivers know the water height." Jackson held his spoon of food very close to his mouth as he spoke. The scoop of turtle soup disappeared in a second.

"Sounds like your pa is right." Captain Whipple always supported whatever Jackson said about his pa. "In a heavy rainstorm, the southbound driver must have been in a hurry. He plunged in, turning over the coach, spilling passengers, baggage, and the mail. The people made it out, but two horses drowned. The mail and baggage, all swept away."

"Yep. My pa is a careful man when it comes to that crossing." Jackson sounded as sure of himself as Eli Cox.

At times Hermie felt irritated listening to Jackson. Nobody's pa knew so much. It sounded like Jackson's pa talked to him about everything.

The next article Eli Cox and Captain Whipple read was about the yellow fever epidemic maybe heading toward Indianola from the eastern states and places like New Orleans.

"My pa says if it gets much worse here, we'll get quarantined."

"Your pa doesn't know Indianola hasn't ever been plagued," Eli Cox said.

"Pa says it's a good thing the new board of health started a hospital. You never know when it'll get bad."

When an article in the paper said the board of health planned to start pushing everyone in town to remove vegetable and animal waste, Jackson nodded his head. "Pa says a lot of experts think mosquitos breeding in low, wet places have something to do with yellow fever."

"How does your pa think the mosquito causes yellow fever?" Eli Cox sounded as tired as Hermie of hearing about Jackson's pa.

Jackson looked up from his plate long enough to say, "Mr. Cox, Pa just told me what the experts said. Pa don't know if it's true."

As much as Hermie wanted Jackson to shut up, he couldn't help being tickled that Jackson got the best of Eli Cox.

With the board of health requiring that all the dung and vegetable waste be cleaned up, Hermie increased his price to four bits for taking away the dried dung and four bits for raking out a hen house. And he raised Jackson's pay to a dollar a day. Every morning he and Jackson increased the number of stops they made to pick up dung and vegetable leftovers. They often had to skip lunch to have time to prepare two garden rows and get home for supper.

Not everyone paid in cash. Widow Lampke paid in two-dozen fresh eggs a week. She insisted Hermie and Jackson stop by on the way home each evening for a few eggs until she paid her bill. Each day she showed them her flowers, or she needed a fresh bucket of cistern water, or she needed them to wring a hen's neck. As they scrambled around doing chores for the old lady, Hermie reminded Jackson that courtesy was part of doing business.

One night at supper Eli Cox said, "Sounds like Huff's Hotel over on Decrow's Point is mighty fancy. Forced Alhambra House and some of the others to do a little upgrading."

"They cater to planters who want to vacation on the coast," Professor Pressler said.

"No one has Herr von Reider's fine stencils and displays of his beautiful art," Frau Pressler said.

Eli Cox motioned to his chair, still the only upholstered chair in the house. "Some people are accustomed to more comforts."

"Jackson and I think this end of town needs a fishing pier like the one Huff's advertises. Boarders could use it free; all others would pay ten cents." Hermie watched to see how they accepted the idea.

"Who in this group will use it?" Eli Cox asked.

"I will," Frau Pressler said. "I love fishing for trout and red fish right at our front door."

"Battina …" Herr Pressler never called her by her given name in public, and everyone turned. "The wind will scald you." He took her hand as though it were delicate crystal.

Hermie thought it odd she never let the professor see her in the kitchen or out in the garden with Gretchen. By the time he returned from the academy, Frau Pressler had returned, like a princess, to her beautiful silk dress. And no one mentioned Frau Pressler running races down the hall with Anna and teaching Mama to cook oysters and corn in so many different and delicious ways.

"You boys may know a lot about hauling dung. Building a pier takes engineering skills," Eli Cox said.

"My pa says a wise man takes advice from folks who have a success record," Jackson said. "Me and Hermie are looking to Captain Whipple for help."

Jackson never spoke ill of anyone, a trait he claimed to have acquired because his pa said to rest assured a man who bears tales about one person will be just as free to carry tales about you. But Jackson's feelings showed in his constant quotes from his pa.

"My pleasure," Captain Whipple said.

Hermie learned from watching Captain Whipple the way to deal with the likes of Eli Cox and Zachary Culpepper was to behave as if they did not exist.

During the summer, Mama moved their lessons to the front porch, where the breeze off the bay kept away the mosquitoes.

That evening, instead of Mama doing numbers, Captain Whipple came onto the porch to smoke his pipe and help Hermie and Jackson do the figures for their pier.

Hermie and Jackson stayed too busy to join in the complaints about summer heat persisting into what should have been fall. When it rained, which it did most every afternoon, they turned their faces up, letting the cooling moisture wash them. Then the rain stopped, and the air turned to hot steam. The wind lay down on the bay, and no place offered shelter from the ravaging mosquitoes.

News spread over town about several people getting yellow fever up in Old Town, or Karlshaven, as the early German immigrants called it. When a few died, panic set in, and people started moving the three miles down the coast to Indianola, walking past Stein House carrying all their goods loaded in carts and on their backs. Finally, they started moving their houses along the road, rolling them on logs pulled by teams of mules. Hermie and Jackson never got to see the strange sights, but it consumed the talk at supper. Anna spent her days watching and reporting on every passing event. One night Anna met them at the back gate reporting excitedly about a house floating past in the bay.

"That can't be true," Hermie said.

"It happened," Mama said. "A man pushed his house into the bay, and it floated past this afternoon. Some men pulled it out of the water near Powder Horn Bayou."

"It's worrisome the number of yellow fever cases being reported," Mama said as she turned back to the kitchen to finish supper.

One day in mid-October, their workload was so heavy that Hermie and Jackson hurried to reach home by dark. Coming down the alley, they noticed only one lamp glowed in the family's back room; the rest of the house appeared totally dark. Captain Whipple and Eli Cox stood just inside the hall at the back door. In the dimness, Hermie noticed Professor Pressler pacing up and down the hall and Herr von Reider standing with his back against the parlor door. Frau Pressler sat as still as stone on the bench in the hall.

"Anna's sick. She started a fever in the night. Dr. Stein is in there with Mama and Tante Amelia," Gretchen whispered.

The door opened, and as Dr. Stein stepped into the hall, Hermie glimpsed Anna lying perfectly still.

"We have a right to know what this is," Eli Cox demanded.

Dr. Stein drew himself up to his towering height, looking down at the stoop-shouldered little man before him. He seemed to be reciting from memory. "Face is flushed, early indications of jaundice, slow pulse, sore throat, and nausea."

"Can we get anything for her?" Captain Whipple said.

"Yellow fever," Eli Cox whispered.

"Ice for her stomach and cold baths," Dr. Stein said.

"I'll go now." Captain Whipple started for the front door.

"The ice house is closed," Professor Pressler said.

"I'll open it," Captain Whipple said.

"You must tell us. How do we protect ourselves?" Eli Cox demanded.

"Leave here." Dr. Stein headed for the front door.

"Will that help?"

"No." Dr. Stein closed the door behind him.

Hermie could hear Dr. Stein speaking to the people gathered outside the front gate. "Face is flushed, early indications of jaundice, slow pulse, sore throat, and nausea."

"Yellow fever." The whispered words sounded like a chorus drifting into the house from the street.

"I must go to her." As Frau Pressler rose, the professor grasped her arm. She whirled, looked him straight in the eye. "I'm going," she said and turned away from the startled man.

Hermie, Gretchen, Paul, and Jackson sank down on the hall floor opposite the bedroom door. Occasionally they caught sight of Anna, heard her begging not to be touched. No one offered to explain yellow fever to them or share their whispered exchanges.

Captain Whipple returned, breathing hard, carrying a tow sack wrapped around a block of ice.

People stood in silence all night outside the gate waiting for Dr. Stein to give them a report. Several women brought food, placed it on the dining table, and left hurriedly. No one ate.

Gretchen slept with her head on Hermie's shoulder, and Jackson's head lay on Gretchen's shoulder. Paul did not sleep. He paced slowly up and down the hall. The gurgling noise began just as daylight came. Tante Amelia called for more water and said, "Black vomit …" before she closed the door.

Captain Whipple motioned for Hermie and the others to follow him onto the back porch. Tears ran down his face and into his shaggy beard. "You know what black vomit means?"

"The Lord God will take her soon," Jackson said.

Hermie felt like exploding. When Captain Whipple folded his big arm around Hermie's shoulder, he did explode in a torrent of childish tears.

Gretchen and Jackson also fell crying against Captain Whipple, but Paul kicked the porch column, said Jackson's Lord God was a murderer, ran out to the privy, and shoved the wooden bolt shut on the inside of the door.

As the wind shifted and a cool, crisp breeze blew out of the north, Dr. Stein came to the back porch, his eyes rimmed red. "Our bright light … has been extinguished."

Chapter 7

HELGA SAT IN COLD SILENCE staring at the lifeless little body that just the week before had skipped up and down the hall announcing her third birthday to the entire house. Anna's face looked serene, the awful contortions from vomiting smoothed away. Had she really prayed for it to stop? Had she really asked God to release the baby from her agony? "I didn't mean it," Helga whispered. "God, I want her back."

"Let me help you wash her." Battina set the basin beside the bed and began gently washing vomit from the soft baby curls. "Eli Cox brought a lovely white casket lined in soft blue velvet from one of his warehouses." Battina spoke softly, soothing the pain with gentle, cleansing strokes of the tiny body while Helga sat motionless, convulsed in tears, unable to lift a hand.

"Did you say Eli Cox gave Anna a casket?"

"Eli wants to help." Battina did not raise her head from the task at hand. "Everyone loved this precious child."

"Frau Battina, the little dress is beautiful. Anna would have loved it." Gretchen stroked the blue softness of the material as she helped Battina slip it over Anna's head sagging lifeless in their hands.

Aroused by Gretchen's voice, Helga whispered, "Oh, Gretchen. I've ignored you." Helga pulled Gretchen onto her lap and crushed the child against her. Anna had been Gretchen's baby from the day she was born. Gretchen had been barely ten at the time, but she had begun immediately carrying the baby everywhere.

"You'll be okay, Mama." Gretchen snuggled against Helga's breast. "I'll help you."

"Come eat." Amelia put her arm around Helga's waist, lifting her from the stool where she'd sat for the past twenty-four hours. "Folks are bringing food. They're too fearful to come inside."

"I can't leave her." Helga knelt, pressing the tiny hand, already feeling cold, against her cheek.

"We'll put her in the little casket and move it into the parlor." Battina guided Helga toward the parlor as Professor Pressler handed Helga and Battina each a cup of tea.

He'd stopped trying to get Battina away from the child. He stared in disbelief at his busy wife as she took charge, directing all the preparations.

They set the coffin in front of the parlor windows where those afraid to come inside could see the child who had called to them when they passed, who had remembered their names and had known where they lived. Now she looked peacefully asleep.

Helga touched Eli Cox on his shoulder. "Thank you, sir, for the lovely coffin."

Eli Cox whispered, "I never gave her a present before now."

Paul began playing the violin. He appeared to be in his own world, separate from the stumbling, tear-filled adults all around him. He nodded to Battina, the only one who penetrated his space, who followed his lead as the music poured forth their grief.

Helga eased onto a bench at the foot of the coffin, allowing the lyrical tones of the violin, the gentle stroking of the harp, and the wail of the wind delivering the first cold front of the season to carry her to a place of deep calm. Finally, lifting her head, she spoke softly. "We'll have a graveside service this afternoon. People are afraid; we mustn't ask them to risk exposure in the church."

* * *

Bundled against the howling north wind, the long procession walked to Old Town, where a sloping oyster reef led up to an open iron gate beyond which the mounds of several fresh graves could be seen among stone markers.

"So many have fallen in such a short time," Amelia whispered.

Paul continued playing the violin, walking just behind the coffin carried by Hermie, Eli Cox, Captain Whipple, Jackson, and Professor Pressler. Helga held firmly to Gretchen's ice-cold hand and leaned into Amelia's tight embrace. Battina kept an arm around Gretchen's shoulder. The crowd stretched a long distance behind them and massed just outside the gate to offer privacy and avoid close contact.

Helga did not hear much of what the pastor said except that the beautiful child had brought so much joy into the lives around her and now rested in the arms of God.

* * *

Their footsteps sounded hollow, echoing through the empty house, as Helga began the long walk down the hall to the family bedroom. Startled, she stopped in the doorway and stared at the perfectly spotless room, stripped of everything: sheets, quilts, pillows, Anna's clothes, even the old sea chest Anna had ridden like a horse on the days too rainy for her to chase chickens in the yard.

"It's in the washroom," Amelia whispered as Helga stared at the bare space where the sea chest had sat since the day they arrived. "We'll start tomorrow getting everything washed. Dr. Stein says the neighbors will be satisfied if they see we've cleaned from ceiling to floor."

"Surely they know we're clean. We aren't peasants." Helga clasped her fist to her mouth, immediately sorry for the outburst.

Battina pulled Helga into a fierce embrace. "Cleaning is symbolic. It calms the hysterics."

At daybreak, after tossing sleeplessly through another long night, Helga, wrapped in the black wool shawl she wore against the winds of the North Sea, stepped onto the front porch and began scrubbing, never looking up as wagons and walkers began their daily routines.

After breakfast Amelia started a fire under the black pot in the backyard, and they all fell into a silent rhythm of boiling, rinsing, and hanging all of Anna's linens and clothing to dry in the icy wind.

* * *

Helga tried not to disturb Gretchen as she crawled quietly into bed, aching with awareness that Anna's hot little body would not be crowding against her.

Gretchen flung an arm around her mama. "I miss her."

Feeling completely impotent, unable to form any words of comfort, she pulled the trembling child into the curve of her body and rocked her as they wept softly together.

The next morning as they began taking their places for breakfast, Battina rushed in, her hair hanging loose and uncombed down her back. "Richard has a high fever. Please call Dr. Stein."

"I'll get him." Hermie grabbed a large slice of bread and headed toward the front door.

"I'll get a fresh basin of water," Helga said.

Captain Whipple followed Helga and Battina to the back porch. "Why don't we move him down to my room? You won't have to climb those stairs in this cold wind."

"I don't want to put you out of your room." Battina's frail fingers combed absently through her disheveled hair.

"I'll be pleased to take the empty front room upstairs."

The sight of Professor Pressler sent a chill through Helga; he had withered overnight. His eyes had caved in, and his skin was parched with fever.

The men and boys wrapped the frail man from head to foot in heavy quilts and gently carried him down the stairs while he moaned pitifully from the pain of being touched.

"I'll go for more ice." Captain Whipple looked at Helga and nodded solemnly.

Dr. Stein arrived in his carriage with Hermie and Amelia seated beside him. He shook his head after examining Professor Pressler. "I'd hoped this cold weather spelled the end of this."

"We'll all have it before it's over," Eli Cox hissed.

No one responded. The children settled on the hall floor. The day dragged on, and the vigil continued until suppertime when the black vomit began.

People gathered at the gate. Young girls from the professor's academy cried silently beside their distraught teachers and frightened parents.

Blessedly, it seemed to Helga, the suffering man drew his last breath just as the sun began sending its red glow across the bay.

Amelia gently moved Battina from the bedside while Helga helped Dr. Stein clean the wasted body. Stunned to see a grown man living in the body of a young boy, Helga realized the irony of this shadow of a man seeing himself as Battina's protector.

The next morning, they processed again to Old Town's cemetery. Battina asked Paul to play his violin. She wore a long black coat and covered her head and face with a black veil. Helga understood the need to be covered from prying eyes, and she understood that tears did not always come when a husband passed.

The townspeople and academy students followed.

As Dr. Stein predicted, the epidemic passed as quickly as it started. Professor Pressler was its last victim.

Captain Whipple insisted Battina keep his room. "I prefer the view from the second floor. I can sit on the porch and see across the bay."

Battina seemed to move in a silent world, not speaking, just performing tasks as she worked beside Helga, Amelia, and Gretchen to complete the symbolic scrubbing and washing of clothing and linens.

The morning after they buried the professor, Hermie and Jackson rushed off to their work and Paul returned to Mr. Fisher's stables. All three stayed away as long as possible in the evenings. They came in after supper each night, scrubbed themselves in the washroom, and ate leftovers in the kitchen before going straight to bed. Helga made no effort to hold classes. Everything about the daily routine felt hollow. Battina no longer dressed for supper. Like Helga and Gretchen, she wore an apron all day and removed it only for meals.

A week after Professor Pressler's passing, Battina helped clear the breakfast dishes and motioned for Helga and Gretchen to sit with her at the kitchen table. "I've decided to return to New Orleans, sell my family home, and settle my affairs. My nanny has been alone all this time. I intend to arrange for her freedom. It's weighed on me for so long. My father would not hear of it. Richard insisted I keep my father's wishes. Since I've no one I must please, I've decided to do what I think is right."

"Please don't leave." Tears creased Gretchen's cheeks. "I can't lose you too."

"Oh, dear Gretchen, I'll return. I want to live here with you and your mama." Battina took Gretchen's face between both hands. "This feels like home to me."

Helga surprised herself by throwing her arms around Battina and Gretchen.

"After Mother died, Richard insisted on taking the position at the academy to increase his chances of being accepted at the University of Louisiana. He dreamed of returning, of moving back into my family home." Battina shook her head sadly. "He wanted so badly to look strong and powerful and in charge like my father."

Helga wanted to tell Battina how very generous she was to allow her husband to believe he cared for a porcelain doll, but she didn't know how to form the words without slurring the proud image of Professor Richard Pressler.

After assuring Gretchen of her return, Battina left for New Orleans on Captain Whipple's steamship.

Chapter 8

JUST AS THEY GATHERED FOR supper, Paul burst in the front door leading a tall gentleman dressed in a silk suit. "Mama, this is Victor Vanderveer. He works for Casimir Villeneuve. He wants me to play at the Casimir House on Sunday afternoons. For tea. He'll pay me." His face flushed, his eyes dancing, Paul's energy electrified the room.

Victor Vanderveer's tiny black mustache looked like a streak of coal dust on his upper lip. "Pardon the intrusion. I see your guests are dining. Shall I return later?"

Eli Cox snorted. "No need to come back. We're like family at this table. What are you offering the boy?"

Stunned at Eli Cox's outburst yet remembering the coffin for Anna, Helga forced herself to look through all the bluster at the heart stirring inside Eli Cox. Offering Eli Cox a nod, she smiled at the gentleman who had stirred such delight in her son. "Please join us, sir. We can all hear what you have to say."

Paul hustled to the kitchen for an extra plate and squeezed onto the bench next to Victor Vanderveer. "Let me extend the Villeneuve's and my condolences on the loss of your little girl and the loss of Professor Pressler. Those tragic deaths brought so many to your gate and to the graveside services. The Villeneuves and I joined both processions and found Paul's musical skill very moving. Actually, forgive me for being so blunt. We attended the professor's services for another opportunity to hear Paul's fine fiddling. His playing's been the talk of the town. Patrons are requesting his musical talent for our Sunday-afternoon teas."

"What will you pay the lad?" Eli Cox bellowed with authority.

"Mr. Villeneuve's able to pay one dollar for an afternoon. Our experience shows a performer of Paul's talent and charm garners many gratuities. And if Paul continues to charm our clientele, he might perform on Saturday evenings in our bar." He quickly added, "The Casimir House enjoys being one of the most popular and luxurious establishments in the state." As he spoke he looked around the table, his gaze settling first on Eli Cox and Captain Whipple. "I'm sure you gentlemen agree?"

Captain Whipple nodded, but Eli Cox, bursting with self-importance, leaned back in his chair and tapped his breast. "I lived at your establishment from the time it opened." He looked around the table like the master of the household. "I discovered an opportunity at the Stein House to help a widow woman get established."

"A dollar and gratuities, Mama. That's better than I get from Mr. Fisher. And Ira won't be robbing me."

Helga felt overwhelmed with Paul's excitement, with the possibility he might pull out of his haunting sadness. "You need to work more than one afternoon a week."

Victor Vanderveer cleared his throat, his black eyebrows rising in pointed arches. "Madam, we also offer a job sweeping the bar and dining rooms. Mr. Villeneuve realizes the boy must work during the week."

"What about your slaves? Will they accept Paul doing their work? I can't employ white men on the dock. Free blacks won't stand for whites taking over their jobs." Captain Whipple's tone emphasized that his employees were free men.

"As you know, sir, Casimir House prides itself on having 150 rooms, and our staff is limited. They'll be happy to have some relief. Since we're beginning to host soirees and hops for the dancing entertainment of our guests, our staff carries even more of a load." He smiled broadly, folding his unspoiled white hands across his breast. "Shall we give it a try?"

Paul sat in rigid expectation, his head thrust forward like an athlete waiting for the flag to start the race.

"Paul is only ten, Mr. Vanderveer."

"Eleven next month," Paul said.

"His youth is part of the fascination. We are all amazed at his talent."

"Why don't you try it for a few weeks?" Helga said. "We'll see how you like it."

"Oh, wow. I'll like it. I promise you I'll like it. Can I wear Papa's suit? I need to look really nice."

Helga felt a jolt at the mention of Max's suit. She had left it in the sea trunk, expecting it to be a long time before one of the boys needed it. "We'll see how well it fits after supper."

Watching Victor Vanderveer join Paul in devouring the chicken and dumplings, Helga found it hard to believe the fancy man who came from the big city of New Orleans would enjoy her plain food.

* * *

On entering the washroom, Helga felt a surge of delight at seeing Paul bent over the sea chest, reverently lifting the black silk suit from storage.

"It still smells like Papa." Paul pressed the jacket against his face. Beaming at Helga, he added, "Papa would be proud of me, don't you think?"

Realizing she'd been holding her breath, she sucked in the refreshing air of relief and motioned for Paul to put on the jacket. "Very proud. You inherited his musical gift. He'd want you to use it well."

"I will. I will." Paul grew taller, swelling his chest in an obvious effort to fill the jacket.

"Your arms are long like Papa's. I don't need to take up much in the sleeves. Her hands moving over the soft silk, stirring the smoky, earthen odor of Max's body, forced a sudden sob she could not hide.

"Please, Mama, try to be happy. Papa always wanted us to be happy."

Helga nodded. "Yes, always."

As the sun rose, Helga completed the last stitch in Paul's fine silk suit. She quietly spread Max's gift to his son on the foot of the boys' bed. All three had started sleeping in the family room after claiming it felt too cold on the porch the night after Anna died.

Jackson made no effort to go upstairs to the room Eagle paid so handsomely to rent for his son. Instead, he stayed as near Hermie as Hermie allowed. Now they snuggled together against the chill under one of the feather comforters from home.

* * *

Although she tried to stop glancing up the hall to check on Anna and looking out toward the hen house where Anna had rushed every morning to gather eggs, she felt helpless to halt the constant ache pressing against her chest. Gretchen's bubbling effort to add cheer to long, dreary days kept Helga on edge as she tried not to cry in the face of so much love.

The evening classes became routine again, and the household

activities continued at a profitable pace. Drovers and ship captains, upon hearing about the clean quarters and good food, continued coming for a few days or a few weeks.

In late November, after Helga and Gretchen finished canning the last of the beets, the front door burst open and Eagle Stone hurried down the hall with a bundle of red-tipped Swiss chard under his arm.

"My God, Hel, I just heard about Anna." Tossing the greens on the hall bench, he threw his arms around Helga. Then, holding her at arms' length, he said, "You are so skinny. You feel like a skeleton."

Helga couldn't speak. The sudden strong embrace forced an audible sob. She felt herself melt against his sweat-stained chest in a rush of violent shaking.

He did not move, and he did not speak. He squeezed her tight against him and just held on. "She'll be okay," he said to Gretchen, but Helga couldn't raise her head to comfort her child.

Finally, he pulled her down with him on the hall bench, took a cool cloth Gretchen brought to him, and began gently washing her face. His voice made soothing sounds a parent might offer a suffering child. She did not know what he said; she just absorbed the comfort from this man she hardly knew.

Gretchen knelt before them. "Mama, are you all right? You're scaring me."

Embarrassed to look at Eagle, Helga took the cloth, quickly wiping her face. "Yes, I'm much better. I didn't mean to frighten you." How could she have allowed him to hold her so intimately?

"A person needs to get the grief out." Eagle kept one arm around her shoulder, his hand patting her as hard as if she were one of his mules.

"Oh, look at the beautiful greens." Gretchen gathered the Swiss chard from the floor.

"It's too late in the season to bring you bluebonnets like I promised. I know a man in Victoria who raises a huge garden."

"They'll be wonderful for supper. Thank you for your kindnesses." Helga stood, smoothing her hair back, wishing her housedress looked fresh.

Eagle rose awkwardly. "I guess Jackson's off somewhere?"

"Working with Hermie at the community gardens. You'll be impressed at what a flourishing fall garden those boys are producing. They're selling everything they grow in town." Helga laughed. "We have to insist they bring some of the vegetables home."

"How's his schooling? Is he working hard?"

"His reading is very strong. He's quickly mastering arithmetic. His spelling is terrible." She laughed again, surprised she'd not thought about the amusing way Jackson invented his spelling words. "He's as creative with spelling as he is with his story telling."

By the time Jackson and Hermie arrived, darkness had settled over the house. When Eagle heard them enter the back door, he rushed down the hall and grabbed Jackson in a fierce hug.

The boy threw both legs around Eagle's body, and the two laughed and yelled and beat each other powerfully with both hands. Then Jackson leaned back, still straddling Eagle. "Did you know yellow fever got little Anna? It's been a bad time, Pa." Jackson rubbed quickly at his eyes.

"Yes, boy. I heard when I got to town." Eagle wrapped his arms around Jackson's shoulders and rocked him gently.

Helga watched something profoundly beautiful in the way the two were able to love one another.

Eagle beamed with pride as Jackson read that night. He kept shaking his head in disbelief as Captain Whipple worked with Hermie and Jackson on their plans to build the fishing pier.

* * *

Helga heard Paul sobbing before he reached the back door. Both pockets on the work pants he wore to sweep the Casimir House were ripped open, exposing his underdrawers, and his face from his cheek to his eyebrow swelled in a bloody pulp. "Ira's after me again. I hate the damn drunk." Paul's tears seemed to come from pure rage. He looked as if he might explode.

Helga wrapped a piece of ice in a rag and held it to Paul's face. "I'm going to see Henry Fisher. He's got to stop that thief."

"No. I've got to take care of myself." Paul spoke through clenched teeth. His tears were gone, his jaw set in determination. Helga crawled into bed that night torn between the soft pleasure Eagle Stone stirred in her and her deep concern for Paul.

Just before sleep came, she jolted awake remembering that Eagle had called her Hel. No one had ever shortened her name in that fashion.

Chapter 9

TWO WEEKS BEFORE CHRISTMAS, THE weather cooled off enough for the boys to wear coats, and Helga and Gretchen covered their heads with shawls when they stepped outside. Helga reminded the children that in Germany their former neighbors were shoveling snow and the animals were safely stabled in the barns. The weather made this new land seem very strange.

* * *

The constant rumble of passing mule trains stopped. Then she heard the mules snort and Eagle shouting her name. Trying not to run, trying to hide her delight, she stepped off the porch and melted eagerly into the circle of his embrace.

"I just killed a young buck on the edge of town. Will the boys be home soon?"

Helga nodded, not trusting her voice.

"I'll show them how to butcher it. I gutted it and washed it out after the kill. Keeps it from tasting gamey. You'll have great roasts and sausage." Chattering nonstop, pulling her toward the wagon, grinning like a boy, he shoved back a tarpaulin to reveal a large cedar tree. "The prairie's full of cedars. I found some painted laurel seeds in New Braunfels for decorations. Maybe the children can paint some shells."

He carried the tree into the parlor and then scaled the wagon, proudly lifting the deer carcass from behind his bench seat. "Isn't he a beauty?"

"Mercy, yes." Helga felt her excitement mounting. "What wonderful Christmas surprises."

"I'll hang the deer on the back porch before taking my team to Ole Man Fisher." His shirtsleeve, ripped from the shoulder to the cuff, exposed hardened muscles as he lifted the carcass and carried it easily with one hand raised over his head around the house and all the way to the back porch.

"We've never eaten deer meat," Gretchen squealed as Eagle suspended the carcass by its hind legs from the edge of the porch roof.

"It's venison. Call it venison. Most folks think it's a delicacy."

As soon as he secured the deer, he hurried back to his team. Helga noticed as he drove away that his infectious grin was just like Jackson's.

The boys arrived just before Eagle returned.

Swaggering with pride, Jackson crowed, "My pa shoots a deer between the eyes every time. He guts it so fast you can't tell its wild game."

Eagle strode quickly to the porch and pulled a knife from a holster on his waist. "First, we cut off the head and front legs." He worked quickly, the boys watching in giddy anticipation.

Gretchen went back to the kitchen, shaking her head. "I'll help Mama cook it. I don't want to see you cut it up."

After carefully wiping the cavity, Eagle said, "As long as this cold weather continues, we'll let it age for a few days before we skin it."

As she followed the rambunctious boys racing to see the cedar that almost touched the twelve-foot ceiling, Helga felt an easing of the deep sorrow that had gnawed at her middle.

After supper and evening lessons, most of the household gathered to watch the children hang the painted seeds along the thick cedar branches. "I'll gather shells tomorrow, and we can paint them," Gretchen volunteered as they hung the last of the seeds.

The next day as Helga and Gretchen began preparations for lunch, Captain Whipple returned unexpectedly from New Orleans. "I have a surprise," he announced, shoving the front doors open wide to reveal Battina standing next to a beautiful woman with honey-colored skin who looked as elegant as Battina.

Both Gretchen and Helga dashed into Battina's open arms.

Captain Whipple led the colored woman into the hall before closing the doors against the strong north wind.

Laughing, Battina reached for the stranger. "This is Orilla Bernard. We grew up together." She pulled Orilla into a tight hug.

With their faces touching, they looked almost identical—the same jet-black hair pulled back in a smooth bun, the same full black eyes and slender little pointed noses. Only their skin differed. Orilla's looked like cream blended with rich coffee.

As Helga reached for Orilla's hand, she shyly curtsied, keeping her eyes on the floor. "I'll do my share of the chores, madam."

"Call me Helga. What a wonderful Christmas surprise."

"She insisted on staying with me." Battina's face twisted, and she seemed about to cry.

"We're delighted to have her." Helga pulled Battina into a hug.

"We arranged to return on Captain Whipple's boat. He told me it's against Texas law for a free person of color to enter the state. I must pretend Orilla's my slave."

"I don't understand." Helga stared at Captain Whipple. "We have freedmen here. They work on your dock; they pick up the slop for the swineherds ..."

"The Texas constitution makes it illegal to bring freed slaves into the state. Slave owners set free some of the men in Indianola. Some bought their own freedom. I watch after the men working for me because in places like Galveston freedmen are often sold back into slavery."

"How can they do that?"

"In Galveston and other places in the state, a free Negro breaking the law, even a minor law, risks being sold to his accuser to pay for the cost of his offense. I've told Battina and Orilla they must be very careful. We're more tolerant in Indianola, but we don't want to stir up the slavers."

Captain Whipple began unloading both their trunks into his old downstairs room.

"I want her to stay in my room, just the way we lived as we grew up." Battina scooped her arm around Orilla's tiny waist. "I've missed her."

The afternoon passed quickly with Battina relating her adventures in New Orleans and her good fortune selling her family home. "I'll be comfortable for the rest of my life because of my father's wise planning."

Gretchen and Helga helped Battina unpack, their excitement mounting as Battina unwrapped her Christmas decorations from New Orleans: candles stuffed in tin holders clipped like clothespins on the branches of the cedar tree, and beautifully painted glass balls made the tree shimmer in the afternoon sunlight.

Paul surprised them by returning before supper, but he said very little after meeting Orilla. In an unusual move, he had brought his violin home with him for the first time since Ira Fisher started robbing him again.

"This is the first time in months we've eaten supper together," Helga said as they took their places.

Spurgeon Platt, a plantation owner from over on the Colorado River who stayed with them when he came to town for business, looked up and frowned as Orilla took her seat next to Battina. "What's going on here? You have a slave sitting at the same table with whites!" He stood quickly, towering over the table, his hands jammed stubbornly in his coat pockets.

"I wondered that myself," Eli Cox said.

Helga, Eagle, and Captain Whipple all rose together as if directed by a concertmaster.

"She's welcome at this table, sir." Helga stood perfectly still.

Captain Whipple nodded his white head in agreement and did not move.

Eagle also nodded, his hands moving to his hips, his elbows pointing out like a schoolboy responding to a dare.

"What's a respectable white man to do at this hour? What if all the establishments are filled?"

"They may be." Helga looked at Eli Cox, waiting for his comment.

"I'll be out of here immediately after breakfast," Spurgeon Platt mumbled, resuming his seat.

"And you, sir?" Helga kept looking at Eli Cox.

He shook his head, straightened his jacket as though it had become rearranged in a scuffle, and began eating his roast venison.

"Let's hear the latest news," Helga said, resuming her place on the end of the bench, her voice sounding as lively as if nothing out of the ordinary had happened.

"I took care of my business in New Orleans, ate more than I needed of gumbo and fried oysters, and enjoyed the theatre on St. Charles Avenue. And the weather cooled off enough to merit a coat." Captain Whipple laughed easily.

Battina took a deep breath. "This was New Orleans' worst year ever for yellow fever. Orilla said by June hearses were making constant trips to the cemeteries. By August, two hundred were dying every day. All together ten thousand died over the summer." Battina reached for Orilla's hand. "Including Orilla's mama, who cooked for us before I was born. She was more of a mother to me than my own mother."

"What about the slave rebellion?" Eli Cox looked suspiciously across the table at Orilla.

"That was a wild rumor," Battina said dismissively.

"It made the paper."

"Mr. Cox," Battina said, exasperation in her voice, "being in the paper doesn't make it true."

"Pa says they started building the governor's mansion in Austin," Jackson announced in a poorly disguised effort to improve the supper table atmosphere.

"It should be ready next year," Eagle added. "So much construction is going on in Austin I'm expecting a load of yellow pine from Pensacola. I'll need a train of about ten wagons to haul it to Austin." He cleared his throat and added, "Have any of you seen my hunting knife? I'm sure I put it back in the holster and left it beside the bed. I couldn't find it this morning."

"I saw it," Gretchen said. "You dropped it on the floor by your door. I set it on your wash stand."

"Really?" Eagle frowned and rubbed his jaw. "I'm usually more careful than that. It's sharp enough to cut a bear wide open."

Instinctively Helga glanced at Paul, who sat stone-faced, his food barely touched.

Captain Whipple came to the kitchen after supper holding a book pressed against his chest. "On this trip I bought this book. I decided not to present it during supper." He held it up with the cover facing them.

"*Uncle Tom's Cabin; or, Life Among the Lowly*, by Harriet Beecher Stowe," Gretchen read.

Battina and Orilla both gasped. "How'd you find it? No one in New Orleans dares sell it." Battina looked closely at the cover drawing of a slave family gathered outside the door of a primitive log cabin.

"A friend sails between New Orleans and Boston. It's out of print now, but he found a copy for me. I thought you might want to include it in your nightly studies." Captain Whipple sounded conspiratorial. "I'm not sure it'll be welcome tonight in this household."

"Oh, it's welcome," Gretchen said, taking the book and reverently opening the cover. "We should start it tonight."

"May I listen?" Orilla asked.

"Of course," Helga said.

Eli Cox, unable to stand being left out of a conversation, even one held in the kitchen, ambled into the room. "Nobody around here has a copy of that book. Slave holders don't fancy it being spread around."

"We need to know the story so we can judge for ourselves." Eagle followed Eli Cox to the kitchen. "How about reading in the parlor so we can all hear?"

Without looking at Eli Cox, Helga motioned the children toward the parlor.

Spurgeon Platt had left the table immediately after eating his fill and hurried upstairs to his room.

Gretchen started reading and was soon captured by the thought of Arthur Shelby selling George away from Eliza and their little son Harry and by the whippings George endured on the new plantation. No one wanted to stop with the first few chapters, so Jackson and Hermie took turns reading as Arthur Shelby decided to save his farm by selling Uncle Tom and little Harry to a slave trader.

When Gretchen started reading, Paul left abruptly and began playing the violin on the front porch. Helga called him twice when his turn came to read. He stumbled over the words and seemed upset reading of Eliza running away with little Harry to keep him from being sold. As soon as they reluctantly agreed to stop reading, Paul went to bed, saying he was too tired to help finish the tree decorating.

Helga followed him to the back room and insisted on feeling his forehead for a fever. "I'm just tired, Mama. Don't worry over me so much. I'm not a baby."

Helga kissed her fingers and pressed them against his cheek. "I was hoping you could have some fun decorating the tree."

Paul shook his head and turned away to pull his nightshirt over his long johns.

That night as Helga slipped into bed, Gretchen threw her arms around her mama and whispered, "This has been the best day. I'm so glad Battina has come home."

"Yes, it's been wonderful." Her concern over Paul dampened an otherwise wonderful day. It felt good to have Battina home, and Eagle's presence made her eager to rise early to hear him whistling softly under his breath, hauling water from the cistern, gathering eggs, and checking the garden for the latest growth and the slightest sign of a weed.

* * *

The guttural scream jerked her from deep sleep. Bounding blindly from bed, she met Paul stumbling from his bed in absolute terror. She pulled him into her arms, smoothing his hair gently, trying to calm the sobs raking his body.

Eagle stood in the doorway, his long johns showing white in the darkness.

"It's a nightmare," Helga whispered.

She guided Paul, still shaking like someone with a violent chill, to her bed and pulled him in beside her. After some time, he settled down, slipping into a restless, thrashing sleep.

On Saturday, the kitchen buzzed with excitement as they began Christmas baking. Orilla made the bread pudding that Battina claimed had made Orilla famous all over New Orleans. Battina shucked oysters to bake for Sunday lunch.

At suppertime Eli Cox barely closed the front door before he announced, "They found Ira Fisher, that no-good son of Henry Fisher, dead this morning behind the Casimir House. Got his belly ripped wide open. Must've been drunk and tried robbing the wrong fellow. From the looks of him, he's been dead for a day or two."

Helga's body flushed hot. "How awful."

"Some people need killing," Eli Cox said. "Look at the way he robbed Paul. He got what he deserved if you ask me."

The murder dominated the conversation at supper. Paul, the only one missing, was playing at the Casimir House during the holidays on Saturday afternoons and evenings.

Gretchen, Hermie, and Jackson eagerly continued *Uncle Tom's Cabin.* Orilla took her seat very close to the circle of children.

Most of the household retired long before Paul came home. Looking exhausted, he insisted he had eaten at Casimir House. "I'll read tomorrow night. On Sundays we don't have late-night shows." He climbed quickly into bed with Hermie; Jackson had moved upstairs the first night Eagle came home.

Helga had barely slipped off to sleep when Paul's nightmare started. Hermie woke and helped arrange both beds so Helga could touch Paul to calm his fears.

"Please tell me what's upsetting you." Helga held fast to his trembling hand.

"I'm just tired."

"Sleep. I'll be close by." Sleep did not come to Helga as she tried to trace the events leading up to the nightmares.

Chapter 10

THE DAY AFTER CHRISTMAS, EAGLE ate breakfast, keeping one arm around Jackson and watching Helga. "That steamer from Pensacola arrived last night loaded with yellow pine. I'll be leaving for Austin as soon as we get the wagons loaded."

"You need me for this trip, Pa. I can manage one of the teams with no trouble at all."

"You can. You're a skilled driver. But I want you to have more knowledge than a mule driver. This is the best place in the world for you to grow into a smart man." His eyes never left Helga as he spoke.

After everyone left for work, Eagle continued slowly moving his gear down to the front porch.

Battina, Orilla, and Gretchen went out to the washroom to begin the weekly washing of linens.

Eagle came to the kitchen door. "I'm going to miss it here." He spoke very softly, keeping his head down like an embarrassed child.

"We'll miss you."

"Will *you* miss me?" When his face flushed, his freckles turned to big brown spots.

"Yes." Helga wanted to touch him.

"I'll get back as soon as I can. This is a good place."

"Eagle?"

"Yes?"

"Hurry back."

He took one step toward her and stopped. "If I touch you, I won't leave." He turned quickly, rushing up the hall and out the front door.

She stood in the middle of the kitchen clutching her fists against her pounding chest, her breath shallow. "When he returns, I will not stand like a scarecrow and wait. I'll go to him," she whispered.

The reading of *Uncle Tom's Cabin* continued to be an evening event for the entire household. As Gretchen read about Uncle Tom being taken to New Orleans by Augustine St. Clare, Orilla began crying very quietly. "The story seems so real with Uncle Tom in my city. I'm trying to imagine it's make-believe because Master didn't sell me or separate my family."

Battina knelt beside Orilla, taking both her hands. "What Orilla is too kind to say aloud is my father refused to sell his own daughter."

"You're sisters?" Gretchen laid the book on her knees and stared wide-eyed at the two women.

"Yes, Gretchen. White slave owners often father children by their slave women. Orilla's mother cooked for our family. Orilla was only two when I was born, and she was expected to care for me. She was wonderful to me."

Orilla laughed, leaning her cheek against Battina's. "At first she was my big doll. Then she became my friend."

"Didn't your ma get mad about it?" Jackson looked angry enough to make up for any lack on the part of Battina's mother.

Battina held fast to Orilla's hands. "In slave-owner families, white wives usually pretend they don't know their husbands fathered the new mulatto baby."

"It was honorable for your father to see Orilla got an education. That's illegal across the South." Eli Cox spoke with authority.

"There was no honor in my father's deed. Besides the unfaithful act, he never acknowledged Orilla, and he refused to free her or her mother. The honorable person in the situation was Orilla's mother. She served our family faithfully and loved me like her own child. Never uttered a word of complaint."

"How long have you known Orilla's your sister?" Gretchen stroked Orilla's fingers, which were spread widely across her knees like frightened birds desperate to take flight.

"For as long as I can remember. I knew it like I know my hand belongs to me. She's always been my sister and my best friend. That's why I set her free as soon as I returned to New Orleans. Now I'm pretending she's my property."

"Master allowed me to have a profession. I'm a seamstress. I have a large clientele in New Orleans."

"You called your pa *Master?*" Jackson sounded incredulous, his eyes as big as saucers.

Orilla nodded.

Captain Whipple spoke for the first time. "You and Battina have lovely clothing. Are you a dressmaker?"

"Yes, sir." Orilla barely spoke above a whisper. "I sew all our clothing."

Captain Whipple's cheeks took on a rosy glow. "I'm sure you'll enjoy a large clientele here. I'll talk to Abe Swartz about displaying some of your garments in his dry goods store."

Battina clapped her hands in delight. "That's wonderful, Captain. I'll help her get things ready."

That night as Helga settled eagerly into bed so ready for a full night's sleep, Gretchen scooted close and whispered, "Do we get babies like the cows? Does the papa jump on your back?"

Helga was startled into full wakefulness as she realized that she had neglected Gretchen's education. She had insisted that Max talk to both boys after discovering them laughing at the antics of cattle in the landlord's fields. It had been easy to imagine that Gretchen did not notice what the animals were doing. "It's not violent like the old bulls. We aren't animals. Getting babies with humans is a loving exchange."

"Did Battina's papa love Orilla's mama? Do masters love their slaves?"

Lying in the dark, listening to the peaceful surge of waves washing over the shell beach, Helga pulled her daughter against her body and prayed she could find a way to tell this child about the cruelties of the world without destroying her innocence. "From reading *Uncle Tom*, you see there's nothing loving about slavery. It's one human owning another. When humans own something, they think of it as an object intended to meet their needs. If slave owners have babies with their slaves, they're using the women only to satisfy themselves."

"But we let them do it. We don't try to stop slavery."

"Slavery's a dreadful thing in this country. It's turned decent people blind to their own failings and to the failings of their neighbors."

"I'm glad Battina freed Orilla."

"I am too."

After Christmas Paul continued having nightmares, but he no longer cried out. Instead, the boys' bed stayed next to Helga's, and Paul clung to her hand in a death grip. Despite her questions, he insisted he didn't know why he was so upset.

The holiday events continued through New Year's at the Casimir House, and Paul stayed gone most every day and into the evening. The day after New Year's the festivities came to a close, and Paul arrived in time for supper.

Eli Cox rushed in breathing like he had run all the way from town. "Sorry to be late. I just heard they've arrested Ira Fisher's killer. It was one of those Casimir House slaves. Oddly enough, it was the youngest and the smallest."

"Benjamin? Was it Benjamin?" Paul jumped up.

"That's the name."

"He didn't do it. He's innocent. I did it. I killed Ira Fisher," Paul shrieked, gripping the edge of the table like he might fall over. "I've got to tell them. They've made a terrible mistake." He turned and seemed to stagger as he ran toward the front door.

"Wait, I'll come with you." Helga realized her voice sounded hysterical.

"I'll come too." Captain Whipple, like everyone at the table, seemed to require a moment to comprehend what he was hearing.

Hermie and Jackson kept up with Paul's pace with Gretchen not far behind. Helga, Captain Whipple, and Eli Cox ran as fast as each of them could shove the breath in and out of their lungs.

Paul beat on the marshal's door until the giant man opened it to the hysterical boy.

"I did it, Marshal. Benjamin didn't do it. I killed Ira Fisher. I'm the killer. You have to let Benjamin go!"

"Now, now, boy." The marshal, his supper bib still tucked in the collar of his shirt, bent low in the doorway to stare into the tear- and snot-streaked face of this strange boy. "Come in and let's talk." The marshal looked into the agonized faces panting to regain their breath. "All of you. Come in."

Paul took the marshal's arm, keeping a firm grip on his sleeve as they stepped into the tight quarters packed with a bed, table, chair, and iron stove still radiating heat from supper. Rusty bars fronted a jail cell extending into a low alcove.

"Paul, you came." A very black boy stretched his arm through the bars. "I didn't snitch, Paul. I didn't snitch."

Paul waved at the prisoner. "It wasn't Benjamin who killed Ira Fisher, Marshal. It was me. I cut him wide open and covered him with tow sacks."

"Calm down. Tell me what happened." The marshal sat in the only chair looking directly into Paul's face.

"Ira was going to rob Benjamin again. He did it every time Benjamin got a tip." Paul looked at Benjamin, who nodded in agreement.

"Yes, boss. Every time."

"Tell me what happened," the marshal said again.

"I told Benjamin I wouldn't let Ira do it again. That was Benjamin's savings to buy his freedom. I wasn't going to let Ira rob him again."

"Tell me what happened."

Helga realized she was holding her breath, feeling like fainting in the hot little hut. She wanted to hold Paul's hand, to help him talk, but Captain Whipple took her arm, holding her close to his side.

"I went home during supper. I got Eagle's knife out of his holster next to his bed." The tears had stopped. Paul spoke in jerking, breathless sentences.

"Tell me the rest of it."

"I told Benjamin I'd stay until we finished cleaning up and I'd walk him across the alley to his place where all the Casimir slaves sleep. Ira was waiting." Paul held both hands together and began pumping his arms up and down. "That knife is so big and heavy. I thought it would scare Ira."

"Did it?" The marshal's eyes did not leave Paul's face.

"No, sir. He laughed and reached for me like he was going to hit me again."

"He hit you?"

"When he robbed me. He always beat me up and tore my clothes."

"He robbed you many times?"

"When I worked for his papa. If he wasn't drunk, he always robbed me."

"You never reported him to me. I'd remember."

"No, sir. Ira would've killed me if I reported him."

"Then what happened?"

"I stuck him with the knife. Real hard right in his stomach. But—" Paul suddenly vomited slick bile all over the marshal's knees and shoes. "I'm sorry. I didn't mean it." Paul bent to wipe the marshal's pant legs with his hands.

As if nothing had happened, without even looking down, the marshal said, "Then what happened?"

Paul wiped his mouth with the sleeve of his shirt. "Ira kept grabbing at me like he wasn't hurt. So I pulled down on the handle. The knife kept slicing right down his middle."

"Then what happened?"

Paul wiped the sweat from his face with his vomit-covered sleeve. "He fell down, and I pulled the knife out. I grabbed some old tow sacks and threw them on top of him."

"Did Benjamin help you?"

"No. I think he ran away when I stuck Ira. I didn't see him when I covered Ira. Then I ran home."

"Have you told anyone before now?"

"No, sir. Will you let Benjamin go now? He didn't do any of it."

"What about all of this, Benjamin. Is this young man telling it the way it happened? Did you help him?"

"No, boss. When Ira started reaching for Paul, I ran to my place. I was afraid he'd kill me for sure. He'd told me if I told anyone he'd kill me."

"How often did Ira rob you?"

"When he was sober. He waited in the alley. I don't know how many times."

"You were saving to buy your freedom?"

"Yes, boss. I already have four bits Ira don't know about."

"How much do you need to buy your freedom?"

"Lots. I don't know how much the Villeneuves wants. But I'll keep saving my tips."

"Do you get lots of tips?"

"No, boss. Only from Mr. Weil when he urps in the hall. He likes me to clean it up fast. He gives me a nickel."

"Has Paul given you any money to help you buy your freedom?"

"No, boss. Ira keeps robbing Paul too."

"Did Ira rob the other slaves who work for the Villeneuves?"

"Yes, boss."

"Do they know who killed Ira Fisher?"

"No, boss. I didn't tell nobody."

The marshal uncoiled his huge body from the little chair with its cowhide-covered seat and took the key from a nail above the stove. "I'm going to let you out, Benjamin. Then I'm going to get Ira Fisher's pa to come have a chat with these folks."

Benjamin rushed from the cell and grabbed Paul in a tight embrace. "I be praying for you, Paul. You're a good man." With that Benjamin disappeared through the door.

"Are you putting me in there?" Paul hugged his arms together as if a cold wind pierced his clothing.

Without answering, the marshal lifted the bucket of water next to the stove, stepped to the door, and splashed it over his vomit-covered legs and boots. Then he poured the rest of the water on the floor and swept it out the door. He took his hat from a nail by the door, looked back inside, and said, "You folks wait right here while I go for Henry Fisher."

"I can't believe he'll charge Paul. The boy was defending himself and that slave boy." Eli Cox paced the floor, his dingy white handkerchief pressed to the sweat on his face.

"I'm sorry, Mama." Paul threw his arms around Helga.

Helga squeezed him against her. "I wish you had let me help you. Using force never solves problems."

"Benjamin doesn't know how old he is. He can't read or write. They sold him away from his mama. He wants to buy his freedom and go back to the plantation where his mama lives. He doesn't know where, except in Mississippi. He says it's two days east of the Mississippi River."

Captain Whipple patted Paul on the shoulder. "Benjamin doesn't stand much of a chance of getting back there, does he?"

"No, sir. But I couldn't let Ira ruin his dream. Everybody's got to have a dream to keep going. Especially if they're a slave. They don't even get paid."

"The Villeneuves feed and clothe their slaves very well. I bet Benjamin has a better life with them." Eli Cox looked pleased with himself.

Dead silence followed Eli Cox's comments. Only the sound of the waves pounding on the pilings along the docks demanded an answer.

Henry Fisher looked like a whipped man. His shoulders slumped, and one side of his shirttail hung loosely from his pants. His hair stood up like he had been running his hands though it in absolute frustration. "Hello, Paul. I thought the marshal had a vicious killer in that slave. Now I'm hearing you're the one what killed Ira."

Paul pulled his shoulders back and stood at attention like someone facing a firing squad when Henry Fisher entered the cabin. "Yes, sir. I killed Ira. I'm sorry, Mr. Fisher. You were good to me. I'm sorry I killed your son."

"The marshal tells me that Ira's been robbing you."

"Yes, sir."

"Why didn't you tell me? I'd have taken a horsewhip to the sorry thing if you'd just told me. You wouldn't a had to kill him. I could've beat some sense into him."

"Excuse me, Mr. Fisher." Captain Whipple laid a hand gently on Henry Fisher's shoulder. "Did the horsewhip ever change any of Ira's behavior? I know you used it often enough when I stabled my horse with you."

Henry Fisher shook his head, hugged his arms around himself in utter desolation. "Never did no good to beat that boy. He was no good from the time he was a little kid. Always beating on the other kids. Always refusing to work. But he shouldn't a been killed. Nobody had no right to kill him."

The marshal stepped around in front of Henry Fisher and bent low to look him in the face. "I agree with you, Henry. He shouldn't have been killed for robbing these boys. He should've been put it jail. He should've been put in jail when he beat you up. He should've been jailed when he beat up his ma before she died. He should've been jailed all those times he threatened to whip my deputy. But ..." The marshal took a very deep breath. "It took this eleven-year-old kid to finally stop Ira."

Henry Fisher only nodded as he rocked himself, enfolded in his own arms.

"So unless you convince me otherwise, I'm going to let this boy go."

Henry Fisher nodded. He turned slowly, put his crumpled old felt hat on his head, and walked out the door.

"Thank you, Marshal. I can't thank you enough." Helga took the gnarly, bear-size paw in her hand.

"Now, boy, you stay out of trouble. And you leave those knives alone. If you have trouble, you come to the law. I'm here to keep down trouble."

Paul nodded and then grabbed the big hand and shook it with all his might. "Thank you, Marshal. I'll stay out of trouble. I promise. I promise."

Helga wrapped her arm around Paul's shoulder, and they led the procession out of the cramped, hot quarters and started the walk home. The cold dampness blowing off the bay penetrated her clothing, producing a freeing energy that forced a smile as she imagined Paul's troubles were finally behind him.

Chapter 11

1854

INDIANOLA'S *SAENGERBUND*, A GROUP OF German men that presented musical programs all over town for church and civic events, planned a trip to San Antonio for the Second Annual Saengerfest, a musical competition between groups from all over the state. Helga had been glad when Hermie joined the group; his sweet tenor made him a popular member. Then the Villeneuves had insisted Paul join to increase German patronage at the Casimir and Alhambra houses, and his playing delighted the members.

The boys burst in the front door gasping for breath after running all the way from the saengerbund's downtown rehearsal. "Everybody wants us to go to Saengerfest. They keep saying they need us." Looking to Paul, who kept nodding his support, Hermie rushed on with his argument: "The stage costs twelve-fifty each way. We have enough to pay for it."

Startled by the prospect of the boys going so far away, Helga stammered, "Where'll you sleep? What'll you eat?"

"We'll stay with San Antonio saengerbund families. They made the trip last year. We're welcome again this year," Hermie said.

"I've been to San Antonio many times in the spring. The trip's beautiful. Wildflowers spread a blanket of color all the way." Jackson mimicked Eagle even in the way he gazed into the distance as he spoke as if he could see the countryside. "I can handle our garden while Hermie's gone."

"The Villeneuves want me to go," Paul added. "They think the local Germans will like having me there."

"That settles it," Hermie said. "We can go, can't we, Mama?"

"It will add to your education … if you think you can afford it."

"We can. We can." The boys' voices sang out in unison like they were speaking from the same songbook.

* * *

After the boys left with the saengerbund on the early-morning stagecoach loaded with a basket of food to share on the trip, Helga hurried to the smokehouse for some of Eagle's venison sausage. As she stepped into the dark, smoky enclosure, she stopped, suddenly startled by the slight swaying of meat hanging from the rafters. She heard her own voice speaking in a commanding tone: "Who's there? I know you're in here. I saw the meat move. I won't leave until you show yourself." She held the door open, but it was too early for light to penetrate the dark cavern.

"It's Sylus Brown, ma'am. Please, ma'am, don't expose me." A black face appeared between the suspended links of sausage.

"You're the slave boy from the auction at the Casimir House."

"I am that, ma'am. I'm running. Please don't expose me."

"I won't turn you in. I'll get you some food. Unless you've eaten so much of my smoked meat you aren't hungry."

"No, ma'am. I ate one sausage. I'll work to pay for it."

"Stay where you are. After my boarders leave, I'll come back." She hurried to the kitchen, cut a large slice from a loaf of bread, and carried it out to the smokehouse. When she entered, the meat hung perfectly still. "Sylus, are you here?"

"Yes, ma'am." His face peeked out. "I'm not bumping the meat."

"How long have you been here?"

"Since before light. I left my master two days ago. Kept to the woods and walked only at night."

"Where's your master's plantation?"

"Up the Guadalupe River. I'm not going back."

"I'm probably the only one who will come in here," Helga whispered, "but you must remain very quiet. I'll speak to someone who may know how to help."

"I don't aim to go back to my master. Not alive, I ain't."

"You can trust Captain Whipple."

At Helga's soft knock, Captain Whipple opened his door with a book in his hand. "I was just rereading Frederick Douglass's book. I thought the children might enjoy it."

Helga nodded and leaned close to whisper, "We have a runaway slave in the smokehouse. Can you help him?"

The captain nodded. “Wait until everyone leaves. Meantime, keep him out of sight.”

Helga hurried down the back stairs.

After breakfast, Captain Whipple went back up to his room and didn’t return until everyone was gone. “We must be careful with this. The marshal won’t be so cooperative if he finds out we’re helping a fugitive.” He paced the parlor. “How large is he?”

“Hermie’s height, but very thin right now. He still has very broad shoulders.”

“You know him?”

“He’s the boy we saw auctioned off on the day we arrived.”

“I remember … No, he won’t fit in one of your empty flour barrels. Let’s ask Orilla to help us with this.”

Orilla pressed her fingertips so hard against her lips they seemed to pale as Captain Whipple explained about Sylus. “Let me see how large he is,” she whispered as though she thought the marshal might already be lurking nearby.

“I’ll bring him into the washroom. He needs cleaning before you measure him,” Helga said.

By the time Sylus was safely in the washroom, he was trembling violently. “You’re safe here,” Captain Whipple assured him. “Frau Heinrich is heating water for your bath. Then Orilla will measure you for some clothing. Do you think if we dress you as a free woman of color, you can walk to the docks without letting people see how frightened you are?”

“Yes, Master. I can do whatever you say.”

“Don’t call me master. My name is Captain Whipple. I am not your master.”

“No, sir. I won’t call you nothing but Captain Whipple.”

“Now you bathe yourself real good, and we’ll get busy.”

Orilla began measuring Sylus, who stretched the limits of the clean shirt and pants Helga had put back for Paul to grow into. As Orilla worked she murmured softly, soothing the fright continuing to grip the boy in violent tremors.

“I’ve got a ship bound for Matamoros loading right now. That boy’s too frightened to walk in broad daylight to the docks. I’ll hire a buggy and drive him down later tonight.” Suddenly Captain Whipple burst into a broad smile. “I’ve just decided I need to handle some business in Matamoros. How handy I have a ship leaving so soon." With that, Captain Whipple walked out the front door.

Since Captain Whipple insisted Sylus not be dressed in finery that would draw attention to him, Orilla decided to alter one of her work dresses to fit him.

At supper Captain Whipple seemed extra jubilant, speaking of his planned business meeting with Richard King and Mifflin Kenedy, the riverboat captains plying the waters of the Rio Grande.

"I heard King bought an old Spanish land grant and started a ranch south of Corpus Christi," Eli Cox offered.

"I went with my pa to Corpus Christi, hauling army supplies to the new headquarters. Our train of wagons stretched for miles. They had the first Lone Star Fair while we were there, and I ate a dried meat biscuit. It wasn't near as good as the inventor claimed. We slept under our wagon because it kept raining." Jackson seemed as proud as Eli Cox to demonstrate his knowledge of the greater world.

* * *

Captain Whipple's buggy arrived just as Gretchen and Jackson finished their studies, and the entire household began settling down for the night.

Captain Whipple loaded his bags and walked around the house to the darkened smokehouse. Sylus Brown, wearing Orilla's altered dress over Hermie's outgrown clothes, trailed Captain Whipple to the buggy.

All the following day Helga listened for the slightest hint of trouble. Orilla and Battina paced the floor, glancing down the road for some hint that the scheme hadn't worked. That evening Eli Cox didn't mention anything at supper, which brought much-needed relief. While Orilla and Battina helped with the supper dishes, Helga whispered, "If they caught Sylus or arrested Captain Whipple, Eli Cox would have known all about it." Orilla and Battina both stifled their giggles.

While Helga prepared breakfast the next morning, a clumping on the front porch startled her. Her heart stopped, and then a surge sent it racing as she hurried to the door and looked up into the stern face of the marshal.

"Morning, ma'am. I'm here to see young Paul." The marshal held his crumpled felt hat between his hands like a prayer book.

"Paul and his brother left three days ago on the stage to San Antonio.

With the saengerbund." She could hardly control her voice. Her knees felt like they'd give way. "What's wrong, Marshal?"

"The Villeneuves discovered Benjamin missing yesterday morning. I thought maybe Paul decided Benjamin couldn't save enough to buy his freedom. Maybe Paul helped him run."

Helga clutched her breast in shock, hoping to quiet her racing heart. "What'll happen to him? He's just a child. Paul said he can't read or write."

"None of them can. It's just as well. Usually keeps them around. If they've got any sense, they know they can't make it on their own. Sorry to bother you, ma'am." The huge man lumbered off the porch and mounted the biggest horse Helga had ever seen.

Battina opened her bedroom door and whispered, "I heard every word. Do you think Captain Whipple had anything to do with Benjamin disappearing?"

"I can't imagine. We'll have to wait until the captain returns."

In a week Hermie and Paul returned from San Antonio, bursting in the front door just as everyone sat down to supper. They took their seats and began hungrily eating. "We had a scary time while we were there," Hermie said between bites. Before Helga could ask what he was talking about, he added, "This little group of really smart people at Saengerfest got up a petition calling for freedom for everyone. They passed it around. We knew it meant freedom for slaves."

"But we didn't sign it," Paul quickly added.

"Some of the San Antonio people came round asking if we had slaves. When we said no, they said that meant we were going to overturn the South. They called us abolitionists." Hermie shook his head. "We didn't know how to convince them. They acted like we were traitors."

"We're glad to be home," Paul said. "We've had all the travel we want for a long time."

"So they weren't friendly?" Helga asked.

"They were really nice to us except for right there at the end when that petition got passed. Then it was only a few troublemakers. Everyone else tried to defend us." Hermie reached for more chicken and dumplings. "It feels good to be back home where we don't have people like that."

Helga glanced across the table at Battina, who looked near tears. "I'm afraid there are people who want everyone to believe the same way they do. It really threatens them to have someone disagree with them. Sometimes they can be dangerous."

"Pa said that very thing when he came home this last time," Jackson said. "He said the editor of a paper in New Braunfels wrote that even if Germans don't own slaves, they shouldn't talk against slavery. They need to get along with their American neighbors."

"Your pa's a wise man," Helga said.

"Yes, ma'am. I know he is."

"I hope you won't decide to stay home forever. If you travel, you learn about all kinds of people, how to get along with them." Eli Cox spoke like a man who knew all about getting along with people.

"I couldn't agree more," Helga said, as surprised at her quick response as she was at Eli Cox's sentiment.

"Did you hear Benjamin ran away from the Villeneuves?" Eli Cox asked.

Paul caught his breath, covering his mouth with both hands. "What'd they do to him?"

"They haven't found him."

"He doesn't know anything about the world. He's only been on that plantation and at the Casimir House." Paul began wiping tears. "I promised to teach him to read, but by the time we finished work, we were too tired."

After Helga went to bed, she heard Paul sniffing and flailing about in the bed next to hers. She reached for his shoulder and patted him until she finally felt his body relax and settle into sleep.

Captain Whipple returned in great spirits from his trip to Matamoros. "I made some good contacts, and I brought back a shipload of coffee, including a barrel for this house. I'm starting a regular run down there."

"Did you hear Benjamin's missing?" Eli Cox seemed to relish being the one to tell the news.

"When did that happen?"

"Right after you left. If the other slaves know anything, they aren't talking."

"I hope he didn't get sold down the river," Paul said as he tried to keep back tears by rubbing his face with the cuff of his sleeve.

Captain Whipple kept nodding. "I hope so too."

After supper they finished *Uncle Tom's Cabin,* having delayed the story at the request of Hermie and Paul until they returned from San Antonio.

Captain Whipple went to the back porch to draw fresh water and then waited there until the other boarders went to their rooms. Then he motioned Helga and Paul to follow him into the backyard. "I want to ease your worries. Benjamin is safe in Matamoros with the Garcia family. I've known them for years. They lost a son about Benjamin's age. They're delighted to have two boys to love."

"Two boys? Did another slave run with Benjamin?"

Helga and Captain Whipple told Paul the story of Sylus's escape.

"Wow! Two slaves freed together. And your friends wanted both of them?" Paul was incredulous.

"They have a big mercantile store in downtown Matamoros. They plan to teach Benjamin and Sylus to work in the store."

"How'd you get Benjamin on your ship?" Helga was stunned.

"After I left here with Sylus and got him safely stowed in my cabin, I kept thinking about Benjamin trying to save nickels to buy his freedom. I walked back to the Casimir House and saw him sweeping the front porch. It was late and no one was around. I told him I'd take him to freedom, but he must wade out into the bay and climb the pilings to my dock. He leaned his broom against the wall and walked away like he was taking an evening stroll. He waded out over his head and had to really struggle to get to the dock. He was a determined young man. He and Sylus curled up together on my bunk. They were both so relieved they slept for the next twelve hours. I'll go back to Matamoros as often as possible to see how they're doing."

"I wish I could go with you," Paul said.

"Maybe you can one of these days."

"Will you take more of the Villeneuves' slaves?"

Captain Whipple shook his head. "I can't say what'll happen. Time will tell us the answer."

Chapter 12

BY MID-APRIL ORILLA ALREADY HAD her dresses in Swartz's Dry Goods, and they were becoming so popular that Amelia arranged for a showing at a ladies' meeting and luncheon at Casimir House. Amelia invited Gretchen to go. "You've earned an outing, and you'll appreciate how much the ladies like Orilla's work."

"I can get the bread made, and the stew will cook itself," Helga said. "You must go. It'll be fun."

Gretchen finally admitted that she really wanted to attend.

Helga had just set the dough to rise under a cloth when she heard the front door open. Wiping her hands on her apron, she peeked into the hall as Eagle, saddlebags slung over his shoulder, hugging a bundle of bluebonnets that matched the blue of his eyes, strode toward her.

"Hello, Hel." His eyes never left her face. "It's been a long one."

"Very long." She wanted to look away, to appear calm, but he held her gaze, held her as surely as if his arms were around her.

"I've not seen a tub in a week. Is the washroom available?" He took her arm above the elbow, firmly guiding her down the hall and around the porch to the washroom. His hand dropped from her arm as he reached for the bucket beside the cistern.

She almost staggered from the sudden loss of his touch. "Everyone's gone."

"Will you help me?"

"Yes."

"I have a caring for you, Hel." He didn't look at her now, keeping his eyes on the tub as he poured the water.

She could not move. It was as if she were held in suspension, waiting as he went to the kitchen for both teakettles, added the steaming water, and reached for her so quickly it felt like one motion.

His body felt hard, lean, and insistent. His mouth moved against hers, forcing her lips to open to his eager tongue. His hands moved urgently across her back, stroking her, caressing her hips as he pulled her to him. "I want you, Hel. Let me get clean for you." He lowered his head, moved his mouth in wide sucking motions across her throat, down the collar of her dress. "You smell so delicious." He pulled back, took a deep breath, and grinned at her. "Why don't you help me get cleaned up?"

Helga could only nod as she began helping him unbutton his shirt, which was stiff from days of sweat, and take down his dirt-caked pants. His body, hard with muscles that never saw the sun, was pink as a baby's, while his hands and face were parched in almost solid brown freckles.

He eased into the steaming tub, his white knees curled up almost to his chin.

Helga knelt beside him and began a slow, sensual movement with the rag across his hard, taut shoulders while he lathered his hair and face and scrubbed himself like a man in a terrible hurry.

She brought the rinse water. As soon as she poured it over his head, he rose from the tub and took her in his arms, his wet body soaking her bodice as he pressed his legs into the folds of her skirt.

He began unbuttoning her dress, whispering hard against her mouth. "Let me do it. Please don't stop me."

"I won't stop you."

They sank to the floor, his hands caressing every part of her, gently rousing her to an urgent need. When he came into her, she clung to him, a moan of pleasure surging through her.

* * *

The day progressed like all the others; people ate lunch; the dishes were washed and preparations started for supper. Jackson was jubilant at the return of his pa and could be heard throughout the house as he updated Eagle on every detail of the past four months.

Helga felt every motion of her body as though she had come suddenly alive to every movement, every whiff of air that touched her. The smell of him lingered all day. She washed herself, washed her hair, and finally soaked in the tub, but the smell, the feel of him, the essence of his presence stayed with her. She didn't remember smelling Max afterward. Even in the first days, his odor didn't linger. She'd have remembered that.

At supper Eli Cox was bursting with delight at what he announced was "the financial boom" around Powder Horn Bayou. "I knew when I settled my business here that Indianola was the up-and-coming place to be. The lawyers are moving down from Old Town. Even William Varnell is arranging to float his warehouse down the bay to Powder Horn."

Eagle nodded agreeably. "Aren't Powder Horn Bayou and the lake behind it a lot closer to sea level than Old Town?"

"Shouldn't cause a problem. The lake offers plenty of room for flood waters to spread back there." Eli Cox pursed his lips like a man of vast knowledge.

* * *

The following September a storm convinced Eli Cox he had been proven correct about the safety of Indianola's shore. The storm wrecked every ship in Matagorda Bay, tore out the wharves at Old Town, and caused a lot of damage up the coast at Lavaca while leaving the Powder Horn area of Indianola relatively unharmed except for fishing piers like Hermie's and Jackson's. The destruction of their pier was the first financial setback the boys had experienced.

"We'd finally started making some money on that dock." Hermie shook his head and frowned at Jackson. "We're not sure it pays to build it again. It cost so much to get the pilings stabilized."

"We don't need a pier. We can fish near shore," Battina said. "The reds are biting just a few feet out." She often stood on the pier very near the shore, and she always returned with enough fish for a full meal.

"You're the best fisherman in this house," Jackson said. "My pa says you got to listen to the experts."

The decision on rebuilding the pier was made by default. Nothing more was said.

* * *

Eagle missed the storm, having been on another long trip hauling Saxon sheep from the Rhineland up to Fredericksburg. Helga was washing the front porch when she saw him coming home on a mule. She recognized him from the stoop of his shoulders and the slight swaying motion as he approached. Finally, she could see the red beard, thick from weeks on the trail and the parched face, creased from the sun and wind touching it. Almost immediately she envied the sun and wind for touching him when she could not.

But he was approaching too slowly. The mule seemed in charge.

"Hel, I came ahead … Can you help?" His eyes looked like bright blue marbles rolling back into his head as he slid like a limp rag from the bare back of the mule.

She caught him and managed to ease his burning hot body to the ground. A passing freight wagon stopped, and the driver jumped out to help her get him into the house. She called to Gretchen to get Dr. Stein as they carried him back to Helga's room and placed him on her bed.

Battina and Orilla brought water, and Helga began gently washing the road dirt from his face and neck, rubbing his calloused hands and arms to cool the raging heat.

"Hel, is it you?'

"I'm with you. I'm taking care of you."

"You'll stay?"

"Always."

He closed his eyes. Chills began to rack his body.

Dr. Stein led her from the room and shook his head. "Yellow fever's been increasing since the storm. We'll watch him, but I fear this is it." He touched her shoulder very gently. "Amelia said you care for him. I'll do my best."

Helga nodded, wiping at tears just as she saw Jackson rushing in the back door.

"Where's Pa? They said he's sick."

Helga opened the door and followed the terrified boy to his father's side.

"Pa, this is your son, Jackson. Open your eyes, Pa." The boy bent low and spoke into the sick man's face.

Eagle's eyes fluttered. He tried to speak, even tried to lift his arm.

"Don't tire yourself, Pa. I'll stay right here beside you. I'll take care of you."

As Helga stroked Eagle's body with cool cloths, Jackson did the same. He sat on the floor next to the bed throughout the night. With the arrival of morning, the fever had not let up. It was as if it was trying to burn right through his body.

When Dr. Stein arrived just after daylight and bent low with a lamp to gaze into Eagle's drawn, flushed face, he shook his head in amazement. "It hasn't killed him yet. Let's hope the black vomit doesn't start and wipe out the rest of his strength. He's tough, holding his own."

Jackson jumped from the floor and embraced Dr. Stein. “Thank you, sir. I know he’s going to get well. He’s awfully tough.”

Dr. Stein seemed to melt at the touch of the exhausted child. “He’s mighty lucky to have a boy as tough as you. I guess you learned it from him, didn’t you.”

“Yes, sir,” Jackson said and struggled to keep back tears.

Throughout the day and the next night, they cooled his body. Neighbors came to the gate asking for a report. The household waited. The next morning, just as the sun began peeking over the rooftops and the noise of wagons increased on the road, Eagle began to sweat. Finally he opened his eyes, looking first at Jackson and then Helga.

“Do you have any of that ice water left that you’ve been pouring on me?”

“Aw, Pa, we do. We do. I’ll get it right now.” Jackson stumbled out of the room, his clumsy boots so loud that those who had dozed off in exhaustion were roused. “Pa’s awake,” he shouted.

Eagle’s sunken eyes crinkled in a smile. “I had dreams. Some were awful. One I want to remember. You married me.”

“We’re having the same dream.” Helga held his rough hand to her lips.

“Here’s some icy water, Pa.” Jackson helped Helga raise him enough that he could sip the cool liquid. Then he took a deep breath, relaxing into a sound sleep as he continued sweating off the fever.

Jackson refused to get in the bed next to his pa. Instead, he curled up on the floor, falling immediately into a sound sleep.

Everyone stayed out of the room, leaving Helga alone with the sleeping boy and man.

She lay next to him, sleeping when he slept and rousing to offer cool water and chicken broth when he awakened.

The next morning’s sun peeked into a room where three exhausted people looked at each other with loving smiles.

“Pa, Dr. Stein said you were tough and I was tough too.” Jackson grinned at Helga and rubbed his tousled hair into a wild bush. “And Helga’s tough.”

Helga kissed Eagle on the forehead and tousled Jackson’s hair a little more as she headed to the kitchen to begin breakfast for her boarders.

* * *

The pastor performed the wedding in the parlor in October. Orilla baked a beautiful cake with sugary icing. The day of the service, Eagle moved into Helga's room; the boys moved upstairs to Eagle and Jackson's room; and to Gretchen's delight, Battina and Orilla insisted that Gretchen move the extra bed into their room. The morning after the wedding Helga rose as usual to prepare breakfast for the boarders.

Eagle made one more trip before Christmas. He returned with a long train of gamagrass hay bound for New Orleans and Mobile. And to no one's surprise, he brought home a giant cedar tree and a fresh young buck.

He warned that the wildflowers would be scarce for the coming spring if the rains didn't begin soon, watering the very thirsty earth. But the bay lay still, a silent presence hoarding its moisture.

By late April, cisterns began drying up. At supper one night it was Captain Whipple who said, "The *Perseverance* arrived from Galveston this afternoon. They're saying the drought there's so bad people are paying two-fifty a barrel for drinking water."

"I'm getting harassed by clients demanding to know when the ice will be in from New England," Eli Cox complained.

"At the Casimir House, we're charging seven cents for a glass of water," Paul said. "A stein of beer only costs a nickel."

"A few people are beginning to build extra shellcrete cisterns. Jackson and I want to start a cistern-building business before there's too much competition. We planned it out today while we were sitting in the market." Hermie smiled across the table. "Captain, will you help us draw the plans for the frames? We could build them six feet in diameter and nine inches high. Connect them to downspouts on the gutters. They're selling for forty-five dollars."

"We'll make that your arithmetic lesson tonight," Captain Whipple said.

Eli Cox shook his head. "I've never seen two boys so busy thinking of ways to make money. One of these days you'll need my services to sell your goods to all the inland towns."

Jackson and Hermie laughed, but it was obvious they were pleased to be admired, even by Eli Cox.

"I heard the Saengerfest is in New Braunfels this year. Are you boys going?" Eli Cox asked.

"I'm too busy," Hermie said. "Our garden is suffering in the drought, but not like the others. All that fertilizing's paid off. Our soil's holding the moisture." He smiled sheepishly at Helga, a private acknowledgement that she had been right. "We're about the only vegetable venders in the market. Building the cisterns will take so much time we're going to hire some blacks to keep up the garden."

"I won't be going either," Paul added. "The Villeneuves don't need to advertise. Customers keep coming even though they have to pay for water without ice." Paul looked accusingly at Eli Cox.

"I can't do anything about the ice. It'll get here when it gets here." Eli Cox laid down his fork and scooted his chair back. "I hope you aren't going up on our board for a simple glass of water." He looked accusingly at Helga.

Everyone in the room laughed. Even Eli Cox.

Chapter 13

HERMIE AND JACKSON CLAIMED THE spring of 1856 was their best season ever. The entire ten-acre garden plot flourished with an abundance of produce, and their vegetable stand in the downtown market paid off handsomely. Their cistern-building enterprise of the previous year introduced them to the town as very ambitious and reliable young men. In early spring they took advantage of their newly won respect to arrange business deals with several of the hotels and boarding houses in Indianola to deliver fresh produce to the back door of each establishment in plenty of time for lunch preparation. They hired several freedmen who were too old to work the docks to make all the deliveries and to maintain the garden.

When the dung pickup business grew too large during the winter, they employed freedmen and provided carts for hauling the fertilizer to the city garden, where the other gardeners, anxious to produce a crop as abundant as Hermie and Jackson's, eagerly paid for the delivery.

"If we can buy more eggs, butter, and milk we can supply all the hotels and boarding houses," Jackson announced as he and Hermie ate their breakfast in the kitchen well before the rest of the boarders. "We need more farmers to supply us."

"We're going to have a regular store in a downtown building one of these days," Hermie said as he finished his eggs and sausage.

Helga stood on the back porch watching seventeen-year-old Hermie, who no longer resembled a boy, and twelve-year-old Jackson, who had grown as tall and tough as Hermie, trudge off by the light of their swinging lantern to gather their day's produce. She smiled, remembering when they had started this early-morning regime. Hermie had explained they wanted to beat the other gardeners to the vegetable market. She didn't mind rising a little earlier to get them off. In the early mornings, when they were rested, their dreams fed her energy, kept her moving through her hours of constant work. When the days melted into each other and it seemed she finished a task only to begin again, Hermie and Jackson's grand plans buoyed her.

* * *

In midmorning, with preparations well underway for lunch, Helga heard Hermie shouting, running up the front steps. "The camels are here. They're unloading thirty-four camels at the Powder Horn dock. You've got to see them." Sweat ran down his very red cheeks.

The previous April the suppertime talk had revolved around an article in the Indianola *Bulletin* reporting the War Department's construction of a huge corral in Old Town to hold camels. The federal government had appropriated $30,000 to experiment with using camels out West as pack animals for carrying military supplies and even ammunition.

"Why don't they hire Pa and other teamsters to haul supplies instead of bringing camels all the way from northern Africa?" Jackson had asked.

"Jeff Davis, the secretary of war, heard when he was fighting in the Mexican War that camels survive, even do very well in dry regions. They go a lot longer without water and carry heavier loads than mules or oxen," Captain Whipple had said.

"Mules are mighty strong. I've got to see those camels beat Pa's mules."

Helga tried shaking off the sadness she felt over her sons never having a papa whom they admired with such intensity.

Now, hurrying with the rest of the household, following her almost hysterical son, she realized the newspaper story had been true. People along the road streamed out of their houses and businesses, rushing toward the docks to witness the most exciting event of their lives.

Crowds filled Water Street, and people leaned out of every second-floor window, watching and shrieking with laughter at the excited, almost uncontrollable camels decorated with red blankets, kicking, rearing up, and crying pitifully as they struggled to regain their land footing. The handlers, three dark-skinned men who came from the Mediterranean, finally managed to get halters and saddles on the nervous beasts.

Helga and Gretchen hurried home to finish lunch for any boarder who might return. In late afternoon they heard a man shouting, "Get out of the road. The camels are coming." Before reaching the front porch, they heard the jingling of tiny bells announcing the procession of plodding camels, sweating, turbaned handlers, and droves of Indianola residents, young and old, scurrying behind the seven-foot giants.

Teamsters tried to control their mules, and horses reared and snorted as the camels approached. One horse threw his rider over the fence edging the road, and some of the teamsters tried turning their wagons around, actually driving into the edge of the water to face the mules away from the approaching camels.

At supper, Hermie and Jackson bubbled with excitement, because the swarms of people in town for the camel invasion had made a rush on their vegetable stand, completely buying them out by midafternoon.

Gretchen glowed with importance, seizing the opportunity to tell of the excitement that had occurred in their front yard. "The horses and mules hated those camels. But the old oxen kept poking along with their heads down, not even noticing all the bedlam."

Paul made it home for supper that night. For months he had spent more and more time submerged in the livelier entertainment world at the Casimir House, so distant from the activities of the rest of the family.

After finishing their studies, the boys started with their mosquito nets to the back porch where they had been sleeping since the weather grew too hot to sleep upstairs. Helga heard Paul yell, "I'm your God-damned brother. That's why."

Shocked to hear such language, she stepped onto the porch in time to see Hermie double his fist in a threatening lunge at Paul.

"What's going on?"

"He wants me to go upstairs to sleep." Paul clutched the mattress.

"He thrashes all night. It's hard to sleep in the room with him. Sleeping on the same mattress is impossible." Hermie spoke through clenched teeth.

"I can't help it. I try to be still." Paul's anger passed, replaced by an almost desperate tone to his voice.

"Maybe you need to get a real job. Work like Jackson and me. You'll be too tired to move when you go to bed."

"Okay. You win. I'll go upstairs." Paul whirled, rushing up the back stairs.

Jackson stood off to one side of the porch, his head down like he was trying to remove himself from the whole scene. When Paul reached the top of the stairs, Jackson made a dash to follow him.

Hermie shook his head. "I'm sorry, Mama. I know he's still dreaming about killing Ira Fisher. But we're tired of being kept awake."

"I don't know how to help him," Helga whispered. "I tried to believe that time would heal those scars, but I don't suppose you can kill someone and forget it. Not if you've got a decent soul."

"Paul's a good person," Hermie said. "Maybe he's too good for such a heavy burden."

"I'll see what I can do." Helga climbed the back stairs, praying for wisdom to say the right thing to her miserable child.

Jackson sat in the dim room on the bed beside Paul, who was violently rubbing his face, trying to stop the tears.

"You feel like my flesh-and-blood brother. I've tried imagining how it feels to keep remembering old Ira Fisher and how he robbed you and Benjamin and beat you up. You didn't give in; you stood up to him. I keep thinking how brave you are."

"I can't stop dreaming about that gush of blood, the way he kept reaching for me like he was going to get me. Then I shoved the knife down his middle easy as your pa cut off that buck's head."

Jackson put his arm around Paul's shoulders. "If you hadn't done it, he would've killed you. Even his pa and the marshal knew you were defending Benjamin and yourself."

Paul nodded. "Okay, I'll sleep upstairs. Maybe by winter when you and Hermie get so cold you move back up here, I'll be done with my nightmares."

"You better be, or we'll throw you out the window." Jackson tousled Paul's hair and suddenly kissed Helga's cheek as he went out the door.

Helga took Jackson's place on the edge of the bed beside Paul.

"Jackson is nice like his pa," Paul said.

"Yes, he is."

"I never told you I'm glad you married Eagle. Hermie's glad too."

"Oh, Paul." Helga wrapped her arm around her son and buried her face in his surprisingly thin shoulder. "It means so much to hear that."

"I guess we haven't told you because we don't want to be disloyal to Papa. After seeing how Eagle treats Jackson, I'm beginning to think Papa wasn't much of a father."

Helga closed her eyes, letting Paul's words sink in, and finally said, "A sign of growing up is beginning to see the faults in those you love and still being able to love them."

"I do love him. Sometimes I think I'm like Papa—the audience loves me like people loved him."

"You are loved, Paul. You look and act so much like your papa I often think he's still with us."

"I can go to sleep now." Paul laughed, real low in his throat. "Maybe by winter I'll let those guys come up here to sleep."

* * *

The camels continued to be the source of suppertime conversation. Jackson finally admitted camels were stronger than mules. He spoke with amazement in his voice. "Today, one of the handlers led a camel to the quartermaster's forage house to pick up hay. First he made the camel kneel down. Then they loaded two bales that weighed a total of 613 pounds on its back."

Hermie interrupted, "Ole Jackson said it'd never be able to stand. Then they piled on another two bales for a total of 1,226 pounds."

"I was positive that camel could not get up with all that weight. But it did. It just walked away like it didn't even know it was carrying a load."

Hermie giggled. "We heard that when they ran out of lumber to build the camel corral they used prickly pear, but the camels ate the fences; they loved those sticky pods."

"Prickly pears are all over the country west of here." Jackson could barely speak for laughing. "I bet they eat prickly pear all the way to Camp Verde."

* * *

After three weeks of entertainment watching the camels being led about town for exercise, the docile beasts started off on their trek to the western frontier.

A week after the camels departed, Eagle returned loaded with corn for shipment out of the port.

Helga watched in patient amusement as Jackson ran up the hall to meet his pa.

"Did you see the camels?" Jackson yelled as he jumped into Eagle's arms, almost knocking his pa to the floor.

"You weigh a ton," Eagle gasped. "I'm going to have to start jumping on you. Yes, I saw the camels on the road to San Antonio."

"Your mules weren't afraid of them, were they?"

"They were. Some of the teamsters almost had a runaway. I sent word back to get off the road and turn the mules away. When they did that, the mules finally settled down."

Jackson shook his head in disappointment. "I thought your mules would be better than that."

Eagle wrapped his arm around Jackson's shoulder, walking toward Helga and shaking his head at his son. "My mules are just like all the others. They're animals; they get afraid of strange sights and strange smells just like other animals. And believe me, those camels have a terrible smell the mules sense long before humans."

"Okay, you can kiss her," Jackson loped away toward the back porch.

Eagle wrapped his arms around Helga. "I can't wait to get you in bed," he whispered. Then he kissed her on both cheeks and headed to the washroom.

At supper Eagle said, "When I came through Victoria I heard a woman knitted a pair of socks out of camel hair for President Pierce. The major in charge of the camels plans to send them to the president."

"I bet those socks stink." Jackson laughed.

Eli Cox cleared his throat for attention. "Did you hear Lavaca started building a railroad? If that thing gets built, it'll kill our business. And you, my good fellow, will have to find work other than being a teamster."

"That should encourage all you commissioners to get a railroad line started from Powder Horn." Eagle burst into laughter. "If it takes you as long to get a railroad in here as it's taking to get the courthouse built, I've got a long time to keep driving my teams."

"We're working on it. Trying to get the legislature to incorporate the Powder Horn, Victoria, and Gonzales Railroad Company." Eli Cox sniffed and began hurriedly eating. "I must say this is fine turtle soup."

"Why thank you, sir," Helga said, barely able to stifle a smile.

Word had apparently spread among the planters that a slave ate at the table with the white owners at the Stein House, because after Spurgeon Platt left, the planters who occasionally stayed one or two nights in the upstairs rooms did not return. Ship captains who knew Captain Whipple came in even greater numbers, and none of them seemed to notice Orilla's presence.

Samuel Vogel, who proudly captained the *Jolly,* a steamship plying the Gulf between New Orleans and Indianola, became a regular boarder, staying a night or two as often as he could. "I look forward to a steady bed under me and meals that taste like real food," the wiry little German said.

Captain Vogel returned in the fall from a trip to New Orleans and Galveston. After everyone asked about the latest news, Captain Whipple said, "What are you hearing about armed filibusterers sailing out of Galveston to liberate Nicaragua?"

"What are filibusterers?" Jackson laid his fork down, looking totally perplexed.

"They're men who take control of another country. In this case it's Nicaragua," Captain Whipple said.

Captain Vogel shook his head in disgust. "It's a clear violation of our neutrality laws. While I was in Galveston the customs agent got word from the secretary of the treasury to stop the *Fashion* because she was picking up men headed for Nicaragua. The agent ignored his orders and allowed another load of armed men to leave the port."

"Did you say the steamer was the *Fashion?"* Captain Whipple asked in dismay.

"That's the steamer that lightered the camels into port," Hermie almost shouted.

"Exactly." Captain Vogel smacked his lips with the first taste of Helga's dumplings.

"The *Fashion*'s been sailing in and out of Indianola since 1850." Captain Whipple seemed completely shocked. "I know her captain. How'd he get involved in all this?"

"You've heard of William Walker?"

"He's the one they call 'the gray-eyed man of destiny'?"

"That's him. He's a strange and ruthless little man. He got involved in a political revolution in Nicaragua and managed to become commander-in-chief of their army."

"But where's he getting the ships to move the filibusterers in there?" Captain Whipple kept shaking his head.

Captain Vogel massaged his temple with fingers from both hands. "It's a complicated and confusing series of events. For years Cornelius Vanderbilt and Charles Morgan have had a major shipping rivalry all along the East Coast. Then Vanderbilt got the deal to dig a canal across the isthmus of Nicaragua and provide all the shipping for the new water route to California. When Walker claimed control of the army, he took the concession away from Vanderbilt and gave it to Charles Morgan. In return, Morgan and his partners are moving filibusterers to Nicaragua from all along the Gulf Coast. Every eighteen days a ship departs Galveston with a load of filibusterers. It only costs each man thirty-five dollars, and he's guaranteed a large Nicaraguan land grant and fifty dollars a month."

"What's behind Walker settling all the new emigrants in Nicaragua?" Captain Whipple asked.

"That's the big question," Captain Vogel said. "A lot of people think it's a grand scheme to funnel more slaves into Texas. We produce a half-million bales of cotton a year. The land in Texas could produce three million bales if the plantations could get cheap labor.

"And slavery's the answer?" Helga could only whisper.

Captain Vogel nodded and looked seriously around the table. "Nicaragua is a good place to hold African slaves until the law is repealed. If it's not repealed, then Nicaragua's a way station for bringing them in illegally."

"Do you really believe the US government will repeal the law?" Battina looked horrified.

Captain Whipple shook his head. "Slaves are being brought in even if the law isn't repealed. On my last trip to Matamoros, I heard that slavers are landing along the lower coast during the night, unloading their cargo, and are back to sea in three hours."

Captain Vogel nodded. "The soil along the coast is porous and doesn't hold the prints from all that foot traffic. They can hide what they call 'black diamonds' all along the coast in the thick brush and high grass."

Eli Cox added, "If the government would legalize the African slave trade again and regulate it to keep down the abuse, the Negroes would be a lot better off."

"Eli Cox," Battina blurted, "are you saying Africans are better off in this country where they are turned into Christians instead of remaining heathens in their own country?"

"Plenty of church people believe that very thing."

"Do you?" Battina looked coldly across the table at Eli Cox.

"Well, I'm not sure. It seems sensible as a Christian nation we would want to find a way to bring all people to God."

"And make them slaves to do it?" Battina did not move her eyes from the squirming Eli Cox. "Mr. Cox, this is one time you can't keep your feet on both sides of the fence."

"The slave issue is tearing this country apart." Eli Cox stood. "We've been fortunate in this town. We haven't had abolitionists holding meetings and making demands. I worry that day may come." He looked accusingly at Battina and left the room.

"Things have been calm in Indianola," Captain Vogel continued as if he hadn't noticed Eli Cox leave the room. "For a long time slave ships have been outfitted and sailed out of East Coast harbors. The profit's so great that shippers in Galveston are openly converting cattle boats into slavers."

* * *

Soon after Captain Vogel left, Captain Whipple made a trip to New Orleans and returned looking very tired. "A New Orleans newspaper editor wrote that in the previous sixty days the port had been very busy with the arrival of fast sailing vessels for what the editor called 'the blackbird trade on the coast of Africa.'" Captain Whipple stopped and took a deep, exhausted breath, "With no apparent thought given to what he was saying, the editor wrote that they could have more ships outfitted if suitable craft became available. He claims there were no problems with getting through customs."

"So slavers are working openly?" Eagle said.

"That's not all. When I got to Galveston, the place was abuzz with the story of a large, fast ship arriving with a cargo of only a thousand dollars worth of Cuban cigars. Despite a few questions at customs about why such a large vessel carried such a small cargo, the ship was cleared and returned to Cuba. It was understood by everyone involved that the cargo of slaves had already been dropped on the Texas coast."

"That's what I've been pointing out; the African slave trade is such a big business it'll never be stopped," Eli Cox said.

Captain Whipple nodded. "There's so little federal effort to catch them on the high seas, and no effort's being made at all in our Southern ports. It's worth the risk for big-time investors."

"Are any of the slave ships coming into our harbor?" Helga asked.

"We don't see any evidence of filibusterers leaving from here or slavers using our port. Even the ships outfitted for cattle seem to be used strictly for that purpose," Captain Whipple replied.

By late November Captain Whipple's opinion regarding the presence of filibusterers was proven wrong. Seventy-five volunteers from Austin and San Antonio arrived in Indianola and boarded the steamship *Mexico,* a Morgan-owned vessel heading for Nicaragua.

* * *

Despite worry over the slavery issue, businesses thrived. Ships came in such numbers that they stacked up at the wharves and remained at anchor in the bay waiting for machinery, clothing, furniture, molasses, and other goods to be unloaded into the warehouses to wait for commission merchants like Eli Cox to move the products onto waiting wagons and ox carts for transport to western Texas.

By the end of 1856, Charles Morgan and his partner began construction of a new long wharf near Powder Horn Bayou to provide better accommodation for Morgan's vessels. Many prominent citizens, excited at the surging economy, eagerly bought stock in the new endeavor.

As confirmation of the business community's belief in a positive future for Indianola, right after the New Year, Morgan's old nemesis Cornelius Vanderbilt's steamship *Daniel* arrived in Indianola on its maiden voyage. The supper-table conversation grew lively over what better proof anyone could need of Indianola's positive business climate than having the two major shipping magnates competing at the port of Indianola.

February brought the thrill of another shipment of forty-one camels, encouraging the belief that Indianola held financial power recognized by the distant government in Washington.

Chapter 14

WINTER'S LATE ARRIVAL FINALLY DROVE Hermie and Jackson off the back porch and upstairs to share the room with Paul. Helga waited anxiously to hear loud complaints, but they didn't come. She stopped worrying, soothed by the belief that Paul was finally sleeping through the night without the nightmares.

Life felt good as the year moved at a more predictable pace. Hermie and Jackson continued expanding their year-round market. They made arrangements with two dairymen in the Guadalupe River Valley to haul in their milk, butter, and eggs every morning. Paul remained in constant demand at the Casimir and Alhambra houses. And Gretchen, at sixteen, had blossomed into a lovely young woman who outpaced the boys in their studies, especially in her command of Spanish and of *Paradise Lost*, one of Captain Whipple's books.

One evening after their lessons, Eli Cox surprised everyone by entering the kitchen and blurting, "Gretchen, you'll make an excellent teacher. You should come to commissioners court and present your application. We need hard-working scholars teaching our children."

Gretchen flushed crimson from her throat to the blonde braids wound across the top of her head. "Thank you, sir. I hope to do that."

"Will you recommend her to the court?" Eagle placed a hand protectively on Gretchen's shoulder.

"I'll be proud to."

At times Helga could not resist liking that irritable little man.

* * *

As the holidays approached word spread about young men coming into town, some by the wagonload, others on stage lines and even by foot. The estimate grew to 500 eagerly awaiting a steamer to take them to Galveston and on to Nicaragua to fulfill the dream of settling on their land grants and establishing a slave empire.

"Our town has lost its innocence," Battina whispered as they watched young men, their faces alive with excitement, hurrying toward the docks.

Helga nodded, struck by the memory of her ignorance such a short time ago in not believing Captain Whipple when he insisted Battina always accompany Orilla when she stepped beyond their fenced yard.

Captain Whipple had kept his voice low when he warned of the danger, which had seemed so remote at the time. "Slaves are in such demand, they bring high prices. Unsavory characters won't hesitate to stuff Orilla in a wagon or haul her on board a ship for sale to the highest bidder."

"Then I'd have to show her papers and prove she's free," Battina argued.

Captain Whipple had patiently explained, "Free people of color have fewer rights than slaves. Orilla, as your slave, has the protection of being your property. Taking someone's property is against the law."

As time passed, Orilla's skills as a seamstress—her tiny stitches seemed to disappear in every garment—built her reputation among the wives and daughters of the prosperous mercantile and professional men of Indianola. She and Battina spent a lot of time in the homes of wealthy ladies and came home with stories that convinced Helga of the wisdom of Captain Whipple's words.

One afternoon Helga heard the front door slam and watched Battina coming down the hall, her face twisted in an angry scowl. "Did you know families in this town who display such genteel airs are buying slaves and renting them to plantations up the Guadalupe and Colorado rivers for as much as $300 a year?" Her voice shook with fury as she paced up and down the hall.

"One of Edgar Samuel's slaves stole some jewelry from their neighbor. The slave's going to prison, and Mr. Samuel will get paid by the penitentiary for their use of his slave." Battina kept shaking her head in disbelief.

Eli Cox peeked out his door, and Captain Whipple came down the back stairs in time to witness Battina's rage. "If a free person of color stole jewelry from the neighbor, he'd be sold back into slavery and the slave's purchase price used to reimburse the neighbor," Captain Whipple said. "Being free can be a dangerous blessing."

"The slave trade's such big business it'll never be stopped." Eli Cox stuffed his hands in his pockets and hunched his shoulders, looking glum as he repeated his mantra once again. "Every newspaper in the state supports repeal. If we don't find a solution it's going to rip the country apart."

Captain Whipple nodded. "There's little federal effort to catch the slavers on the high seas, but British naval vessels do give chase. In many instances the naval officers are working with the slavers. The slavers pay twenty-five dollars per slave to the British vessel when it allows them to continue on their voyage with their cargo."

* * *

Eagle returned on the Saturday before Christmas with his usual offering of a giant cedar and a fresh, young buck. He didn't wait to get Helga alone to grab her in a fierce bear hug. "I didn't think I'd ever get home," he shouted as he swung her in a circle until they were both dizzy.

Jackson stood grinning until Eagle unclasped Helga and turned toward his son. For the first time, Jackson didn't jump into Eagle's arms. Instead, he grabbed his pa in a tight embrace. "I've gotten so big, I might hurt you if I jump."

Helga thought Eagle and Jackson both looked sad that the old ritual had ended—Jackson at twelve had shot up almost as tall as his pa.

After supper, Hermie and Jackson went out on the back porch with Eagle and seemed to be talking privately. After some time Eagle came in, put his arm around Helga, and hugged her tight against him. "Hermie and Jackson need to talk to us."

Helga's throat tightened in dread as Eagle took her hand and led her toward the two boys, who had strained, fearful expressions on their young faces.

"What's wrong? Did something happen to Paul?"

"That's what we need to talk about," Hermie said.

"Tell me. Is he hurt?"

"Not hurt," Jackson said. "He'll be along later."

"Mama, we're worried about Paul. He's drinking. Every night."

"He says it makes him sleep," Jackson said. "We shouldn't have kicked him out last summer. He's drinking to make himself sleep so we won't kick him out again." Jackson's voice caught as he fought back tears.

Eagle wrapped an arm around each boy. "I told them we had to talk to you. We can't keep it a secret."

Helga felt numb. "I haven't smelled it," she whispered, unable to understand how she had missed something she usually smelled on a man as he approached her on the street.

"He brings it home with him and drinks after we go to bed," Hermie said. "We both smell it. I've started lighting the lamp to let him know that we know what he's doing."

"What does he say?"

"He says we shouldn't care because he's not keeping us awake." Jackson kept shaking his head. "I feel like a snitch to tell you. But we're scared. He's drinking a lot every night."

"How long's this been going on?"

"Since we went back upstairs." Jackson kept swaying from one foot to the other like a nervous rocking horse.

"I'm afraid he'll be like Papa," Hermie said. "Remember how Papa drank to go to sleep?"

"I remember."

After the boys went to bed, Eagle and Helga sat silently on the bench in the kitchen. Warmth from the iron stove kept the room comfortable as a cold north wind whipped the waves into a whistling gale that rattled the windows.

"I don't know what to do," Helga finally whispered.

"I don't either. We need to talk to him."

Finally, they heard his soft steps on the back porch. He walked into the kitchen and stopped as he saw them in the dim light. "I thought you'd be asleep."

Helga smelled him before he stepped in the door. "What do you need to tell us, Paul?"

"About what?" He began to back toward the door.

"You needn't back away. I can smell it," Helga said. "Tell us what's making you drink."

"It's the holidays. There was a big party. I accepted a sip after I finished playing."

"You're drinking every night," Helga said.

"So they had to snitch. They are so perfect. They had to get me in trouble." Paul's voice rose. "I'll knock their heads in for this."

"No, you won't. You'll sit down here and talk to us." Helga kept her voice low and firm.

"I'm too tired. I've worked since early this morning. You don't understand how hard it is working like this. I clean all day and play all night. It's not easy to do what I do."

"Paul, I don't want you to start drinking. It will destroy you. Working hard doesn't give you an excuse to drink."

"I'm not destroying myself. I'm not like Papa. I can have a drink without killing myself." Paul was near tears. "I'm so tired, I've got to go to sleep. Can we talk later?"

"Tomorrow morning after breakfast." Helga stood and looked down at her son crumpled in a round heap on the bench next to Eagle. He looked as miserable as she felt.

As soon as they climbed into the ice-cold bed, Eagle pulled her to his shoulder and began patting her like he was soothing a colicky infant. "I don't know what to do, Hel. But I'm with you."

"Having that job with all the attention and praise seemed to be good for him. Now I'm not so sure."

"He's running from demons. Taking away the place where he finds satisfaction won't stop the demons," Eagle said.

Helga kept waking, sometimes sweating with fear; other times the cold crept over her entire body. Each time Eagle's arm reached protectively for her, smoothed the damp hair from her forehead or wrapped her in his warmth—offering what she needed. Just before morning, Helga roused from sleep, eager to make love with the man who had gentled her all night.

When she walked into the kitchen, ready to start breakfast, she saw the torn piece of an old newspaper with Paul's scrawl across the top: "I have to be at work to help serve breakfast at Casimir House. Love, Paul."

* * *

Eli Cox stayed true to his promise to recommend Gretchen to the commissioners court. "Mama, it was so easy. They accepted my application. They didn't even ask me many questions." Gretchen took a deep breath and smiled. "Tonight at supper I'll thank Eli Cox in front of everyone."

Helga pulled Gretchen into a tight hug. "I'm proud of you for getting the job. And I'm proud of you for thanking Eli Cox in front of everyone. He'll be so delighted."

"I know. Sometimes it's hard to be nice to him. He can be so aggravating. But somewhere down in his chest there's a good heart."

That night at supper Helga could barely keep from laughing as she watched Eli Cox bursting with joy as Gretchen praised and thanked him.

"He's very influential. We're lucky to have him living here." Gretchen beamed across the table at Eli Cox.

* * *

As 1858 began and Gretchen started teaching, Amelia began coming for a visit each morning after breakfast and spending most of the day helping Helga with the increased workload. She insisted, "It feels like the old days—we're alone with our secrets, looking out at the crazy world. Now it's not our papa and the nutty neighbors. It's the whole world going crazy."

Helga didn't mention her secret. As much as she loved Amelia, and as close as they had always been, Helga had never talked about Max's drinking. Even when Amelia came for a visit and found Max disheveled and barely moving around, neither sister spoke about it. And now, the sad story was repeating itself. Only this time it was Paul—Helga and Amelia's own flesh and blood. And just as the whole village had been aware of Max's drinking, Helga knew the entire town was aware that the young, lively musician at the Casimir House couldn't stay away from the bottle.

* * *

The Casimir House kept all 150 of its rooms full and offered a growing schedule of entertainment, which meant Paul worked from early morning until late evening most every day. And he came in at least once a week too drunk to get upstairs.

Helga had started waiting up for him, believing her presence discouraged his drinking. To keep from disturbing Hermie and Jackson and the other boarders, or perhaps to keep them from knowing when Paul was drunk, Helga often walked Paul to a mattress on the washroom floor, where she stayed with him until exhausted sleep finally stopped his thrashing. Each morning when she went to the kitchen he was always up, having cleaned himself and washed his clothing from the night before. He hustled about cheerfully filling the buckets with cistern water, starting the fire in the iron stove, and placing the teakettles on to heat. Never speaking of the previous evening, he appeared to be showing Helga, and possibly himself, that he had changed, that last night was a thing of the past. Helga felt relieved that he at least spared them both the pain of promises about starting over that Max had offered after every episode.

Spring brought continued prosperity to everyone in town and to all members of the household—something Helga wanted to celebrate. But turmoil raged within her. Eagle's prolonged absences left a constant ache in her body, and Paul's drinking grew more frightening whether he staggered home or bounced in smelling like a tavern and acting as if he had not a care in the world. During the gay times, when he looked most like Max, she found it increasingly difficult to keep from slapping his face.

Chapter 15

THE WHIRLWIND OF BUSINESS ACTIVITY generated by immigrants surging through Indianola continued into 1859. Merchants from the East Coast looking to make a fortune in the new western settlements stayed in town long enough to make financial arrangements for shipping merchandise to their businesses. Like all the hotels and boarding houses, Helga's rooms stayed full.

Orilla and Battina spent more and more time in their thriving dressmaking business. "I want her to have her own money and feel like a free woman. Even if we pretend she's my slave."

Mrs. Campbell opened her Millinery and Fancy Goods Shop on Main Street, thrilling Battina and Orilla by inviting Orilla to display some of her finer gowns in the store.

When the weather grew too cold to continue selling at the open vegetable market, Hermie and Jackson rented the first floor of a downtown building and opened H & J Grocery. "We can pay the bank loan in six months," Hermie said. "Our customers have been very loyal for over a year. And"—he grinned sheepishly at Helga—"since we both speak Spanish, the Mexican cart drivers are some of our best customers."

Eagle barely found time between freighting trips to spend one night at home. The only delay in his turnaround time came from getting his wagons through the traffic and up to the docks for unloading and then moving to a nearby warehouse to fill the wagons for the outbound trip.

"We're about to finish the courthouse," Eli Cox announced as soon as he sat down for supper. "We've fenced it, added trees, and the exterior will be scored to look like stone. And we've added a water closet, the first one in this town." Eli Cox leaned back in his chair, stroking his ample chest. "I read in the *Courier* about plans to build a public bathhouse with five or six compartments. It should be busy all the time with all the business we're getting."

Helga heard the kids snickering in the kitchen after supper. "Pa saw them installing that fancy water closet. He said its discharge pipe flows into the bay right in front of the courthouse. And he also said building the courthouse right next to the water is asking for a good storm to wash through its first floor."

Helga couldn't keep from smiling. Eagle often warned of Indianola being vulnerable to ravages from the sea. She didn't argue with him, but she couldn't imagine all the smart businessmen establishing such a thriving town, one beginning to rival Galveston, on land dangerously exposed to the sea.

* * *

While Helga carried her secret worry over Paul's drinking, the growing tension at supper each evening centered on the political climate, which fueled every conversation. The anger in town over the slave issue seemed like a festering sore just below the surface, ready to explode in the streets and at the supper table.

One of the boarders, a Mr. Sanger from Virginia staying in town while he arranged shipment of merchandise for his new mercantile store in Victoria, asked about Sam Houston running again for governor. "I hear he opposes reopening the slave trade. Folks in Galveston say if the law doesn't get changed, Texas will secede—either join other Southern states or return to a republic. How can Houston win in such a climate?"

Captain Whipple's whiskers trembled as if suppressing a big smile. "He's the hero of San Jacinto, the battle that won Texas's independence from Mexico. If he's elected it will be because he's still our war hero. His support for the union won't matter."

"He's very coarse," Mr. Sanger said. "I hear he travels the state in a buggy, wearing an old linen duster. When he gets hot during one of his long speeches, he strips to his waist. There's not an ounce of dignity in the man."

"Well"—Eli Cox leaned back in his chair, hooking his thumbs in his coat lapels—"Hardin Runnels beat him two years ago. He shouldn't have any trouble doing the same again this time."

"I'm not so sure Runnels is a shoo-in," Captain Whipple said. "In the last two years under Governor Runnels, filibustering picked up. People worry it'll come down to a serious break between the Southern plantation owners and those who want to stop the spread of slavery."

"With all the movement west and fertile bottom land just waiting for cotton planting, the price of a slave's gotten out of hand. We've got to have the labor if we intend to thrive." Mr. Sanger raised his chin like a peacock about to open its tail feathers. "I'm an example of a businessman seeing potential in this state. In addition to my store in Victoria, I've purchased land along the Guadalupe. I'll need slave labor to get it ready for planting."

"Why don't you hire help?" Hermie asked.

"German immigrants or Southern lads aren't suited to hard labor. You can't command them."

Helga sucked in a relaxing breath when Battina lightened the conversation with a compliment for the delicious baked red fish. "We're fortunate Hermie and Jackson bought this huge catch this morning. And shared with us."

Jackson's face lit up. "We keep buying everything we can. The more we buy, the more the business grows."

The following evening Eli Cox arrived with a gift—a Bateman's Patent Safety Gas Lamp—placed it on the dining table, and filled it with Bacon's Fluid Gas. "It's warranted not to explode and should provide more light than ten candles." Beaming like a kid, he added, "I saw the ad in the *Courier.* Bought it at the new Gas Lamp Depot."

To everyone's delight, it brightened the room; however, so many bugs swarmed to the light, he blew it out before supper ended.

"You can read by it and not worry about bugs in the food," Jackson offered.

"Try it with your studies tonight," Eli Cox said. "See how much better you see."

"It's a deal," Jackson said. "I'll read first."

Paul came in sober and asked to read by the new light. "Maybe we can buy one if it works so well."

Helga felt such relief at seeing Paul sober and wanting to be part of the evening that she wanted to hug Paul and Eli Cox.

With the increase in business, the competition grew stiff. Hermie and Jackson brought home a copy of the *Courier* and pored over ads. H. Runge & Co. was offering German prunes just arrived from Bremen.

"We've got to start buying off the ships," Hermie said.

"You can buy from me," Eli Cox said. I'll sell you small amounts of northern potatoes, sacks of white corn, and even garden seeds. Most of it's contracted. I can let you have a little to make you more competitive."

"Really?" Jackson said. "You'd do that?"

"Of course. I want to see your business grow."

Helga clasped both hands across her breast in shocked wonder. She took a deep breath and said, "Sir, we're eternally grateful to you. Thanks to your influence with the commissioners court Gretchen has a teaching job, and now you offer to help the boys. We can't thank you enough."

Eli Cox rocked back in his chair and looked as though he might cry. "Frau Heinrich, I'm proud to do it."

Helga wished for some way to tell Eli Cox he could call her Helga.

* * *

Otto Schnaubert arrived in town and came immediately to the Stein House. "I'm offering lessons in drawing to ladies and gentlemen of this city. I've been told your establishment has lovely stenciling. If I may display my work here and offer lessons in your parlor, I'd like to become a boarder."

"We have a room available upstairs." Helga looked over the tall, thin young man wearing a slightly shabby coat in the July heat. "It's the room the artist who did the stenciling occupied while he was in town."

As he followed Helga through the house, Otto whispered, "The stenciling is lovely. My sketches will be comfortable here."

* * *

Summer brought more changes, disturbing almost everyone. The city council, concerned over the city's rapid growth and its need for expanded city services, instituted Indianola's first taxation. An ad valorem tax on property displeased Dr. Stein. Eli Cox as a commission merchant and Hermie and Jackson as grocers were unhappy about a ten-dollar-per-year license fee. The Villeneuves weren't happy about a twenty-dollar tax on each billiard table, two dollars and fifty cents for every theater performance, and ten dollars for each tavern and restaurant.

In an effort to keep the city clean and improve health, the city started weekly garbage pickup enforced by the marshal. Residents who did not place their refuse in the street or alley for convenient pickup received a five-dollar fine, 10 percent of which went to the marshal for his troubles, which encouraged him to diligently enforce the law.

The most draconian laws resulted from fear growing among the residents over the influx of so many new arrivals. Concerned that abolitionists might be among the newcomers and stir up the Negro population, the council declared a curfew for all slaves and free Negroes within the city limits. No Negro or slave could leave the premises of his owner or employer after 9:00 p.m. without written permission. The council charged the marshal with jailing any offending free Negro or slave, and it authorized white people to apprehend any violator and deliver him or her to the marshal. The offending free Negro or slave received neither less than ten nor more than thirty-nine lashes and remained jailed until the owner or employer paid a two-dollar fee and all costs. The punishment could be suspended with the payment of five dollars and costs.

If caught playing cards or any gambling game in the city, free Negroes or slaves received thirty-nine lashes and a fee of one dollar.

The alderman had authority to appoint five citizens to assist the marshal in patrolling the city whenever the marshal deemed it necessary to keep the peace.

Battina trembled during the reading of the provisions. "That scares me."

Eli Cox shrugged. "These laws don't apply to Orilla. She doesn't go out at night or gamble. There's no reason for you to worry."

"It's the fear. When people become afraid of a whole group, they stop being rational. They punish the entire group out of fear of what one might do."

Helga wanted to comfort Battina, to tell her that she was being foolish, that she was letting her imagination run away with her, but Helga feared Battina was right. No one knew where all the unrest might lead.

One night in July, just as they were finishing supper, the conversation ended with the sound of a thud as someone leaped on the back porch and began banging on the door. Eagle rose quickly, stepping protectively in front of Helga.

A heavily sweating Negro stood at the door, his breath coming in such gasps he could barely speak above a whisper. "Please, can I see Captain Whipple?"

Captain Whipple called out, "Samuel?" He rushed to the door. "What's wrong?"

"It's Joseph, Captain. He be arrested for defending his self against a drunk white man. We needs you to come to the marshal's fast. That white man he says he's going to own him a slave before this night's over."

"We better get down there." Captain Whipple looked at Eagle. "Would you mind going along with us?"

"Sure, Captain." Eagle touched the captain's shoulder. "It's faster to take the road."

"Better not. We don't know what may be waiting between here and town." The captain followed Samuel down the back steps.

As Helga watched them rush out to the alley, her throat closed in fear. Captain Whipple would never have asked for help unless he needed a strong man's protection.

Long after bedtime, Eagle, Captain Whipple, and Paul returned with a terrified-looking Negro.

"I told the captain Joseph would be okay staying here." Eagle's voice held a question; his eyes pleaded.

"Of course." Helga reached to shake Joseph's crusty-hard hand.

"I be grateful, ma'am." Joseph kept his head down. Only the bloodshot whites of his eyes showed in the lamplight.

"He can stay in my room," Captain Whipple said as they headed toward the kitchen.

While they ate ravenously, the story came out. Paul had seen it all from the front porch of the Casimir House. He had followed the angry crowd to the marshal's office.

"Paschal James got fired before I started working at the Casimir House, but he comes in and gets drunk every night. They kick him out when he gets too rowdy." Paul kept his head down, only looking at Helga out of the corner of his eye as he talked. "Everyone at the Casimir House has heard Paschal James boasting about hating Negroes, especially the free ones like Joseph. Paschal always says he's going to get him a black SOB one of these days."

Eagle wrapped his arm around Paul's shoulder and shook him like he was a hero. "Paul had the courage to push his way through that crowd. They were ready to hang Joseph right then. Paul told the marshal Paschal had been following Joseph, shoving him every few steps as Joseph carried a load of sugarcane from a freight wagon up to the dock. As Joseph stepped on the dock, Paschal hit him with such force Joseph and the cane went into the bay. When Joseph scrambled to get the cane, Paschal started to hit him again. That's when Joseph let Paschal have it right in the face—probably broke his nose. Sure made a bloody mess." Eagle's grin spread as he beat Paul on the back.

"I've put up the bail," said Captain Whipple. "I'll hire a lawyer in the morning. We need to let folks calm down for a while. Could Joseph pay his board by helping you around here until the trial? It'd keep him away from downtown." Captain Whipple smiled at Joseph. "I can tell you he's a good worker. He's worked on my dock since buying his freedom five years ago."

"I've wanted to expand the garden all the way to the alley. I've got the boards to enclose it. I'd be grateful for the help."

"It'll be a while before the hearing," Captain Whipple said. "The law says a Negro can't testify against a white man. None of the Negroes on the dock who saw what happened will be allowed to testify. So Paul's testimony is the key to Joseph's defense, unless someone else steps forward. Plenty of folks were on the street. They may be waiting to test the water."

"Surely more witnesses will step up," Helga said.

"So often it's easier to look the other way, to ignore what's happening," Captain Whipple said. "There're fewer and fewer free Negroes in Texas since they can't legally stay here. In Galveston, some of the freedmen are asking men they think will make good masters to buy them back into slavery. They're afraid they'll get accused of something and sold onto an outlying plantation."

"If they're free, how can they be sold?" Paul shook his head in amazement.

"They're sold to pay off their debts. If Paschal can convince the judge that Joseph harmed him, Joseph can be fined so much for personal injury that he can't pay it. The judge can rule Joseph be sold to Paschal to pay his debt. Indianola's been pretty liberal, but I'm afraid attitudes are changing." Captain Whipple looked genuinely worried.

Despite the tragedy swirling around her, Helga slept soundly that night wrapped in the comforting arms of Eagle. Paul had shown real maturity. Maybe this would be what he needed to stop drinking. And Eagle gave him the fatherly support he needed.

Chapter 16

JOSEPH PROVED TO BE AS hard a worker as Captain Whipple claimed. He expanded the garden and prepared it for spring planting, and he kept the house in spotless condition inside and out.

Amelia insisted on preparing lunch on the day of Joseph's hearing to allow Helga to attend.

Helga tried not to worry about Paul's ability to stand the questioning. He came home sober the night before the hearing. Helga could not keep herself from fearing that he was waiting to drink until he got upstairs. That morning he was up as usual doing all the chores he seemed to have assigned himself—drawing water, heating the teakettles. And as usual, he was alert and cheerful.

Eagle rode in the night before on a mule, leaving the other teamsters to bring in the wagons. Hermie and Jackson closed their store for the day. Battina and Orilla canceled all their appointments for measurements and fittings. Gretchen asked another teacher to take her classes. Eli Cox, Captain Whipple, and Paul sat on the front row behind Joseph. Townspeople packed the courtroom.

Paschal James's facial injuries had all healed; however, he wrapped his right arm in a cotton sling. When his lawyer directed questioning, Paschal said, "I'm still unable to work. That Negro damaged my arm until I can't do no lifting on my job."

Joseph's lawyer, whom Captain Whipple claimed as one of the best in Indianola, questioned Paschal. "What's your job, sir?"

"I'm unemployed right now."

Eagle reached for Helga's hand and squeezed it.

"What was your job before you became unemployed?"

"I swept out the Casimir House."

"Why aren't you still doing that?"

"I got fired."

"Why?"

"For coming in drunk."

"When was that?"

"Two years ago."

The courtroom burst into laughter. Eagle squeezed Helga's hand even harder.

Paul stepped up to testify, walking straight as a military officer, his chin up like he was waiting for orders.

After Paul finished telling his account, Paschal's lawyer stepped forward and leaned menacingly toward Paul. "Are you the only one who saw what happened?"

"No, sir."

"Where are the others?"

"I can't say, sir."

"Why were you out on the Casimir House front porch?"

"I was getting some fresh air. The smoke's very thick."

"Do you smoke?"

"No, Sir."

"Do you drink?"

Paul did not blink and continued looking straight at the lawyer, "Yes, sir."

Murmurs rippled through the hushed courtroom.

"A boy your age? Let's see … you are sixteen. And drinking? Were you drinking on that afternoon?"

"No, sir."

"You like the slaves who work with you at Casimir House?"

"Yes, sir."

"Would you testify against a white man to protect one of your Negro friends?"

"Not if he was guilty."

Helga held her breath and prayed the judge was a man without hate in his heart for Negroes and young boys who drank. Hermie took her other hand, and she realized all the family members spreading along the bench were clasping hands.

Finally, the lawyers rested, and the judge looked gravely across the courtroom. "Since Joseph doesn't have any witnesses to speak for him except this one boy who admits to drinking, I have no choice but to fine the defendant three hundred dollars for personal injury to Paschal James and one hundred dollars for court costs."

Helga gasped and then covered her mouth with both hands. She could see Paul's head drop liked he was whipped. Joseph, his black face immobile, stared straight ahead.

Several people in the courtroom clapped. Others sat silently, apparently as shocked as Helga.

Captain Whipple stood. "Your Honor, as the employer of Joseph, who has been an excellent worker for the five years he's been in my employ, I wish to pay all costs."

The murmur in the courtroom grew to a roar.

The judge's eyebrows shot up. "That will cost you four hundred dollars. Is that Negro worth four hundred dollars to you?"

"Yes, sir. May I pay the debt now?"

Helga fought back tears of frustration and anger building until she wanted to stand and scream, "How could you be so blind? How can you sit there and let another human be so degraded?" And then she saw in the pleased expressions on most of the faces surrounding her that they believed Joseph was guilty. They did not believe Paul's story. They thought Joseph deserved what he got.

As soon as it was over, Helga tried to speak to Paul, but he looked away from her and said he had to get back to work. Everyone scattered, going back to work, except Eagle, who continued to hold her hand and walk silently beside her back to the house.

"Home so soon," Amelia said as they walked in the door.

"It doesn't take long to deny justice for a Negro," Eagle said.

Helga was grateful he didn't tell Amelia about Paul's embarrassment. The word would spread quickly enough.

Paul came home sober late that night. "I thought I might get fired. Mr. Vanderveer waited to see how the customers reacted to me after I testified. I played the best I could, and I think the customers still like me. I got three dollars in tips. That's real good for the middle of the week."

"I'm proud of you," Helga said. "I've wondered all day if I have that much courage."

"The way it turned out, I didn't help Joseph at all."

"You helped truth and decency."

Paul sighed deeply. "Maybe. Mr. Vanderveer told me to watch my step when I'm on the street. He says plenty of folks are mad at me, especially old Paschal James."

"Were you scared walking home tonight?"

"Yes. And I'll be scared in the morning. But I'll do it." Paul went to the washroom and took down the straw mattress. "I better sleep in here tonight. I may thrash so much that Hermie and Jackson will want to kick me out."

Helga fought tears as she sat down on the floor beside her son, whose stooped shoulders made him look as if he had been physically whipped. "I'll stay here until you go to sleep."

Helga offered Joseph a permanent job helping her enlarge the chicken house, get the spring garden planted, and care for a second milk cow. She realized worry and the fatigue from staying up each night to wait for Paul had slowed her down, and Joseph seemed to always be there when she was too tired to keep going. He refused, however, to eat at the table with the family. He took all his meals in the kitchen after helping serve. Then he washed dishes and swept the dining room.

* * *

There seemed to be no pattern to Paul's drinking. Some nights he came home sober. Other times he could hardly get up the back stairs. Helga wondered if the nights he drank were the result of customer comments, but Paul refused to talk about it.

* * *

April brought wonderful rains and Eli Cox brimming with excitement over being asked to serve as a director of the Indianola Railroad Company. "Raising money will be a huge challenge. We don't have wealthy capitalists in Texas. The eighty-mile railway between Harrisburg and Alleyton got its funding through investors in Massachusetts. We need to find investors that recognize the potential for Indianola. We are sitting on a transportation gold mine." He grinned mischievously, "You better watch out, Eagle. When we get a railroad in here, your business will see its last day."

Eagle laughed good-naturedly. "I'll worry when the railroad gets built."

The next month everyone at the supper table teased Eli Cox when the commissioners court raised taxes to pay for a new jail.

"That iron jail cell we have now sat on the beach rusting for thirteen months before the commissioners got it installed, Mr. Cox." Jackson took up the taunt in his pa's absence. "If we pay more taxes to build the new jail, are you sure it'll get done?"

Everyone laughed so hard Helga felt sorry for Eli Cox. No matter how much he tried, he couldn't explain why it took so long for his commissioners court to get anything done.

In August, Gretchen sat down at supper ready to take on poor Eli Cox. "Why are the commissioners requiring teachers to sign an oath saying English is the primary language in our classes?"

Eli Cox shrugged sheepishly. "It's from the legislature. They don't want our schools teaching the language of immigrants. In Indianola, it would be German ..." His voice faded as he looked helpless for a better explanation.

"I teach English, German, and Spanish. I signed the oath because I won't get paid if I refuse. It feels like we're separating people into us and them."

Eli Cox nodded, and again Helga felt sorry for him. After supper she found him sitting alone in the parlor listening to Battina playing the harp. "Eli," Helga said, "since you've been part of this family for so long, why don't you call me Helga, and I'll call you Eli?" She felt moved to tears as she watched Eli's face crumble like that of a child about to cry.

"I'd like that very much, Helga." He ducked his head and flushed bright crimson.

* * *

Tensions mounted in Indianola as more and more Northern agitators got off ships and headed inland to garner support for the Union. Most of Otto's drawing students wanted private lessons in their homes, but a few came during the day to Stein House, and despite the doors being pulled shut between the parlor and dining room, Helga often heard comments about newcomers who might be abolitionists coming into the state to create discord. After one man was forcibly placed on an outgoing ship following a charge of planning to set a fire at the port, Helga heard two of Otto's students, wives of the town's prominent businessmen, complaining more to each other than to Otto that something needed to be done to stop the criminal element coming in from the North. Helga never heard Otto respond to the comments. Instead, he gently moved them on with their art lessons.

The city appointed a patrol to keep the peace that some residents called "the vigilance committee."

Captain Whipple brought home a copy of the Indianola *Courier* dated October 10, 1860. "This article quotes Judge Hawes at Saluria down on Matagorda Island saying if Lincoln wins the presidency, he'll contribute a thousand dollars to arm and equip the first Texas company of a hundred men. And he'll give each man a hundred dollars. He also says any appointees that accept an office under Lincoln must be expelled from Texas. Hawes says they're the most dangerous enemies to the peace, prosperity, and continued union of the States."

"Judge Hawes is convinced we don't have sufficient protection along our coast. He's expecting a Union invasion at any minute," Eli Cox added.

The suppertime conversations revolved around the increasingly radical political climate. Eli Cox and Captain Whipple brought copies of the Galveston *News,* the Houston *Telegraph,* the Austin *State Gazette,* the San Antonio *Herald,* and any other newspaper that came into port.

* * *

In late October, the captain entered the dining room, obviously distressed. Holding up two more papers, he said, "All the Texas editorials support secession. The political speeches are becoming more inflammatory. Threats of secession are a constant drumbeat among those claiming the election of Lincoln will destroy the nation."

Eagle had returned with news that Governor Sam Houston was traveling the state calling for cool heads. As boarders began taking their places at the table, Eagle said, "I heard Sam Houston give a fireball speech in Austin. He's insisting the South isn't going to get alliances with European nations against the North. Houston says the only way the South will get British support is to pledge to end slavery." Eagle looked around the table shaking his head, "Can you see Texas agreeing to end slavery?"

"The tragedy is that most elected officials in Austin think the South is powerful enough to beat the North," Captain Whipple said.

Then Eli Cox rushed in for supper waving a paper with the news of the October 16 raid on Harper's Ferry. "Thirteen white men and five Negroes under a man named John Brown killed the mayor and one

Negro freedman and captured the arsenal and rifle works. Robert E. Lee led some marines and captured or killed them all."

"Was it a Negro rebellion?" Battina asked, her black eyes wide with horror.

"No." Captain Whipple shook his head in disgust "I read that story this morning. John Brown sounds like a crazy man. He thought he could start a mass insurrection, arm Southern slaves, and establish an Abolitionist Republic in the defeated South. His group forced some Negroes to take part. No one with a lick of sense joined his scheme."

As more news poured in of Brown's conviction and hanging, it became clear the incident had not accomplished exactly what John Brown intended, but it did create more divisions in the country. To Helga's surprise, Eli and the captain found mutual agreement on the troubles Harper's Ferry created.

"Some Northern thinkers like Horace Greeley, Emerson, Thoreau and a lot of others argue that despite John Brown being insane, what he did was noble because slavery's so vile." Eli Cox shook his head and looked at Battina and Orilla. "Slavery's evil, but killing people won't stop slavery."

Battina and Orilla both nodded as if to reassure Eli they understood and agreed.

Orilla, who rarely spoke at supper, said, "Both sides see the other as evil. How will we ever reconcile?"

When Joseph finished sweeping the dining room, he came quietly into the kitchen. "Missy." He shook his head, "I mean, Ma'am," it's sounding bad. I plan to lay low and do my work. If I am the cause of any trouble for you, I'll ask the captain to take me off to Mexico on his ship."

"Joseph, we're not going to make any plans for you to leave. You work for me. And, you are welcome to call me Missy if you prefer."

"You can say you bought me if you want to, Missy."

"I think most folks believe the captain bought you when he paid your fine and court cost. We know it's not true. But just like in Orilla's case, we are letting folks think what they will."

Joseph nodded. "Sure is a mixed-up world."

When Paul came in that night he was sober and very upset. "Who is John Brown? What's Harper's Ferry? Two customers I've never seen wanted to know if I supported what John Brown did at Harper's Ferry. They said I was a nigger lover, that we had niggers living in our house."

He looked at Helga accusingly. "This is when I need a drink—when I can't make sense of anything."

"Drinking won't make it better." Helga wrapped her arms around her trembling son and silently thanked God Paul did not pull away.

Finally, she explained all she had learned from newspaper accounts and the captain and Eli about Harper's Ferry. Paul lay motionless on the mattress in the washroom, covering his face with both hands.

"If I can't play music in a place like Casimir House where nobody cares about anything but having a good time, I won't be able to work in this town."

Helga could not answer. For some things, she had no answer.

As the election neared, Eli Cox and Captain Whipple brought more disagreement to the supper table, although they were more courteous than the rhetoric chronicled in newspapers and speeches coming from every corner.

"The commissioners and I don't believe we'll actually secede," Eli Cox said. "We think this saber rattling is just so much noise. The North isn't about to allow a war that will force business to a standstill. Look at all the traffic we get in our port from the Northeast."

Captain Whipple rubbed both hands through his scraggly white beard. "I agree business will grind to a standstill. But the North has the industrial might to continue building ships, blockade our coastline, and shut down the international cotton trade. Cotton is all the South produces. The North can destroy our economy."

"That's what Governor Houston's saying," Hermie said. "If the Yankees blockade our coastline, our business will be destroyed."

"The commissioners don't think they can do it," Eli argued. "We have two busy shipyards. We're not going to allow the North to stop our port traffic. We have so much activity downtown it's hard to move all the wagons and carts waiting at the docks. Even with some crop failures this year, we've got such a variety of products coming in from all over the West we're not dependent on any one crop." Eli stopped and grinned broadly. "And there's the railroad. With the roadbed graded and the delivery of so many ties, we're in a position to grow into a full-sized city."

"But we've run out of ties. Jackson and I walked the new roadbed around the backside of town. The ties stop on the other side of Old Town." Hermie grinned at Eli. "It looks like we may get a rail line. Someday. We're not there yet."

A few nights later Eli came in with the *Courier-Bulletin*. "The editor thinks our rosy financial picture will continue indefinitely. He touts both the railroad and Charles Morgan increasing the number of steamers between here and New Orleans." Eli folded the paper into quarters. "And look at this piece of news. Morgan's latest steamship with its steel boiler is one of the largest iron ships ever built in this country, and it's come into our port."

The news trickling in of Lincoln's election stirred patriotism for the former Republic of Texas. Caution was thrown aside as Texas newspapers called for secession instead of living under the evils of Lincoln's "Black Republicanism."

On the night of November 21, a well-advertised mass meeting took place at the courthouse, preceded by a parade. At the insistence of the entire household, Helga agreed to attend.

"You need to see it yourself instead of waiting for us to tell you all about it," Gretchen argued.

Sam McBride, who owned one of the shipyards on Powder Horn Bayou, led the parade, carrying a flag emblazoned with a Lone Star, the symbol of the former republic. Sewn by local women for the event, the flag drew such wild applause it drowned out the band's rousing march music. Marchers carried poles topped by huge, transparent pieces of glass with candles or kerosene lamps illuminating phrases like The Issue is Upon Us; Who is not for us is Against us; The Time Has Come; States' Rights; Millions in Number, One in Sentiment; and The North has broken the Symbols of Union.

After the parade passed, Jackson shouted above the noise of the crowd, "I counted twenty-eight of those giant signs. I wish Pa could have been here to see this."

"I do too, Jackson." She did not say how badly she needed him to be there.

The crowd filled the courthouse to overflowing. Helga stood outside, pressed by the throng against an open courtroom window from which she heard Judge J.J. Holt give a rousing speech saying they must take decisive action. Then he appointed a committee to draft resolutions representing the views of Indianola citizens. While the crowd waited for the resolutions to be written, the band played the French national anthem, which Helga recognized as a revolutionary symbol. After another loud and emotion-laced speech, the committee returned.

Their statement began by saying when the North cast its vote for Lincoln, it declared its intent to use the federal government to destroy the institution of slavery in the South and subvert the rights of Texas. The statement said Texas ought not to submit to the rule of a Black Republican administration. It called for the governor to convene the legislature to support a secession convention. It asked federal officials in Texas to keep their offices for the time being and to immediately resign after the state took action, asserting Texas's right to peaceably retake the powers it had delegated to the federal government when it accepted statehood. The document made it clear that if the resumption of Texas's rights was denied, the citizens recommended minutemen be organized and equipped in each town. Finally, it called for sending a copy of the proceedings to the governor and having the document published in newspapers.

As Helga walked home with members of her household forming a silent brigade, the events of the evening roared in her head as loudly as the waves crashing against the shore. Helga made tea, and they settled in the kitchen around the warmth of the iron stove.

"When Texas joined the Union, Amelia's letters sounded so hopeful. She called it a great day for Texans. Now they want to leave. Texas has prospered and been at peace while it's been part of the United States." Chilled by the shock of what she had just witnessed, Helga clutched her teacup to warm her fingers.

A few days later when Eli Cox read in the *Courier* that a company of Home Guard had started enrolling men and money was being collected for purchasing arms, Hermie carefully laid his fork across his plate. "Jackson and I signed up today with the Home Guard."

Helga suppressed a gasp as she covered her mouth with both hands.

"We had to, Mama. We can't live in this town and have a business here without supporting the volunteers."

"He's right," Captain Whipple said. "Every one of us is a Unionist. We don't want to see this happen. But we're Texans first, and we're Indianolans."

"I think Pa would agree. You got to support your own, even if you disagree."

"Paul signed up too," Hermie said. "He looked pretty upset, but he did it."

"What will this mean? Will you be going to war?" Helga could feel her throat tightening.

"We'll be drilling and doing exercises for now. It won't be all the time. We can continue working for now." Eli did not speak with his usual assurance.

Otto rarely spoke at supper, but he always appeared genuinely engaged in every issue. He cleared his throat. "I'll be serving in the artillery ... as a first lieutenant."

"Will you be going out to the island?" the captain asked.

"We're waiting on two twelve-pounder cannons from General Sidney Sherman in Galveston. And we're converting a six-pounder into a five and getting it mounted." He flushed and looked embarrassed. "May I keep my room? And leave my sketches displayed here? I really don't have any other place for them."

"Of course," Helga said and hoped her relief at not losing a boarder didn't show.

That night Helga waited anxiously for Paul to get home. He was drunk, but just drunk enough to be willing to talk. "If I'm going to keep my job, I've got to support the volunteers." He sat at the kitchen table holding his head in both hands. When he looked up at Helga, his face was sketched in agony. "They're raising money to arm us. I can march and do exercises. But Mama, I can't kill another man." Tears streaked his face, and he allowed Helga to wrap him in her arms.

A few days later, the notice arrived that South Carolina had seceded from the Union. "This is it," Helga whispered as Captain Whipple read the account in the paper.

* * *

When Helga saw Eagle pulling his team off the road just before Christmas, she rushed down the front steps and threw herself against him as he climbed down from his bench. "I don't know when I've needed you so much," she cried, clinging to this man who smelled of sweat, mules, and dung. "The world has gone crazy. All three boys have volunteered. The town's raising money to arm them."

"Hel, I hurried. I felt you calling." He held her against him, his hands stroking her back, smoothing her hair, gently rocking her as they stood in plain view of wagons clanging past. "Those boys are doing what they need to. We can't turn our back on our homeland. We're all Texans."

The news Eagle brought to the supper table was of secession talk everywhere, the Lone Star flag hoisted on downtown squares, and anger almost out of control. "People who've said anything against slavery or supported Negroes are being called traitors. A sixty-year-old pastor who actually supports slavery, preached against flogging Negroes. A gang tied him to a post and gave him seventy lashes, almost killed him. They're blaming some fires in barns and other buildings in north Texas on abolitionists."

"I'm wondering if I should take Orilla to Boston. My mother has relatives there." Battina closed her eyes. "I don't want to leave you. And I don't want to start over, but attitudes are changing. Even Orilla's beautiful dresses are receiving senseless criticisms. It feels like the air we breathe is filling with venom."

Captain Whipple nodded. "I don't want to see you go, but it may be wise to leave before you can't get away."

Eli nodded. "We're seeing the split already. It's hard to tell just where it'll end. With all the secession talk, the New York commercial house planning to fund the railroad has withdrawn its support. Henry Runge is heading to Germany to get funding there. We're going to lose most of our freight traffic if we don't beat the Buffalo Bayou Railroad to Austin. It's already built past Houston."

Eagle didn't tease Eli about the railroad dream. Instead, he looked at Battina and shook his head. "The anger isn't rational. That's why it's scary."

"We must stay through Christmas." Battina seemed to be asking rather than stating her feelings.

"I'll help you when you're ready," Captain Whipple said.

All over town the Christmas season was the liveliest Helga or Amelia could remember. Casimir House hosted soirees and hops. Little boys shot firecrackers day and night. Battina and Orilla stayed busy sewing fancy ball gowns. Eli even sold Hermie and Jackson a shipment of mangoes fresh off the boat from Central America. Cedar trees were decorated all over town with painted mountain laurel seeds and shells and fragile glass ornaments German families had brought with them from the old country.

Battina and Orilla stayed up late helping Helga cook mincemeat pies and fruitcakes. Helga made *lebkuchens* that Jackson said were the best cookies he'd ever eaten. In addition to the annual young buck, Eagle brought home a big fat goose that was late flying south and a wild turkey.

Helga wondered if the frenzied activity was the result of Indianola's continued prosperity or the desperate effort to mask unease about what the future held.

Chapter 17

THE DAY AFTER NEW YEAR'S, Battina and Orilla came home early. "It's time for us to go," Battina said as she and Orilla entered the front door, their arms full of dresses.

"What happened?" Gretchen dropped the mop handle and rushed to Battina's side, wanting to throw her arms around her, wanting to beg her not to leave.

"Now that the holidays have passed and they've worn all of Orilla's elegant dresses, she's no longer welcome in the store. Several customers said they prefer a white seamstress measuring and touching them." As Battina spoke her black eyes flashed with fury, and yet she held her head high like a swan ready to fly above the churning waters of an ugly lake as she swept into their room and carefully spread the dresses on her bed.

Orilla stared straight ahead as if she had moved to another world as she followed Battina into their room and sat down on her bed still clutching her dresses against her breast.

Gretchen had made herself into a sponge, absorbing every gesture, every way of speaking, and every detail of the dignity and charm of both women. Now she must fight her desire to cry and rage and hit someone. She must not act like a peasant. Finally she said, "I'll bring you some tea," as she eased their door shut behind her.

At supper Captain Whipple said a ship should be leaving port in two days with only brief stops in New Orleans and Mobile before sailing on to Boston. "It's safer to take as direct a route as possible."

Gretchen could not listen another moment. She whispered, "Excuse me," and quickly left the table after only a few bites. This couldn't be happening to the world she had crafted so carefully. Sharing the room with Battina and Orilla, being allowed to touch and actually experience the varieties of elegant fabrics and laces, and learning how the delicate stitches controlled the drape and flow of each garment had opened the world like an unfolding flower in a way her mama could not even imagine. She had become a new person, a woman of breeding. She threw herself on her narrow little bed and gave in to the tears.

By the time Battina and Orilla returned from supper to begin packing, Gretchen had forgotten her determination to be dignified. She beat her bed with her fists. "I want to go with you. I can't live in a place where you aren't welcome."

She felt Battina easing onto the edge of the bed, her soft hand gently stroking her hair away from her face. She knew she looked awful—red-faced, tear-streaked—but she couldn't get control of herself.

Battina's voice stayed soft and comforting. "We'll meet again when all this turmoil ends. And it will end."

Gretchen rolled over and flung her arms around Battina. "You and Orilla are the most beautiful women I've ever seen." Then she saw her mama standing there with her arm around Orilla's waist.

"Gretchen's right. You're beautiful women. You've been good examples for us."

She hadn't intended to say things to hurt her mama, but since Battina entered her life she had felt open to more than hard, knuckle-bruising work. Wiping her face on her sleeve, she got up and began helping with the packing. "If you don't come back here I'll be coming to Boston as soon as I can save the money."

* * *

Captain Whipple brought a buggy around after dark, and Hermie and Jackson loaded the trunks and the enormous crate holding Battina's harp. The captain gently patted Gretchen's shoulder, his pale blue eyes crinkling with concern. "I'll get them settled in their stateroom tonight. The ship sails at daybreak."

Gretchen could only nod. She appreciated his kindness. She knew it was another of the captain's ways of trying to please Mama. Captain Whipple and Eli Cox were probably in their sixties, but they both cared about her mama in a way she couldn't figure out. She noticed it in the little things they did for her, the way they made themselves part of the family even though they were boarders, the way they always waited for Mama to come to the table before sharing their newspaper articles or the latest events in town. She also noticed they looked at Mama when they talked, always including her in the conversation even though she rarely took part. Mama didn't seem to notice their attention was anything out of the ordinary. She always told Tante Amelia she was imagining it when she teased Mama about being lucky to have two old men who cared about her.

As the buggy rolled away, Gretchen's future looked as frightening as the darkness into which her dear friends disappeared. Mama wrapped her arm tightly around her shoulder, silently allowing her to weep even though she must have known how desperately Gretchen wanted to be away from this place.

* * *

The following week, Paul bounded onto the back porch with more enthusiasm than Gretchen had seen from him in a long time. He had been so morose and self-pitying he had become an embarrassment. Mama thought she was keeping his drinking a secret by waiting up for him and getting him to bed in the washroom every night, but only politeness on the part of everyone in the house kept a cloak spread over the family shame. No one wanted to add to Mama's trouble except Paul, who was the source of it.

"Everybody from the Casimir House went to see the most amazing show at the courthouse," Paul said. "Three Germans from San Antonio landed this morning after a tour up the Mississippi. They have pictures of things you've never seen, like waterfalls and a ship and a house on fire. It's sort of a magic lantern show. You've got to go tomorrow night. And go early, because the courthouse will be packed."

Mama looked so thrilled to see Paul's enthusiasm that she obviously would have done anything to encourage him. Besides, Gretchen thought, the show would lift all of their spirits.

Everyone in the household rushed through supper and hurried to see the show at the courthouse. Some folks in the crowd were wearing blue cockades made of ribbons shaped into rosettes.

"They're badges," Hermie explained, "in support of secession."

"Are we the only people in town who don't want to secede?" Gretchen whispered.

"Just about. It's going to happen for sure."

The program, accompanied by music from behind the curtain, began with an exciting display of huge photographs of kings, actors, temples, and cities. Then wheels within wheels began to turn as if they were

This Civil War wood engraving by Thomas Nast, is titled Union Troops in the Streets of Indianola, Texas. It was published in the *New York Illustrated News*, April 6, 1861. From the collection of the Calhoun County Museum, Port Lavaca, Texas unfolding, and sparks darted off into diamonds and stars while the whole scene advanced and receded in a pulsing motion. Every picture and every movement drew expressions of astonishment from the crowd.

They walked home refreshed by the spectacle, glad to have had an hour of distraction from the continuing bad news.

* * *

Despite the warnings of Governor Houston and other Unionists that separating from the Union would harm Texas, those who could voted three to one to secede from the United States.

After Captain Whipple read the results of the referendum, Mama looked exhausted. "I feel like a death sentence's been declared. I wish I could have voted."

On March 2 the votes were tallied, and three days later Texas began the process of joining the Confederacy.

On Saturday morning, hearing the strains of "Yankee Doodle," Gretchen rushed with Mama and Joseph to the front porch to watch federal troops from Fort Clark briskly marching to the lively tune. Captain Whipple explained that since war had not been declared, Union soldiers were allowed to come into Indianola and board the *Daniel Webster* and other ships to take them back up North. They looked so serious, young men stepping quickly four abreast with the American flag leading the column.

Gretchen wondered where they were from. Were they going to Boston? If only there was a way to go with them, to slip aboard undetected and arrive in beautiful Boston harbor.

"I feel scared, Missy Helga." Joseph kept his voice very low. "Them army boys look mighty serious."

"I'm scared too."

Gretchen had never heard her mama admit to being afraid. Perhaps it explained why Joseph refused to leave despite all the roiling anger; like the others, he wanted to protect Mama. Captain Whipple offered to take him to Matamoros, reminding Joseph he was a free man and could find a new life of real freedom in Mexico.

"Captain, I needs to stay here. Missy stays alone so often with Mister Eagle always gone."

* * *

Word came of South Carolina firing on the US garrison at Fort Sumter. As quickly as striking a match, the handsome young men from Fort Clark instantly became the enemy, people she should hate, not courageous men who recently had protected the western settlements and might take her with them to Boston.

The town buzzed with talk of Union soldiers from Fort Clark waiting at nearby Green Lake on the Guadalupe River and at Saluria on the eastern end of Matagorda Island to be lightered out to ships lying at anchor in the Gulf.

Captain Whipple was incredulous when he came to supper. "The Confederates captured the warship *Star of the West* off Pass Cavallo." Captain Whipple shook his head like he couldn't believe his own story. "She and three other war vessels have been anchored right off Pass Cavallo, waiting for the wind to die down to take on federal troops. The Confederates, under cover of darkness, sailed out and boarded her without the crew realizing they were enemies. The *Mohawk*, charged with guarding the *Star of the West*, didn't realize until too late that its charge had sailed away in the darkness to Galveston harbor."

Eli Cox breathed a heavy sigh of relief. "Looks like the South will have no trouble ending this war if the Yanks can't keep watch over their own ships."

As Indianola celebrated capture of the *Star of the West*, they heard that Confederates had cut off escape for the federal troops waiting for evacuation at Green Lake and Saluria. The Federals surrendered to Colonel Earl Van Dorn. Gretchen hurried home from school each day eager to hear the news and wondered at her split feelings of loyalty to her home and her longing to be part of that other world from which the Federals had come.

A few days later Hermie rushed in the front door, red-faced with excitement. "A bunch of us are meeting Colonel Van Dorn in Victoria. The last of the federal troops from West Texas forts are heading this way to escape through our port. We aim to cut them off."

"What about Jackson and Paul?" Mama asked.

"We tossed a coin, and I won. Jackson stays here with the store. It's the weekend, and the Casimir House wants Paul to stay here. I think he's glad."

Gretchen and Mama followed Hermie upstairs and watched silently as this stranger, a young man with a tiny moustache and arms as muscled and lean as a teamster, threw a change of clothes in a knapsack and rushed past them. He hurried downstairs and grabbed some ham Joseph was slicing and a handful of rolls. Then, stopping abruptly, he kissed Mama's cheek, hugged Gretchen fiercely, and shook hands all around the table with an almost violent force. "Don't worry, Mama. I'm going to be okay." Just like that. He was gone.

Events moved like a whirlwind. News arrived of Governor Houston's removal from office when he refused to swear allegiance to the Confederacy. It seemed like a crazy contradiction. Sam Houston had been everyone's hero. The old-timers loved talking about Houston leading Texas to victory over Santa Anna; he had served as the first president of the Republic of Texas. Then, like the clank of a guillotine, he was no more—as worthless as a dead man.

* * *

After Editor Yancey ran an article explaining that as the Union began blockading ports along the Gulf, including Matagorda Bay, the *Courier-Bulletin* would be printed only as a half-sheet to conserve the stock of paper, Jackson started bringing the smaller newspapers home. Gretchen wondered if it made him feel like an adult or if he wanted to impress Mama.

"Aren't privateers the same as pirates?" Jackson asked as he held the *Courier-Bulletin* ready to share the latest news.

Captain Whipple chuckled. "Some would say that's true. The Confederacy doesn't have a navy. It's using privately owned ships to go into the Gulf of Mexico to capture and rob Northern vessels. The Southern ships are operating as privateers."

"Robbing?" Jackson shook his head in amazement. "It says here that a Confederate privateer out of New Orleans captured a Yankee ship loaded with limes. Limes? Rob a ship for limes? They're expecting about twenty more fast steamers to be outfitted with guns to work as privateers out of New Orleans. Is that how we're going to get the goods we need in our stores? Robbing Yankee ships?"

"I'm sure we will. Now that the Union is blockading our ports, the Confederacy will do whatever it can to get through the blockade."

Gretchen agreed with Jackson; the world felt crazy.

Toward the end of May Hermie returned, tanned to a deep bronze and terribly excited. He grabbed Jackson in a fierce hug. "I saw your pa in San Antonio."

"What was he doing there?"

"Colonel Van Dorn sent two of your pa's teams to Fort Clark to get four twenty-four-pounder guns. He's going to bring them here to protect the battery at Pass Cavallo. He's a volunteer in the army now."

"Why were you in San Antonio?" Gretchen asked.

"We headed for the El Paso Road to catch the last of the federal troops coming this way from far West Texas. We intercepted them just outside San Antonio. We outnumbered them by almost four hundred men. They surrendered without a fight. Not a shot fired."

"Next time, it's my turn to go," Jackson declared.

Gretchen noticed that Mama smiled at the enthusiasm of these eager boys. Like most of the young men, even the little boys in Gretchen's class, they were eager to be part of the war. Many of the older men like the captain and Eli Cox seemed less sure war would settle things.

As more and more men were needed to defend the Texas coast, a draft appeared certain. Many of the original guard, including Hermie and Jackson, joined the newly incorporated Company B under the command of Captain Leon Rouff.

"We wanted to serve under Rouff because he's a German emigrant who just became a naturalized citizen of the United States." Hermie sounded very proud. "In a matter of a few weeks Captain Rouff went from a German citizen to a US citizen, and now he's a citizen of the Confederate States of America."

Paul started out of the dining room. "I'm waiting until I'm drafted. That'll come soon enough."

"You may not like your captain," Hermie argued.

Paul turned and looked solemnly at Hermie. "I won't like any of it. So what does it matter?"

Gretchen noticed Mama's eyes film with tears as she listened to Paul and Hermie. She usually kept her feelings hidden as if she had a reservoir where she stored pain away for some future time that never arrived. Even when Anna died, she had worked harder and harder as though the physical effort would erase all the hurt.

Gretchen was relieved her mama didn't have the pain of family members supporting both sides in the war. Some of Gretchen's students had families that were falling apart with sons and fathers choosing to fight on different sides. She couldn't imagine anything worse than having your family shooting at each other.

* * *

When Eagle walked in the door after delivering the guns to Pass Cavallo, Mama threw her arms around him. "Having you here makes this world feel less chaotic," she said.

Each time Eagle came home, Mama livened up, seemed so much younger. Gretchen had seen Eagle's hands touching her mama's shoulders and stroking down her back. She tried not to think of what he did when they closed the bedroom door. Thinking about it made her ache between her legs in ways she knew she must control.

At supper everyone wanted to hear about the twenty-four-pounders. "While we were getting the guns over to the island, a Yank sloop of war, a really fast little ship, came in sight and spent several days moving up and down the coast. First thing Captain Shea did when we got the guns in place was fire some rounds of warning, letting the Yanks know we can defend ourselves."

"Can we actually defend the pass?" Captain Whipple asked.

"It's vulnerable from land and sea, and so are our troops. For instance, if they wanted to withdraw, there're several bayous cutting off retreat."

"That sloop may be watching the entrance to Pass Cavallo because we sent a couple of ships loaded with cotton to Matamoros some time back. They should be returning loaded with coffee any day." Captain Whipple looked worried.

"Captain Shea is moving the men to a better position at the mouth of the pass. It'll be called Camp Esperanza."

"Brigadier General Stapp called several of us to his headquarters asking for help building our defenses." Captain Whipple shook his shaggy white head. "Since my ship is fast and shallow-drafted, I'm getting it painted gray to make it less visible for running the blockade. I'll be taking cotton and hides out of our port."

"Where'll you go?" Jackson looked shocked.

"I'll go to Bagdad on the Mexican side at the mouth of the Rio Grande. There're hundreds of ships, mostly British, anchored off the coast waiting for Texas cotton. The mills in Manchester and Bremen are eager for our cotton."

"You'll be gone for a long time?" It dawned on Gretchen that the captain was headed into a very dangerous job. It scared her.

"This is something I can do for my state."

* * *

In August Jackson rushed in for supper in a state of glee. "It's my turn this time. Benjamin Terry and Thomas Lubbock are back from a battle at Manassas, Virginia, asking for volunteers. They're cavalry, and I'm leaving with them right away."

"Where will you get a horse?" Mama kept shaking her head like she was trying to say no.

"I'll buy what I need on the way to Virginia."

"Can't you wait to tell your pa good-bye?"

"Pa may not be back for weeks. We're going now. Besides, I may be back before he gets home."

"Really?"

"Yep, this war may be over before we can even get there."

Gretchen felt a sudden chill as if a fierce storm had just blown in.

Chapter 18

NO WORD CAME FROM JACKSON or from Battina and Orilla. The federal blockade of Pass Cavallo brought all commerce, including mail delivery, to a halt in Indianola and Lavaca and all the inland towns dependent on the shipment of goods coming in through the pass. Helga's business disappeared except for her regular boarders and the ship captains, who seldom spent more than one night while they waited for cotton to be loaded on their ships in preparation for another trip through the blockade.

* * *

Just before Christmas, Hermie announced he was closing the store. "I can't stock the shelves. Nothing's coming in. The army rounded up the Negroes who worked our garden to build reinforcements at Fort Esperanza. Most of the farmers who kept us supplied joined Major Forshey at the fort."

"What're you going to do?" Helga held her breath, dreading his answer.

"Major Forshey needs volunteers along the coast. If we don't step up, when the enemy makes its big push to invade, we won't be able to keep them out of Indianola."

"At least Captain Whipple and the other blockade runners are getting through." Helga felt foolish as soon as the words left her lips. It sounded like she was grasping at straws.

Eli Cox looked exhausted, his black suit threadbare and wrinkled from wearing the same clothing for months. "Hermie's right. Business is stalled. Despite all their maneuvering behind the barrier islands and cutting through the bayous and back bays, the blockade runners aren't bringing in enough commercial goods. It's mostly military equipment and medicine. We can't run our businesses with the limited supply of dry goods, liquor, and coffee that's getting through."

Just before Hermie went up to bed, he drew Helga aside. "I'm taking our money out of the bank. I know Jackson would approve. If the Yanks get in here, they'll clean out the bank. Can you keep it? In a safe place?"

"Joseph dug a hole in the garden so I could bury my jars of money. We can dig another hole."

"I'll dig one tonight and get the money tomorrow. I've been keeping back gold pieces and silver dollars at the store. I'm not sure we can depend on Confederate bills."

That night Captain Whipple came in from a long blockade run down the coast looking haggard, his beard and hair grimy from days at sea, his eyes sunken from lack of sleep. He settled his bulk at the kitchen table while Helga dipped some leftover stew. "After I unloaded at Bagdad, I went on up to Matamoros. The town is so dry, it looks like white powder has settled over everything. But the Brits keep coming after our cotton."

"Did you see Benjamin and Sylus?"

"They're doing well, working hard in the store, and seem to be thriving. They send you good wishes. Benjamin wanted to hear all about Paul." Captain Whipple lowered his voice. "How is Paul?"

The captain finally asked the dreaded question. When this kind man with the bloodshot eyes looked at her with such gentleness, all the months of hiding the truth, of pretending Paul slept in the washroom to avoid waking the household, felt like a foolish lie.

"Not so well. His job at Casimir House is tenuous. The soldiers are giving him some rough talk about not volunteering at Fort Esperanza."

Hermie suddenly appeared, a shovel in one hand and his arm wrapped around Paul's waist. "I found him in the garden digging for your jar of coins."

"I'm getting out of here. It's going to cost a fortune to hire someone to get me out. You've got a pile of gold pieces buried out there someplace." Paul was so drunk Hermie had to hold him up.

"Hello, Captain. I suppose you knew about Frau Heinrich's drunkard son. It's the talk of the town." Paul looked defiantly at Captain Whipple, pulling away from Hermie and swaying as if in a strong wind. He grabbed the corner of the kitchen table.

Captain Whipple nodded, rising from the table. "I'll be leaving for Brownsville as soon as we get this next load of cotton on board. Would you like to take a wild ride on a blockade runner?"

Paul's mouth fell open in surprise. "You'd take me?"

"Only if you are sober by the time we leave. You've got twelve to fifteen hours." Captain Whipple patted Helga on the shoulder. "I'll see you in the morning." Without another word, the captain walked past Paul and Hermie and quietly climbed the back stairs.

"You weren't really going to take Mama's money?" Hermie looked accusingly at his brother.

Paul folded himself like a pretzel onto the bench beside the table. "Why not? I don't have enough to finance getting out of here." Garden soil caked the knees of his black pants and his worn jacket cuffs. The buttons on the white silk shirt lay open, exposing his chest. His hair looked like he had been running dirty fingers through it as he crawled through the garden rows.

Helga stared at the drunk swaying defiantly on the bench, looking up at her with a stupid grin on his face. The rage she had worked so hard to keep at bay unleashed a shaking fury that spit words of cold finality. "I've waited up for you for the last time. I've helped you get to bed for the last time." She started out of the kitchen and then stopped. "Be on that ship with Captain Whipple tomorrow. Stay in Brownsville until you get sober."

Lying in bed, staring at the ceiling, hearing Hermie climb the stairs to his room, she wondered if she had sent her son to his death. Then she heard Paul clanging around in the washroom, setting up the washtub to wash his clothes. At least he still wanted to be clean. Staring into the dark, she remembered that it had been the same with Max. He had always kept so clean, made sure he wore the best, even when they couldn't afford it.

At dawn, Paul met Helga in the kitchen. Washed and combed, cheerfully going about the morning chores, he planted his usual kiss on her cheek. "I'm all packed. And I didn't take your money."

"Thank you, Paul. I'm glad to hear that." She no longer wanted to pull him into her arms to comfort him.

"Will you pray for me?"

"I've prayed for you every day and every night. I always prayed for your papa. I finally understand I have no power to help. You must take charge of yourself."

* * *

She stood on the porch watching Paul go. Or was it Max? The black suit hung loosely from his frail shoulders, the violin case tucked under his arm as he casually swung his satchel in the other hand. He towered above the dumpy little captain as they walked toward the docks. He never looked back.

As she turned to go back inside the house, an aching hole opened inside of her.

Hermie arrived just before lunch, his eyes red-rimmed with tears. He reached for Helga and hugged her against his scratchy wool jacket. "I said good-bye to Paul. And I asked him to write." His voice broke. "A rider came into town with this letter."

Helga drew back, afraid to touch the paper.

"It's Jackson. He was killed with Colonel Benjamin Terry in a battle at Woodsonville, Kentucky, December 8. It's signed by Colonel John Austin Wharton." Hermie carefully folded the letter and slipped it back in the envelope, tears rolling unchecked down his cheeks and dripping onto the front of his jacket. "I'm glad I closed the store. After I got the letter, I went back to take a last look. So many good times poured over me that I had to get out of there. Jackson was my best friend in the world. Better than a brother. He always said I was his brother."

Helga wrapped her arm around Hermie's waist, and they walked back to the kitchen, where Joseph was hurrying to finish the fried chicken. As always, he had heard their conversation, and tears ran along his wrinkled old face as he continued cooking. "Won't be no more lively talk around this place. Mr. Jackson kept ever'body thinking all the time."

Helga moved in a fog of pain. Everywhere she looked, something reminded her of the happy days of children moving eagerly about the house. Now the losses were coming so fast. The gnawing ache she felt for Eagle made her long for him to come home, and at the same time she dreaded his arrival. He would burst in the front door all smiles and loaded with his usual Christmas treats. Then he'd hear the joy of his life was gone.

The next morning Hermie finished cleaning out the boys' room, carefully setting Jackson's things in a box for Eagle.

"I'm sorry to leave before Christmas. I hope Eagle makes it back to be with you and Gretchen. Keep paying Joseph as much as you can so he'll stay and help you. He's a good man, and you need him."

Helga could only nod. If she spoke, she wouldn't be able to hold back the tears. She wanted to throw herself on Hermie and beg him not to leave.

* * *

The day before Christmas, just as expected, Eagle burst in the front door grinning, a turkey in one hand and a goose in the other. "Hey Hel, can you help me?"

As Helga rushed into his arms, Joseph took both birds, carrying them quickly back to the kitchen.

Eagle swung her off the floor, nuzzling his whiskery face into her neck. "I almost ran those mules to death to get here, Hel. God, I've missed you."

Helga clung with all her might, not wanting to stop the rush of joy his presence brought.

Finally, as his breath began to come in gasps, he eased her feet to the floor. She took his face in both hands. "Come to the bedroom."

"Not yet, Hel." His laughter was infectious. "You've got to let me get all the stuff off the wagon and take it in."

"Let Joseph do it. I need to talk to you."

His face darkened to a frightened stare as he let her lead him like a blind man.

"I can unload," Joseph said. "And I knows how to drive a team to Mr. Henry Fisher's."

Helga took the letter from her apron pocket as she closed their bedroom door.

Eagle stared like it was a poisonous snake. Finally, he began opening it, his fingers trembling. The sound came like the yelp of a suffering animal. He buried his face in the paper and sank onto the bed.

Helga clutched him in a fierce embrace and did not stop holding him as he rocked in the agony of his loss.

Throughout the night Helga held the suffering man in her arms. As the sun rose bright and clear on Christmas morning, Eagle got up and went to the washroom. "You've got things you need to do. I'm okay now." Then he pulled Helga into a tight embrace. "Thank you for taking care of me again."

When he came to the kitchen, fresh shaven and clean, he began the morning routine of helping to get breakfast finished. He checked on his mules at Henry Fisher's and returned with a soft gingham dress. "This is for you. I found it in San Antonio, and it looked like it would fit. It makes your eyes and hair look extra pretty."

Helga clutched the dress to her body, delighted with its beauty and thrilled to have a gift from Eagle that was so personal.

As they were seated for Christmas lunch, Gretchen said, "I feel so bad to have all this food. I've got several children in my class whose families need help. Their fathers have volunteered over at Fort Esperanza and along the coast. The family gardens are being depleted; the meat supply is about gone; everything is getting too expensive."

"I'll help you take the goose and some of this food to one of your families." Eagle's eyes flashed with some of their old sparkle. "We've got way too much ... with the boys all gone ..."

"Good idea," Eli Cox's voice boomed. "I'll help."

Helga felt like hugging Eli.

That night as soon as their door was closed Eagle grabbed her, pressing his body against her, caressing her with a hunger that made her ache for him. The long weeks of absence, the pain of so much loss, the uncertain future all disappeared in the urgent need for each other at that moment. Their first act was rough and fast. Then they both relaxed and enjoyed the long, slow pleasure of bringing each other to full satisfaction.

Finally, just as Helga was drifting into contented sleep, her body tucked against Eagle's warmth, he whispered, "Hel, I've got to leave tomorrow. Baby, don't tense like that. I've committed to hauling cotton to Matamoros."

"Why can't the blockade runners haul the cotton?"

"Not enough is getting through. It's stacked up where the railroad ends at Alleyton. It's the Confederacy's white gold. The British and several European countries are eager to feed their mills with our cotton."

"Won't the Federals start blockading Matamoros?"

"Mexico's neutral. They're lightering the Winchesters, all kinds of other military equipment, and medicine into the port at Bagdad in exchange for the cotton."

"Will you ever get home?"

He buried his face in her breast. "Oh, Hel, I don't know. I hate to leave you in this mess. I expect the Yanks will be here soon. Then we'll never get cotton out."

Just before dawn, they both woke and enjoyed their last sleepy arousal.

As he dressed in the lamplight, she curled onto her knees in the bed, watching his back as he pulled on his socks. His shirt stretched tight across his shoulders, and the tendons in his neck expanded as he tugged at his contrary left boot. His movements, things he did every day, things she rarely got to see, made her want to touch him, pull him into her, and beg him not to leave.

The bed bounced. He stood, and her dream of keeping him with her ended with an abrupt jolt.

Chapter 19

1862

IN EARLY SPRING, HELGA OPENED the front door to a man holding his hat over his chest, a woman so work-worn it was hard to judge her age, and two little, barefoot girls whose dresses barely covered their wiry bodies.

"I'm James Carter. This here's my wife, Emma, and my girls, Effie and Sarah. Major Shea ordered the evacuation of Mustang Island. We hear you have good rooms."

Helga opened the door to admit the tattered family. She couldn't stop looking at Effie, whose golden ringlets hung uncombed down her back.

"I don't mean to stare at Effie. She's about the age my Anna would have been. Her blonde hair curled just like Effie's." Helga shook her head. "I have one nice front room on the first floor and two upstairs."

"I can pay you with that steer hooked to the back of my wagon."

Staring at the giant grey animal with stubby thick horns, Helga thought it looked as frightening as the bawling hoards of cattle that used to pass along the road on the way to the docks. "We can use the meat. But I don't have a way to slaughter it."

"Missy Helga. I knows about beef cattle. I worked in the slaughter house on the docks before the captain hired me." Joseph raised both bristly eyebrows. "If Mr. Carter give me a hand, we can do it today."

"I'll certainly do that, ma'am. The Federals bombarded some of the ranches without notice, burning some houses. I really need to get my family to safety."

"Of course." Helga smiled reassuringly, not at all sure of the beef's value or what Dr. Stein would expect as his percentage.

"I'll be heading back to the island. I've got to defend my place and sell my cattle before the Feds wipe me out. Soon as I can get back, I'll bring another good one."

Joseph helped the Carters move their mattresses and trunks into Battina and Orilla's room. The girls tiptoed down the hall, shyly peeking into the parlor and then the kitchen.

"Please excuse them, Frau Heinrich. They've never seen such a grand house," Emma Carter said, pulling at her loose-fitting dress and smoothing her hair back, revealing a very young face.

"Let them look all they want. This is their home. And call me Helga."

At supper, Gretchen invited both girls to walk to school with her each morning.

"They can't read," Emma said as though that disqualified them from school attendance.

"They'll be reading right away," Gretchen said.

Helga felt she might burst with pride at her confident, schoolteacher daughter.

* * *

After Christmas, Gretchen continued taking extra bread and venison sausage for children who came to school hungry. One night, Eli had barely taken his seat at the supper table when Gretchen said, "Eli, churchwomen are trying to feed families whose men have gone to the coast. The numbers have grown way too big for the churchwomen to handle. Now we're hearing that the commissioners court actually allowed sixteen dollars a month for a destitute old man." Gretchen's voice began shaking with emotion. "One of my students came to school today clutching the hand of her three-year-old brother who is so frail his eyes sink in like an old man's. She insisted he could read and that made him ready for school. I couldn't turn him away. He desperately needs the food we're serving at school. Eli, if the court can take care of one old man, why doesn't it provide for these families?"

Eli kept nodding his head as Gretchen spoke. "Okay, okay, I'll see what I can do, Gretchen. You know we're hearing of more and more destitute people." His voice rose as if he were asking a question.

"I'm sorry, Eli. I know you're trying. I'm not blaming you." Instead of blushing a bright red as Gretchen had done in the past, her face paled, exposing a hollowness in her cheekbones that Helga had not seen before.

Within weeks the commissioners began a welfare assistance

program. When Eli announced the plans at supper, he seemed hesitant to add, "To cover costs, the court ordered a war tax of twenty-five cents per hundred dollars of taxable property."

"Thanks, Eli." Gretchen reached for his hand. "I know it's hard for you to raise taxes, but a lot of families who were poor before the war are about to starve with their men gone."

Eli nodded. The old bombast was gone.

"James and I support the Confederacy. This is our home." Emma looked around the table uncomfortably. "But with so many planters staying home to oversee their slaves and their crops and the small farmers going to war, some folks are saying it's a rich man's war and a poor man's fight."

Eli Cox laughed deep in his throat. "You're right. The planters are bringing their wagons to my warehouse demanding supplies. They say getting in the cotton crop is their contribution to the war. The men are off fighting so the planters can keep their slaves." Eli shook his head. "It seems backward."

"Backward is the word, Eli." The captain stared into the middle of the table, a hollow tone in his voice. "I've raged against slavery, and here I'm siding with the forces that want to keep it alive. I keep asking myself if love of homeland is worth all this."

* * *

In early September Eli came to supper with upsetting news. "I just heard about forty German boys murdered as they slept on the banks of the Nueces River."

"Who did such a thing?" With Effie and Sarah at the table gazing with wonder at their beautiful teacher, Gretchen seemed to have found her voice and joined the conversation more and more frequently.

"Confederates," Eli said. "Captain James Duff heard from an informant about these young men—they were all Union sympathizers—leaving Comfort and heading to Mexico." Eli seemed to notice Effie and Sarah staring in disbelief at what they were hearing.

"It's a long story." Eli stopped and looked at Emma, waiting for permission to continue talking in front of the girls. After she nodded reassuringly, he said, "When federal troops left the western posts, the men around Comfort organized a militia to protect settlers from the Indians. But the Confederates declared martial law because they suspected the militia intended to overthrow the government. The men disbanded the militia and headed to Mexico. They planned to evade the Confederate draft in Mexico, and some of them would have joined the Union troops down there."

"So they just killed them?" Gretchen kept shaking her head.

"Some of them got away in all the confusion." Eli looked again at Emma, who had placed an arm around each of her daughters.

"It's okay, Eli. My girls are strong, and we can't hide the truth of the war."

* * *

October brought news of four federal warships overpowering the Confederate troops protecting Galveston. The city surrendered. With Galveston's fall, despair settled like a damp fog over the household.

Eli tried being reassuring. "I heard Fort Point overlooks the channel leading into Galveston's harbor, and it only had one operational gun. The others were logs painted to look like cannons. Faced with the Yank fleet, Confederates just abandoned the island. We're a lot better protected at Fort Esperanza. The Yanks won't find it so easy to get through the pass." But before the month was out, Indianolans heard the boom of cannon at Fort Esperanza.

The following day Helga was glad to see that Captain Whipple had returned from a blockade run, but he was rushing with such urgency that he couldn't get his breath when he reached the top of the front steps. He held up a leather bag of his business papers. "I cleared out all my files. Our forces abandoned the fort. They're coming into town before the Yanks cut off their retreat."

"Did you see Hermie?"

He shook his head, still gasping for breath. "Too many rushing around getting ready to stand up to the Yanks on our docks. Make sure you've got any valuables hidden away."

"Lemme wrap the meat in the smokehouse up real tight in oilcloth. I got me a smoothed-out place under the house where I can hang it near the potatoes and onions." Joseph grinned, proud to be part of the plot to outsmart the Yanks.

"That's a good idea. I'll make sure all the jars in the garden are well covered."

"You needn't worry, Missy Helga. I check those jars ever'day."

Helga smiled at the wiry little man. He had requested his own pickle jar when she asked him to bury one for her. She didn't think he had spent a dollar of his salary.

* * *

Gretchen returned from school with Effie and Sarah in tow. "The school's closed until further notice. If it continues for long, may I move my class to our parlor?"

"Of course," Helga said as she wrapped a reassuring arm around Effie and Sarah, who were fighting tears.

Union forces under Captain William B. Renshaw moved easily through the pass and anchored in the bay. The next morning, Amelia arrived driving Dr. Stein's carriage.

"The Union's *Westfield* is flying a flag of truce. The ship's commander says he's taking every town on the bay. We can move about, continue receiving wood and provisions. He just wants to buy beef for his men. If we refuse, he'll take it."

All the time Amelia talked she and Helga were handing food, silverware, and lace tablecloths from the carriage to the waiting arms of Joseph. "Dr. Stein insisted I come here to get away from the shells when the battle starts. It'll start soon, because Dr. Stein says we're not doing business with the enemy. The Yankees say women, children, and the sick can leave town." She stopped and looked at Helga. "No, my dear sister, I have not seen Hermie."

Joseph crawled under the house and added Amelia's food and valuables to the supply.

* * *

By noon the bombardment started. They stood together, feeling the vibration on the upstairs porch as each volley from two Union gunboats shattered the air. Effie and Sarah buried their faces in Emma's breast. Helga and Gretchen moved close to Emma, wrapping their arms around the shivering trio.

In a short time the cannonade stopped, and they waited for Yankees to come demanding food but the road sat eerily empty.

Captain Whipple patted Helga's shoulder. "I'll go downtown and check out the wounded."

They watched in despair as the two Union gunboats moved on up the bay toward Lavaca.

* * *

Helga saw Captain Whipple returning with Hermie in tow. He towered over the captain; his shoulders bulged at the seams of his shirt. His beard looked thick and curly—he had been transformed into a man, no longer the boy who bounced home so filled with energy and excitement over his next moneymaking plan.

"Sorry I couldn't get here. The captain said I had to come and show you I'm okay." He kissed Helga on the cheek.

"What about casualties?" Helga asked, hoping to delay his departure.

"Looks like one Union and two of our boys. We've got several wounded."

"Be careful," Helga whispered as Hermie kissed her again before turning to leave. Then, looking back, he grinned, his former charm showing through the hairy face. "That's my top priority."

Eli came home in late afternoon. "They cleaned us out. Took all the cattle waiting for shipment, emptied what little remained in my warehouse." He kept rubbing his hands through his thin, wiry hair in angry frustration.

Soon after Eli arrived the guns roared at Lavaca in a thunderous barrage indicating Major Shea also had refused to surrender.

Later they heard that despite being weak from cases of yellow fever, the troops at Lavaca manned their twin cannons and fired relentlessly. The Yanks moved out of range into the bay, firing their long-range guns until dark. The next morning the bombardment began again despite the fact that there was no return fire from Lavaca.

Near noon, Effie and Sarah rushed inside to report Yankee steamers sailing back down the bay. Helga, Gretchen, Emma, Joseph, and the girls climbed to the porch on the second floor, watching the ships gliding calmly through the surf like monsters dragging one of their injured to safe harbor for repair. They exited the pass and steamed northeast toward Galveston.

With the departure of the Federals and the Union gunboat *Kittatinny* forced to remain out in the Gulf because it drew too much water to cross the bar at Cavallo Pass, the Confederate soldiers returned to Fort

Esperanza and, under the watchful eyes of the Union gunboat, began reinforcing their defenses.

* * *

Helga kept watching for Eagle and Hermie, hoping to see them before Christmas, but no word came from either of them.

On Christmas Eve Captain Whipple said, "I heard General John Magruder is convinced the Yanks intend to capture the entire Texas coast and go inland from here." He shook his head like an aging lion. "The overland cotton route down to Matamoros has become so important to the Southern economy that Magruder believes the Yanks aim to destroy it and take control of our cotton production. The mills in the Northeast are loudly demanding our cotton."

Helga's heart lurched in fear. "Aren't the blockade runners getting through with cotton?"

"Just barely. It gets harder every trip."

"Eagle will be a sitting duck."

"That's not all. Magruder has ordered a scorched-earth policy for the entire coast."

"Scorched earth?"

"To keep anything of value out of the Federals' hands, Magruder's sent orders to Major Shea to burn the railroad ties, warehouses, and wharfs at Indianola. Even the bridges here and the railroad at Lavaca. He ordered burning the lighthouses at Saluria and Pass Cavallo and the houses at the pass. His one caveat is that if we cut the railroad ties in two, we can keep them for firewood."

Helga could not believe what she was hearing.

"I wouldn't be surprised if the Yankees burned everything, but I can't believe we'll be destroyed by our own military." Eli Cox's face had turned ashen as Captain Whipple spoke.

"I don't think our people will do it," Captain Whipple said. "When the Yanks actually come will be time enough to destroy everything."

"Absolutely," Eli said. He pulled out a yellowed handkerchief and swabbed the sweat from his face.

"I'll chop those railroad ties," Joseph said as soon as Helga came to the kitchen after supper. "I got me an axe that'll work just fine. We'll show Magruder and them Yanks. And we'll have us plenty of firewood."

The next week Helga moved around in a state of icy fear. Every noise, every loud jangle of wagon teams on the road startled her. She tried to control her restless energy to keep from upsetting Gretchen and Emma and the girls. Her only outlet was constant work.

Joseph worked each day until well after dark, hauling the railroad ties home from Canal Street and chopping and stacking them under the house. He moved in a fury that matched Helga's agitation.

The great news came: on New Year's Day, the Confederates thoroughly beat the Yankees and chased them out of Galveston. Confederates burned the bridges and ferries between Matagorda Island and the mainland, but locals refused to destroy their own property.

Chapter 20

1863

THEY CONTINUED TO HAVE ENOUGH to eat thanks to the plentiful garden, all the fish Joseph caught, and the second fat steer James Carter brought just before the Yankees took his entire herd, sending him as an angry new recruit to fight with the Confederates. Gretchen took as much food to her school children each morning as she and the two girls could carry.

When the salt supply ran low, Joseph offered a proposal. "Missy, will you mind if I scrape up the bottom of the smokehouse? There's lots of salt in that dirt. I can leach it out. Boil it down. Get us plenty of salt."

Helga looked at the agile little black man, who maintained a slight body stoop when he spoke to her, who never really looked into her eyes, and her heart broke at what he must have endured to cause such a humbling posture. "Joseph, you are one of the most skilled men I've ever met. You are keeping us alive." Her voice broke, and she could only nod and smile.

"I'm happy to help you, missy," Joseph spoke barely above a whisper as he backed out of the kitchen.

A few nights later at supper, Helga announced that the salt had come from Joseph's ingenuity.

"Come in here, Joseph," Eli called like the master of the manor.

Joseph took one step into the dining room and stopped.

"You have performed a miracle. We're going to spread the word around town. You've provided the solution for our salt shortage."

Joseph beamed. "Thank you, sir. I'm proud to help."

* * *

At supper in early April, Eli Cox said, "Today the commissioners set aside money for corn, flour, and other food necessities." He sighed dramatically. "It won't please a lot of folks to have a war property tax of fifty cents per hundred dollars." He added quickly, "It's not permanent. Financial aid stops when the head of the family ends his military service. We're not starting a permanent charity."

"That's the best news I've heard." Gretchen clapped her hands. Effie and Sarah began clapping, which started wholesale applause around the table.

Eli Cox, his face red with pleasure, rose from his frayed blue chair and took a little bow.

Helga felt like laughing out loud as she made a mental note to offer appreciation to Eli more often.

* * *

Toward the end of April, a company of men and wagons from Seguin rolled into town headed for Fort Esperanza.

Joseph rushed back to the kitchen. "A young couple's coming through the gate. They're part of that army bunch."

Helga smiled to herself at the irony—an old Negro man now watched the road and reported everything with all the eagerness Anna had once displayed. Shoving the aching memory away, she opened the door to a handsome young man and a tiny companion who stood behind him and peeked around his arm like a timid child.

"I'm Lieutenant Samuel Henry, ma'am, and this here's my wife, Mary." He pulled her protectively under his arm. "We met your husband on the way down here. He said you might have a room for my wife. And … you'd take good care of her." He lowered his head and looked up through thick brown lashes, a childish plea in his voice. "We just got married. She's really scared about me leaving her."

Helga felt the heat of excitement flood her body. She knew her face was blazing as she stammered, "Is my husband well?"

"Yes, ma'am. And he sent this letter." Samuel Henry fished inside his breast pocket. "Sorry—it's a little wet with sweat. I put it close to my vest …"

Helga grabbed the thick letter and held it against her breast. "You don't know how much it means to me. I don't care if it's wet."

They all three laughed at her delight. Helga hurriedly showed them the room and rushed to her bedroom to read the letter and hold it against her face to breathe in Eagle's presence.

The pages of random sizes were wrinkled from Eagle carrying them stuffed inside his shirt. He had added pages until he met the Henrys. He kept saying he was okay, that he was traveling back and forth between San Antonio and Matamoros. He made no mention of the cattle thieves that Helga kept hearing roamed the wild area between Corpus Christi and the Mexican border. When he crossed the Rio Grande to Matamoros, he had seen Paul, who sent his love. Paul was playing in a very big hotel and bar in Matamoros. He didn't mention Paul's drinking. He said the route crossed Wild Horse Desert, which was white with spilled cotton blowing like giant snowflakes and sticking like Christmas ornaments in the chaparral. He said he always demanded payment in gold for his men; sometimes they hauled for the Confederacy, and other times they hauled for Richard King's company. He put his money in a private bank in San Antonio, where Helga could get it if he didn't get back. When the war ended, he wanted to buy farmland in Washington County, far away from the mosquitoes and storms of the coast. He missed her on every page. He went to sleep at night looking at the stars and thinking of her. He told her to look at the moon each night before she went to bed, because he would be looking at that same moon.

She folded the thick pages back into her apron pocket, felt its bulk against her hip, and touched it again and again. That night she began a new routine: she sat on the porch, her knees tucked against her chest, and watched the moon with Eagle. When it shone full, she imagined his face smiling as they lay together washed in the contentment of its glow. When clouds rolled in off the bay, wrapping the moon in undulating mist, she felt the gentle stroke of his hand.

One evening, watching the moon, which showed only as a tiny sliver, she imagined Eagle whispering about darkness allowing the stars to pop out even brighter. A movement at the back gate startled her, and a man materialized out of the darkness.

"It's me, Helga," Captain Whipple whispered. As he approached, she realized he was wet and covered in mud up to his hips. "They got my ship, loaded with coffee and medical supplies for Esperanza. A little shallow-draft gunboat hid in one of the bayous. Just waiting. Sank me and blocked the channel."

"Are you all right? You look awful."

"Just wet and nasty."

"I'll get you some hot water. And some supper."

"Sounds like heaven."

* * *

The year dragged on with Captain Whipple unable to run the blockade. "As long as Lincoln puts his main Union force along the Mississippi, the guns and medical supplies that teamsters like Eagle are hauling over the Cotton Road are keeping the South alive. The real problem will come if the Yanks capture Vicksburg and Port Hudson. That'll stop everything crossing the Mississippi from the East. That's when Lincoln will flood Texas with enough troops to halt the traffic along the Cotton Road. He's under tremendous pressure from the East Coast textile industries desperate for our cotton."

The captain's prophecy came true in July when the Union cut the South in two with victories at Vicksburg and Port Hudson.

In September word arrived that a Union task force of more than twenty ships and five thousand men had tried to enter Texas through Sabine Pass along the Louisiana border. A little band of forty-three Confederates stopped the invasion and captured the *Clifton,* one of the ships that had taken part in looting Indianola the year before. But the good news didn't last long. In November, Eli Cox reported that a man had ridden in from Brownsville with news that the Feds had steamed up the Rio Grande to occupy Brownsville. "Confederates set fire to the town before moving out. That ends our cotton crossing the river to Matamoros."

"What about Eagle?" Helga heard the demand in her voice and didn't care.

"I didn't mean to scare you," Eli said. "The teamsters had already moved upriver to the Laredo crossing. It's three hundred extra miles from Laredo down the Rio Grande on the Mexican side of the river to the port at Bagdad. Foreign ships are still waiting off the Mexican coast loaded with military equipment and medical supplies. All we have to do is lighter the cotton out to them."

* * *

The unrelenting Union advance came up the coast, capturing Point Isabel, Corpus Christi, and Aransas Pass. Firing on Fort Esperanza commenced at daybreak on November 29.

Overwhelmed by the sheer number of Feds, Confederates set fire to the stores, blew up their magazine, and abandoned the fort overnight. Near daylight, noise of the infantry marching along the road toward Old

Town woke everyone. Standing on the front porch huddled against the fiercely cold wind whipping off the bay, they watched Samuel Henry break rank and run up the steps to grab Mary.

"It's going to be okay, baby. We're heading to Lavaca. I'll be back as soon as I can." He didn't give her time to argue as he turned and dashed back to his place with his company.

Mary didn't say a word. She buried her face in her hands and cried great, choking sobs. Helga squeezed the hysterical girl in her arms while she scanned the faces, looking for Hermie amid the passing troops.

Later in the day, the air split with the thunder of Union gunboats pounding the docks and the immediate response of Indianola's guns roaring to life. The house shook as they watched from the second-floor porch. Helga wrapped one arm around Mary's trembling shoulders and helped Emma and Gretchen hold onto Effie and Sarah.

Suddenly the guns stopped. The stench of gunpowder and smoke rose in dense clouds over the town. They could see Union boats moving up toward the docks to disgorge a contingent of soldiers. Then the gunboats, like sinister, black drays having delivered their passengers, moved back into the bay and sailed up the coast toward Lavaca. Again the earth shook as the bombardment began at Lavaca.

In late afternoon Joseph rushed down the hall. "They're coming, missy. They're marching straight for our door." Joseph grabbed leftover food off the stove. "I'll get this under the house."

The sharp knock on the door caused Helga to pick up her step. The young Union soldier shivered with the cold. The knees of his britches looked wet, and sand clung in wet clumps to his boots.

"I'm Lieutenant Jethro Pickle of the Sixteenth Ohio Volunteers. We've been ordered to occupy or dismantle your house. If we stay here, your house will remain standing."

"And if you don't stay here?" Helga wasn't sure she had heard correctly.

"We'll dismantle it. Use the lumber to erect suitable quarters." Jethro Pickle didn't blink. His blue eyes, bloodshot from wind and sand and lack of sleep, held no sign of sensitivity. He was following orders; no forays into pleasantries.

"I have two available rooms upstairs."

"We need four. We'll bring in our bunks for six men to a room."

Helga heard banging under the house. The Yanks had already discovered Joseph's stash.

Joseph helped Gretchen move her things into Helga's room. They gathered all Otto Schnaubert's sketches and carefully stacked them under Helga's bed. Mary Carter moved her bed downstairs, eagerly crowding in with Emma and her girls.

Joseph hurried outside and returned in a fury. "Them bastards have found Missy Amelia's silver and her pretty lacy things." He bowed his head. "I sure am sorry."

"You've done all you could."

"They're digging rifle trenches in the front yard. They already have a fire going with our railroad ties. Cooking up meat I hid under the house. They've got a big pot going with potatoes and carrots and a bunch of other vegetables. They've about wiped us out, missy."

"What about our jars?"

His eyebrows danced in delight. "Not yet. They is buried deep. I'm keeping the mulch thick, and the winter squash makes a nice blanket of vines. The greens is thick for mighty good eating. Nobody bothered to look real close underneath."

Lieutenant Pickle returned before supper. "I'll take my meals in the house. The men will come in after they eat to get out of this cold. We didn't expect cold in Texas. The bay froze last night out on Matagorda Peninsula."

"What do you suggest I cook? Your men confiscated our meat and have almost depleted the garden. And this is the first day." Helga looked the blue-eyed boy straight in the eye.

"You'll have to excuse the men eating your vegetables and smoked meat. We've been on Matagorda Peninsula for days living off rations. Citizens who house troops are eligible for rations."

Helga did not give him the satisfaction of an answer. She stood perfectly still and looked at the young man, waiting to hear a solution.

"I'll go now and get rations."

Gretchen and the girls returned the next morning with the entire class in tow. Each child carried an armload of books and supplies. "The school building's damaged beyond use. We'll have to use the parlor." She pulled the benches in from the dining room. Her student enrollment had fallen to ten, because every family with the means had left for the safety of the interior.

Communication became a whisper campaign. Captain Whipple spread the word about Union Major General Dana instituting a propaganda campaign encouraging Confederate desertions. "They've copied letters written by our deserters and placed them atop poles stuck along the shore. The letters claim deserters are well received by the Union forces, encouraging more Confederates to join them."

"Is it working?"

The captain shrugged. "Who knows? There're always deserters in a war. The other side always looks better fed and better armed."

The men marched, performed exercises, and went out into the prairie looking for Confederates during the day. The evenings until bedtime were rife with the noise of boots scraping and clunking, songs of young men missing home, and arguments that settled down after Helga or Captain Whipple stuck their heads in the door. Some of the young men settled in the parlor, preferring to read away from the noise of their upstairs quarters. Others played cards after supper on the dining table. Often they hung around the kitchen when something smelled better than the food cooking on their own fire.

Helga and Joseph gathered vegetables from the gardens of the abandoned houses, but it became more and more difficult to find anything that hadn't already been confiscated by the Yanks. Joseph found potatoes no one had bothered to dig up in the abandoned city garden. He took Hermie and Jackson's little boat out fishing every morning and evening. Mushrooms with delicate pink undersides grew out on the prairie, but Eli and the captain insisted it wasn't safe for Helga to walk by herself away from town. Mushroom picking became a Sunday-afternoon partnership between Eli and the captain.

When Helga ground and boiled peanut hulls as a substitute for coffee, Lieutenant Pickle found a way to requisition enough coffee for everyone at the breakfast table.

One afternoon, Joseph stepped onto the back porch carrying two headless rattlesnakes by their tail. "I kicked into the edge of a low bluff up at Old Town, and rattlesnakes fell out by the hundreds. They make good eating, Missy." The things were about four feet long and still squirming. Helga shuddered.

"I'll drop them in salty water for a while and they'll get still. You wait. They taste really good." He grinned mischievously. "With them Yanks around, rattlesnake's a lot more plentiful than beef cattle."

He hung the creatures and began carefully skinning them. "They is good lots of ways. They can be fried, put in soup, or baked."

He had to fry his catch in cornmeal since flour was no longer available. To his delight, Eli Cox proclaimed the meal a winner. "Since rattlesnakes are as plentiful as mosquitoes, I suggest we harvest the crop as often as Joseph is willing to go after them."

Even with fishing becoming impossible close to shore as the bay became contaminated with the carcasses of beef the Feds threw out, Lieutenant Pickle never convinced his men who were cooking in the backyard to capture and cook the plentiful snakes.

The Union camp set up on the prairie behind town lay between Indianola and Old Town. It formed a grid of tents for the enlisted men. Other structures for officers and headquarters rose from lumber taken from the abandoned houses and businesses in town.

One morning when Helga and Joseph heard the fife and drum, they hurried to the edge of the field behind the house and watched the review of what they were later told were three brigades.

"Look at that dandy," Joseph whispered as he nodded toward a general wearing a continental hat with a plume. Gold-tipped epaulets dangled from his shoulders as he sat astride a coal-black charger prancing up and down the line. That night Lieutenant Pickle explained that the man in the old-style military dress was Brigadier General Fitz Henry Warren, commander of the post at Indianola.

Captain Whipple delighted the household with whispered information in late February. "About fifty Confederates came upon twenty-five mounted infantrymen out gathering fresh beef. When the Yanks fired at the approaching Confederates, the noise startled their poor old nags, who reared up and threw fourteen off their mounts." The story, provoking gales of laughter among the boarders with each telling, circulated in whispers throughout the house.

One afternoon just before supper, a thundering cavalcade of horses strung out over a mile raced along the road toward town. The entire household, including Lieutenant Pickle, rushed to the front porch to watch the Union men dashing past.

The next evening Captain Whipple could hardly contain himself as he started the whisper chain: a captain of a Union provost guard, ignoring orders to stay within eight or ten miles of Indianola on his scouting mission, had strayed beyond Lavaca to Chocolate Bayou, a good eighteen miles from camp, and stayed for dinner at a Mr. Foster's house. Despite Foster telling him rebels patrolled nearby, he had continued enjoying his meal. Suddenly realizing a hundred-rebel cavalry was bearing down, he had ordered a hasty retreat, leaving his men racing as fast as they could behind him. Despite many opportunities to engage the pursuing Confederates, the captain gave no orders to return fire. The rebels had captured six provost guards.

* * *

As suddenly as they came, in mid-March the Union forces started leaving. The men upstairs packed and dismantled their bunks. Gossip spread that the Yanks were heading for an invasion of Texas from Louisiana.

After all the men left the house, Lieutenant Pickle returned and very formally led Joseph to the parlor. Joseph's voice carried loudly throughout the house. "No, sir. I ain't going nowhere. This here's my home."

Lieutenant Pickle's voice stayed low.

"No, sir. I'm a free man. I ain't no slave. You can't do no liberating of me."

Without another word, the front door slammed and Lieutenant Pickle was gone, leaving Joseph in a huff.

"Them bastards told Lieutenant Pickle to take me to freedom." Joseph shook his head in amazement. "Why'd I want to go with them thieves? No sir. I ain't going off with no thieves."

Later, they heard the Yanks had taken several slaves from the Casimir House, and a few slaves who wanted to get away from their masters had left some of the local homes. The soldiers also took silver, jewelry, fine china, and anything appearing to be of value.

On Sunday afternoon troops boarded three pontoon boats that they lashed together. The evacuation quickly developed into a Sunday-afternoon show for the entire household. The troops were ferried down the bay toward Pass Cavallo and beyond Fort Esperanza. When the third trip began, the evacuees included several women camp followers who had been seen around town gathering supplies for the men. As the last pontoon moved out into the bay, the incoming tide swamped the vessel, throwing all passengers into the water. Screams carried by the wind reached shore as the struggling people grabbed at the sinking pontoons.

"Find some extra quilts and make some hot tea," Captain Whipple shouted as he and Joseph grabbed Hermie and Jackson's little fishing boat and rushed to the water's edge. Several other small craft began rowing out to the struggling people. Townspeople without access to boats watched helplessly as frightened swimmers sank beneath the waves. Others managed to swim and float with the tide back toward the boats heading out to meet them.

The death toll reached twenty-three. The commander, grateful for local rescue attempts, left some of the regiment's supplies and castoff clothing for the townspeople when he returned for the survivors.

Gretchen, Helga, and Emma helped neighbor women boil the uniforms in lye water to fade out the blue color, and then they boiled pecan hulls for dye to stain the cotton fabric a reddish orange. The boys in Gretchen's class received their first new pants in four years, and the girls discovered pants legs could be unstitched to form new skirts. They continued to use prickly pear thorns as substitutes for pins, which had been impossible to find throughout the war.

Joseph continued to row out early each morning in search of water fit for fishing beyond the dead beef floating in the bay. Across the bay he found diamond-backed turtles and even caught a giant sea turtle large enough to share the meat with several families. The Feds had cleared out the prairie chickens and quail.

Late in April news confirmed the gossip that had spread around town about the reason for the sudden departure of the federal troops. The Union had tried a major invasion of Texas through Mansfield, Louisiana, but the Confederates had stopped them.

Joseph expressed the feelings of the entire household: "They got their comeuppance."

Still no word arrived from Hermie or Eagle.

Chapter 21

1864

GRETCHEN TAUGHT HER CLASS CHRISTMAS carols, hoping their sweet, clear voices would ease the aching sadness spreading through the house as everyone watched Helga search the road several times a day for Hermie and Eagle. Without mentioning the missing tree, Gretchen helped the children dye shells with pokeberry juice and hang them from the mantel and the parlor door facing. They made wreaths of salt cedar to take home, and the entire household joined them in strolling through town on Christmas Eve singing carols. The New Year arrived with no word from Hermie or Eagle.

In mid-March, a soldier appeared at the front door with a letter addressed to Mary Henry. Gretchen stared at the official-looking envelope, wrinkled from riding stuffed in a saddlebag. It carried the scrawled name of a captain in the Army of the Confederate States of America. Sucking in deep, calming breaths, she carried the news to the bedroom, where Mary was listening to Effie and Sarah read. Seeing Gretchen holding the letter, Mary's hand flew to her mouth, her eyes wide with terror.

"It's Sam?"

Unable to speak, Gretchen held out the letter.

"Would you read it to me? I don't want to touch it." Mary dropped to her knees with her head bowed, her hands folded like a child saying bedtime prayers.

Gretchen kept breathing deeply, trying to steady her hands as she fumbled with the envelope. It advised Mary Henry that Lieutenant Samuel Henry had been killed on February 22 in a skirmish with a Union gunboat patrolling the coast.

Mary sat down cross-legged on the floor, burying her face in both hands. She looked like a child sobbing uncontrollably.

Gretchen knelt beside her, finally sitting on the floor to better hold the grief-stricken girl.

Mary raised her head. "I don't know where to go. My parents disowned me when I married Sam. He's Catholic. They think I'm going to hell."

"Stay here. Help me with my classes." As soon as she spoke, Gretchen wondered if Eli Cox and the commissioners would pay Mary. Had she just committed to sharing her very low salary?

As she feared, hiring Mary became her responsibility. The county was struggling to feed destitute wives and children of soldiers. They did not consider Mary destitute, because she lived under the good graces of Frau Heinrich.

* * *

The children remaining in Gretchen's classes came from families too poor to leave town and very grateful to send their children to school, where they received the food Gretchen provided. The number of families dependent on the county grew to 297. More taxes were assessed for land, town lots, slaves, horses, cattle, and Confederate notes. Money became so scarce for paying taxes that the commissioners accepted produce and beef cattle at Eli's warehouse, where it was quickly redistributed to hungry wives and children of the soldiers.

Confederate military authorities donated beef for support of the families, and the county received cloth for the destitute from the textile mill at the Huntsville penitentiary that made denim and other heavy materials for the Confederate Army.

* * *

In late April, Eli Cox and Captain Whipple came in for supper at the same time. Eli stopped just inside the front door. "A rider just came in from Austin with news that Robert Lee surrendered at Appomattox." He held his hand up before anyone could respond. "Five days later, while President Lincoln attended a play, someone shot and killed him. Andrew Johnson is the new president of the United States."

"Lord, have mercy. What's gonna happen now?" Joseph's voice carried from the kitchen door.

"We'll have to wait and see, Joseph. It'll depend on what the Union decides to do." Captain Whipple went to the washstand on the back porch and began silently scrubbing his face and hands for supper.

Gretchen felt strangely removed as the household continued with its regular supper routine. Relief that the war had ended was tinged with fear of what lay ahead as the government in Washington took control. Would they have been better off under Lincoln? Would Union soldiers return and take over their town again?

Several weeks after Lee's surrender, Eli Cox rushed from town, almost giddy to be the first to share the latest news. "We beat the socks off a Union force on the Rio Grande at Palmito Ranch. Apparently they didn't know the war's been over for a month."

Gretchen caught herself suddenly hugging Eli Cox. Then, feeling awkward, she backed away. "You think our boys didn't know the war was over?" Placing her fists on both hips and sticking out her chin defiantly, she said, "Whether they knew or not, it feels like sweet revenge."

Eli Cox, obviously thrilled to be hugged, turned a blazing red from the top of his wrinkled collar and wrapped both arms around his thick waist. "My sentiments exactly."

A few days later Tante Amelia rushed to the house, gasping for breath. "Come quickly. Hermie's injured. Dr. Stein's operating."

Gretchen left Mary in charge of her class and ran with her mama and Joseph to Dr. Stein's office. They heard the howl as they reached the front porch. The guttural shriek pierced the air—the sound of Hermie in the depths of agony—and then ended.

Amelia stopped them at the door, pulling them both against her. "Dr. Stein had to do it. Gangrene had set in."

The sudden silence was more terrifying than his scream.

Finally, Dr. Stein stepped from the room, his body and even his hair covered in Hermie's blood. "He's passed out. Let's hope he stays out for a while."

"Can we see him?" Mama trembled like a leaf.

"Stay very quiet. The bleeding's almost stopped. If we keep him quiet, it should seal over."

Hermie looked dead, the same pasty white as the table holding his mangled body. His left leg, missing from just above the knee, looked like a white-bandaged stub propped on a mound of blood-soaked rags.

"You and Missy Gretchen stay here. I'll cook the supper. You don't need to worry none," Joseph whispered as he backed out of the room.

Gretchen clutched her mama's hand as they eased onto a bench against the wall. Mama didn't say a word; she seemed to be breathing for Hermie. Finally, she took his hand and pressed her lips against his blood-encrusted knuckles.

Dr. Stein returned, his clothes changed and the blood washed away. "He needs to stay here and remain as still as possible for a few days. Bleeding will be the biggest thing to watch for. It'll be a while before he can manage for himself."

As the days wore on, watching Dr. Stein wait to give Hermie morphine until the pain seemed beyond endurance became more than Gretchen could bear. Finally, she followed her uncle out of the room. "Why do you wait so long? Why do you let him writhe in pain before you relieve him?"

Dr. Stein pressed his lips together, seeming to search for the right words. "Morphine's very addictive, Gretchen." His voice stayed as gentle as it used to be when he played with Anna. "I don't want Hermie to come out of this with a worse problem."

"You mean like Papa and Paul?" Gretchen made herself look into Dr. Stein's face.

Dr. Stein laid both hands on Gretchen's shoulders. "I've seen patients never get well after too much morphine."

Gretchen nodded, afraid she might cry if she spoke.

In a few days Hermie began thrashing around, his eyes like a wild man's. "He cut off my leg, didn't he?" He reached for the bandaged nub and then pulled his hand back in horror. "I'm a cripple. He's made me a cripple."

"Gangrene had set in," Mama said. "Dr. Stein said you'd die if he didn't cut it off."

"Why didn't you let me die? I'm no good like this." Hermie's face contorted in fury.

Mama only shook her head in pained bewilderment, obviously unable to find words to soothe Hermie.

* * *

Hermie withdrew into himself. Even after getting home and settling upstairs in his old room, he stared at the ceiling, turning his head away when anyone tried talking to him.

After being home a few days, Gretchen followed Mama upstairs with Hermie's supper tray. She decided to ask the question that had been hounding her since Hermie came home. "I heard it happened at the Battle of Palmito after the war ended."

"Yeah. Someone had a New Orleans paper. It said Lee had surrendered and Lincoln had been assassinated."

"Why'd you keep fighting?"

Hermie rolled his head back and forth in frustration. "We couldn't back out on Rip Ford. We'd been with him since February when he took volunteers in San Antonio. He found equipment and horses for us and trained us as we headed south. Rip was determined the Yanks weren't going to retake Brownsville. So when we heard the Yanks were massing at Brazos Santiago, heading to Brownsville, we took three hundred men down river to meet them. We didn't lose any, but some of us got hit."

Mama laid her hand on his shoulder. "You've always been a loyal person."

Hermie turned his head toward the wall. "I'm changing that."

Mama pulled her hand back like she had touched a hot stove.

* * *

Indianolans went about repairing the town with a vengeance. They began reconstructing the wharves, shoring up buildings on the docks, and reopening for business. Families rebuilt the houses and businesses the Yanks had burned or torn down for the lumber.

Joseph seemed obsessed with filling the rifle pits the Yanks had dug all over town. As soon as he finished with those around their property, he went down the road, helping neighbors fill their pits.

One day after working all along their road, Joseph came in hot and angry. "The neighbors said those bastards took their jewelry and family dishes from the old country. I told them about Missy Amelia's silver and lacy covers. Did they take your jewelry, missy?"

Mama laughed. "I'm fortunate, Joseph. I don't have a single piece of jewelry. When the soldiers were packing, Lieutenant Pickle wanted to see in our sea chest. I hid my mama's hand-painted cookie plate under Anna's little dress. My heart jumped in my throat, but I stood my ground. I told him my dead baby's dresses were in that trunk, and he'd take them over my dead body."

"What'd he do?"

"He backed off. Said he didn't know I'd lost a baby girl."

Gretchen could see mist gathering in her mama's eyes. "I'm glad Paul has Papa's violin. They'd have taken that for sure." Then, from the pained look on her mama's face, she wished she hadn't mentioned Paul.

"We're lucky they never dug in that garden." Joseph could hardly stop cackling over the buried jars of coins.

Mama smiled. "Lieutenant Pickle wasn't about to allow his men to damage the garden; it served their appetites too well."

* * *

Hermie continued to make no effort to get up. They carried his meals to him on a tray, and he talked as little as possible.

A month passed, and the neighbors stopped dropping by, tired of being told Hermie didn't feel like having company. Dr. Stein checked on Hermie a few times and came back downstairs shaking his head. "I don't know how to rouse him. If he doesn't move soon, he'll be a cripple."

After visiting day after day for the entire month, Amelia came back downstairs with tears making her eyes a shiny blue. "I'm afraid our precious boy has turned into a bitter man." She wrapped both arms around Mama and whispered, "Dr. Stein and I think he should be moved to our house. Gentle coaxing is not working."

Mama nodded and turned away to hide a racking sob.

Gretchen offered to carry the supper tray that night.

"I'll carry the food tray if you'll bring a fresh pitcher of water for the basin," Mama said. "I'm going to insist he wash himself." She sounded determined.

As Mama entered the room, Hermie muttered, "I'm not hungry." He turned his face toward the wall.

Mama set the tray down on the bench beside the bed. "Gretchen has some water so you can wash up."

"I don't want it."

As quick as lightning Mama grabbed Hermie's shirt at each shoulder and jerked him into a sitting position. Bending low over his face, she howled, "What?" At the same time she grabbed his shoulders, jerking violently at him like she was trying to rip him apart. "Don't you dare keep lying there feeling sorry for yourself. I will not let you throw away your life because a terrible thing happened to you. I will not let you end up like your brother. Like Papa." The last words came out as a weak whisper. She slumped back on Jackson's bed, still clutching the front and sleeves of Hermie's shirt in her hands.

Hermie's mouth had dropped open during the onslaught, and his eyes bulged in complete surprise. He had not resisted or made a sound. Finally, he looked down at his bare chest, where only the collar of his shirt remained. "That's my only shirt ..."

Mama toppled over onto Jackson's bed as if she had been slapped, both hands still clutching the scraps of shirt. Covering her face with the pieces of cloth, she cried without making a sound, her body shaking like she was having a seizure.

Slowly, almost dreamlike, Hermie reached across the space separating the beds and began stroking Mama's cheek, smoothing back her hair. Finally, he pulled himself off the bed, and kneeling with the stub of his leg on the floor, he cradled her in his arms. "Mama, I'm sorry. I'm so sorry, Mama." Then, for the first time since he lost his leg, he began to cry, his tears running onto Mama's hair. Gretchen knelt beside him; wrapping one arm around his waist, she held her mama with the other.

Slowly Mama stopped shaking and slipped into an exhausted sleep.

Hermie looked at Gretchen and shook his head. "Take the tray back to the kitchen. I'll clean myself up and come down there to eat."

Gretchen threw her arms around her almost naked brother. "You're back. Thank God, you've come home."

The next morning Mama came to the kitchen as usual before daylight. Washed and her hair brushed, she looked fresher than she had looked in a long time.

Hermie came to the breakfast table wearing a white shirt with sleeves way too short. "Eli Cox offered me his extra shirt. Joseph helped me dig up Jackson's and my jar of money. I'll buy one today." Moving awkwardly on his crutches, he did not utter a word of complaint as he hobbled toward town. Mama watched him until he got out of sight and then turned to Gretchen. "He's going to be okay, isn't he?"

Gretchen threw her arms around her mama. "Oh, yes. He's going to be just fine."

* * *

Standing on the front porch in early June watching her students scatter toward home, Gretchen heard Eagle shout, "Hel, I'm home. Hel, are you there?"

Gretchen opened the door and yelled, "Eagle's home," and then watched her mama run toward the grizzly-looking man, whose red hair had faded to a dull gray.

Gretchen watched them embrace, watched Eagle's powerful hands stroking her mama's back and then her hair like he was touching the finest jewel in the world. She turned away, heading to the kitchen, praying that someday she would find a man who would love her so completely.

Chapter 22

EAGLE PULLED HELGA DOWN ON the top step beside him as he gazed out across the bay, waving excitedly to passing wagons and shaking his grizzly head in relief at being home. "I've missed you. I've missed everything about this place. I want to sink into life here and just be with you." He squeezed her tighter against him. "You wouldn't believe how fast we moved when we heard the federal blockade was over. We headed back to San Antonio, loaded the cotton stacked up there, and hauled it down here as fast as we could." He sucked in a deep breath, "Thank God we're done with that long haul to Mexico."

He suddenly stopped talking and focused intently at Helga. "You've let me ramble on and not said one word about why you're so skinny. I can feel the bones in your shoulder. What kind of hell have you been through?"

She leaned against his shoulder. "Having you gone so long has been the hardest part." Then she told him about Hermie renting a small store and rehiring freedmen to get the garden ready for a fall crop. When she saw Hermie coming around the bend in the road, she told him about Hermie losing his leg. She hadn't expected to see Eagle so physically shaken as he watched Hermie gamely swinging himself along toward home. Eagle's face twisted with pain as he leaped to his feet, raced down the steps and out the gate, and grabbed Hermie in a fierce embrace. Hermie dropped his crutches as they laughed and cried and beat each other on the back.

With tears streaking the dust on his face and running into his shaggy beard, Eagle kept shaking his head. "I worked like a mad fool on that damn Cotton Road. I thought I'd eased the agony over losing Jackson. Seeing you missing your leg and still coming along the road without Jackson loping along trying to keep up, I realized I'd been imagining that things would be the same when I got home. I didn't let myself think about Jackson being gone and all the torn up things the war caused."

"I miss him every day. He was my brother." Hermie looked guiltily at Helga. "Mama, Jackson and I had a lot more in common than I had with Paul."

Helga nodded, achingly aware the war Paul fought had long ago taken him to a place where there was no room for family.

* * *

At supper, Helga began noticing Hermie and Mary always sitting together, talking quietly to each other. One evening, Hermie came home early and asked Helga what she thought of him hiring Mary to help him in the store. "I take forever to stock the shelves. I spill more than I put up."

"Gretchen would be grateful. She gave Mary a job without thinking how hard it would be to pay her."

Hermie hobbled away. The next thing Helga knew Mary began leaving each morning with Hermie, and Gretchen seemed very relieved to be teaching without a helper she couldn't afford.

* * *

When Union Major General Gordon Granger arrived in Galveston on June 19 to announce Lincoln's Emancipation Proclamation freeing all slaves in Texas, it caused barely a ripple in Indianola or Calhoun County. Unlike East Texas and the other Southern states, where the act resulted in planters' financial destruction, no real planter class existed in their area. The property assessment of the entire county at the end of 1864 showed only 175 slaves. Indianolans looked to the sea and to their own personal industry for their prosperity.

When the army of occupation arrived soon after Granger's announcement of emancipation, residents warily watched Union troops descend in droves, clogging the streets as they roamed about downtown. Word spread that officers were being billeted in private homes until they built permanent quarters behind the quartermaster and general headquarters office. The enlisted men set up tents near Powder Horn Bayou.

* * *

Captain Hershel Avery stood politely holding his hat over his chest when Helga opened the front door. His head almost reached the top of the door facing, and his shoulders bulged against the spotless uniform jacket. His boots were blacked to a sparkling sheen. "I'm looking for a room overlooking the bay. I'll pay your going rate." He bowed slightly toward Helga, and she noticed his black hair receded slightly at the part and his steady black eyes crinkled at the edges, almost offering a smile.

"I have two rooms upstairs. They aren't on the front. You can see the bay from an angle."

"May I see them? My home's on the Hudson River in New York. I want to see water during my stay."

Helga led him up the front stairs, where he stopped and gazed at the bay lapping gently against the shell beach. "How's the fishing?"

"Excellent. We have a lot of red fish and trout. Shrimp and crabs are plentiful, and oysters when they're in season."

"Terrific." His smile spread wide, exposing straight white teeth, making it hard for Helga to maintain her rigid disdain for the occupier.

He strode up and down the hall, examined the room, and fluffed the pillows on the bed. Then he looked over the downstairs and exclaimed over the stenciling and Otto Schnaubert's sketches, which he had placed on display again after returning from the war. "You mean the artist actually lives here?"

"He offers classes at times. Usually he goes to homes." Helga found herself smiling at the young man, the first Union soldier who had noticed the stenciling.

"Perhaps I can take lessons." Captain Hershel Avery obviously meant to take the room.

At supper the conversation became animated after Captain Avery, who insisted on being called Hershel, made it clear he didn't want his stay to be unpleasant for anyone. "Our men have orders to keep the peace and make sure the freedmen have their rights protected. We've been told this county had few slaves and the freedmen who were here before the war were part of the community."

A collective sigh went around the table. Then Hershel moved easily into questioning Otto about his art, where he studied, and where he served during the war.

Suddenly Gretchen smiled broadly and asked, "How far is it from your home in Albany to Boston?"

"About 170 miles. You know Boston?" Hershel's eyes rested on Gretchen's face glowing in the soft light cast by the setting sun.

"We have friends there." Gretchen's face blazed a fiery red. "We've been expecting a letter."

"There's a backlog. So much mail stacked up since the end of the war." Hershel kept glancing at Gretchen as the conversation moved back to Otto's sketches.

A letter from Battina arrived the following week, filled with encouraging news. Orilla had started a thriving dressmaking business and planned to marry a returning soldier. Battina begged for news and for Gretchen to escape Indianola's summer heat and mosquitoes for a long visit in Boston. Helga watched Gretchen read the letter and tried to ignore the pain pressing against her chest at the sight of her daughter's longing to be away from Indianola. Immediately Gretchen set about writing a long response. Helga added her news, and they sent the letter off by return steamer. Gretchen made no further mention of going to Boston, although she stuck to the plan she had laid out when Battina and Orilla left to save money for the trip. Hershel began filling her time and her conversation. It didn't appear his charm centered entirely on his living so near Boston.

"He's a Harvard man, Mama. And he speaks German. He's a lawyer. He'll work for his family firm when he gets out of the army." Gretchen's excitement showed in the staccato sentences and the new bounce in her step. "He didn't want to come here. When the war ended, he still owed the army a year."

"So he'll be leaving next June?"

Gretchen nodded, her thoughts moving into a faraway future.

* * *

The Chihuahua Trail opened again, bringing long lines of Mexican carts loaded with silver, lead, and copper rumbling down the road on the way to the docks. As evacuees returned to town, they repaired and rebuilt their houses and businesses with the lumber flowing into the port. Businessmen from the East looking for investment opportunities began arriving on the increasing number of ships, and the Stein House enjoyed its share of guests who willingly paid in gold or silver dollars.

Eli Cox took on new vigor and even bought a new black suit as he began receiving merchandise for his commission business. Captain Whipple hired a team to lift his submerged ship. Palmetto logs arrived for reconstruction of his and the other damaged docks. Charles Morgan quickly reopened his shipping operations along the Gulf, buying new ships and refurbishing his fleet. Both Confederate and Union confiscation of his ships had taken a toll on his business, and he aimed to get it back.

Although jobs became plentiful, soldiers' families didn't rebound as quickly from the increased business activity. The farmers returned to land suffering from years of neglect, and their livestock had been sold to pay for their families' survival. The commissioners repaired the school, and Gretchen, Effie, and Sarah eagerly began their early-morning trek back to their classroom, but they continued to carry food for children who arrived hungry.

The destitute received supplies that had been left in the Confederate commissary in Victoria, and the collector of customs at Matagorda Bay gave $132,000, the balance of his custom duties, to the county for purchasing corn for hunger relief. The state controller's office refunded some of the taxes collected during the war.

* * *

James Carter appeared on the back porch, his eyes sunken and watery like those of a very old man. Coarse threads stuck up from the shoulders and sleeves of his uniform jacket, outlining ripped-off Confederate insignias; his pants were frayed at the knees. "I can't see a way to take Emma and the girls back to our ranch. The Yanks stripped it clean." He sounded weak, like a man so bone-weary he could barely speak.

"They'll be thrilled to see you."

"I wanted to talk to you first." He shuffled his feet, staring at his mud-caked boots. "I can't pay you a thing right now. I fought in the Red River Campaign. We stopped Banks with awful losses. Then they told us to go home. Just like that. We got nothing for our effort. Confederate notes aren't worth a damn." He shook his head as he spoke as if he couldn't believe his own words. "I fought with Shanghai Pierce on the Red River."

"Isn't he ...?"

"Yep. He's the cattle rustler. But he don't need to rustle no more. With all the cold winters in North Texas during the war, millions of unbranded cattle roamed down south. They're just waiting to be claimed. He'll pay in gold for every head I bring to him over in Matagorda County. He ships them out to Cuba, New Orleans, and St. Louis. If I treat him fair, he'll be fair with me." James Carter stopped and looked intently at Helga. "What I'm saying, ma'am, is I'll pay you in gold just as soon as I can get some cattle sold to Shanghai."

Helga patted the distraught man on the arm. "I'll be glad to help." She saw no need to remind him that his family had been getting free board for over a year. She'd need to continue paying Dr. Stein's percent from the buried jars.

Effie saw James Carter the minute he stepped in the back door and ran screaming, "Mama, he's home. Pa's here." She leaped wildly into his open arms.

"You've grown up. I can't believe how big you are," James cried as he struggled to hold both girls in his arms and reach for Emma.

As Helga watched the reunion, she realized the girls looked healthy, no longer frail and thin; their cheeks were rosy, and Emma no longer wore the gaunt, hollow look of hunger.

Helga didn't have to mention the board to Dr. Stein, because he came by that evening and seemed pleased to see the Carters reunited. When he realized James Carter planned to leave the following morning, Dr. Stein drew Helga aside to ask about the family's board. "Shanghai Pierce's a rough customer. We may be taking on Emma and the girls permanently with her husband taking up with that riffraff," Dr. Stein said.

Helga nodded. "I believe he'll pay as soon as he can."

"Keep a record. We'll worry about collecting later."

Helga felt relieved at his generosity. She wasn't about to test him by admitting the Carters did not pay in cash. She made sure Dr. Stein received his percentage from her dwindling supply in the jars, and that was all he needed to know.

* * *

Eli Cox cleared his throat to get attention. "I waited to make this announcement until I knew Hershel would be out drilling with his men. He seems like a nice young man ..." Eli shrugged. "It's awkward with him living here and all. Governor Hamilton received instructions from President Johnson ordering Texans to sign an amnesty oath."

"Amnesty?" Hermie's knuckles turned white as he gripped his fork, pointed it accusingly at Eli Cox.

Eli shook his head. "The copy I've seen says you'll support the Union, abide by its laws, and renounce slavery. Some people are signing just to get the war behind them and get on with their lives." He looked around the table like a man canvassing for support. "I think I'll sign to get back to business as quickly as possible. I didn't own slaves anyway, and neither did most folks around here."

Hermie laid his fork down and gazed at the faces around the table. "We've lost so much, and yet we're well-off compared to the rest of the South." He finally shook his head. "I've got to think about this for a while. I never wanted the war. Then I fought for the South because it was my home."

"It feels like we've given up enough," said Gretchen. "We lost Jackson. Hermie lost his leg. Signing some paper swearing loyalty seems like one more insult." She rose stiffly from the table. As she reached the kitchen door, she turned, an angry frown on her face. "I guess I should be glad I'm a woman. Nobody wants my signature."

Eli Cox looked like he didn't know where to hide. Captain Whipple broke the silence. "I plan to support the Union. I supported it before the war."

Eli Cox sighed like he had been holding his breath. "Folks respect your judgment, Captain."

* * *

Eagle made good on his plan to be home more often. He hauled supplies to the western army posts that were being reestablished and returned with a wide variety of exports—cotton, bales of wool, barrels of pecans, and corn. Each time he returned, he talked about buying farmland in Washington County. "You should see the countryside around Chappell Hill. Lush, grass-covered hills roll real easy up to the edge of the forests thick with big, healthy trees. The cotton crops used to be huge. Now the planters can't afford to pay Negroes to work the fields. They're land poor, ready to sell off pieces of their property." He hugged Helga against him and nuzzled her neck as he whispered, "If I buy a place and hire someone to run it, would you think about going up there with me? Someday?"

Helga always asked when, and he always said, "Someday." She knew it would be a long time coming, because Eagle was a roving man. He would not be ready to stay in one place for a very long time.

By Christmas the house was filled with energy and anticipation. Gretchen and Hershel and Hermie and Mary spent evenings on the front porch singing Christmas carols in English and German. Mary didn't know the German songs, but her sweet soprano rang clear on the English versions. She still reminded Helga of a fragile little child. She trailed behind Hermie, absorbing his every utterance.

When Eagle arrived with the cedar tree, they sang while they decorated it, adding more delicate ornaments Hershel had bought at Reuss's Drugstore.

As they prepared for bed, Eagle laughed softly. "Gretchen and Hermie seem mighty preoccupied with their new friends. Hermie can't keep his eyes off Mary. And Gretchen's radiant."

Helga nodded and leaned close to whisper, "Hershel didn't move out when they completed the officers' housing. Gretchen brushes her hair and pinches her cheeks constantly. I wonder if she does that at school."

"Has Hermie signed the loyalty oath? I'm signing it on this trip. No sense waiting any longer."

"It's due after Christmas. If Hermie doesn't sign, I don't know how Hershel will take it. I think getting to know Hershel has softened Hermie's attitude about the Yanks."

The surprise on Christmas morning came when Hermie and Hershel, on a prearranged cue, knelt before their girls and presented their gifts—beautiful diamond engagement rings.

Helga laughed with delight at their gallantry, the success of their secret plan. She felt Eagle stroke her back and knew he was as pleased as she with the timing and the sweet, fresh love bringing so much joy to the house.

That night as Eagle helped her undress and ease into the warmth of their bed and their own vigorous lovemaking, he whispered, "I wish I'd known you when we were young."

* * *

In May Hershel came home in midafternoon. "Miss Helga, you know I want to marry Gretchen and take her home with me when I leave. I don't want to make it hard on your family with Gretchen marrying a Yank. May we have a quiet little ceremony here before I leave?"

Until Hershel said he planned to take Gretchen away, Helga had avoided thinking of the inevitable. "I think that's a wise plan." She forced a smile.

* * *

When fabric began making its way into town, Gretchen started sewing her wardrobe. "I know his family's wealthy. I don't want to look like a peasant."

Helga laughed to hear Gretchen adopt her own favorite denial. "You're beautiful and educated. You're no peasant. You can hold your head high in any company."

Together with Emma and the girls and Mary's help, they sewed a lovely wedding dress and trousseau. "Battina would be proud of your sewing and the designs you've created," Helga said as she helped Gretchen pack and fought to keep her profound sadness from showing.

Helga wasn't the only one dreading the day Gretchen left. Effie and Sarah trailed Gretchen's every step, and Mary helped eagerly with all the preparations and cried over every new dress and detail of the plans. Effie and Sarah spent more and more time questioning Gretchen about her trip and about New York. Even Hermie grew quiet as more and more talk centered on the approaching wedding.

Mary surprised them all with her beautiful arrangements of wildflowers throughout the house and her skill at decorating a cake.

* * *

Hershel beamed, looking as if he might flap his long arms and take flight when he returned following his official release from the military. "I've got the steamship tickets for in the morning." Then he stopped and gazed around the parlor and dining room. "This place is beautiful. I'll miss it. I'll miss the entire family. But honestly, I won't miss patrolling this town."

The parlor looked beautiful for the wedding that evening, and the bride and groom beamed with so much joy that it spread like a warm blanket over the whole household, which allowed everyone to push aside their dread at seeing Hershel and Gretchen leave.

They all gathered on the dock the next morning and smiled and waved until the ship moved out of sight toward Pass Cavallo. Then the pretense ended, and to a person they cried as they made their way slowly back home.

"It's awful hard to watch her go," Hermie said as tears streaked his cheeks, and he hugged the sobbing Mary under his arm as they walked.

"I'm reminding myself that I raised you to grow up. Have lives of your own," Helga said as she swung onto the comfort of Eagle's arm. When bedtime finally came, Eagle held her on his shoulder while she cried until she could cry no more.

Effie and Sarah clung to Mary as their new companion. No longer the little girl playing dolls, Mary drilled the girls each evening on their schoolwork and borrowed Captain Whipple's books, including *Uncle Tom's Cabin,* for their reading.

In August Eagle led all his freight wagons as they hauled more supplies to the military posts on the western edge of the state. He made it home in early September in time to witness a fierce storm blow a ship transporting lumber from Pensacola through the wharf and directly into the street in front of Casimir House. "I'm going to start looking for a farm in Washington County. This town is too near sea level." Helga rocked him contentedly in her arms, knowing his wagons were already loading for another trip out west.

Gretchen wrote faithfully, describing Hershel's welcoming family and living in the big house while they built their new home. She mentioned plans to add a nursery. She told of an exciting trip to New York City with Hershel's mother to meet some of the kin who lived in the city. She still had not seen Battina and Orilla, but she planned a trip to Boston as soon as they finished construction on their house.

Hermie and Mary planned to delay their marriage until Eagle came home for Christmas. Surprisingly, Mary did not want Hermie to fix the quarters over the store for their home. "I love it here," she said shyly. Then she reached for Helga's hand. "May I call you Mama?"

Helga pulled the tiny girl into her arms and hugged her fiercely. "I'd love to have you call me Mama."

As Christmas and the wedding day approached, Emma and the girls threw themselves into the decorations and sewing with just as much enthusiasm as they had shown for Gretchen. "Even if they are staying right here, we want it to be as grand as Gretchen and Hershel's wedding," Emma said as she held the lovely white satin wedding dress against her cheek. "Did you have a beautiful wedding, Helga?"

Helga shook her head. "Gretchen's was the first I've ever seen."

"Me too," Emma said. "And this will be my second."

They moved a larger bed into Hermie and Jackson's old room, and the only difference in their lives was the change in quarters. Mary settled happily into her new life as Hermie's wife.

Chapter 23

1867

IN SPRING RECONSTRUCTION OF THE South became far harsher than anyone expected. Eli hustled to the supper table carrying a very wrinkled newspaper. "I wish the captain were here to talk about this. Congress has passed the Reconstruction Act over President Johnson's veto."

Hermie came in right behind Eli, shaking his head in disgust. "They've divided Texas and the South into five military occupation districts. All the Southern states have to write a new constitution guaranteeing Negro suffrage." Hermie wedged onto a bench beside Mary and quickly kissed her on her cheek before continuing. "We have to allow Negroes to vote in an election selecting new government officials." He looked around the table. "Negroes can't read or write. How are they going to know anything about voting?"

Eli interrupted, "The part about ratifying the Fourteenth Amendment making Negroes citizens doesn't bother me. I'm worried about the part that gives military commanders of each district the authority to remove previously elected officials. I don't know how far people can be pushed around here. I don't want Indianola to have a race riot like New Orleans had last year. Too many people died."

Helga felt relieved when Hermie said, "Eli, let's not talk riot talk. We don't want to stir people up. Our troubles aren't near as bad as they had in New Orleans."

"You're right. You're right." Eli kept shrugging his shoulders like an embarrassed child.

* * *

The weather brought more bad news: rains came in steady torrents all through May, filling the bayous and overflowing the lakes on the backside of town. Water stood in low-lying fields, and humidity increased as a harbinger of the torrid temperatures of an early summer.

* * *

Despite anger over the loyalty oath and the latest draconian laws, the military occupation force in Indianola maintained a harmonious relationship with the citizenry by judiciously enforcing the edicts. Unlike those in other parts of Texas and the South, Indianolans were accustomed to business dealings with the North. Most of the Northerners who came to town and received appointments to official positions were capable businessmen. They made real efforts to become part of the community. Still, resentment grew like a slowly festering boil.

* * *

In July Eli stormed in to supper. "We can't vote. Now we can't hold office. The damned Yankee radicals are taking over. In some places they're rounding up freedmen, ex-slaves who can't even read and write, and handing them political offices."

Helga had never heard a curse word pass Eli Cox's lips. Now his face blazed and sweat streaked the front of his shirt. Serving as commissioner meant so much to him. He looked like a man stripped of everything he valued.

Hermie appeared as riled as Eli. "They're not reconstructing the South. Kicking out our local officials, not letting citizens serve on a jury if they supported the Confederacy—it's subjugation. The radicals want us to suffer. Winning isn't enough for them. They intend to dominate us. Forever."

"As much as I miss her, I'm glad Gretchen and Hershel are safely out of here. It would be terribly hard on Hershel to enforce these laws. How could he ever tell a man like Eli that because he held office during the war he's forbidden to hold office now?" Helga hoped that reminding them of Hershel's discomfort with the law might ease some of the fury sweeping the household.

Helga wished Captain Whipple or Eagle would return and offer some calm to the venom spreading around the table. She felt uncomfortably aware of Joseph eating in the kitchen. Usually at the end of the meal, Joseph hustled to the dining room to help clear the dishes by the time Helga rose from the table. That night Joseph did not enter the room, and he was not in the kitchen.

After she washed the dishes, Helga found Joseph sitting in the garden, his back leaning against the wall of the washroom. "I'm sorry you heard the anger at our table tonight."

"Yes, ma'am. I'm sorry too. I been thinking about what I should do. I never cared for voting. I only wanted freedom. Hermie's right. I can't read or write. Every time I go into town them people asks me to sign up to vote."

"As a freedman, you have the right to vote, Joseph."

Joseph rubbed a gnarly hand over his graying, nappy head. "I know, but sometimes a man's got to trade power for being happy. Missy, I was born a slave, and every family I ever had got sold away from me. Since I been here, you treat me good. You treat me like I'm a man."

"Oh, Joseph." Helga crumpled to her knees, laid her hand on his bony shoulder.

"I don't want to go away. I want to live the rest of my days helping you keep this place going. But when I hear that mean talk I think I'm a fool to stay in a country where I'm hated."

"The men are angry because they can't vote, and now they can't continue holding the offices they've been so proud to have. Joseph, I can't guarantee that when you are away from this house you won't find men who'll take their anger out on you. Blame you for something you can't help. But if you want to stay, I'll see you aren't harmed at this house." Helga wondered how she'd stop a mob of angry white men.

* * *

Captain Whipple returned from New Orleans just before supper. His cheeks were so red that they showed through his white beard. He ate only a few bites, drank copious amounts of ice water, and excused himself before the meal ended.

That evening, as Helga sat on the back porch looking into the moon's steady glow and imagining Eagle sitting beside her, Joseph hurried down the back stairs to draw water from the cistern.

"He's mighty sick, Missy. I heard him groan and found him blazing with the fever."

Hermie met them at the captain's bedroom door and took one look at the man lying lifeless under the glow of the lamp. "I'll get Dr. Stein. Mary will get some ice."

Joseph and Helga applied ice to his fevered body as quickly as Mary hauled it upstairs. Finally, they heard the rattle of Dr. Stein's carriage.

"I was at the hospital when Hermie found me. I've seen a rash of yellow fever in the last few days. All the cases are folks living or working downtown. The hospital's overflowing. I could smell it as soon as I stepped from the carriage. Their bodies are emitting a musty odor in a lot of these cases."

The captain moaned and tried to pull away when Dr. Stein touched his chest. "I'll apply a mustard plaster to ease this congestion. We're thinking it may be best to keep these yellow fever patients away from the sun. Move him to the west side of the house in the morning. Return him when the afternoon sun lights the west room. And keep his body cool."

For the next three days Helga, Emma, and Joseph gently carried the captain's bed from the east side of the house in the morning. Each afternoon they returned him to his room. On the fourth morning, his fever broke, and he asked to be relieved of the cold clothes. Only when his strength began returning did Joseph consent to leave his side. "I thought you was a goner, Captain. Scared me nearly to death."

"It scared me too," Helga said.

"Me too." Mary looked up at Helga and smiled, obviously very proud of how much she had helped Emma manage the house and prepare meals during the long days while Helga and Joseph tended the captain.

Before the epidemic ended, almost six hundred suffered with yellow fever and close to eighty-five died. Then it spread inland to new areas of the state, killing hundreds.

* * *

In October, Eli came to supper with a very worried look on his face. "The Union troops ordered our new commissioners to impress all men between eighteen and forty-five to work on roads within the precinct where each man lives. They can't come in here, free the slaves, and then force white men into bondage who've never owned slaves. There'll be a rebellion."

Eli was right. The local troops could not enforce the ruling.

* * *

Despite his plans to take shorter freighting trips, Eagle's business continued to grow, and he accompanied more and more of his wagon trains on extended trips to Austin and to the army posts on the western edge of settlement. He made it home for a wonderful Christmas that was made perfect by a long letter from Gretchen saying they would have a baby in the spring. Helga held the letter a long time. "I'm trying to imagine Gretchen heavy with a child," Helga said as she and Eagle sat on the back porch enjoying the chilly December evening.

"I am too. You never said if you had a hard time giving birth."

Helga leaned her head against Eagle's shoulder. "No, having babies was not hard for me. I'm hoping Gretchen has a body like mine."

"She's built like you—tall and slender. Strong too." Eagle pulled Helga into a tight embrace. "I hope she's as good at loving as her mama. That'll make Hershel a mighty happy man."

"I hope Hershel is as good a lover as you. That'll make Gretchen a mighty happy woman."

Eagle left again by the first of the New Year.

* * *

The days in April dragged as Helga, Emma, Mary, and the girls all waited eagerly for a letter letting them know about Gretchen and the new baby. Amelia kept assuring them that Dr. Stein said Gretchen was a big girl, well built for having healthy babies. Finally, Hermie and Mary rushed in before lunch with a letter from Gretchen glowing with the news that Helena Avery was a beautiful blonde baby. Gretchen hardly mentioned the delivery except to say Hershel's mother and sister helped the doctor. She expected Battina and Orilla to visit before summer.

"This is when I feel jealous of Hershel's mother. I should have been there."

Emma laughed. "I feel jealous, too."

"So do I," Mary said. "We'd be wonderful midwives."

They all laughed as Helga stuffed the letter in her apron pocket and rose to finish preparing lunch.

* * *

With the arrival of summer, Captain Whipple came to supper with news. "Since yellow fever was so bad last year, the military district in New Orleans ordered quarantine stations all along the coast. Indianola's station is that old Morgan steamship wreck in the bay. It's going to be marked with a yellow flag. Dr. Stein is the new quarantine surgeon. Ships have to anchor and wait for Dr. Stein to come aboard. He'll examine everyone on the ship before they dock." The captain shook his head in disgust. "As if we don't have enough taxes, each ship must pay a fee for the boarding."

"I hope Dr. Stein can spot yellow fever that easily," Hermie said. "Seems like a big burden for him to carry."

"You don't think Dr. Stein would get blamed if we had another epidemic?" Helga asked as she set the last dish on the table and slipped onto her end of the bench.

"Who knows what this Reconstruction government will decide," Eli said as he began devouring his oysters.

* * *

The handsome young black man standing at the door wore a beautifully tailored brown suit with a gold watch fob draped across his vest, the image of the wealthy businessmen who preferred staying at the Casimir House. His smile spread as he gazed down at Helga. "Frau Heinrich, I'm Sylus."

Helga's heart leaped wildly as she threw her arms around the startled young man. "Oh, Sylus, come in here. Let me look at you. I can't believe you're here. You look wonderful." All the time she spoke, she led him toward the parlor.

"I'm on my way to New Orleans on business. I wanted to stop and thank you and Captain Whipple for saving my life." He smiled sheepishly and bowed slightly as his arm swooped down to indicate his beautifully tailored suit and highly polished boots. "I've tried to live up to the faith you put in me."

"Tell me about yourself." Helga wanted to ask about Paul, but she forced herself to hold back.

"I've continued working with Benjamin at the mercantile store in Matamoros. When the Garcias died, they left the business jointly to Benjamin and me. We've expanded over the years. It's been successful."

"I can tell you've been successful. Do you and Benjamin have families?"

"Both of us have wives. I have three children and Benjamin has five." Sylus allowed Helga to continue holding his hand. Then he squeezed her fingers and said, "Paul sends his love."

Helga couldn't keep from clutching her chest as the hot flood of emotion swept over her. "How is he?"

"He's still playing at the hotel and bar."

"But how is he?"

Sylus shook his head. "Paul gets by as best he can. He still plays like an angel, and he's got a loyal following."

"Could I visit him?"

Sylus' facial muscles twitched. "I don't think he'd want you to come down. He gets upset when anything unusual happens."

"Is it the alcohol?" Helga forced herself to look directly into Sylus's soft brown eyes.

"That's about right."

Helga wrapped her arms around herself and rocked to ease the pain that tore at her body. "I sent him away, you know. I told him not to come back until he sobered up."

Sylus nodded. "He couldn't stay here with the war coming. Benjamin makes sure he has everything he needs. He remembers what Paul did for him. He won't let him down. You needn't worry."

"Have you seen Captain Whipple?" Helga tried to force a smile.

"I stopped by on my way out here. My ship sails later this afternoon. It's taking on some cargo." He pulled out his watch. "I need to get back in case they move faster than they estimated. They didn't want me to debark. I told them when I bought my ticket I planned to see folks in Indianola."

"Sylus, I'm so glad you came." Helga fought to hold herself together and wished he'd leave quickly. "Please send my love to Paul. Tell him his sister has a little girl. And thank Benjamin for me." Her voice broke, and she could not stop the flood of tears.

Sylus folded her in a tight embrace. "I'll tell them both of my visit with you. I'll tell Paul his mama is still a handsome and very kind lady."

Helga could only nod. She watched Sylus stride confidently back toward town, and she could not believe he had been a frightened slave boy so few years before.

1869

Although Francis Stabler came from Baltimore after the war, townspeople viewed him as an inventor and a businessman, not one of the hated carpetbaggers who took financial advantage of a defeated people.

Eli could barely contain himself when he realized the inventor had chosen the Stein House for his residence.

"I understand you have a method for canning raw meat?" Eli could not stop shaking Mr. Stabler's hand.

"We use carbonic acid gas. The meat keeps for long periods. It's perfect for ships at sea and for travelers crossing the country." Francis Stabler withdrew his hand and patted Eli on the shoulder. "You'll have to visit our canning plant when it's complete."

Not only did Eli get to see the plant, he got to sample some of the first products at supper when Francis Stabler brought home a fifteen-pound can of beefsteak. "It's delicious, as tender as fresh butchered," Eli exclaimed. "I know I can offer you a market."

Francis Stabler seemed as pleased as Eli to find a mutual business arrangement.

* * *

Captain Whipple beamed with sheer pleasure as he announced that the fast little ship he had used so successfully as a blockade runner looked as good as new after it was raised from where the Yanks sank it during the war. "Now that it's refurbished, I can join the Corpus Christi and Indianola United States Mail Line. We're offering passenger and mail service to connect with the Morgan Line steamers going to New Orleans."

"So you're trusting that outfit?" Eli leaned back in his chair, a smug look on his face.

"I'm sort of like you, Eli. I want to make a little money in this growing economy. Morgan's steamship services are the best bet for you and for me."

"Yes, yes, you're right, Captain. We just need to watch what he does next. Some folks are worrying that he's trying to monopolize the railroad and the shipping business."

Captain Whipple chuckled. "That's one thing you and I agree on wholeheartedly. But you see what's happened. We rounded up enough local support to build the depot, repair shop, and thirteen miles of track.

Then the money dried up. That railroad's got to have outside investment, and Morgan looks like our best bet."

* * *

In May Amelia excitedly announced that Dr. Stein was getting gas lighting for his office and for their upstairs living quarters. "Most all the downtown business houses are hooking up to the line." The whole household made a nighttime tour to see both Amelia and Dr. Stein's and Hermie and Mary's brightly lit buildings. "Now we can stay open at night," Hermie said as he reached to circle Mary under his arm. "If Mary decides to move above the store, we'll have gas lights upstairs." Mary smiled sweetly, turned away, and busied herself with a turkey duster on a row of cans.

A few days later the captain came to supper wearing a broad grin. "Guess who just arrived?" He didn't wait for an answer. "None other than Charles Morgan and two gentlemen from New York and New Orleans. They're impressed by how much progress Indianola's made on the railroad."

Helga couldn't remember seeing the captain so animated. Before she could say a word, Eli bustled into the room wearing a smile even larger than the captain's. "Morgan's worried about Midwestern railroads heading toward the Gulf coast. Thinks they'll cut into his steamship business. Looks like he's going to put his money into the Indianola Railroad."

Then it was the captain's turn to interrupt. "I hope he can convince the San Antonio and Mexican Gulf Railroad to extend its line down here. That'd open our markets all the way to California."

In July a Morgan steamship carried the world's first shipment of beef in refrigerated containers from Indianola to New Orleans. It was hard to tell who was the most excited that night at supper. Hermie kept squeezing Mary's shoulder as she snuggled beside him at the table. "Refrigeration will open our market to fresh fruits and vegetables coming all the way from the Indies."

"When we get refrigerated warehouses," Eli said, "we can slaughter the beef here, keep it just above freezing, and ship it all over the world." Then he lowered his chin and shook his head at Emma. "You know refrigeration spells the end of your husband's and Shanghai Pierce's cattle-driving business. It'll put an end to moving beef on the hoof." Then he looked at Francis Stabler. "What about your canning process?"

Stabler smiled like a man sure of his place in the world. "It'll be a long time, if ever, before all the ships will be refrigerated. I think there's room for more than one preservation method in this economy."

Emma nodded. "Maybe James will come home if he can't sell beef to Shanghai Pierce. He'll have to sell his cattle to Mr. Stabler."

Helga couldn't help smiling to herself. Whatever happened, Eli was the first to read doomsday in it for someone. At least Eagle wasn't there for Eli to remind him that the long-awaited railroad was certainly going to end his freighting business. That night as she sat on the back porch looking at the moon, she couldn't keep from hoping that traffic on the railroad would put a dent in Eagle's business. Maybe force him into shorter runs.

* * *

Hermie and Mary always delivered the mail, because Hermie made it a point to meet every mail ship. When Gretchen or Battina or Orilla's mail arrived, they usually rushed home early to hear the news. Hermie always said getting the letters felt like a family reunion. Gretchen's letters were always long and filled with news about Helena's growth and their family trips to New York City for shopping or to visit Hershel's relatives. Battina and Orilla visited as often as their business allowed and then always wrote long letters filled with how happy they were and exclaiming over Gretchen's new home and good life. Gretchen's late-summer letter was even longer than usual, and at the end she wrote in large print, "Baby due in spring. Hooray!"

After lunch, when Hermie and Mary headed back to the store, Emma stopped washing dishes and looked seriously at Helga. "Did you think Mary seemed upset over Gretchen's news? I wonder if she's wanting a baby and not able to have one. They've been married almost three years."

"Mary's so tiny. I worry about her carrying a child." Helga shrugged. "They've never mentioned having children. Mary seems content to be working at the store all day with Hermie."

* * *

Charles Morgan steadily increased the arrivals of his ships along the Gulf coast, and he bought into railroads that ran from Gulf ports to inland cities. In August Morgan paid a total of $6,750 in gold dollars for town lots next to the docks on Travis Street where the railroad would eventually run. It looked like Indianola would finally get a railroad.

* * *

Not all news was good in 1869. A storm carrying tornadic winds destroyed the Episcopal Church, ripped off roofs, knocked down chimneys, broke windows, and drove boats onto the beach. But with no lives lost, the storm reinforced the local belief in Indianola's safe location.

* * *

The election in November reawakened anger as new voter registration lists were drawn up eliminating even more voters than the previous election. Eli and the captain still could not vote, and on election day they came home in a fury. "The army's herding freedmen to the polls and standing around watching who votes. E. J. Davis is going to win for sure." Eli paced up and down the dining room.

"When Rip Ford recruited some of us in San Antonio, he said he was having to fight that turncoat E. J. Davis along the Rio Grande," Hermie said. "Davis left Texas for the Union, and now he's back wanting to be the governor."

"With the new constitution giving freedmen the vote and cutting so many whites from the registration lists, we might as well accept that E. J. Davis is going to win." Captain Whipple's beard shook as he clinched his jaw. "If Democrats ever decide to work with moderate Republicans, we can get rid of this bunch. The moderates don't want these radicals any more than we do."

* * *

When Eagle came home, he was as angry about the changes in the government as anyone at the supper table. "It's crazy in Austin. Davis got the legislature to extend his time in office for two years. Claims it's to make local and federal elections coincide. And he's gotten the militia bills passed. Now, on his own, he can call every man between eighteen and forty-five into the military. He's planning a state police force that'll be under his control."

Eli Cox added, "Instead of being under military rule, our good governor is going to be appointing our mayors and even our city officials. I tell you, he's become the king."

"You know the sad part? The freedmen got him elected. And they aren't going to get a thing for it." Eagle seemed to hear himself for the first time and lowered his voice. "We should all speak to Joseph and make sure he understands this has nothing to do with him."

Helga breathed a sigh of relief and felt Eagle's hand stroke her back.

"Sorry, Hel," he whispered. "I should be more careful what I say. Joseph doesn't need to hear all this."

* * *

Two days before Christmas, James Carter stood proudly at the front door dressed in a leather shirt and pants, his face shaved clean and his hair groomed like a man just out of the barber's chair. "I've come to see my family, Miss Helga. And to pay my debt."

He paid his debt in gold coins. And he brought gifts for Emma and both girls and paid for two rooms so he and Emma could have a room and the girls could have separate quarters. "I'm building my fortune. I'll have a good spread on Mustang Island before long. We'll be going home to a fine house."

The thrill of the gifts and having two rooms showed in the faces of the two little girls, but when it became clear that he planned to leave again the day after Christmas, they set aside their beautiful new dolls and clung to his every move.

Emma kept looking down and smoothing the skirt of her lovely new calico dress with its yellows and browns that brought out the color in her face. Finally, just as Christmas lunch was coming to a close, she said, "Maybe next Christmas we will all have our own homes. I don't really care if ours is grand. I just want it to be ours."

For just a moment the room fell silent, and then conversation began again with everyone talking and pushing back quickly from the table.

That night as they prepared for bed Eagle said, "I feel sorry for Emma and the girls. It's so obvious that James has touched the golden hem, and he wants the entire garment."

Helga turned around and fell into Eagle's arms, pressing her face against his chest. "Women want their men with them, Eagle. We hate watching you ride away from us."

"I'm just like James, aren't I? I shouldn't be doing so much talking."

"No, you shouldn't."

Chapter 24

1870

IN LATE APRIL, WITH THE arrival of Western Union Telegraph lines connecting Indianola with the rest of the world, a message arrived from Gretchen: "Hershel Avery born April 20. Mother and son well. Letter follows."

At supper everyone gathered around the message, eager to see something that could arrive so quickly.

"Just imagine how fast we can receive orders. And with the new refrigerated steamships, there's no limit to our business," Eli crowed as he shoveled his mouth full of supper as quickly as he spoke.

"Not having to wait on a ship to bring news from Gretchen and Hershel makes them seem so much closer," Helga said.

Hermie slipped his arm around Mary's shoulder. "We think this is the best time to add our good news. We're planning to get a baby of our own. Probably in December."

"We didn't want to tell anyone until we were sure," Mary laughed. "At last we'll have some babies of our own around here."

Helga and Emma had been privately worrying that Mary might be too small to conceive a child. Their delight with the news soon led to speculation that she might not be strong enough to carry a baby. She proved to be healthy and filled with energy the entire time.

Hermie surprised Mary in August with a new Howe sewing machine for her birthday. "I thought you could sew baby clothes so much faster with a machine," Hermie said as he looked questioningly at Mary. She stepped back from the wooden table holding the machine and stared down at its black metal treadle. "Don't you like it?"

Mary shrugged her tiny shoulders, her hand fluttering toward her belly protruding only slightly under the fullness of her dress. "It's too early to sew baby clothes. My mama always said we tempt the devil if we make plans for a baby too far in advance."

Helga hugged Mary. "There's no big hurry. We'll all help when you think it's time."

Hermie looked at the people still gathered around the supper table. "How about putting it in the parlor? Maybe Effie and Sarah would like to learn to sew on it."

Both girls squealed and rushed from the table to run their fingers over the amazing new machine.

Helga burst into laughter. "I bet several of us will enjoy learning to work that thing."

Mary suddenly began laughing. "Maybe I'll learn to use it too. But not to make baby clothes."

Mary continued going to the store with Hermie and coming home each evening without showing any interest in the sewing machine. Effie and Sarah started immediately, under Emma's supervision, sewing secret nightshirts and blankets for the new baby that they tucked away before Mary and Hermie returned from the store each evening. Before they returned to school in the fall, they were proficient enough to sew lovely little dresses.

Finally, in early December Mary stopped going to the store each morning and asked Helga, Emma, and the girls to help her sew some clothes for the baby on the machine. Effie and Sarah decided to keep their baby clothing a secret until the baby arrived.

Eagle returned with the annual Christmas venison, wild turkey, and cedar tree. They spent Christmas Eve decorating the tree and sampling all the sweets prepared for the season. Finally, Helga and Eagle were preparing for bed and their eagerly anticipated evening alone when they heard Hermie rushing down the back stairs.

"We've got to get Dr. Stein. Mary's having the baby."

"I'll get the doctor," Eagle volunteered, squeezing Helga's arm in a mutually shared farewell for the evening.

The labor moved rapidly, and by the time Dr. Stein arrived, Helga realized Mary's tiny body could not open for the baby's passage. Dr. Stein agreed. As the night wore on, the grinding labor drove Mary's body in hard contractions without producing any dilation.

"Can't you do something? Can't you relieve her agony?" Hermie's fingers gripped Dr. Stein's sleeve, his face wet with sweat.

Dr. Stein shook his head, wiped his own brow with the back of his sweat-soaked sleeve. "I've given her two doses of ergot and two of morphine. I'll kill the baby if I give her any more morphine."

"Do it. Save Mary," Hermie hissed.

Dr. Stein nodded and slipped a vial into her half-opened lips.

Hermie sat by her bedside, swabbed her face with cool clothes, and cried silently as he watched his love slip out of reach. She cried out for a time and then grew silent, too exhausted and too drugged to fight the pain racking her tiny body.

At daylight, Dr. Stein shook his head. "The baby's gone. It's just a matter of time until Mary succumbs."

By midmorning both mother and child were dead, and Hermie was reduced to exhausted tears. "I knew she was too tiny. She was like a little elf. I shouldn't have let her have a baby."

They buried Mary next to Anna, and as they walked home Hermie said, "I miss Paul more today than in all the time he's been gone. I needed to hear his music."

No words of comfort relieved his pain. And no one knew what to offer to make him better. Helga watched her son hobble from room to room and then roam the yard and finally heave his exhausted body up and down the beachfront like a wild animal searching endlessly, unable to fathom the loss of its mate.

* * *

After the funeral, Hermie felt like a caged animal flailing against invisible restraints. One night as he paced the empty aisles of the store, he heard his own voice snarling at the forces he couldn't conquer. "I'm better than this. I don't intend to continue being a helpless victim of this agony. I'm not a weakling who needs to nurse a whiskey bottle."

The words rang loud, echoing off the pressed tin ceiling of the store and jolting his body like a flash of lightning. He'd always felt superior to his papa and to Paul, drunks too weak to live in the world with ordinary men.

He crumpled to the floor, his hands covering the tears that ran unchecked down his face and soaked his shirt. Like a searing vision, the truth opened a great hole in his middle. How could he possibly know what burden weighed down his papa and his brother?

That night he knew it was time for him to see Paul. He locked the door of his store as the wind picked up and a cold front brought pounding winter rain. The increasing chill soaking through his jacket dampened some of the fire burning within him. When he dried himself and crawled beneath the heavy quilts where Mary had slept so recently, he drifted to sleep easily for the first time since her death.

* * *

The moist, tropical breeze caressed his body as the ship moved into the mouth of the Rio Grande and made its way along the shallow, twisting river between overhanging sabal palms. The river made another wide bend and then opened to a view of the old Casamata Fort and the docks at Matamoros teeming with wagons, cattle, and big-wheeled Mexican carts.

Hermie walked into town along the street lined with lush tropical foliage. Around him, the clatter of so many languages blended together in lively confusion. Many of the buildings looked like they belonged in New Orleans—tall open doorways and elegant wrought-iron balconies. The shops, filled with goods from all over Europe and the coastal cities of the United States, offered a cosmopolitan mix of goods to all of northern Mexico.

The hotel commanded a full block and boasted the same high, arched doorways. As he stepped into the cool semidarkness of the sprawling lobby, the sweet strains of Paul's violin washed over him, almost buckling his one good knee.

He sat at a table at the rear of the large room and watched the late Sunday afternoon crowd sitting in quiet appreciation of Schubert, Brahms, Bach, Beethoven, and Mexican and French songs Hermie did not recognize. It wasn't a crowd like those at the Casimir House who came for lively entertainment; these people were attending a concert.

Had he never listened to Paul's mastery of the violin? Or had Paul over the years developed into a musician of the first order? It was the sweet sound of the familiar music—violin strains Papa had played and Paul had recaptured that Hermie had longed to hear at Mary and the baby's funeral—the connection with Papa and Paul that he had ignored for so long.

When the performance ended to loud applause, Paul moved easily among the tables, speaking to people, friends who admired him. Then his eye caught Hermie, who stood smiling as Paul approached.

"Hermie?" Paul stopped for only a second and then bolted into Hermie's outstretched arms.

"This is my brother," Paul shouted, turning to the upturned faces beaming like family at the musician they loved.

Applause thundered as Paul lifted Hermie's arm in a tribute of triumph.

The two brothers clung to each other, waiting for the tumult to end. "Excuse me for the night. I've got to be with my brother." Paul laid his hand firmly on Hermie's shoulder as they moved together out of the room.

"I thought you were Papa. As I watched you play, I felt like Papa'd returned."

Paul looked sideways at Hermie as they walked across the lobby. "Was it good? To see Papa again?"

Hermie bowed his head and hobbled beside his brother. "I don't know. I've shoved the feelings away for so long I don't know what's there."

"I have a room at the back. You can stay with me."

"Is it okay?"

"That's Hermie—always wanting to follow the rules. It's my room, Hermie. I give you permission to stay with me."

Hermie nodded, embarrassed by his rigidity.

The room obviously was one the hotel couldn't rent. It provided one window high above the back alley and walls of sweating brick. The bed, piled with twisted quilts, looked barely wide enough for one person.

"Even though we were small, our bed at home was no larger than this." Paul collapsed on the thin mattress and motioned for Hermie to take the only chair next to the tiny table that held a pitcher and bowl filled with greasy water.

Paul reached for a bottle of whiskey, filled the glass partway, and handed it to Hermie. "Do you drink?"

"Sometimes." Hermie took the glass and swallowed the burning liquid. "I try to leave it alone."

"I don't." Paul refilled the glass and threw the contents into his mouth. "So what happened to your leg?"

"I made it to the last battle of the war."

"Palmito Hill? You were down here?"

Hermie nodded. "With Rip Ford at Fort Brown."

"I never knew you were over there. Those guys came in here all the time. Did you come with them?"

Hermie shook his head. He refilled the glass and drank the contents.

"Why've you come now? All this way?"

Hermie reached across the space, almost touched Paul's arm before he drew back and rubbed his fingers roughly through his hair. "I'm not exactly sure. I know I needed to come. I needed to tell you to your face." Hermie dropped his hands and in one motion reached for Paul's hand that clutched his drink. "I finally realized you and Papa endured pain I never understood."

"I killed a man—drove a knife into his gut until he buckled to his knees. Then I became the town coward for not wanting to go to war and kill more men. What pain did Papa have?"

"Failure. He was a peasant to Grossvater and Grossmutter. Sometimes, when he was drunk, Mama dismissed him like a peasant. He found acceptance in the faces of strangers who laughed at his jokes and loved his music."

Paul tossed down another glass. The muscles of his face sagged. "And that's what you see here? Strangers who make me feel successful?"

"No. They love you. Paul, I knew you were loved when I was at Fort Brown. The men who came to hear you talked about your beautiful music. It was my view of success keeping me away."

Paul brushed at the air as if dismissing an intruder. "Tell me about Mama. Sylus said she's well."

"She sent her love. She grieves over sending you away."

Paul shook his head. "She didn't send me. I had to leave. Casimir House guests kept asking what unit I was with, when I'd be going out to the island. When the soldiers came in they started out kidding me about my easy job. As they drank more, their comments became threatening."

"So many families came apart by men fighting on both sides. Our family started coming apart before the war, even before Papa drowned in the Weser."

Both men felt the warmth of the whiskey and passed out on the narrow bed without awareness of its confinement.

Hermie stayed for almost a week. Paul slept every day until late afternoon when a beautiful Mexican woman who introduced herself as Maria knocked softly on his door carrying a fresh basin of water and towels. After Paul washed and dressed in the clean clothing Maria laid out on his bed, she returned with mounds of steaming eggs and coffee.

She always nodded at Hermie and then bowed slightly as she slipped out the door.

The first time she appeared Paul nodded toward the door after she left. "She's the best thing that's happened to me down here. I guess you could say we're like a married couple who don't live together." Paul shrugged as if helpless for a better explanation. "Actually, she does all the giving. I just take. And play music." With that, Paul turned to the tiny mirror hanging on the inside of the door, tied his tie, and carefully combed his hair.

Hermie spent the days roaming the dusty streets and visiting with Benjamin and Sylus, who assured him Paul enjoyed a community of friends who cared for him. And, of course, they agreed Maria saw to his personal needs.

Each evening Hermie joined the adoring audience as the poignant music flowing from Paul's bow seemed to nurture the crowd as they listened, tapped to the rhythm, and sometimes broke into full-throated song. Each night he fell asleep in an alcohol-induced fog.

Paul rose on the last morning and walked to the dock with Hermie, who still suffered from the headache their last night had produced.

"Tell Mama I'm okay. I have a good life here. Like Papa, all I need is an audience that appreciates me and a bottle of whiskey for my bed partner."

Hermie allowed his crutch to drop as he clutched his brother in what felt like their last embrace.

* * *

By the time the ship reached Indianola, Hermie's restless spirit had calmed into a quiet grief. As soon as he stepped on the front porch, Helga rushed out the door, eager to hear his news. He dropped his crutch and let his valise fall from his back as they sat together on the steps. Squeezing Helga's cold hand, a faint smile showed beneath his three-day beard. "Mama, we've been wrong about Paul. He may not be able to stop drinking, but his spirit touches every person who hears him play. I watched people set aside their problems as they listened to the sweet sound of Paul's violin. He's a master at finding the place where his audience experiences pure joy."

* * *

Eagle returned at the end of April at a perfect time for Eli to enjoy a new line of taunts. Before Eagle got both legs onto the bench for supper, Eli hurried to his chair, saying, "Did you hear that Charles Morgan's in town again? His outfit's laid a new rail line clear out to the end of his dock."

"Sure did." Eagle grinned. "Coming through Clark Station yesterday, we stood around with the crowd to watch the San Antonio & Mexican Gulf lay the last track to complete its connection with Lavaca."

"Doesn't that worry you—all these railroads coming in? Indianola's laying a mile of track every day. Won't be long until we connect with the San Antonio. If Morgan gets control of both railroads, you'll be left high and dry." Eli looked around the table, nodding gravely at anyone who made eye contact.

Eagle laughed and dived into his baked hen. "If the freight business ever dries up, I'll stay around here and help Helga raise these fat chickens." His hand stroked her back. "Right now I'm plenty busy. San Antonio's given me the contract to move an iron bridge up there.

"A bridge?" The question came as a chorus from around the table.

"Yeah. We've brought oversized wagons down here to carry it back to San Antonio in pieces. It'll be here any day."

"Why'd they want an iron bridge?" Eli's excitement seemed to grow with every little detail.

"Heavy rains swept away an old wooden bridge on Houston Street. I guess they want one that'll last. It's their first iron bridge."

The bridge arrived in pieces up to forty feet long. The entire town gathered to watch the tremendous effort required to hoist the heavy iron pieces onto fourteen mule-drawn wagons.

The night before Eagle left for San Antonio, he could barely contain his glee as he told Helga about Eli Cox. "Hel, he strutted up and down the dock telling everyone who'd listen and plenty who didn't care to listen that he lived at the Stein House, that he had known me for years. It was the funniest sight to see a grown man so anxious to show off for the crowd."

* * *

C. A. Ogsbury, editor of the Indianola *Bulletin*, started a campaign to get the downtown streets graded and filled in where the constant ebb and flow of the tides left deep puddles. Hermie brought home one of Ogsbury's editorials. "He's right. Improving our streets will raise property values."

"But what's it going to cost? We're already gouged by Governor Davis's taxes. If we get rid of Davis and his Reconstruction government we might have a little left to take care of local needs." Eli quickly squelched further talk of street improvement but not before the captain said, "If Democrats and moderate Republicans start working together, we'll get rid of Davis."

"I'll believe it when I see it," Eli snorted.

No one picked up on the captain's comment. Instead, the conversation veered off toward the anger festering over still being governed by officials who had been placed in office by the government and the continued presence of the army patrolling the streets.

* * *

A storm in June flooded the downtown around Powder Horn Bayou but caused only minor wind damage. Galveston wasn't so fortunate. When the captain returned a few days after the storm he brought news of serious damage to Galveston's shipping. "We were mighty lucky our little ship rode it out. It was a fierce blow."

Eli beamed and reared back in his chair at the table. "That's more proof that Indianola's not in as much danger from low sea level as Ogsbury claims in those editorials. He's not doing any good for Indianola to keep ranting about the streets flooding."

The captain shook his head and sighed wearily. "Ogsbury's not trying to chase away business, Eli. We need to raise the level of the streets. There's no reason to have water standing in pools every time the tide comes in."

* * *

In late summer Eagle came home with news of voter registration meetings planned all over the state. "It looks like the Confederates and Unionists are finally working together. We've got to forget the war, combine forces to get rid of Davis's carpetbagger government."

"Davis's state police are so out of hand that people in Galveston have lost all respect for the law," Captain Whipple said.

"It's like that everywhere I've been," Eagle said. "In Gonzales a kid named John Wesley Hardin who everyone knows is a killer just shot two black state police. And the town's standing behind Hardin. They're claiming Hardin can't get a fair trial in Davis's Reconstruction courts."

Eli interrupted, "The state tax rate in 1860 was twelve-and-a-half cents on a hundred dollars. Today it's two twenty-five on a hundred dollars. And the state's going broke."

"Plenty of people are mad," Eagle said. "Davis declared martial law in Huntsville and Walker County, places where he thinks people are protesting too loud."

"Do you think he'll put us under martial law?" Hermie asked. "We've gotten along with the military. Davis can't get by with sending state police in here."

"No, no." Eagle shook his head. "Indianola's quiet compared with most of the state. I doubt Davis is paying Indianola much attention."

"You're right," Captain Whipple said. "We're having a voter registration drive at Casimir Hall in September. If we can get people to register to vote, to believe we can beat Davis, we'll avoid some of the upheavals going on around the state."

* * *

Helga was astounded at the number of people crowded into Casimir Hall, the largest building in town. It opened for public concerts and for the traveling theatrical companies that came in on ships and performed a few nights before heading west. She always felt awed by the elegance of the place—chandeliers and wall fixtures lit the room with artificial gas, and large panels edged with gilt molding highlighted the gleaming white walls. White columns and a massive arch framed the stage on which the Indianola City Brass Band played rousing music and speakers stirred passions Helga hadn't seen since the secessionist mass meeting back in 1860. The announcement that Davis had tried to stop a similar meeting earlier in the month in Austin added energy to the voter registration drive and determination to vote on October 3 regardless of how many state police descended on the polling places.

* * *

Election talk came to a halt at the end of September with the arrival of another storm that caused the tide to rise at an alarming rate. When

Hermie, Eli, and Captain Whipple did not come in for lunch, Helga and Emma helped Joseph load food onto one of Hermie's carts and pull it to town through the ankle-deep, fishy-smelling water that high tide left behind. Hermie and his crew of freedmen were shoveling sand out the double front doors of his store. "This is the worst we've ever seen," Hermie said as he and his crew wolfed down slices of ham stuffed between biscuits.

They found the same destruction at Eli's warehouse, where he and his employees were digging through crates of fresh fruit, stacks of farm implements, and pieces of furniture that had been waiting for freight wagons for delivery to inland communities. Eli and his men dived eagerly into the food. "Did you hear the railroad's shut down? The tracks are washed out." Eli looked sheepishly at Helga. "Ogsbury's got it right. We've got to build these streets higher. They're too vulnerable to all this water."

As they pulled the cart of food toward Captain Whipple's office, Joseph kept chuckling. "I never thought I'd hear Mister Eli say something needed doing about all this regular flooding. It's a new day, ain't it?"

Helga and Emma burst into gales of laughter. "You're right, Joseph," Helga giggled. "I wish Eagle were here to witness it."

The sight of Captain Whipple's office still under water sobered them. "Do you mind, missy, if I stays here and help the captain? He's got a mighty load, and nobody works for him." Joseph spoke as he grabbed a shovel and began scooping the smelly water alongside the captain, who made no effort to stop for lunch.

"Stay as long as he needs you, Joseph." Helga and Emma unloaded the last of the lunch and pulled the cart back toward Dr. Stein's office. Amelia and the doctor were washing the front wall and porch.

"We're higher than the folks near the bayou. We've already gotten the front rooms cleaned up." Amelia's dress was soaked through with sweat, her face red from the hours of sweeping in the rising heat and humidity.

"Come, we'll get you some lunch. Heat some water for you to clean up. Give this place a little time to dry out," Helga said to the exhausted pair.

"Amelia needs to go. I've got patients who'll be coming in."

"I'll stay here to feed the doctor." Amelia swept vigorously at water pooling on the planks of the front walk.

"Then we'll bring the food to you."

* * *

One morning in mid-October soon after the entire household finished breakfast and headed to their jobs, Amelia arrived waving a copy of the *Bulletin*. "I told Dr. Stein I had to tell you the news. Every congressional seat in the state has gone to Democrats."

Helga grabbed Amelia and Emma in a fierce embrace. "I've been bursting with hope since the meeting at Casimir Hall. Even with Eagle bringing home stories of fraud charges in Austin against Davis's government, I've felt full of energy."

"It's Eagle coming home that's filling you with energy, even if he brings bad news." Emma's blue eyes pooled with tears. "I wish James would come home."

* * *

The Stein House thrived with a constant stream of guests coming to town on business connected with the surge in shipbuilding and home and commercial construction.

Each time Eagle came home, he insisted Helga go with him to Rundell & Nolda Confectioners for a dish of ice cream or an iced soda water. "Since I'm hauling their hard candy to San Antonio and Austin, we need to support their business."

Helga loved the outings. She liked walking beside Eagle, feeling the brush of his hand on her shoulder, the tingle of his fingers taking her arm as they approached a puddle of water. As they walked home with the moon rising high over the bay and the breeze softly touching her skin, she burned with anticipation of their time alone after the household grew quiet.

The greatest surprise came when Eagle pulled his wagon to the back fence in the alley. His eyes danced with delight as he pointed proudly to a new washing machine anchored between feed sacks in his wagon. "Hermie and Eli told me washing machines were coming in, so we ordered the first one for you. From now on you're not going to be stooping over that black pot in the yard."

Helga and Emma stood clasping each other in amazement as Eagle and Joseph, too impatient to wait for the other men to get home for supper, heaved the contraption off the wagon and got it set up on the back porch next to the cistern.

"That's some fine instrument, Mister Eagle," Joseph said as he wiped his sweaty face on his shirtsleeve.

Eagle wrapped one arm around Helga and the other around Emma. "It's about time these ladies had something to make their work easier."

"I can't wait for the girls to get home from school and see this thing," Emma whispered.

Helga leaned against Eagle's sweat-soaked body. "I've never seen a washing machine except in one of Hermie's catalogs. I wonder how it works?"

"It looks easy enough." Eagle lifted the lid, stared at the paddle inside the tub. "Put the clothes in the tub, pour in hot water and some lye soap, and turn this wheel." He cranked the wheel as they all bent over the wooden tub watching the paddle move easily in a circular motion.

"Let's try it first thing in the morning," Emma said as she turned her back on Eagle and rolled her eyes at Helga.

"I'll start right now with my shirts and pants," Eagle said as he rushed to the wagon and hurried back carrying a wad of dirty clothes.

In a flash Joseph returned from the kitchen carrying a kettle in each hand. "Look at that," Eagle crowed as he cranked the wheel and they watched the clothes swirl amid pieces of melting lye soap.

"It's working," Helga laughed as she reached for the wheel and began to crank.

The new machine occupied the suppertime conversation, and the next day the neighbors began coming to see the new invention at the Stein House. For two days, while Eagle kept an eye on the loading of his freight wagons he eagerly demonstrated the operation using clothing contributed by members of the household. Early on the third day, Helga stood on the front porch listening to the slow rumble of Eagle's line of wagons as they started on a trip to Fredericksburg. Turning away after the last wagon passed, she saw Emma standing in the doorway wiping tears on the tip of her apron.

"Do you ever feel like running out to the road and jumping in the wagon with him? You could leave Stein House. Forget all the backbreaking work and constant problems?"

Helga stared at Emma's tear-streaked face. "Leave Stein House? Spend days just riding?"

"Helga, you'd be with Eagle. Riding with Eagle every single day."

Helga shook her head. "After Max died, being able to run Stein

House gave my family a future. I can't imagine abandoning it." Helga turned and started hurrying down the hall.

"Helga, your children are grown. You could be with the man who makes you glow. It's so plain to see how happy you are when he comes home." Emma laid her hand gently on Helga's shoulder.

"And when he's gone, I stay so busy I don't think of him."

"Until you go to bed." Emma's smile made her look like a young girl.

Helga laughed. "Stop that talk, young lady. We've got sheets to wash in our fancy new machine."

Joseph had already placed the sheets from his and the captain's room into the tub and was busily pouring hot water from two kettles. "This is the big test, ain't it, missy? We're getting this job done mighty fast."

Immediately the wheel began to bind, and when they opened the lid, the sheets had twisted into snarly knots. Joseph tugged at the sheets until they began to rip. "Let's get the fire going under the pot," Helga said as Joseph pulled the split sheet from the tangled mass. "Eagle doesn't need to know this thing doesn't work on everything."

Joseph nodded. "I'm worn plum out turning that big wheel."

* * *

A few weeks later, Hermie came home for lunch with a big grin on his face. "Tante Amelia wants you to come this afternoon to see her surprise." Hermie kept laughing throughout lunch, obviously enjoying Helga's questions and eagerness to know Hermie's secret. As Helga approached Amelia's, she began running when she heard the strains of Schubert's "Der Lindenbaum."

Rushing up the stairs, she burst in the door squealing, "Amelia, you can still play." Her sister sat at a lovely Steinway piano, an image Helga had not dreamed of ever seeing again.

Amelia grinned mischievously. "Dr. Stein surprised me." She began playing "Der Wanderer," a song their papa had sung over and over when Amelia decided to leave for Texas.

Helga pulled a chair next to the elegant rosewood instrument and closed her eyes as Amelia's fingers moved effortlessly over the keys. "I can imagine being at home, Papa's pipe smoke filling the room, and Mama rushing from the kitchen to watch your beautiful hands."

Amelia looked at her chafed hands and work-toughened knuckles. "These are not the hands Mama always called musical instruments." She clasped her hands across her breast and smiled at Helga. "Life's been good with Dr. Stein. He's a kind man."

"I know. Mama and Papa would be pleased."

* * *

During the spring baseball season, Eagle returned bubbling with excitement. "Coming through Cuero, I heard the Crescents were in town for a baseball game. Several of the teamsters and I went to see them play. Will you go to a game with me next Sunday?"

"I don't know a thing about baseball."

Eagle roared with laughter. "I don't either, but I loved watching."

On his next trip home, he burst in the front door and pulled Helga into his arms, swinging her in a circle. "I just heard there's a dance at the new German Casino. How about us going? The brass band's playing. I know you can dance. You're a German."

Helga laughed as she clung fiercely to his powerful shoulders. "That I can do. I can dance." And dance they did as the music filled the casino and enlivened the spirits of a crowd celebrating their new prosperity.

* * *

In early October the first cold front had not arrived, and Helga spent the hot Sunday afternoon weeding the garden until she heard Eagle calling her name as he pulled his team up to the front gate. She rushed around the house, trying to push the sweaty hair back from her face as she met Eagle coming toward her. He grabbed her into a fierce hug and then pulled her back as his hand caressed her cheek. "You're so hot. What've you been doing?"

"The greens are thriving in the garden. I was doing some weeding."

"Where's Joseph?"

"He's still at church. They hold services all day on Sundays. It's usually after dark before he comes in." She swung onto his arm as they walked back toward the wagon.

"He ought to be here doing that. You shouldn't have to spend Sunday afternoon working so hard."

Helga stopped and stared at Eagle's angry expression. "You didn't know I work hard all the time? Are you gone so much that you're not aware of my work?"

Eagle's face softened. "Hel, I know you work hard. But it's Joseph's place to relieve you of that heavy stuff."

"Joseph's place? You're never here. Never around when there are big problems, and you dare to say that our hired black man is not taking care of his duties?" Helga's voice rosc, and she pulled her arm away from Eagle's touch.

Eagle's face twisted like she'd slapped him. He stared at her, his mouth forming a silent O. He slowly shook his head, and his fingers touched her trembling chin. "I'm so sorry, my love." He turned and walked toward his waiting team. As he took the reins he looked back at Helga. "Will you ride with me to Ole Man Fisher's while I put up my mules?"

Helga rushed into his arms and squeezed him around the waist with all her strength. "Forgive me, Eagle. I don't know what came over me."

He lifted her up to the seat and gentled the mules as he went around to the other side to climb up beside her. He kissed the tear coursing down her cheek. "I don't know what came over me either. I do know I hold a mighty love for you."

* * *

That evening as Helga and Eagle sat on the back porch watching the giant harvest moon light the yard in a warm glow, Joseph hurried through the back fence and headed toward the garden. When he saw them he called out, "I got me a plan."

He knelt at the edge of the garden and began digging into the loose soil with his hands. "I been helping a little to take care of the old folks and the orphans. We're getting incorporated. Official. We started the Indianola Colored Benevolent Society. I been hoarding this money you pay me. Now I got something important to do with it." He carefully wiped the soil from his heavy jar of money.

"That's the best news I've heard, Joseph." Helga leaned her head on Eagle's shoulder.

He murmured into her hair, "I should be ashamed of myself for getting mad at that fellow."

* * *

A few days before Christmas, Eagle proudly presented Helga with an enormous package wrapped in white paper and tied with a huge red bow. "I bought this at Mrs. LeGros's new ladies' shop right here in Indianola." As Helga eagerly unwrapped an elegant white satin gown with a wide lace collar, Eagle couldn't contain himself. "Mrs. LeGros showed me a picture of Jenny Lind wearing a dress just like this one. I told her your body didn't need a corset."

"It's so fine." Helga breathed in the softness of the fabric. "Where'll I ever wear it?"

"When I got to the dock this afternoon, the *Thomas P. Ball* had just come in on her maiden voyage from New York." Eagle swelled out his chest and executed an elegant bow. "We're invited to come aboard. There'll be an orchestra, and Barratte's Restaurant is catering a huge buffet." He winked mischievously. "And there'll be wine and plenty of speeches."

Emma and the girls slipped shyly into the hall and eagerly watched as Helga spread out the beautiful dress and delicate slippers. "The girls and I can help Joseph get supper," said Emma as she stroked the gown. "You must go and remember everything so you can tell us all about it."

The *Thomas P. Ball* was finely appointed for the wealthiest traveler. Barratte's, which advertised itself as a "Parisian and New York experience," kept its reputation as the fanciest restaurant in town.

Walking home that evening with her hair fashionably tucked into a soft bun and her dress swirling all about her, Helga felt elegant for the first time in her life. Eagle seemed equally proud in his new black suit and handsome boots. She could not remember ever feeling so thoroughly loved and admired.

"When you touch my arm, my whole body tingles," she whispered.

"Then I won't let go for a minute."

1872–1873

When Gretchen wrote early in the year that they were expecting their third child in November, Helga tried to hide her concern. She argued with herself that the loss of Mary and the baby had nothing to do with Gretchen. After all, Gretchen was strong, had shown with the birth of the first two that she was like Helga, a woman blessed with easy child deliveries. When the telegraph message finally arrived at the end of November saying that mother and baby Elizabeth were both well, Helga couldn't hide her sudden relief.

Amelia brought the message and stood in utter shock as Helga crumpled to the bench in the hall in a rush of tears. Emma, who had greeted the news with a loud squeal, knelt beside Helga. "I've been afraid you were worrying all this time." She looked up at Amelia. "She's almost worn the mail out writing to Gretchen to check on how she's doing."

* * *

For over a year each time Eagle came home the supper-table conversation revolved around how far the railroad had progressed. In May, Eagle's news that the railroad had finally covered the sixty-five miles to Cuero was soon dampened by newspaper accounts of a worldwide financial panic and widespread bank and business failures.

The captain, Eli, and Hermie all brought newspapers to supper with articles declaring that there was no available money to continue constructing the railroad on to San Antonio.

"How's all this going to affect you?" Eli looked solemnly at Eagle. "Cattlemen are loading their beef on rail cars in Cuero. When they get here, the train pushes the cars onto the railroad pier. Then cowboys herd the animals through chutes right onto waiting ships. It won't be long until all the freight business will be coming in that way."

Eagle nodded. "So far more freight needs hauling than we can handle. Downtown's about as congested as it's always been. I don't think you need to worry, Eli, about all the business skipping your warehouses and going directly from the ships to the train." Eagle could barely suppress a grin as he slyly turned the taunting back on Eli. "My wagons will be using your warehouses for a long time, and I bet other freighters will be doing the same. We can move our wagons onto the piers and load the cargoes directly into the ships, but we still need your warehouses to store and sell freight."

* * *

James Carter appeared at the front door wearing a handsome black suit and a string tie at the neck of his white shirt. Emma and the girls fell into his arms as he tried to tell Helga of his fine herd of longhorns assembled on their ranch on Mustang Island. "I left a crew of the cowhands rebuilding our house," he said as he wrapped both arms around Emma and the girls, who didn't seem to hear a word he said as they clamored with questions about when they could go home.

He paid Helga generously for his family's extended stay, and before Emma and the girls climbed into their handsome new wagon, they all three clutched her in a fierce embrace.

"I'll miss you every day," Emma whispered. "You have been like a sister to me and a mother to my children."

Helga pressed her cheek against the face of the beaming young woman. "You have your man again. That's all that matters."

"Don't forget your lessons," Helga said to the girls. "Be sure to write Gretchen and tell her all about your new house."

As Helga watched them drive toward the docks to be loaded on a waiting schooner, she tried to suppress the profound sense of loss flooding over her.

* * *

For the remainder of the year Helga shoved the sadness, the sense of loss, away by staying busy with the steady stream of guests. Prosperity became the driving force that kept everyone moving, and the conversation at supper often revolved around how fortunate they were not to be having the outlaw problems that plagued the rest of the state.

One night all the men returned from town with differing versions of how Mayor John Barlow and four aldermen had handled a bunch of rowdies who had caused trouble in one of the downtown saloons.

"I heard that the mayor and aldermen armed themselves with shotguns and arrested the men," Hermie said.

"Then the Mayor marched them to city hall, where he appointed himself ex-officio judge of the police court," Eli added. "He confiscated their guns and fined them for disturbing the peace."

"Can he legally do that?" Hermie asked the captain.

The captain smiled broadly. "It looks like he did it. And from what I've heard the men got out of town a lot faster than they came in."

"So long as everybody stays happy with the mayor's actions we'll avoid a feud like the one going on around Cuero," Eagle said.

"I saw an article in the paper saying it all started after the war when Charles Taylor joined a bunch who started stealing horses," Hermie said. "They arrested Taylor in Bastrop, and on the way back to Cuero a deputy named Bill Sutton shot Taylor in the back when he tried to escape. That started the whole thing."

Eli chimed in. "They're calling it the Sutton-Taylor feud, and the killings still haven't stopped."

"In Cuero," Eagle said, "folks claim the Taylor family creed is 'Who sheds a Taylor's blood, by a Taylor's hand must fall.'"

"That's the silliest thing I've heard," Helga said. "Why would a family want to live like that?"

"It beats me," Eagle said. "It seems to be part of the times we're living in."

"At least we don't have foolishness like that around here," Helga said.

* * *

The following March, Bill Sutton brought the feud to Indianola. In midafternoon Amelia rushed in the front door still wearing her apron. "Did you hear two men were murdered, shot dead right before the eyes of one man's wife who is expecting their first child?"

Amelia stayed and helped Helga and Joseph get supper prepared. "I know the men will come in tonight with all the details. Dr. Stein never pays any attention to what's going on, and if he hears anything, he won't talk about it."

The guest rooms were all filled, and the rush for supper turned into a scramble for who could provide the most details of the killing. Eli walked in the door announcing that one of the dead men was Bill Sutton. "He's at the center of that feud."

"I can tell you for sure that he's the fellow who did the first killing," Gerald Hastings said. "I've been loading my cattle at the Cuero railhead since it opened, and that's the God's truth. He started the whole thing."

"It was two Taylor boys, Bill and Jim, who shot Sutton and the other man," Eli said. "I hear they followed them as they came in here on the train."

Captain Whipple said, "I was in the sheriff's office when they brought Sutton's wife in to protect her in case someone might be lurking around wanting to kill her too. She was hysterical but finally calmed down enough to tell them that when Sutton found out they were having a baby he decided to quit the whole fight and go to New Orleans to start a new life. The other man had decided to leave the state with them."

"They almost made it. They were going up the gangplank to board the Morgan steamer *Clinton,*" Hermie added.

"Last I heard almost three hundred men have died in that feud. It's been crazy," Gerald Hastings said.

* * *

The US Signal Service named Indianola and Galveston as Texas's two coastal weather observation and reporting stations. The station's chief signal officer, Sergeant C. A. Smith, moved into the first-floor front room that Emma and the girls had vacated.

Eli Cox pumped Sergeant Smith's hand as all the guests listened eagerly to his introduction of the interesting new boarder. "Tell us how all this equipment works. I hear you have to report to your Washington headquarters every day."

When Sergeant Smith smiled, which he did almost constantly, his rosy cheeks rounded so high they almost closed his deep blue eyes. "Call me Charlie, if you don't mind. Yes, I'll telegraph my daily observations of atmospheric conditions, even water temperature, to headquarters. All the stations are connected. The changes we observe along the coast affect shipping, commerce, and agriculture." His face rounded into a pink ball. "In the last ten years this new scientific method of weather observation has spread all over the United States. We'll soon have telegraph lines to all the military posts out west." Charlie seemed as impressed with his job as were the guests around the table.

"Can we visit and see all the instruments for ourselves?" Hermie became an immediate admirer.

"I'll enjoy showing you around."

Helga couldn't help smiling at seeing everyone excited about the reporting station instead of fretting about competition from the Galveston, Houston, & San Antonio Railroad, which had reached the new town of Luling the first of the year. Every businessman and ship owner had been eager to get the Indianola Railroad completed to San Antonio and Austin before the Houston line undercut their business. It had become painfully clear that their railroad had lost the race.

Since flour was available again, Helga enjoyed serving biscuits instead of the cornbread they had eaten during the war. Charlie Smith seemed to love the biscuits and white gravy Joseph had taught Helga to make. When supper ended, Charlie leaned back on his bench and rubbed his round belly with obvious satisfaction.

"Miss Helga, this is the finest meal I've eaten in many a day. I thank you for it and for allowing me to join your household."

Chapter 25

1875

DESPITE SUMMER HEAT SCORCHING THE city, turning the streets into billowing dust bowls and the colorful buildings a dull gray, mid-September brought excited visitors from all the surrounding counties to witness the trial of Bill Taylor, who had killed William Sutton and his friend Gabriel Slaughter the previous year.

Eagle had left in late August with a huge load of lumber for Fredericksburg. "I'm going to try to get back in time for the trial, but I'm not sure I can make it."

Helga stayed so busy getting ready for the onslaught of guests who would be coming for the trial that she had no time to miss him during the long days, and she was so tired by night that she barely crawled into bed before she fell into exhausted sleep.

So many people needed a place to stay that guests crowded into the Stein House, and strangers willingly shared the upstairs rooms that held several beds. Helga sent word for Amelia to come help.

Tuesday morning Charlie Smith didn't linger over his breakfast as usual; instead he gobbled it down quickly and asked Helga to pack a lunch for him to take to the signal station. "I don't like the looks of the weather. I may not get back for a while."

All day the wind increased in gusts. Heavy clouds hung low over the bay and moved over the city, opening for brief moments to reveal the sun and then shutting again like an ominous vise. Helga and Amelia kept the oven hot baking bread and stacking it in the pie safe. "If this storm keeps up, we'll have to pack lunches tomorrow for everyone spending the day at the trial. We can't expect them to come back here in pouring rain." Helga fried chickens as quickly as Joseph could pluck them.

When the trial ended for the day, the guests returned for supper in the gathering chill of early darkness. The wind blew with a steady force, sending Joseph scurrying to close the storm shutters and move all the loose garden implements and the washing machine into the washroom. As a precaution in case salt water flooded into the cistern, they set out buckets and tubs along the edge of the back porch to catch rainwater.

Amelia sent word for Dr. Stein to join her at the Stein House for supper, but he didn't come. "He has two babies due. Ironically, this kind of weather always gets him out for deliveries." She laughed and continued flouring pieces of chicken for the frying pan.

After supper, Amelia and Joseph helped carry quilts to all the rooms as the guests huddled in the parlor around the fireplace trying to ward off the sudden chill settling over all the rooms.

When Charlie Smith did not return that night, Helga drew the captain aside. "Charlie must be worried about this storm."

"I'm afraid so," the captain said. "It would have let up by now if it were just an early norther."

In the morning, rainsqualls moved in off and on, causing the water level to rise in the bay. A few men, the most determined of the guests, wrapped themselves in their light coats and hurried to the courthouse, determined not to miss a minute of the trial.

Amelia and Helga continued preparing food. "If this storm lets up and doesn't do any major damage, all our cooking will feel like old times when we cooked day and night to get ready for a holiday." Amelia hugged Helga. "I love being here with you. Let's pretend we're preparing for a party instead of worrying about a storm."

Tears welled before Helga caught herself. "If it's a party, way too many are missing."

Amelia kept her arms around Helga. "Try to imagine they're all still here."

Helga pulled away. "I can't. You've always been the one who believed in fairy tales. I wish I could."

The wind steadily increased to gale force, and the incoming tide drove the level of the bay ever higher. Waves, frosted white on top, pounded the shore, causing the visitors gathered on the front porch and on neighboring porches to watch in amazement as the water surged beyond the beach and onto the road.

In midafternoon, as Captain Whipple and Helga stood on the front porch with the guests chatting excitedly about waves lapping beyond the shore, Francis Stabler slogged up the road pulling a cart loaded with several cases of his canned beef. They helped him drag his load to the back door. "I'm the only one concerned about this weather. I shut down the packing plant. The cattle will have to wait in the holding pens until this thing passes. When I told my workers to go secure their homes, they thought I was crazy."

"You're not crazy," Captain Whipple said. "This is no ordinary storm."

Suppertime was festive, with the guests laughing about the added attraction of a good storm story to tell those back home who couldn't come for the famous trial.

Eli Cox was in his glory. A house full of strangers hung eagerly on his every word. "You'd better enjoy the cool temperature this evening. By morning the sun will bear down and send a new army of mosquitoes to feast on us. Let's hope the heat doesn't turn the courthouse into a sweatbox."

Thursday morning did not bring a beautiful dawn. The water continued to rise overnight, and the wind drove the bay in massive waves over the road. Still, some of the men insisted on braving the waves lashing at the front fence. They waded off toward the courthouse, ignoring the current tearing at the foundations of neighboring houses that sat near street level.

Eli and the captain helped Joseph bring in all the meat from the smokehouse. Then they joined Hermie nervously pacing the hall, speculating about how high the water might be downtown, trying to estimate how soon the vicious weather would blow over.

Joseph came into the kitchen wearing his winter coat. "Missy, I'm mighty worried about them Negroes living in those little shacks along the bayous back of town. Mr. Hermie says I can take his and Mr. Jackson's boat in case I need to get them out of high water."

"This is the highest I've ever seen the water."

"I know, missy. That's why I'm scared for them folks."

"Bring them here if you can. We'll make room in the halls."

Joseph smiled broadly, exposing yellowed teeth. "Thank you, missy."

Captain Whipple gave Joseph his rain slicker. The men stood with Helga and Amelia on the back porch watching the withered old man half carrying, half dragging the boat as he splashed through ankle-deep water covering the alley.

"I can't let him go alone." Captain Whipple stepped off the porch.

"Take my rain slicker." Hermie struggled to get out of his coat, and the captain, patting Hermie's shoulder, accepted the offer.

Helga clutched Hermie's arm, trying to quiet her mounting worry as they watched the two men disappear into the sheets of rain.

By lunchtime nearby houses sitting low to the ground had begun ripping apart, planks and timbers moving like battering rams into neighboring houses. Waves pounded the front steps of the Stein House, climbing relentlessly higher. The house shuddered like a giant suffering from a terrible chill.

Wives of the men who had gone to the courthouse gathered in Charlie Smith's front room and strained to see through the cracks in the tightly closed shutters.

Neighbors came down the alley in fours and fives carrying children and a few valuables. Most had lashed themselves together with ropes to keep from being swept away. The water in the alley reached their waists. As they struggled up the back steps, they kept saying how grateful they were for the Stein House, because they had watched it being built with the steel rods driven into the ground to add stability.

The frantic wives, eager for something to distract them from their worry, wrapped the newcomers in quilts and served them hot tea.

Helga and Amelia kept watching the alley for Dr. Stein and Joseph and the captain, but all they could see between the torrents of rain was water surging into what looked like a sprawling new bay spreading across the prairie behind the house.

"They'll never get back in this." Amelia hugged her arms around her waist and stared into the sheets of rain pounding the backyard.

Hermie's voice sounded urgent. "Water is seeping under the front door."

Helga and Amelia stepped in the back door as Hermie's voice rose loudly over noise of the pounding rain, "Everyone needs to move upstairs. The water's rising."

In silence, without being given instructions, everyone, including the children, carried food and buckets of water up the back stairs. The rain sprayed in sheets under the second-floor porch, tearing at their clothing.

The few men who were able hauled furniture up the stairs and stacked it in the hall. When Otto Schnaubert started gently removing his sketches from their displays in the downstairs rooms, the guests almost reverently accepted a frame in each arm and carried them to Otto's bedroom on the second floor.

Hermie hobbled in from the washroom, an axe tucked awkwardly under his arm. "The waves are pushing at the floor. We've got to relieve the pressure."

"That's something I can do." A neighbor who had refused to accept a blanket and a cup of tea because he had not been able to bring food for his family reached for the axe and began chopping holes down the center of the hall. Seawater spewed several inches high through the openings. He continued driving the axe into the floors in all the downstairs rooms. The water came up in dancing fountains, immediately rising over the tops of their shoes.

"Let's get upstairs." Hermie's voice sounded strong, full of authority.

The out-of-town guests made room for the neighbors to sit with them on their beds. Some of the neighbors settled in the captain and Joseph's room, and Otto Schnaubert welcomed others into his room. No one complained as they wrapped themselves in quilts in the dim light filtering through the shutters. Although the children's eyes were wide with fear, they stayed strangely quiet, huddled against their parents, listening to the raging wind beat against the house.

Several wives cried silently. No one mentioned that the great adventure had turned into a horrifying experience.

Eli Cox moved between the rooms, reassuring the cold and terrified people that by morning it would be over. "The courthouse is strong. I'm sure all your men are huddled on the second floor worrying about you just as you're worrying about them." He finally gave up when it became clear he wasn't easing the concerns of anyone. They weren't listening to him; the steady roar of the wind held their full attention.

As night turned the rooms to complete darkness, Helga lit lamps in each room, and the women helped lay out cold biscuits, sausage, and greens from the garden. Francis Stabler opened cans of his beef.

They pulled the buckets off the back porch as they filled with rainwater and set them back out as they were emptied.

By midnight, the wind screamed, piercing the air like the shrieks of a torture victim. The house moved like a rocking chair, and water filling the first floor caused the few pieces of remaining furniture to knock against the walls like a monster trying to make its way to the cowering people above. Objects flew against the outside of the house, crashing into the shutters. Each blow made Helga jump as she feared a hurtling missile would pierce the wall.

"We need to get the buckets off the back porch." Hermie's voice rose over the storm's din. "After the eye passes, the wind will drive those buckets like cannon balls through the house." The men acted in unison, moving the last supply of water into the hall.

Suddenly the wind ceased, and the house stopped heaving. The only sound was the breathing of terrified people and the roar of the storm moving away. Then came Hermie's reassuring voice. "We're in the eye of the cyclone. The wind will return soon from the opposite direction."

The words had barely left his lips when the sound of water rushing seaward caused a gasp of horror and the house shuddered as the wind slammed violently against the back porch.

Few words were spoken for the remainder of the night. Children slept. A few people stretched out on the floor next to the already occupied beds or in the hall. Everyone remained perfectly still, listening to the howling wind and the rush of water hurtling seaward. By dawn Friday morning, the winds had settled to a stiff gale. Almost all the water had been sucked back into the bay. The husbands, who had weathered the storm on the second floor of the courthouse, burst through the front door and rushed through the mud-caked downstairs in a state of terror, expecting to find wives gone, swept away or drowned like so many of the bodies they had seen strewn along the road from downtown. To reach the Stein House, the men had waded through mud and had swum across two new bayous cut by the raging water.

When they saw their spouses were safe, they fell upon each other in delirious exuberance, crying and praising God.

Amelia and Helga kept scanning the road and the alley for Dr. Stein, Joseph, and the captain, who failed to return. The front stairs to the second floor were twisted and hanging loose. The smokehouse and privy were completely gone.

The women helped lay out the remaining vegetables and the meat and bread for breakfast on tables in the upstairs hallway while the men recounted the devastation. The business area was wiped clean of all buildings from Powderhorn Bayou to the railroad tracks. Bodies lay everywhere, many of them damaged beyond recognition by the debris that had slammed into buildings and into people. The wharves were ripped to splinters. Only a few downtown buildings had survived, and those were heavily damaged. Clothing, linens, furniture, and much of the merchandise in the buildings filled the streets in wet, twisted mounds.

One of the men took Helga aside. "Your garden has been stripped bare, and the tops of four large jars are sticking out of the soil. Would you like some of us to scoop up the mud on the first floor and cover those jars?"

Helga's breath escaped in a relieved sigh. "It's so kind of you to help."

"We're glad to. You've saved our wives. You're still caring for this mob."

"The mud's so salty you'll never grow anything in that garden, but it'll cover your jars for a while."

"You've never used the bank?" Amelia was incredulous when she saw what the men were doing.

"Let's see if the banks made it through this storm. Then I may reconsider."

Townspeople began walking past, headed toward Old Town—some were clutching children, others were crying, reciting almost to themselves the horror of their children and wives being washed from their grasp. Still others simply stared straight ahead, resolutely placing one foot in front of the other. No one remembered seeing Dr. Stein or the captain or even Joseph. A man who seemed to be pulling a tiny woman along by her hand kept calling out to no one in particular, "Don't try to take the train. The track's eaten away and ripped up. The railcars are flipped like toys."

As time passed with no word from Dr. Stein, Amelia became more and more anxious. She bolted suddenly toward the front door. "I'm sorry to leave you with all this mud and people, but I've got to find Dr. Stein. It's not like him to stay gone so long."

"I'll go with you." Hermie swung in behind his tante Amelia.

Everyone helped shovel mud out of the first floor, using the saltwater that filled the cistern to scrub the walls and floors. Then Helga realized people on the road were heading back into town, calling out to those they met, "We can't get away yet. The water's too deep. The road's washed away."

Charlie Smith appeared at the front door, his clothes soaked through with mud and his eyes framed in hollow, dark circles. As Helga led him up the back stairs to the room on the front of the house, he spoke in halting breaths, "The wharves are gone. Most of the businesses are gone. Dead bodies are everywhere. Whole families are wiped out. We thought the signal office was tearing apart. Water tore around the corners of the buildings like a raging river. A skiff floated by and we grabbed it." Without a word of resistance, he fell on a bed next to the open window and was asleep instantly.

Amelia and Hermie finally returned late in the afternoon, mud-soaked and wet from having crossed the storm-dug bayous on makeshift rafts. Amelia kept sweeping her fingers through matted, wet hair. "It's over. The town's gone. Dr. Stein's missing. People saw him at the hospital. Then he went to a home to treat someone hit by flying debris. No one saw him after that." Amelia looked at Helga with an expression of utter disbelief. "There's a raft of twisted lumber and boats and animals and humans spreading for miles back of town. It's a heap of stinking, rotting death."

Helga held her trembling sister until the setting sun brought complete darkness to the house.

As Helga opened more of the Stabler canned meat, Hermie followed her, his voice low. "Stabler's whole operation's gone. Cattle, fences, everything wiped clean. Both banks are heavily damaged, but they saved the safes and all the records by latching the safes to cotton bales. The town's a wasteland."

"What about Dr. Stein? Did you hear anything about Captain Whipple and Joseph?"

Hermie shook his head. "Dr. Stein and Tante Amelia's building's gone. And Joseph's African Methodist Church is destroyed. A man told me Joseph and the captain put some women and children in a boat and were pushing it out this way." His voice trailed off, and he turned abruptly and went out on the back porch.

Helga looked at her son and shook her head. "And what about your store?"

"Gone. Even the canned goods have washed away."

Despite all the help shoveling mud out of the first floor, scrubbing the mud off the walls and floors, and scouring rust already coating the iron cook stove, the smell of fish and wet wood made the downstairs intolerable. As everyone wearily climbed the stairs for supper, Hermie's voice rose for all to hear: "We need to conserve the food and especially the water. It'll be a day or so before relief comes." After sharing the meat and bread and taking tiny sips of water, every person voluntarily crowded together in an effort to spread the mosquito nets as far as they would extend.

Amelia and Helga slipped onto the front porch in search of a breeze to keep away the buzzing pests. Amelia leaned against Helga's shoulder. "I keep looking up the road expecting Dr. Stein and Captain Whipple and Joseph. Have them tell us how foolish we've been to think they were lost."

"I'm doing that too. I try to stop myself, but I forget and look again. And every time I do it, I think my heart will burst through my chest." Helga clutched Amelia's hand. "I'm also watching for Eagle. He'll come as soon as he can, but we need him right now."

Amelia nodded. "I feel lost. You're all I've got in this world." The two grieving sisters clung to each other and cried until sleep finally claimed them.

At dawn Helga set out loaves of bread and the last of the sausage, saving Stabler's canned meat for as long as possible. Her chest ached with a strange mixture of pride in the strength and leadership of her son and profound sadness as she watched Hermie hobble away with the men to continue burying the dead.

Helga and the women spent the day using the salty cistern water and lye soap to continue scrubbing away the rotting fish smell. They gathered pieces of twisted window frames and shutters scattered about the yard to build a fire in the big iron stove to dry out the lingering moisture. Occasionally the air echoed with gunshots, causing everyone to stop and listen.

When the men returned, they brushed aside questions about the gunshots and hurried to the washroom to scrub as best they could the smell of death that penetrated their clothing.

Again they gathered upstairs for supper, which consisted of the last of the bread and Stabler's canned meat. When the upstairs grew quiet as they huddled under mosquito nets, Helga heard mummers among some of the couples about looting. Motioning Hermie to follow her to the back porch, she whispered, "Looting? What are they talking about?"

"We've found several looters. They're being shot on the spot." Hermie reached for Helga's shoulder to steady her. "Mama, we've got to stop the looting. No one will be safe if we allow a handful of men to rob our businesses and mutilate the dead for their valuables."

"The dead?" Helga covered her mouth to stifle her cry.

Hermie kissed Helga's forehead. "Some things are too horrible to think about. If you can't control it, Mama, you're foolish to let it torment you." He moved back toward the doorway into the upstairs hall. "Let's not talk about it anymore."

Helga stood alone on the back porch. Stars lit the sky in a brilliant canopy; the chirping of crickets erupted like a symphony; and mosquitoes droned a steady hum that finally drove her into the silence blanketing the second floor of the Stein House.

* * *

Sunday morning, reporters from the Victoria *Advocate* arrived after nine hours on horseback, bringing word that relief was on its way. The men distributed a few loaves of bread that they had carried in sacks flung over both sides of their saddles.

The burials continued as rapidly as the hungry men could work. The stench of rotting flesh penetrated everything. The water along the beach was too polluted with human and animal remains to allow for fishing.

Monday morning, everyone rose by dawn and watched in silent hunger for the expected relief from Victoria. When the wagons rolled into town, people eagerly gathered round to gulp the water and clutch loaves of precious bread. As each wagon emptied its supply, the out-of-town visitors climbed aboard for the ride back to their homes. They all assured Helga they would gather more supplies and send the wagons back immediately.

Local residents also crowded aboard, many of them saying good-bye to Indianola forever. By the time the last of the wagons pulled away, a few loaves of bread, smoked sausage, and a tin of coffee were all that remained for the boarders and two families who planned to stay while they rebuilt their houses.

Tuesday, enough relief items arrived from residents of Cuero that Helga and Amelia cooked cornbread and a big pot of potato soup. When the wagons pulled out of town, they carried more Indianola residents to meet the train at a place about twelve miles out where the railroad tracks had not been destroyed. At that point, fresh supplies were switched from the train to the wagons, and the Indianola residents boarded the train for the trip to new lives in Victoria and as far away as Cuero.

With all the wharves ripped from their foundations, ships moved into Powder Horn Bayou to unload relief supplies. Morgan Lines had suffered serious damage to its fleet, but as its vessels brought in food and water, the captains offered free transportation to anyone who wanted to get away from the destroyed city. Many accepted the offer.

On Wednesday Hermie returned in the early afternoon, his clothing filthy and reeking of death. He slumped on the bench at the kitchen table. "Every living thing on Mustang Island got swept away. There's no way the Carters could have survived."

Amelia broke into racking sobs as she sank onto the bench, bowing her head into her folded arms on the table. "Who else must we lose?"

Helga and Hermie, empty of any words of comfort, sat on the bench gripping Amelia tightly between them. As Amelia grew quiet, the only sound filtering through the open windows was the innocent and gentle slapping of the waves against the shell beach.

* * *

Helga and Amelia dealt with their grief in the only way they knew: they worked. "We're either getting rid of the fishy smell or we're getting used to it," Helga said as they came back in the house after hanging clothing on the makeshift clothesline that extended along the back porch.

Late Thursday afternoon they finally opened the door to Captain Whipple and Joseph's room. During the storm, the neighbors had crowded into the room, but when it became clear the men were not going to be found, one of the women had closed the door. "It feels like we're invading their privacy to use their room now."

The neighbors had stripped sheets from the two narrow beds and left every book and personal item, even Captain Whipple's big comb he used on his beard, neatly arranged on the stand next to his bed.

Helga sat abruptly on the captain's bed, burying her face in both hands. "I can't believe they're gone." She looked up at Amelia's stricken face. "They were our family. During the war, Joseph taught me how to survive, to feed the whole household from the prairie and the bay. And the captain …" Helga choked back a sob. "He was like a wise grossvater for the children."

Amelia leaned against Helga, stroking her sister's hair. "I don't know how we're going to manage. But I know we're going to do it."

Helga stood and took a deep breath like a swimmer about to dive into the icy waters of an ocean. "Shall we start with moving all these wonderful books to the parlor? It'll take years to read all Captain Whipple's treasures."

On Friday, Eagle and his line of wagons arrived loaded with food, water, crates of live chickens, two milk cows, and clothing from towns along the route from Fredericksburg. Helga was too weary to run to him, but her relief was profound at the sight of his grizzly, bearded face.

"Hel, I came as fast as I could shove these damn mules. We haven't stopped except to rest them when we had to." All the while he was squeezing her and then pushing her away to see if she was okay.

Then he saw Amelia standing in the front door, and he knew without her speaking that Dr. Stein was gone. He pulled both women against him as they all three sank in tears on the front steps.

Chapter 26

HERMIE RATTLED THE DISHES AS he angrily maneuvered his stub leg under the dining table and heaved himself onto his end of the bench. "Did you hear? Charles Morgan didn't send one nickel for the relief fund. People from all over the country contributed. Morgan sent a letter of sympathy." The serving dishes reached his plate. Without looking at the gumbo, he filled his bowl and kept talking. "We're fooling ourselves if we think Morgan's going to help deepen Powder Horn Bayou all the way back to the lake."

Hermie's voice was so animated Helga had to bite her lip to keep from smiling. She couldn't remember when she had seen him so alive, even if it was anger stirring him.

"If Morgan would help us move the port just three miles up into the lake, we'd have a protected inland harbor." Eagle shook his head in disgust. "What makes Morgan so hard to convince?"

Eli Cox's puffy cheeks trembled. "The Morgan Line may have built Indianola. But Charles Morgan looks only at his bottom line. not Indianola's future."

Francis Stabler looked grim. He carefully removed his tiny wire-frame glasses and smudged the tallow-splattered lens with the cuff of his white shirt. "Morgan's in such poor health. Those two from New Orleans, C. A. Whitney and A.C. Hutchinson, are running the whole operation. Whitney thinks deepening the bayou into a good ship channel and moving the port back on the lake is the right thing to do. Hutchinson's dead set against it. Claims it's too costly."

"Hutchinson knows it's a death sentence for Indianola to continue sitting so near sea level," said Eagle, growing angrier by the minute. "With all Morgan Steamship has invested in our port, you'd think he wouldn't want to see it wiped out."

Hermie's jawbone bulged as he clenched his teeth, a habit Helga had noticed often since the storm. "It never seems to bother Morgan to dump one port and establish a new one. Remember, that's what made this place thrive. Lavaca raised its wharf rates, and Morgan moved down here and helped turn this place into a thriving port. And"—Hermie looked at the faces around the table—"you remember he even dumped all his business in New Orleans three years ago and dredged the Atchafalaya River at Brashear in Louisiana to turn that place into a major port. Brashear is where we've been sending our shipments ever since."

"That's why it doesn't make sense for him to refuse to dredge our little bayou that runs into the lake. It's already deep enough for small vessels. It won't cost near what that Louisiana project cost." Eagle's face had become so red he looked like he might explode.

"Businesses are waiting to see what Morgan will do. Reuss Drug and Runge Bank are smart to open second businesses in Victoria and Cuero." Eli stared at the center of the table and seemed to be speaking to himself. "So many are moving inland to safer locations."

"If it weren't for Eagle's teamsters making that twelve-mile trek every day to meet the train and hauling the food and water back here, we couldn't keep this place going." Helga said, hoping to ease the tension as she touched Eagle's hand under the table.

Eagle hadn't been going with his men to get the supplies. Instead, he worked from dawn until well after dark repairing the Stein House. As soon as shipments of lumber and hardware arrived, he replaced the downspouts that had been ripped from all sides of the house and cleaned out the cistern. He rebuilt the privy and smokehouse and the damaged front stairs to the second floor. He ordered material to replace the storm shutters that flying debris had pounded into splinters. He was waiting on shingles for a new roof.

In early October Eli Cox came to supper and quietly took his seat in his old, frayed chair. Toward the end of the meal, he cleared his throat and said, "I'm taking my commission business to Houston."

Helga felt sorry for him as he winced at the audible gasp of surprise.

He looked around the table searching for a friend. "For … for … five years a New York steamship company's been bypassing Galveston, taking passenger steamers, barges, and tugs up to Houston. The Morgan Line just dredged a twelve-foot channel in the bayou." He stopped and shrugged defensively. "I think Houston will be the future port. And it's not sitting on the coast."

Eagle nodded. "You're right, Eli. Galveston is in a mighty dangerous spot. And its wharf rates are way too high."

Helga was surprised at her sudden urge to cry. She wanted to hug Eagle for coming to Eli's defense. But she couldn't imagine Eli leaving. It felt like one too many losses. He was the last person she expected to move away.

"Well, I'm not leaving." Hermie's jaw had been popping. "I built a good business here. I'm going to stick it out. I've leased the Westhoff building. Plenty of men are eager to get it repaired. I've hired some Negroes to get the city garden ready for winter. Their wives are scrubbing the mud off the walls of my building. They'll help get the shelves stocked."

"I'm staying," Otto Schnaubert said in his very soft voice. "Before the storm I planned to open a studio downtown. If you don't mind, I'll keep my business here, Mrs. Helga."

"We're happy to have you."

Charlie Smith, who had worked night and day since the storm to rebuild the signal office, raised his hand like a schoolboy. "I'm here for the duration."

"I've ordered supplies for rebuilding my factory," Francis Stabler said.

Helga smiled as she felt Eagle's hand stroke her back. She didn't have to tell him she was counting her boarders as each one spoke up.

"I think this town will come back." For the first time since the storm, Amelia looked as determined as the young girl who had stuck out her jaw when she told Papa she was absolutely going to Texas.

After supper, Helga slipped her hand through Eli Cox's arm. "We're going to miss you, Eli."

Eli dropped his head and blinked his little beady eyes several times. "This is the most family I ever had. You've treated me very well. I'd like to come back for visits. Maybe at Christmas?"

"Of course. We'd love for you to come as often as you can."

"Nothing's left of my business. I'm getting too old to gamble on starting over." He held tightly to Helga's arm, peering into her face as though he needed to convince her.

Helga nodded and kept patting his arm.

"Some say this was a freak storm—never happen again in a hundred years."

"No one knows, Eli." She watched him shuffle toward his room. The storm and his financial loss had turned him into an old man.

The storm had twisted some lives as cruelly as it ripped apart their homes. From the front porch Helga had watched families leaving town in fury at the bay and at God and at each other. They had lost everything, and they wanted someone or something to blame. Others, like Charlie Smith, thrived after discovering some internal power that had been dormant. His rosy, boyish cheeks dissolved overnight into the chiseled face of a confident man. He spoke about his job with new authority: "The Signal Service is calling the hurricane the most severe to reach the mainland since it started keeping records. It flooded all across East Texas and washed out railroad tracks. It spawned tornadoes that tore hundred-foot-wide strips through the piney woods."

* * *

The telegraph lines had been ripped down, so Helga wrote to Gretchen, Battina, Orilla, and Paul immediately after the storm to let them know about all the losses.

Within three weeks, Hermie brought letters home at suppertime from all three women. Helga's hands shook as she tore open the post from Gretchen.

"Dear God, she's coming with the children. They'll be here for Christmas." Helga clutched the pages to her breast.

Battina's letter was filled with concern for all of them. At the end she added that she and Gretchen had planned even before the storm that Battina would accompany Gretchen to help with the children.

Orilla's letter glowed with love and sadness that she couldn't get away from her business during the holidays. "You know this is the party time of year. The ladies of Boston demand beautiful clothes with even more attention to detail than the ladies of Indianola."

Helga felt lighter than air for days and could not stop talking about the upcoming visits and thinking of what special dishes to prepare.

The following week a letter arrived from Matamoros addressed in the shaky hand of an old man. Hermie handed it to her and left the kitchen as though he understood she needed to be alone with the first communication from Paul since he walked so casually to the docks with Captain Whipple.

Paul expressed his love for all of them and his sadness at the deaths from the storm. He said his health was good. His writing grew more uneven as it reached the end of the page.

Helga folded the paper and closed her eyes. She could see his hand trembling as he labored to write. She could feel him straining, pushing himself to finish the letter before he took a drink. She folded the letter and slipped it in her apron pocket. She would have to wait to share it until a later time. For now, she had to keep it to herself.

* * *

In November Eagle and his teamsters hauled wagonloads of sewing machines, ovens, and washing machines to San Antonio and Austin.

The night before he left, he continued to hold Helga long after they made love. "It gets harder every time I leave, Hel. This time, I'm going to send my men back to town by themselves. I'll take the money out of the San Antonio bank. I'm going to Washington County to look at farmland."

"You won't stay up there? You're not going to actually move to a farm?" Helga threw her leg across his hips, pulling him fiercely against her crotch.

"You know I can't stay gone. If this place doesn't blow away, you're going to get tired of running Stein House. I'll get things settled, find some good men to run the farm." As he talked, he began moving his body against her, rousing them both to a heated passion.

Amelia did not stop working. She moved like someone being chased, always alert and always vigilant. The weight she had gained after coming to Texas fell away and continued to disappear. She grew gaunt and pale, yet she pushed herself in the garden and in the kitchen. In the evenings she lit a lamp and bent over the sewing machine patching sheets.

With the day drawing near for Gretchen, Battina, and the children to arrive, Amelia worked more frantically getting an upstairs room ready and helping Helga bake Christmas goodies.

* * *

Walking to the docks, Helga realized she was outpacing Amelia, forcing her sister to gasp for breath. She slowed, wrapping her arm around Amelia's thin waist, practically carrying the tiny woman along the new wharf.

As the ship eased into the dock, Gretchen and Battina waved frantically. Gretchen held Elizabeth, a beautiful blonde three-year-old whose solemn face and questioning eyes looked so much like Anna's that Helga didn't think she could look into that face without breaking down.

Walking down the gangplank, Gretchen broke into a run and rushed into Helga's arms, squeezing little Elizabeth between them.

"You're crushing me, Mama." Even her voice sounded like Anna's.

"Elizabeth, I'm your *oma.*" Helga took the child in her arms and looked into the serious brown eyes. "Her hair curls like Anna's," Helga whispered to no one in particular.

Seven-year-old Helena and five-year-old Hershel were older replicas of Anna. Gretchen, who had rounded into a lovely young matron, smiled with pride as the children willingly hugged Helga and called her Oma.

Amelia surprised them all by crying uncontrollably. "I'm sorry to do this. It's so wonderful to have you here with us. We've been so lonely."

Helga was startled at hearing her sister finally speak of her loneliness, admitting how much she suffered from the loss of Dr. Stein.

Elizabeth willingly placed her tiny soft hand in Helga's as they walked toward home. Hershel skipped ahead, swinging his valise, ignoring his blonde hair blowing wildly in the breeze off the bay. Helena held demurely to Gretchen's hand, as reserved and proper as her mama had been.

Gretchen raced excitedly through the house, exclaiming over how lovely it looked after all the mud and water. "And it smells so good. Your cooking always fills the house with such good aromas."

Elizabeth kept questions flowing about who lived in each of the rooms. "This is a funny house, all bedrooms," she announced as she skipped up and down the hall just as Anna had done.

Before supper Eagle surprised them by arriving with the usual Christmas bounty.

Gretchen ran to him and threw her arms around him. "I've missed you, Eagle. You make the Christmas season so beautiful."

Eagle grinned at Gretchen. "It feels like old times to have you back."

"We've always had the largest tree and the best venison. I miss that at home." She shook her head like someone trying to correct a wrong impression. "We have turkey, of course. But no one brings us a wild bird. And never a fresh-killed deer."

"We have snow," Hershel announced defensively, sounding a lot like Hermie when he was that age.

"Yes, snow." Elizabeth bounced down the hall. "We go down the hill on our sled. Mama said you don't have snow."

"You're right," Eagle said with great enthusiasm. "If the weather is still warm tomorrow, you can swim in our bay."

"Really?" Hershel's eyes popped wide in surprise.

"Yep. I'll take you myself."

"And I'll go too." Gretchen clapped her hands. "I haven't been in the water since we left here."

At supper Eagle announced proudly that he had bought six hundred acres in the hills between Brenham and Chappell Hill. "Acres of rich farmland, fat milk cows, and plenty of trees around the house. It needs a lot of work ..."

"Let's go see it!" Elizabeth chimed in, raising her fork like a flag.

"It's too far to go before Christmas. It takes several days. I've hired some freedmen to get it back in shape. The planter let it go to weeds after the war."

Amelia brightened. "I bet I could get a garden going. With the Negroes helping, we can have a good business selling vegetables in Brenham and Chappell Hill."

Helga noticed Amelia's eyes brighten.

Eagle cocked his head as if he didn't quite understand. "You'd consider going up there? Living out in the country all by yourself?"

"It sounds like home—the hills, the forests, the cows ..." Amelia looked around the table. "Without Dr. Stein here, Indianola doesn't feel like home. I've always missed Germany, but he made living in this humid, fishy-smelling place tolerable."

A hole opened in Helga's middle. Indianola without Amelia seemed impossible. She forced herself to smile. She would not let Amelia know that for her to leave would feel like another death.

After supper, while they decorated the tree, Hermie started the caroling, his sweet tenor voice echoing through the house, which encouraged all the boarders to come to the parlor to join in or listen to the lovely sounds of Christmas.

Helga was delighted to see the children knew all the songs and sang with enthusiasm.

At the end of the evening, Gretchen threw her arms around Hermie and Battina. "This has been wonderful. It would have been perfect if Battina and Paul could play for us."

Helga and Hermie both smiled and nodded without comment.

The next morning Eagle took the children for a swim.

Gretchen came to the kitchen and laid her cheek against Helga's.

"Last night I didn't mean to cause pain for you and Hermie with my wish for Paul to be here. After I spoke, I realized from both your expressions that it's not good with Paul. Can you tell me?"

Helga sat down on the kitchen bench and pulled the well-worn letter from her pocket. "I've read this every day since it came."

Gretchen's breath caught as she looked at the envelope. "Did he address this?" She began unfolding the heavily creased pages. "Mama, this is pitiful. He must be very sick. He can barely form the letters."

Helga nodded.

"It's alcohol?"

Helga could only nod.

"He's completely alone in Mexico." Gretchen lowered herself to the bench, wrapping her very soft, lady's hands around Helga's.

"A woman cares for him. Hermie says he plays beautiful music to a large crowd of loyal supporters."

"How can he play the violin with such shaky hands?"

"I wondered that, and then I remembered the man at home who stuttered so badly he could not carry on a conversation. But he could sing like a bird without any hesitation. It was like singing made him a new man. Hermie says Paul looks relaxed and at peace when he plays."

Gretchen pulled Helga's rough hands up to her face. "Things haven't turned out like we dreamed. You've had so much sadness. Now Tante Amelia wants to go off to that farm."

Helga forced herself to smile. "Hermie's still here. And don't forget Eagle."

Gretchen smiled wickedly. "I used to envy you and Eagle. I always hoped I'd have a husband who loved me like he loves you."

It was Helga's turn to look wicked. "Did you get one?"

Gretchen laughed. "I did. Oh, Mama, I found a great man."

Helga threw back her head in sheer delight as she and Gretchen shared their secret laughter.

* * *

One morning as Helga began preparing breakfast, she noticed a lamp burning in the parlor. Gretchen, with her skirt puffed out all around her, sat on the floor in front of Captain Whipple's bookcase holding a book against her breast.

"I found *Uncle Tom's Cabin.* I loved this book."

"You must take it. And the *Iliad.* Remember when Eli Cox told you to read the *Iliad* so you could convince the commissioners to give you a teaching position?"

Gretchen covered her mouth to muffle her giggle. "Dear old Eli got me that job without me saying two words."

"Take as many of the captain's books as you want. Read them to the children. Let them know how you studied when you were their age."

"They have no idea what it was like when we first arrived. They've had a tutor until this year when Helena went to a girl's school. They don't understand how much we wanted to learn, to become good citizens, to fit into this strange new world."

"Children aren't supposed to understand their parents' world. They're busy trying to understand their own."

The two weeks flew by so quickly Hélga could not believe it was time to say good-bye. Eagle rented a carriage for the trip to the docks because a cold front blew in and the wind off the bay pierced through the heaviest coats.

Helga could not hold back the tears, and neither could Gretchen and Battina. Even the children broke into sobs as they clutched fiercely around Helga's waist and then Amelia's. Finally, all three lunged at Eagle, who had become their *opa* who taught them about mules and cleaning fish and shooting quail. All three had trailed him everywhere.

"Come to see us. You can't swim in our river. It's really big." Elizabeth spoke through halting sobs.

"Come in the winter. We can take a sleigh ride," Hershel said.

Helena just cried and leaned against Eagle, who had taught her the Virginia Reel. He had taken turns swinging first Elizabeth and then Helena, never appearing to grow tired of them.

As Helga watched him with all the children, she was reminded of what a good papa he had been to Jackson and how terribly he missed his son.

When the ship heaved and began pulling away from the dock, Eagle wrapped his arms around Helga and Amelia. As they waved and cried, he made no effort to wipe away his tears.

* * *

Eagle began making preparations to return to the farm, buying equipment he needed to get the fields ready for spring planting. One night as they crawled into bed, Eagle said, "Hel, what should I do about Amelia? I think she really wants to go to the farm."

"She's waiting to be asked. She wants you to need her to help out."

"What about you? How will you manage without Amelia or Joseph?"

"Hermie will help find someone who'll live here and work with me."

"You came from Germany to be near Amelia. Now she's leaving you."

Eagle rocked her gently as she cried, partly in relief over his realizing how upset she felt over losing her sister.

* * *

Amelia jumped at Eagle's invitation to help on the farm. She bustled like her old self, excitedly buying tools she needed for a garden. The biggest surprise came when she went to the docks and bought several crates of Shanghai chickens with feathers on their feet that looked like boots. "Shanghais are the healthiest chickens. They're huge and produce more eggs than most. I think they'll stand the trip to the farm better than the chickens we have around here."

Watching Amelia scamper around preparing for the trip, seeing the color return to her cheeks, and watching her begin to eat again, Helga recognized the same Amelia who had left for Texas all those years ago. She never appeared to think for an instant of the sadness felt by their papa or by Helga.

* * *

A week before Eagle and Amelia planned to leave, Helga hired Ester Harrison, a young widow who had lost her husband and her house in the storm. Hermie was enthusiastic about Ester. "She's been helping me in the store, Mama. She lives in a room behind the livery stable."

Ester was almost as tall as Hermie, and as she walked timidly up the front stairs, her huge black eyes gazed at the surroundings. "I've never been in a house so big. You Germans keep it so clean."

"Thank you, Ester. Having a clean place and good food is the key to our success. Hermie tells me you're a hard worker."

"Yes, ma'am. I can work. And I like to." She looked around the parlor. "Will I live in this house?"

"Of course. You'll have a room upstairs."

"Can I see it?"

As they climbed the front steps, Ester kept blowing a silent airy whistle. "I never thought I'd live in a place like this." She stopped and gazed out over the bay. "It's so beautiful. Can't believe how cruel it can be."

"Yes, when it looks so peaceful, it's hard to believe what terrible destruction it can bring. Hermie told me that the storm took your husband."

"And the house. It wasn't much of a house. We built it ourselves. Together. There's not a nail left."

When they stepped into her room, Ester's airy whistle sounded clear and strong. She moved to the bed and ran her hand over the quilted top. Then she slipped her fingers along the edge of the white washbowl and pitcher. "My own bowl and pitcher."

"Will twenty dollars a month plus room and board be satisfactory?" Helga said.

"Oh ma'am, if I can live here, I'll work free."

"I pay people who work here. And please call me Helga."

"When can I start?"

"As soon as you move in, we'll show you the routine."

By nightfall, Ester was solidly ensconced in her room and helped serve supper and clean up.

That night as Ester headed up to her room, she stopped and whispered loudly to Helga, "I wish Morton could see me now. He'd be proud."

"I'm sure he'd be proud to see you taking care of yourself."

Helga smiled as she listened to Ester making the airy whistle as she hurried up the stairs.

* * *

Eagle and Amelia collected so much equipment for the farm that Eagle hired one of his teamsters to drive a second wagon. Helga stood on the porch with Hermie and watched them pull slowly away. Eagle turned and waved several times. Finally, Amelia turned with one quick wave, but her attention seemed absorbed by the road that lay ahead.

When the wagons moved around the bend in the road and disappeared, Hermie left for his store and Helga turned back to the front door.

Ester stood just inside the hall. "Miss Helga, that's got to be the hardest thing in the world to watch them drive off."

"Yes, Ester, it hurts. You know all about the hurt of saying good-bye. And your good-bye was permanent."

Ester nodded, puckered her lips like a child on the verge of tears, and turned back to the kitchen. "I'll get them potatoes peeled and started for lunch."

Besides the workload she carried, Ester helped fill some of the emptiness causing an ache in Helga's belly. Every room she entered reminded Helga of who had lived in that spot and the memories they left behind.

Ester was overwhelmed by the washing machine, the size of the cook stove, and the number of quilts available for each bed. As she became more comfortable in her new home, her cheerful chatter and appreciation for every detail of the house smoothed the rough edges of Helga's loneliness.

* * *

Eagle came home in late February with a letter from Amelia describing all the trees and the rich, thick soil in the garden. She filled her letter with praise for the land, the neighbors, the Negro workers, and Eagle for finding the farm.

As they crawled into the cold, wintery bed, Eagle said, "Amelia is happier than I've ever seen her. I had no idea she was such a farm hand. The men like her because she treats them well."

"So you're comfortable she can run the place?" Helga stretched her naked body full length on top of Eagle and nibbled his ear.

"God, Hel. To get back here, I'd leave a blind cripple in charge."

In the sleepy aftermath of their lovemaking, Eagle mumbled, "I didn't mean to insult your sister. She is good at running the place. And I'm glad to let her."

* * *

By summer things weren't so peaceful. The railroad shut down without notice.

"Everyone thinks A. C. Hutchinson has a hand in this railroad mess," Hermie said. "That man's determined to kill Indianola's business. And it's destroying merchants in Victoria and Cuero." Hermie looked steadily at Eagle across the table. "Do you think your teamsters would pick up the slack? We need to get deliveries from the ships to the inland markets."

“I expect a wagon train in from Chihuahua in the next few days.” He shrugged. “I’ll talk to my men. They’re making big money hauling silver in here from Mexico. They all know that with the railroads coming our Chihuahua freight business won’t last much longer. They want to haul that silver just as long as they can.”

“I can’t blame them if they refuse. If our port dies because we can’t move stuff in and out of here, they won’t have a place to bring all that silver.”

“That’s the best argument.”

It was only two days before fifty wagons rumbled past, the weight of the silver causing the wheels to grind deep furrows in the gravel road, stirring dust so thick it was hard to see the wearied men looking steely-eyed as they clutched their Winchesters.

Eagle stayed away until just before supper, when he brought Jack Ambrose, his wagon master, around back to the washroom.

“He wants to get cleaned up before supper. I told him his room is waiting for him,” Eagle said as he headed to the washroom with two kettles of hot water.

“Will he haul until the train runs again?”

“He’s thinking about it. Tell Hermie to get ready to grease the gears. He can sweet-talk Jack as good as anyone I know.”

Helga nodded.

When the teamsters were in town, Jack Ambrose always took the extra bed in Hermie’s room, and the two seemed to get along very well despite being as different as two men could be. Jack was short, his face chiseled in sun-dried creases. His eyes held a flash of green when the sun hit just right, but he kept such a squint it was hard to get a good look. Where Hermie was open and friendly to everyone, Jack remained watchful, glancing about constantly as if he expected danger to walk through the kitchen door.

“Good evening, Miss Helga. Eagle tells me you have a bed waiting for my weary bones.” Jack Ambrose shook Helga’s hand warmly. Despite the hot water and lye soap, he still smelled of tobacco.

“We’re glad to have you. We have chicken and dumplings tonight.”

“Sounds like home,” Jack Ambrose said as he eased quietly over to Hermie, who towered a foot above him. “I hear we’re bunking again.”

“Glad to have you.” Hermie offered his most genial smile.

The supper talk centered on all the farm equipment, furniture, and washing machines sitting on the docks that merchants in Victoria and Cuero were expecting.

Finally Hermie's fist hit the table. "Truth is, Jack, the railroad barons are trying to take over the country. The legislature's been giving the railroad sixteen sections of land for every mile of track they lay. It's not going to be long until these foreign railroaders are going to own the entire West."

Eagle took advantage of the opening, "This shutdown of the railroad's another power play. We're convinced Morgan's man Hutchinson's behind it."

"Here's our other worry," Hermie said. "The Galveston, Harrisburg & San Antonio is laying track as fast as it can slam it down. It reached Seguin this month. Be in San Antonio by February. When it connects with San Antonio, it's good-bye to Indianola's chance to control the western market."

Jack rubbed his gnarly hand across his face. "What kept the Indianola railroad from going on to San Antonio?"

"The war stopped it. Then Morgan's outfit never got funding to go beyond Cuero." Eagle grinned. "I never complained, because it kept you and me in business hauling freight. But it's a shame to let them get by with killing business for all these towns around here."

Jack pulled out a sack of tobacco. "I know Miss Helga hates smoking at the supper table. Let's go out on the porch and figure out just how we're going to put them bastards in their place."

Hermie heaved himself off the bench. "I think Mama has a bottle of really good brandy someone gave her for Christmas. Maybe she'll let us sample it with our smokes."

As Helga headed for the kitchen, she heard Jack Ambrose say, "My guys hate them big operators. It's a constant fight with them out of Chihuahua. I think they'll be tickled to keep them from hurting the merchants around here."

Helga took the brandy from the bottom shelf of the pie safe. Looking at Ester, she whispered, "I knew this brandy would come in handy one of these days."

When Eagle crawled into bed smelling of alcohol, Helga felt an old tension tightening her whole body. "I'm glad you got Jack to agree. But I hate the smell of you."

"Aw Hel, don't get all sideways. You know having some brandy isn't turning me into a drinker. I already have a headache from the stuff."

"Good. Did you finish it off?"

"Jack did. The rest of us just had enough to stink like Jack." He pulled her tight against him. "But you're not going to like the deal."

Helga knew what he was about to say.

"I had to agree to go with them. Jack made it clear the men won't be happy to cut out the big money if I don't go with them."

She pulled his mouth to hers. "I want to taste you all I can before you leave."

"Even if I taste bad?"

"Yes."

* * *

Near the end of September, without any advance word, the train service started as suddenly as it had quit. Eagle's freighters had been maintaining a steady supply line to the towns along the railroad track to Cuero, and he had just come in for supper while his wagon was being readied for an early-morning departure.

Hermie stormed in the front door and met Eagle in the hall. "Did you hear the train left Indianola this morning at seven? It made it to Cuero a little after one this afternoon."

"I met it this morning." Eagle shook his head. "I've got some mighty fast mules, but there is no way my mules can compete with the railroad." Eagle laughed and patted Hermie reassuringly on the shoulder. "Too bad Eli isn't here to remind me that the end is near."

Hermie grinned, some of his fury dispelled, as he followed Eagle into the dining room. "It's really clear now that the Morgan Line shut down the railroad to force it into receivership."

Eagle looked around the table. "We may as well get used to Indianola being only a tiny part of Morgan's empire. Railroads are the fastest way to move freight, and that bunch aims to control the railroads and the ports all over Texas and Louisiana. You remember when we thought Morgan had quit New Orleans and moved to Brashear in Louisiana? They weren't quitting New Orleans; they were expanding."

"But the railroads are becoming giant monopolies." Hermie looked around the table for support. "The state continues giving land in West Texas to railroads to pay them for building rail lines in East Texas. Those East Texas lines compete with our business. The legislature's got to put some controls on those thieves."

"It's a shame, of course, to create giant monopolies, but Texas needs those railroads." Frances Stabler smiled kindly at Hermie. "You heard Eagle say his mules can't compete, and it's the business competition that's moving this whole thing."

"Okay, I'll just run my store and stop all the shouting. Besides, Mama will be tickled to see Eagle quit that freight business and stay home."

"And my men will be happy to get back on the Chihuahua Road until the railroads take it over." Eagle reached for Helga's hand under the table.

Chapter 27

SOON AFTER AMELIA SETTLED ON the farm, Eagle introduced her to Albert Waters, the planter who originally owned the land. When Eagle returned after his second visit and the delivery of more equipment, he came home bursting with the news. "Hel, your little sister got herself a beau. And she giggles about him like a young girl."

"Do you think she'll marry him?"

"I bet. He's sure coming around. Had supper there every night. She cooked enough for half the county. He had no trouble downing every bite."

"If they marry, we'll need to find another overseer."

"I'm not so sure she wants to give up managing our place. The Negroes love her. I don't think she'll go live in the big house. She said it's too full of his dead wife's things. I bet he builds them a place near our property line."

Helga shook her head in wonderment. "When Amelia left Germany, she meant to live in the rich farmland Friedrich Ernst described in his letters. When the family she planned to work for died, she settled for life in Indianola. Maybe she's getting her dream home after all."

In late fall, a letter arrived saying Amelia and Albert Waters were happily married. He was building a nice little cottage for them just beyond Eagle and Helga's east pasture.

Eagle made fewer and fewer trips to the farm. "Amelia doesn't really need me, and the freedmen know how to manage the place. They ran all of Waters's property the four years he was in the war. When he got back, he paid them in farmland, so they're okay staying around and working for us and running their own places."

1880

Just as Eagle and his men expected, the railroad took over the Chihuahua trade, but he continued his freight business out west to Kerrville and Fredericksburg, hauling over terrain so steep and rocky in places that they used oxen to pull the wagons up some of the rough grades. Eagle kept the freight business moving in and out of Indianola and made an occasional trip with his men.

In mid-April he returned from a long haul to Fredericksburg followed by a side trip to the farm. He climbed down from his wagon seat clutching an armload of bluebonnets. His grin showed through several weeks of whiskers, but it did not hide the fatigue clouding the blue of his eyes.

Helga scooped the flowers from his arms and pressed her face against his whiskery cheek. “Come inside and rest for a while before you drive the team to Ole Man Fisher.”

Eagle slumped on the bench at the kitchen table sipping iced tea and eagerly eating a slab of leftover pound cake. “This is the best tasting cake in the world.”

Helga slid in beside him on the bench. “We just heard about another robbery of a stagecoach between Kerrville and Fredericksburg. It sounds like it’s as dangerous out there as it was on the Chihuahua Road.”

Eagle laughed and pulled her against him, ignoring Ester busily kneading a huge mound of dough. “Hel, my men are as mean as the bandits waiting to shoot them in the back.”

“But isn’t it too risky?”

“If I stopped the freight business, they’d pool their money and buy their own wagons and teams. Profits keep them going.”

“Is that what’s kept you hauling all these years? Profit?”

“Hel, I’m an old teamster. I’ve been on the road since I was a kid. I finally got worn out.” He stopped and looked over his shoulder at Ester, who was pretending to be too busy to hear the conversation. “And I got to missing you too much.” He kissed the tip of Helga’s nose. “So long as I’ve got men who want to work for me, I’m going to keep those wagons rolling. Besides, the teamster business paid for our farm.”

* * *

Although all the stores in town, including Hermie’s, made daily home deliveries, Ester preferred taking the cart to pick up coffee, sugar, flour, and other necessities at Hermie's store. She always returned bubbling with gossip and reports of business or politics. Just before Christmas, she hurried to the back porch still sweating in the extra humid midmorning air. "Guess what? Hermie's got a lady friend. I can tell the way she acts around him."

Helga grabbed the panting girl in a fierce embrace. "You're not teasing me?"

"No, Miss Helga, he's acting like an awkward boy. Stumbles around when he tries to talk to her. You know Hermie don't have no trouble talking to nobody. But he can't make good sense when he talks to her."

"Who is she? Do I know her?" Helga felt silly to feel so giddy, but she had given up on Hermie ever letting himself be vulnerable to loving again.

"She's Lilly Pearl Davis. Her pa's Bert Davis, that big cattle drover who worked with the McFaddins over at Refugio. I heard he built his wife and Lilly Pearl a big house in San Antonio's King William District."

"What's she doing here?" Helga felt a little less excited.

"Visiting. She's been off at college in the East. She came in on a ship last week with Mr. Regan's daughter. I heard they're real close, like sisters. She's planning on coming back for New Year's."

"You come home with more news. How do you get all this information?"

Ester shrugged her big, square shoulders. "I got my sources. When folks work for other folks, you'd be surprised what they hear."

Helga felt her face burning as she remembered Eagle embracing her as though Ester weren't present. She wondered how many people in town knew all about their affection.

Hermie didn't mention Lilly Pearl, but he moved along the road and made his way through the house like a man hardly able to contain himself. Helga knew when Lilly Pearl returned to San Antonio without Ester needing to report, because Hermie looked like a lost puppy.

The morning after Christmas, Hermie beat Helga to the kitchen. He busily heated kettles for bath water, and Helga could hear him singing softly to himself as he washed before breakfast.

That night after supper, Hermie followed Helga to the kitchen while Ester was busy in the dining room.

"I'd like to bring a friend to supper tomorrow night. What are you planning on cooking?"

Helga looked at her son and suddenly felt sorry for his nervous state.

She had never seen him so anxious and ill at ease. "I can have oysters if you think she'll like them."

Hermie froze and stared at his mama. "How'd you know she's a … lady?"

Helga shrugged. "I just guessed. You seem too excited to be inviting some fellow for supper."

"Yes. Well. Her name's Lilly Pearl Davis. She's visiting from San Antonio. She actually speaks French. She's been to college."

"I'll try to make supper really nice."

"Aw, Mama. I really want her to think we aren't …"

"Peasants?"

Hermie flushed. "It's just that we're Germans. Immigrants. And she's from this old Southern family."

"Hermie." Helga touched his arm. "Remember that you speak Spanish, English, and your native tongue. You are not a peasant."

Hermie nodded. "Thanks for making supper really nice."

That night Ester rushed into the kitchen as excited as a child. "They're coming up the road in a buggy. Hermie's rented a buggy. And she is about the prettiest lady I've ever seen."

Ester was right about Lilly Pearl. Pearl accurately described her clear white skin. Her golden blonde hair hung in perfect ringlets around her shoulders, and her eyes looked like shiny blue marbles. Her blue gingham dress hugged a tiny waist.

"My, you have a lovely big … boarding house." Lilly Pearl gazed around the hall, her eyes examining the stencils just below the ceiling and Otto Schnaubert's sketches lining the walls.

"Thank you, Lilly Pearl. We're glad you could join us for supper."

"I am too. I wanted to meet Hermie's family." She beamed up at Hermie with absolute adoration. Placing her very small white hand on his arm, she glided just the way Battina did into the parlor and took in the room with the eye of a commission agent. "My goodness, Mr. Schnaubert's sketches are lovely in the parlor."

"She's sure taken with him," Ester whispered the minute Helga stepped into the kitchen. "You think I should serve and you just sit like a lady?"

"Of course not. I'm not pretending we're something different than ordinary people."

"You think Hermie will be embarrassed?"

"I can't imagine he'll want me to pretend."

The meal went very well, and Lilly Pearl ate more heartily than Helga expected considering she was about the size of a ten-year-old.

That night as Helga and Eagle finally were able to close their door and crawl eagerly into bed, Eagle whispered, "I hope Hermie has found him a woman as loving as his mama. She looks awful fragile to me."

By spring the romance appeared in full bloom. Lilly Pearl managed to visit the Regan's for a few days every month, spending most of her days at Hermie's store, according to Ester.

"She's busy stacking things on the shelves and gazing at Hermie like he's Zeus just come down for a visit."

"Now, what makes you call Hermie Zeus?" Helga found herself surprised at Ester's observation.

"I went to school, you know. Not for so long, but long enough for me. My teacher used to talk about all them Greek gods and such."

* * *

Hermie found someone to run the store for a few days in June and made the trip to San Antonio to meet Lilly Pearl's family.

The only thing he said after his return was he didn't know how Lilly Pearl could stand to take that stagecoach ride from Cuero to San Antonio. "It's crazy for our train to come to a dead stop in Cuero."

When he crawled into bed, Eagle could hardly contain himself. "Never thought I'd see the day when Hermie floated. But I think he's managed to do it over Lilly Pearl."

Helga wrapped her legs around Eagle's naked body and slipped on top of him. "Did you ever float over me?"

"I still do, Hel. Why do you think I hang around here so much?"

The next morning Hermie came to the kitchen as Helga lit the fire for breakfast. "I asked Lilly Pearl's family for permission to marry her. They like me, Mama."

Helga felt like a mama bear defending her cub. "Did you really think for a minute they wouldn't like you?"

"They're awfully rich. And …" He stopped, raising both eyebrows like a wise old man observing errant youth. "Lilly Pearl has everything. More than anyone could want. I told them honestly about my business. I plan to fix up the rooms above the store. Lilly Pearl thinks it will be a wonderful place to live. She says she likes to be right in the middle of all the downtown activity."

The wedding was planned for November. Lilly Pearl and Hermie came together to ask Helga to come to San Antonio for the wedding. Eagle and Ester both insisted she should attend.

"Ester and I can take care of this place. Ester will tell me what to do, and I'll do it," Eagle said.

Ester beamed with the sudden acknowledgment that she could run the place.

The letter that arrived from Gretchen after she heard about the wedding consisted of only a few large words scrawled sideways across the page: "You are going to that wedding. Orilla and Battina will help me make you some beautiful dresses!"

Helga held the lovely piece of linen parchment paper gingerly with her fingertips. "I don't think my daughter knows we have ladies' dress shops in Indianola."

"Her dresses are so elegant," Ester said. "She wants you to impress Hermie's new family."

"Really?"

* * *

On Eagle's return from the farm, he stopped before taking the mules into town to deliver an enormous trunk and two hatboxes. "Amelia ordered some wedding clothes for you from some fancy dress shop in Galveston." He hauled the dusty containers up the front steps and back to their bedroom.

As Helga watched Eagle drive away, she felt the softness of her plain cotton housedress hanging loosely at her shoulders, giving her plenty of working room. She tugged at the waist, realizing it only cinched in when she tied on an apron. It was clean and practical for running a boarding house. Not what a lady wore for tea. She felt foolish to feel embarrassed, but clearly Gretchen and Battina and Amelia intended to see her dressed properly to meet the Davis family. Her mama would have chided her about false pride. She could hear her mama saying, "It takes a generous spirit to graciously accept a gift given with love."

Ester could barely contain her excitement. "Look at that," she whispered as Helga withdrew a soft, camel-colored coatdress with very slender long sleeves and back folds in the fabric below the waist that flowed to the hem.

"Oh, look at this." Ester pulled a rounded piece of horsehair from the trunk on which Amelia had pinned a note. She giggled as she slowly read, "This is a bustle to make this traveling outfit look perfect on you. Cinch it around your skinny waist."

"Look at this hat." Helga also found herself giggling at the matching brown hat with a high crown and narrow brim. The hat in the other box was a luscious deep blue with a matching feather swooping back away from the brim.

"Look at the dress she's sent to go with that hat." Ester held the rich blue gown with draped satin skirt and tiny waist up to her wide shoulders. "You'll be so elegant in this."

Helga nodded as she pulled out beautiful leather shoes. "She's even sent stockings and some lacy drawers." She held up the corset and laughed at Ester's embarrassment.

"Aw, Miss Helga. You're way too skinny to wear a corset."

Helga carefully placed all the clothing back into the trunk. "I guess my little sister thinks I need all this to make a good impression on Lilly Pearl's family."

In a few weeks, Hermie hired a wagon to deliver a trunk from Gretchen. The letter inside said she and Battina had selected the best Orilla had to offer. The gowns were of beautiful taffetas and satins with bows, lace, and elegant detailing at the high collars and down the front and sides of the skirts. They did not forget the corset, a bustle, hose and drawers. Matching shoes, handkerchiefs, and even a tiny watch fob added the final touch.

As Helga looked at the broad assortment of clothing for the rich, she heard her own voice say, "It looks like my family doesn't want me to embarrass Hermie by looking like a peasant."

"I heard that." Eagle stood in the doorway, his arms folded across his chest. "Hel, your family loves you. They're excited for you. You finally have a chance to travel, to have a wonderful time. They're contributing to your pleasure in the only way they know how. No one in this world thinks you're a peasant."

* * *

Hermie left several days before Helga to arrange for the dinner Helga wanted to host the night before the wedding. And Helga thought he also wanted some time to himself.

Eagle instructed Helga about every step of the trip: how to go from the train in Cuero to the stagecoach, how to make sure her trunks got moved to the stage, where to sit on the train to avoid as many coal cinders as possible. He recited names of all the managers of the stagecoach inns. She was to tell them who she was, because they were his friends and would offer her the best accommodations. As the train pulled away from the station and she watched the slump of his shoulders, she realized he had never been the one to stay behind.

Helga did not allow herself to close her eyes. She wanted to see the prairie rise up into rolling hills as Eagle described. The trees were still green even in November, many of them twisted live oaks and cedars. And there were patches of yellow wildflowers still blanketing some of the fields.

The transition to the stagecoach was far easier than Eagle made it sound. Both train personnel and stagecoach people had a system developed for every step of the way. The stage traveled only a short distance before Helga appreciated the comfort of the train, and she found it perplexing that businessmen who made this rugged trip had not demanded a railroad be built all the way to San Antonio.

As they moved beyond Cuero they passed fields of cotton still being picked and cattle grazing behind barbed-wire fences all along the way. She wondered what kept the cattle from walking into the sharp points on those odd new fences.

On the third very long day, the stagecoach driver knocked on the roof and shouted, "San Antonio's just ahead."

The coach jostled to the top of a hill looking down on white buildings clustered together. Through the middle of town a slender thread of trees edged a river twisting into the hills. On beyond, toward the west, hills rose higher than Helga had seen since she left Germany.

The downtown area was more congested than Helga expected. The stage wound through great lines of shouting teamsters, snorting mules, and ox-drawn Mexican carretas. Streetcars drawn by little mules zipped between the traffic. The cold front that had kept temperatures down disappeared, causing uncomfortable warmth, which made the smell of animal dung and filth penetrate the coach and stifle her breath.

Finally, she saw Hermie and Lilly Pearl and a handsome little couple waiting beside a beautiful carriage. Lilly Pearl, the first to reach the coach, grabbed Helga in a long, tight hug and then introduced her smiling parents.

Lillian Davis slipped her tiny hand into Helga's and leaned close.

"Call us Lillian and Samuel. We'll call you Helga if that's okay." She raised pointy eyebrows when she talked.

"That's so kind of you." Helga had never felt like a big person in her life, but she felt like a giant in this family. And Hermie towered over all of them.

"Come, let's get you out of this hot, smelly downtown." Lillian took Helga's hand as they walked to the carriage, where a Mexican gentleman offered her assistance to climb into the soft leather interior.

Samuel Davis, a very short, barrel-chested man, wore leather cowboy boots and a brown business suit. As soon as the trunks were loaded in a wagon that trailed their carriage, he clambered aboard and squeezed in next to Hermie, who was snuggled against Lilly Pearl. Sitting across from Helga, Samuel leaned forward, wanting to hear all about her experiences on the road. "I used to make that trip when I was driving cattle to Indianola."

"I don't know how Lilly Pearl can make it so often. The stage is a rough ride."

"We think she had a good reason," Lillian said in what Helga realized was her naturally soft little voice.

Hermie smiled contentedly, his fingers tightly entwined with Lilly Pearl's.

"Hermann tells us your husband brought all the iron pieces for our bridge on Houston Street," Lillian said.

Helga pretended not to notice Lillian calling her son Hermann. Occasionally Helga heard businessmen say Hermann, but it sounded strange coming from a future family member. "It was a big project for Indianola. The entire town turned out to watch the pieces loaded on the wagons."

"It was big for San Antonio too." Samuel laughed like a jolly little elf. "Everybody went up there to see it unloaded and put together."

"We can drive up tomorrow," Lillian said. "Tonight you need some rest in a good bed."

The downtown slipped away as they rode between the river and tiny, multicolored houses built next to the street. And then the trees grew tall and towered above two- and three-story houses sitting far back from the street. The carriage pulled into a long, curving driveway, and Helga's heart began to race. Could it be possible Lilly Pearl actually lived in such a grand home?

Three massive archways fronted a porch spread across a house more impressive than the landlords' manor houses in Germany.

Everything moved in a haze of confusion for Helga. Lillian led her upstairs to a room overlooking a garden ablaze in roses of all colors. French doors opened onto a balcony admitting the sweet scent of the garden. Gaslights burned in the halls and in all the rooms, casting a warm glow on the elegant paneling and handsome tapestries lining the halls.

Servants brought cool pitchers of water, and Lillian insisted Helga enjoy the tub with running hot water in the upstairs bathroom before supper.

Their supper was not elaborate as Helga expected, but very tasty roasted chicken and mounds of vegetables served by two Mexican women wearing matching blue dresses with starched white aprons.

Samuel smiled warmly at Helga. "Lilly Pearl says Indianola is building back after that terrible storm. She says your business has a steady stream of boarders all the time."

Helga felt suddenly foolish for being worried about this family. The evening and the following day became a lively time of laughter, delightful stories about Lilly Pearl and Hermie's childhoods, Samuel's cattleman years, and Helga and Lillian's mutual fondness for gardening. The Houston Street Bridge looked as impressive as the Davises claimed, and Helga relaxed completely in the warm embrace of the Davis family.

Hermie had reserved a large room at the handsome Menger Hotel for the family and wedding party. And to Helga's delight, he had arranged for the Menger's specialty—an elegant meal of quail and turtle soup from the San Antonio River.

Lillian wore a scooped-neck satin gown of blue that made her eyes look as beautiful as Lilly Pearl's. As they entered the hotel foyer, Helga was keenly aware she looked just as grand in her silk and velvet gown as any one of the Davis family members.

She imagined Gretchen saying, "You aren't a peasant, Mama."

Hermie even had a pair of new crutches. Helga hadn't noticed the underarm padding was frayed on his old pair.

* * *

At the wedding Hermie looked tall and handsome and very happy watching Lilly Pearl come down the aisle on her father's arm. Lilly Pearl looked like a Dresden doll in white lace with tiny pearls sewn onto her gown.

Lillian did not try to hide the tears spilling down the front of her beautiful dress. Samuel patted her gently and pulled her fingers to his lips several times during the service.

That evening as the music played for the bride and groom, Helga was surprised to see how Hermie managed to dance using one crutch and Lilly Pearl for balance. Her heart filled almost to bursting with joy at how her son had risen up from defeat after he lost his leg.

Lillian placed her tiny arm around Helga's waist. "Aren't they a beautiful couple? I want them to be happy, but it will be so hard to have Lilly Pearl so far away."

"You must come often to visit. We always have at least one extra room." Helga felt suddenly blessed to have Hermie close to home.

"I'd love to come down. Perhaps summer will be a good time. Give Hermann and Lilly Pearl time to get settled. Lilly Pearl says your home overlooks the bay. When Samuel drove cattle to Indianola, I went with him many times and loved bathing in the marvelous clear water."

"You made the trips with Samuel?"

"Oh, yes, until I was well along with Lilly Pearl, I made as many trips as I could. We loved being together. And we loved seeing the countryside." She smiled guiltily at Helga. "I've always loved the water, but Lilly Pearl's simply terrified of it, so I've avoided going in since her frightening accident. Maybe when she's not around I can take a swim?"

"Of course. Many of our boarders find bathing in the bay is the best part of staying with us. But tell me about Lilly Pearl's accident!"

"She fell in the San Antonio River down at the end of our street."

"Was she hurt?"

"Not physically, but it left an awful scar in her mind. She was only three, and we walked down to look at the ducks. I was standing next to her when the riverbank broke off, and she fell in before I could grab her." Lillian's face twisted in pain at the memory. "I jumped in and pulled her up from the water immediately, but she was under just long enough to have terror carved into her forever. She's never walked on the bank again."

"That's terrible for her and for you too. Isn't it wonderful you can swim."

"I don't know what we'd have done. I could never have any more children—" Lillian stopped. Her face flamed. "I am so sorry to talk like this to you. You have suffered such losses. Please forgive my thoughtless comments."

Helga bent her face next to Lillian's. "Dear friend, I'll be eagerly looking for your visit. Plan to come in the spring. Don't wait for summer."

1882

Helga looked forward to the evenings when Hermie and Lilly Pearl came to supper not just for the visit but to hear about all the business activity her transient boarders rarely shared.

"We were glad to hear the legislature's stopped giving railroads sixteen sections of land for every mile of track they lay," Hermie said.

"That was a crazy thing for the state to do. The state's given railroads eight million more acres of public land than are even available for that purpose." Eagle was incredulous.

Hermie shook his head in disgust. "We made railroad men like Charles Morgan fabulously wealthy. Since Morgan's death, we're hearing that Charles Whitney's going to Europe to get financing to continue the Gulf Western to San Antonio."

"That'd be perfect," Lilly Pearl said. "My parents would come more often. We could visit them if we didn't have to take that bouncy stage from Cuero."

Helga smiled at the tiny girl. She had surprised them all with her adjustment to living in the small space above Hermie's store, and she seemed to enjoy working there. According to Ester, Hermie's customers liked Lilly Pearl as much as they cared for Hermie. They made a good business team. Each time they came for a visit, Helga and Ester checked Lilly Pearl's cinched waist.

"It never changes," Ester said. "That girl's waist makes the tiniest V-shape. There's no grandchild growing in there yet, Miss Helga."

Helga didn't have to wait for Hermie and Lilly Pearl to come to supper to get the bad news about Charles Whitney's unexpected death.

Lilly Pearl was out of breath when she reached the front door. "I told Hermie you needed to hear right away. With Eagle gone you might not have anyone coming in here to tell you. Charles Whitney was ready to leave for Europe to get financing for the railroad, but he had a massive stroke in New York the night before he was to sail."

Helga slumped to the bench at the kitchen table. “What a blow. Charles Whitney was our last hope.”

Lilly Pearl sat down on the bench and scooted close to Helga, grinning like a kid with a secret. “You know what Hermie and some of the merchants are saying? They’ve been having night meetings in our apartment.”

Helga waited to give Lilly Pearl enough time to enjoy her tease.

“They think we can make Indianola into a resort town. Look at the beach—the water’s crystal clear. They’re talking about building bathhouses. Our seafood is fabulous. We have excellent restaurants. With the Gulf right here and Pass Cavallo easier to get through now that they’ve widened and deepened it, the men think advertising fishing in the Gulf will be a big draw. And they want to advertise the road right out front. They say the route from Old Town right past the Stein House and into town is the most beautiful beach drive and promenade in the state.” Lilly Pearl giggled. “I almost forgot to add the sea breezes.”

“Do they think they can change the image of the port?” Helga felt overwhelmed with the speed of the change. She marveled at the young people never giving up, planning new ways to keep Indianola vibrant.

* * *

New energy surged through Hermie and Lilly Pearl’s circle of friends. They planned advertising, they led a downtown cleanup and painting competition, and they encouraged more top-quality restaurants to open.

Before the year was out, Helga and Ester noticed the V-shape was not so pronounced in Lilly Pearl’s waist. In early 1883, Lilly Pearl surprised them all with the ease of her delivery of a fat, pink baby boy named Samuel Hermann Heinrich.

“We’re not calling him Hermie,” his proud father said. “We like Samuel. It sounds stable.”

Chapter 28

1886

NEW YEAR'S MARKED THE END of a month of family celebrations and a joyous reunion. Gretchen, Hershel, and the children arrived in early December and made the season one of the happiest Helga could remember. The Davises came down from San Antonio, and Amelia and Albert arrived just before Christmas.

Eagle amazed the family by romping through the days with the adoring grandchildren. He started the holiday excitement by returning from the farm in late November with a pony.

Samuel, who charmed the household by announcing several times a day that he would be three in May, immediately named the pony Sugar. He clutched Sugar's mane and stretched his legs tightly around the gentle pony's neck. "Ride me, Opa," Samuel shouted as Eagle led the little horse round and round the house.

When the other children arrived, Eagle continued the pony rides until well after dark each day.

As the ship pulled away carrying Gretchen's family, Helga wrapped her arms around her body to ease the aching hollow filling her insides.

Amelia waved and sobbed without any attempt to control herself. "I think they'll come every year now that Hershel's parents have passed. I wish they'd move down here." Amelia blew her nose nosily on her already wrinkled handkerchief.

"Gretchen says the law practice stretches back to his grandfather's time. He'll never give it up."

"Still. We can wish."

Eagle stood quietly holding Samuel and watching the ship sail away. "Samuel, it's just you and me now. And you won't have to work so hard to share the rides on Sugar with your cousins."

* * *

Hermie and Lilly Pearl appeared just after supper carrying a long, slender package wrapped securely in rope. Hermie looked stricken as he handed the bundle to Helga.

Helga sat quickly on the hall bench, trying to control the shaking of her fingers as she unwrapped the package plastered with Mexican stamps. Paul's violin case, scarred from years of wear, lay still and black in her lap. She opened the lid and stared in disbelief at the old instrument. Its wooden body shone with a rich patina in the reflection of the lamp Ester held high to provide a better light.

Helga opened the folded paper tucked between the instrument and the faded blue velvet lining of the case.

"Paul passed peacefully Christmas Day. He usually slept very late. On this day, he did not wake. He wanted you to have his violin." Helga folded the paper and pulled the instrument to her lips. "He's gone." Helga looked up at the solemn faces. "He wouldn't part with his violin if he were still alive, would he?"

"No, Mama. Paul would never give up his violin." Hermie slipped the paper gently from Helga's hand. "I'm sure his friend sent this. I wish she'd signed it. I'll write to Sylus and see if he knows how to contact her."

Eagle stood tight against her, cradled her face against him without saying a word.

"I hope she was with him. I hope he didn't die all alone." Her body felt numb as she leaned against Eagle.

"Mama, for a long time Paul kept himself from being lonely, from feeling anything."

Helga nodded. She didn't need Hermie to explain how alcohol worked to erase a man's feelings. "Let's place it on the mantle. Paul loved being part of life in the parlor."

She carried the violin and its bow to the fireplace and was surprised at the warmth of the flames against the aching cold spreading through the house.

* * *

Life did not slow down for Indianola. Business remained brisk at the port, and freighters kept the wagons moving toward the west. Tourist traffic picked up each month as a result of the statewide advertising campaign and the weather warming toward summer.

Even with the summer being hotter than usual, people continued to arrive with plans to bathe in the clear water and enjoy the fresh seafood so abundant everywhere. The weather did not cooperate; the heat grew more intense—rain refused to come to produce the cooling sea breezes the advertisements boasted about.

Drought replaced what residents tried to claim was just a period of no rain. Finally, in mid-July they received a letter from Amelia asking Eagle to come help her sell some of the cattle. She wrote there wasn't enough grass to feed the herd, and the cotton crop was burning up on the stalks.

Eagle held Helga against his naked body, slowly kissing her neck and shoulder. "Hel, I don't want to go. It feels like I need to be here."

Helga pulled him against her breast, nuzzling the back of his neck. "You need to help Amelia. We're doing fine. Samuel's the one who will be lost without you."

Eagle grunted. "That child is the best thing that's happened around here in a long time."

"Then get back fast. For Samuel." Laughing, Helga pushed Eagle onto his back and crawled on top of him. "And for me too."

The cisterns in town were drying up. Everyone rationed each drop of water.

Hope began rising on August 18 as clouds moved in and the humidity began climbing. At breakfast even Captain Isaac Reed, the Signal Service observer who had replaced Charlie Smith when he was promoted to the station at Galveston, seemed buoyed by the change in the weather. "I'll get down to the signal office early and see if we have any special news."

But the rain didn't come. Instead, the wind blew hard from the east, stirring up dust and sand from the parched prairie and along the beach. Ester gave up trying to keep the grit and dirt swept from the front porch.

Isaac Reed hurried in early for supper. "I need to take some food with me, if you don't mind. The Washington station telegraphed that a West Indian hurricane passed south of the Florida Keys. They expect high wind and gales along the Eastern Gulf states tonight."

"You didn't get a warning for our station?" Helga tried to keep the worry out of her voice.

"Nothing so far. I'll watch the telegraph lines tonight."

Isaac Reed did not come home that night. All the next day the wind increased and the tide kept rising. Helga tried not to frighten Ester, who was already tense, constantly going to the front door to check on the bay. They began baking bread for lunch, and Helga continued baking throughout the day. "We can always make bread pudding if we end up with too much," she assured Ester.

Just before supper Hermie arrived in a carriage with Lilly Pearl, Samuel, and a load of food and clothing. "I wanted to bring Lilly Pearl out here before she scares Samuel," Hermie whispered. "She's terrified of the rising water. Samuel's beginning to get upset."

Helga and Ester encouraged Samuel to help them carry all the food from the smokehouse into the kitchen. While Helga and Ester wrung chicken necks and prepared to fry as many chickens as possible before supper, Samuel scampered through the hen house feeling under every hen for more eggs.

Neighbors began arriving with armloads of quilts and food, each one saying it was only a precaution. The Stein House was the strongest place on the coast.

Hermie tried to direct all the new arrivals, get them situated in upstairs rooms, but he was obviously worried about Lilly Pearl, who did not leave his side. She trailed him like a child, not uttering a word but wearing an expression of distracted terror. It was as though she could see something no one else could.

The neighbors helped Helga and Ester lay out food on the dining table for supper. Helga was glad she'd sent a large basket of food with Isaac Reed, because he did not return all evening.

Finally, as people were doubling up on beds all over the house, a man who lived in Old Town banged on the front door. "Glad to see you've secured your storm shutters. I just left the signal office, and Isaac's put up the storm signal. Seems kind of late to me. The wind's already knocked out the telegraph pole."

The wind continued to buffet the house. Everyone maintained silence as though listening for a hint of what was to come. Hermie asked Helga to continue watching Samuel while he tried to get Lilly Pearl to lie down in Ester's back room. "It's furthest from the howling wind, and the shutters aren't so noisy back there."

With Lilly Pearl out of sight, Samuel seemed to forget his fears and visited with all the strangers, who enjoyed the distraction of chatting with the friendly little boy.

As people began getting quiet, it did not take long for Samuel to fall asleep in Helga's bed.

Remembering the importance of fresh water after the last storm, Helga and Ester placed buckets and tubs on the back porch to collect the rain when it started. By one in the morning the rain had not come, but the bay was lapping the edge of the porch. They took up the rugs and began hauling furniture and food upstairs. Helga picked up Paul's violin and carried it upstairs with one of her armloads of food.

Torrents of rain started pounding viciously against the house about three. Water began its relentless fountain spray onto the first floor through the old ax holes from the last storm.

A neighbor man motioned to Helga to follow him to the back porch. "Why don't you let your pony come inside? He's up on the back porch, and it's pitiful to watch his terror." The man grabbed Sugar's mane and coaxed him into the kitchen.

Helga carried Samuel upstairs to a back room and laid his warm little body in the center of a bed next to two other babies who had fallen into fitful sleep. The parents sat quietly on the edge of the bed, gently patting their children and staring into the dim glow from the kerosene lamp in the hall. Across the hall Hermie sat motionless, holding Lilly Pearl as the room filled with exhausted neighbors trying to find a corner of a bed.

Ester followed Helga into the room and sat cross-legged on the floor, her shoulder against Helga's leg. With the hurry to finish chores finally completed, the terror of eleven years ago seemed to come rushing back. Ester trembled like someone immersed in ice. Helga made room for her on the end of the bed.

"We're going to get through this. Stay strong. We can make it together."

Ester nodded. Helga heard the distinctive breathy whistle that Ester always made when excited or stressed.

Almost instantly the house lurched backward and shuddered so hard it felt like the floor was heaving them upward. The ripping sound of wood forced a collective gasp, and screams came from the hall. "Water's coming in the front of the house."

The lamp in the hallway went out, plunging the world into blackness.

Helga gathered Samuel into her arms as he roused up and reached for Helga's cheek. "It's Oma, Samuel. Hold onto Oma as tight as you can. Don't let go of me."

The house lurched again. Shrieks of terror rang through the darkness. Helga tried to brace herself as she and Samuel were thrown against the back wall. Then she felt water rushing across her body. "Stay with us," she shouted to Ester, who had not budged from Helga's side. She felt Ester helping lift Samuel higher out of the water.

Boards slammed against her, and writhing bodies collided as Helga used her free arm and her legs to crawl upward along what felt like the wall tilting onto the back porch. She grabbed a broad piece of wood with her left arm as it slammed against her. Then, realizing it was floating wildly, she tucked her fingers into the edge and held on, kicking vigorously to move away from the churning mass of wood and struggling people. Samuel clutched tightly at her neck, his legs gripping around her body like he was riding Sugar at full tilt.

The board felt like part of the roof with ridges of shingles. Helga gripped the rough edges of the board with all her strength to keep it from floating away. She could feel Ester buoying Samuel with one arm and holding firmly to the board. They kicked in a frantic rhythm, trying to move out, away from the bodies flailing and grabbing at them as the wall collapsed.

"Oma's here. We're swimming together." She spoke against Samuel's ear, trying to calm the frantic breathing she could feel as the baby squeezed against her.

Finally, they seemed to escape the crashing timbers and the bodies frantically clawing at her clothes. They clung to the board as it heaved violently in the raging water.

Every ounce of energy went into clinging to that floating lifeline and trying to guard themselves against debris looming out of the darkness. Helga refused to let herself think of what the softness was that bumped into her, whether it was a drowning victim or an animal. She made herself shove it with her feet and tried to be grateful it wasn't a piece of heavy timber crushing her bones or injuring Samuel.

The water was cold, but the wind that slammed into her bare arm clinging to the board felt like piercing sheets of ice. Keeping Samuel tight against her body was the only way to keep the baby warm enough to survive. Esther's body stayed tight against the other side of the child, her arm helping to form a cradle under his body.

After a time she could not calculate, the darkness began to fade and they could see the objects careening toward them in time to raise their feet to lessen the impact. Sometime during the night Helga realized she'd lost one shoe when something stabbed her bare foot, sending a searing pain up her leg.

"Look." Ester's eyes stared in horror over Helga's shoulder.

Out of the blackness the horizon turned to raging reds and oranges. Something very large burned, shooting sparks upward like the inferno of hell.

They turned enough to watch the flames licking at the sky, melting away the darkness.

Samuel's racing pulse slowed, and he seemed to drift into what Helga hoped was sleep. Should she keep him awake? Could he be slipping away from her instead of just escaping into his own dreams? She prayed to know the answer, and all she knew was she must allow the child to be at peace.

At times Helga's foot touched something before another wave tossed them upward. Were they far enough into the prairie to get beyond the flooding? And did she imagine it, or was the wind dying down? Were they going longer between the violent upward thrusts of the waves?

As morning light crept over the roiling sea, the objects—half-naked bodies tumbling over and over like swollen fish and masses of sea-soaked animal carcasses—made her long to shut her eyes and hide from the horror.

And then she was certain she touched the ground. The waves did not toss her again. She could feel the tide going out, but not in the massive sucking way she remembered from before. It felt like the bay was not so determined to snatch back its water.

"We're touching bottom," Ester said. "Praise God, we're finding the shore."

Samuel opened his eyes and looked at Helga for an instant with a puzzled expression. "Oma? You hurt your face?" He stroked her left cheek, causing her to wince.

"I think I bumped my head," she said and realized Samuel had scratches on his face.

Ester and Helga placed both feet on solid ground, allowing the scrap of roof that carried them to safety to slip away with the tide and head back languidly toward the distant bay.

They began slowly wading back toward town. Mangled bodies of humans and animals lay among twisted pieces of lumber, garden implements, buckets, and ripped-apart furniture. She scanned the death around her for other survivors, but nothing moved. Bodies twisted in horrid shapes of fright, some naked and others with clothing ripped and torn to shreds, did not look like anyone she had ever seen. The earth looked like a field of battle—all silence.

Helga's bare foot had been injured more severely than she realized, and each step sent stabbing pain up her leg and into her groin.

Samuel eased his grip on Helga's neck and began gazing at the receding water and the death scattered all about them. His eyebrows bunched as he clasped Helga's face in both hands. "Where're my mama and papa?"

She looked into the serious eyes, felt the tension in those tiny hands on her cheeks, and thought she might collapse. "Oma doesn't know. We'll look for them."

Satisfied, he threw both arms around her neck and clasped his legs more tightly in their pony grip, his head resting on her shoulder.

She hoped the steady walking would lull him to sleep. She felt compelled to look, felt compelled to see if Hermie and Lilly Pearl were among the twisted and torn bodies. Surely she could recognize them. Then she saw Sugar, his sturdy legs stiff and thrown upward like he had tried to swim. The poor pony had been trapped in the kitchen with no way out until the house collapsed around him. By the time he was set free, he had drowned, captured in the flooded first floor. Looking around at the dead cattle, it didn't look like anything had survived, even those that had been free to swim.

In the distance she saw a man stumbling toward them, his arm raised as if he wanted them to wait for him. As he drew near, Helga recognized Ernest Polk, who ran the store down the street from Hermie's grocery.

He looked crazed. "I'm trying to find my wife. We were holding onto our little girl." He stopped, covering his face with both bloody hands.

Ester reached to touch his sleeve and then drew her hand back as she saw the gash oozing blood down his arm.

"Walk with us toward town. We can look together," Helga said as she began to take one painful step and then the next.

"No. I've come from town. I'm walking the prairie. It's like before. I know they've been washed out here." As he limped away, Helga heard a desperate sob.

Ester reached for Samuel. "Let me carry you so Oma can rest." She had a blue knot on her forehead, and her dress was ripped open like someone had clutched at her back until the fabric gave way.

"No." Samuel buried his face in Helga's neck, clutching at her fiercely with his arms and legs.

Helga stroked his back. "You can stay with me."

The water was only ankle deep. In the distance Helga felt sure she could see the skeletal remnants of the trees circling their house. It was the only house with trees tall enough to offer summer shade. But where was the house? She could see only the twisted circle of bare, bent trees and a clump of lumber on the west side of the property.

Finally, the scene took shape. The washroom was gone. Part of the kitchen floor looked like it had risen up and been anchored by the big iron stove. The concrete steps rose to nothing where the back porch once stood. Beyond the shredded oleanders, the beautiful road townspeople had started calling the Promenade lay under several feet of bay water. Helga wondered if the road was gone, eaten up by the fierce waves. Metal poles, the securing rods that had anchored the house for so long, rose like grasping claws into the gently blowing breeze. Next to the back steps the concrete base of the cistern formed a circle on the ground filled with water and chunks of floating debris. All evidence of the great white Stein House had washed away. Behind where the washroom had stood, still buried deep in the earth, the rims of saltwater-filled jars could be seen. Gold and silver coins silently soaked in seawater.

Shards of dishes, a twisted rug, and a can of Francis Stabler's meat lay where the backyard had been. And then she saw Paul's bow driven like an arrow into the ground. The people were gone. The Stein House could not protect them. They had been washed away, and only scraps of their lives remained.

Helga sat on the top concrete step and immediately felt relief from the pain in her foot, which she could not see for the mud caked up her ankle. She stretched her leg out and dipped her foot through the floating mix of gunk in the cistern, allowing the mud to float away. Pulling the dripping foot back, she could see a long gash that ran from her heel up into her ankle.

Ester looked at Helga's foot. "Stay here with Samuel. I'll look for the others."

"They'll come. If they can."

Ester nodded. Holding the swatch of cloth that had been the back of her dress, she walked toward the alley, past where the hen house, smokehouse, and privy had stood.

Samuel gazed questioningly at the stripped and twisted trees. One rope hung from a branch of the old bois d'arc, all that remained of the swing Eagle had hung for him. "Where's your house?"

"The wind blew it away. We'll get another house as soon as we can."

"I want my mama." Samuel settled his head against her breast, and his eyes began to droop, exhaustion finally forcing his first restful sleep.

She couldn't stop scanning the prairie, imagining Hermie and Lilly Pearl walking home. No life stirred. How could everyone be gone? All the people huddled on the second floor? Didn't any of them get out?

Her mouth felt parched, and the salt dried her skin to a scaly, itchy crust. Even Samuel's eyelashes held drying scales of salt. His cheeks looked like a cat had clawed them. His hair lay stiff and matted against his scalp. She dreaded when he awoke wanting water and food.

After a long time of sitting motionless with Samuel, she saw Ester coming at a slow, deliberate pace, one arm clutching a roll of blankets, a pail swinging heavily by her side. Her downcast look told Helga more than she wanted to know.

Their eyes met as Ester came into what had been the backyard. Ester shook her head. "They were together. To the end."

The pain cut like a knife into her middle. It made her want to vomit, to heave forward on the soggy ground in a ball of agony. Instead, she sat as still as she could to keep from waking Samuel. Tears washed her face and dripped on the orphaned baby in her arms.

"It was a beautiful sight. They held each other to the end." Ester turned her head away and whispered, "I wish Martin and I could have been together like that." She looked down at Helga, her face twisted in fresh loss. "I don't mean to sound ungrateful, Miss Helga. We did everything together. Before the storm."

"Hermie would feel the same way, Ester."

Ester eased onto the step next to Helga and wrapped her arms tightly around Helga's shoulders. "The fire took most of downtown. Hermie's store's gone. I found several cans of fruit and Mr. Stabler's tins of meat. Regan's Dry Goods is destroyed. Mr. Regan's letting people take any clothing they find. I got a pair of work shoes and men's socks for you." She unfolded her great bundle. "I got a blanket for Samuel and one for us." She pulled a small can of kerosene out of the bucket. "I couldn't find the tallow to make a paste with the kerosene. Maybe pouring it on your foot will keep you from getting lockjaw."

Samuel roused, rubbing his salty cheeks. "Let's eat, Oma."

Ester stabbed a knife into the can of fruit. "This fruit will feel good to your tummy."

Samuel took the can and drank the juice eagerly through the slit. "More."

Ester used the knife to stab away the lid. Then she fed Samuel every slice of the delicious-looking peaches.

Ester grabbed Helga's arm, her eyes dancing. "I saw the most amazing thing. You remember when the Catholic Church rebuilt after the storm they placed the statue of Mary, Star of the Sea, on the new building? It survived. The church didn't have any damage."

"That's amazing." Helga could not muster the energy to match Ester's enthusiasm.

"So many other places are totally gone. Lagu's Store, the Villeneuve's Liquor Store, and A. Frank's warehouse all burned to nothing. The fire jumped the street and took out Dahme's Corner. Lagu lost his hotel. The drug store and Regan's Dry Goods got burned. That's why the blankets smell like smoke." She squeezed her eyes shut like she was viewing the destruction. "I can't even name all the wrecked buildings."

All the time she talked, Ester skimmed debris off the water that collected at the base of the cistern. She filled the pail with water and rinsed Helga's foot. "This is going to burn. You better let Samuel sit on the step beside you."

Although Samuel refused to leave Helga's lap, he bent over her foot and watched wide-eyed as Ester poured the kerosene into the oozing cut.

The pain seared through her foot like a hot knife as Helga used all her strength to keep from jerking away. She covered her face to keep Samuel from seeing her gritting her teeth.

"She's hurting you, Oma." Samuel's hand pulled at her fingertips.

"No, Samuel. She's helping my hurt foot get well. It's already feeling better."

Ester propped Helga's foot up on the overturned pail. "It shouldn't hurt as much the next time."

They began to hear voices of people wading along the road toward Old Town. Several stopped, saying they were leaving. "I promised God if he'd save us, I'd leave this place and never return," one man said as he walked along holding the hand of a little girl who looked like she had seen a ghost. A woman walked behind them carrying an armload of clothing.

People continued passing all day, some in tears, others so exhausted they could barely walk, all determined to get away.

Samuel remained very quiet, continued to snuggle against Helga's breast, his eyes roaming the property like he couldn't believe what lay around him. At one time, he said, "See your washing machine?" He pointed where the cow lot had been. Two legs and the crank handle stuck out of the mud. It made Helga think of Sugar's legs stretching rigidly into the air.

"Let Ester get it."

"It's too heavy for Ester. We'll ask Opa to get it when he comes."

Samuel made no effort to go out and take a look. Despite being worried about his reaction to what had happened, Helga didn't want him seeing any more mangled bodies.

As darkness came, the air grew cooler. They gratefully wrapped in the blankets as they stretched out on the wet ground.

The next morning wagons from Victoria began moving through the slushy shell of the old road. They stopped with barrels of water and loaves of fresh bread.

"The damage is terrible in Victoria. The train can only come within four miles of here. We'll go back for more supplies as soon as we finish unloading," the wagon driver said as he slapped the reins on his mules and slowly moved his wagon toward downtown.

All day they watched streams of people walking out of town and others riding in the empty freight wagons heading back to the train.

Ester said, "Miss Helga, shouldn't we plan to leave too?"

"You go if you need to, Ester. I'm waiting for Eagle. He'll come as soon as he can. He planned to leave the farm last Thursday. If he doesn't run into the storm, he should be here by today or tomorrow."

"I'm not leaving without you and Samuel. Don't you think for a minute I'd leave." Her lips trembled, and she wiped the back of her muddy hand across her cheek. "You're my family."

* * *

They heard Eagle screaming, his voice sounding like the bellow of a grieving animal, "Hel! Where are you, Hel?" before his wagon came into view.

"Opa," Samuel yelled and leaped off Helga's lap, running as fast as he could toward Eagle, who scrambled off the wagon and rushed to grab the child.

Helga limped despite her new shoes, but she made the distance across the vacant plot of soil in record time, throwing herself into Eagle's crushing hug.

"I'm so sorry, Hel. I promise I'll never leave you again. God, oh God, I've been scared." He clasped Helga and Samuel in the circle of his arms. He looked down, released her long enough to gently touch the bruise on the side of her face, and then pulled her tight again.

"Ester, thank God you're still here." He stretched his arm and pulled Ester into their circle.

"I've got food and water. Brought the food from Amelia's garden. And I got the water before I reached Victoria. That place is a wreck. You wouldn't believe the storm tore up so much."

He gazed at the place where the house had been and shook his head. "Hermie and Lilly Pearl?"

Helga could only shake her head. "Ester found them. Together."

"Oh, Hel, I'm so sorry. I should have been here."

All the time they talked Samuel kept his face buried in Eagle's neck, his arms and legs wrapped around Eagle's body like he still feared he might be dropped. "Mama and Papa are gone."

Eagle stroked Samuel's salty hair. "You're safe now, buddy. Oma and Ester and I are going to take good care of you."

There was no response, just the tightening of the child's grip.

To get off the damp, fishy-smelling ground, Eagle pulled the wagon onto the property. They all climbed in and devoured the bread and garden vegetables from Amelia.

"Where's Sugar?"

Eagle looked pained as Samuel shook his head and waved his hand toward the prairie. "He got lost with Mama and Papa."

"Maybe we can find another pony when we get to Tante Amelia's," Helga said as she looked across the wagon at Eagle holding the confused little boy.

"Oh, Hel, I hoped I'd hear those words. We can get out of here as soon as we take care of everything." He glanced at Samuel. "Wouldn't you like to go to the farm where we have cows and chickens and horses?"

"And ponies?"

"Ponies, for sure."

Ester showed Eagle where to find Hermie and Lilly Pearl. They lay so near the house Helga wanted to follow. Then she looked at Samuel, who had finally relaxed enough to move away from her side to play in the jars of coins glistening under the seawater. He did not need another trauma.

She watched Ester and Eagle digging, resting, and digging more. Hermie and Lilly Pearl would stay where the vicious waves had tossed them, like Max, lost forever in the icy waters of the North Sea. They were all being left behind—Paul alone in Mexico and Anna in the tiny coffin on this barren, desolate coast.

Helga sat motionless on the steps, drained of all energy, gazing across the horizon for some sign of life. The promise the vast prairie had offered when they first arrived at the thriving little port lay dead and stinking.

"Here's a present, Oma."

Samuel's hands, wet from the water in the jugs, opened wide holding the old silver Thaler emblazoned with the image of the wild man of the Harz Mountains.

The relief came from a forgotten time when she believed the old coin would save them from financial ruin. Helga wrapped her grandson in her arms and laughed. "That's the best present I've ever had."

"What is it, Oma?"

"It's our family's sign of hope, Samuel. You found it at a perfect time when Oma thought hope had gotten lost."